FREE FALL!

First Caine heard the decoy pods breaking free. Then, with a wrench, his team's pod was released from the shuttle, and suddenly they were in free fall.

A second later gravity returned with twin jolts as Caine popped the drogue and main chutes. "Get ready," he said as their flight smoothed again. "Five seconds to breakout ... three, two, one—"

He wrenched the control—and the pod's walls split from floor to ceiling, the floor disintegrated, and the four men of the commando team were flung apart into the darkness as the wall sections they were strapped to caught the inrush of air and separated. Caine got a dizzying glimpse of stars above and black ground below; and then, with a snap, the pod section above him unfolded into a hang glider wing and he was flying ... right into the heart of *Ryqril* territory!

Blackcollar:
The Backlash Mission

Timothy Zahn

DAW BOOKS, INC.
DONALD A. WOLLHEIM, PUBLISHER

1633 Broadway, New York, NY 10019

DAW Collectors Book No. 683.

DEDICATION

For Uncle Timmy—
Who locked up the mountain
and then gave me the key.

First Printing, September, 1986

1 2 3 4 5 6 7 8 9

Printed in the U.S.A.

Prologue

The wind coming northward over Ralston Buttes had been increasing steadily throughout the night, shifting gradually around toward the west with the promise of bad weather coming in behind it. Lying flat on his belly beneath one of the surrounding pine trees, Lonato Kanai listened as the branches scratched at his flexarmor battle-hood and peered through the gloom at the darkened mansion directly ahead. In an hour— maybe sooner—the storm would arrive, drenching the whole Denver plateau and turning the slope he was on into fairly obnoxious mud. But long before that happened Kanai and his fellow blackcollars would be on their way home. It had taken them six hours to crawl through the last hundred meters of forest, but now all the early-warning motion sensors were behind them and the target lay open ahead.

Reasonably open, anyway. There were still the roof-mounted chain guns and hedge mines, their infrared and ultrasonic autotarget systems waiting only for the intruders to move away from the waving tree branches and onto the elaborately sculpted lawn. And, of course, inside the mansion itself would be a dozen or more armed men.

Reaching to his left forearm, Kanai unlimbered the collapsed sniper's slingshot strapped there and unfolded it, setting the brace against his arm and slipping a tiny lead sphere into the pouch. He'd barely managed to make marksman rating during the war, but thirty years of practice had honed his skills considerably. The nearest ultrasonic projector—a small tripartite horn—was nestled under the eave, just barely visible in the cloud-reflected lights of Denver over the hills to the east. Eyes on the projector, peripheral vision and other senses alert, Kanai eased his elbows into a less uncomfortable position and waited for the signal.

It wasn't long in coming. Abruptly, the tingler on his right wrist came to life, tapping the dots and dashes of blackcollar combat code into two sections of skin: *attack*.

Even through the whistling wind Kanai heard the *crack* as his

5

lead shot drilled its way deep into the ultrasonic projector. Quickly he set up his second shot as the sounds of other freshly ruined sensors reached him. Ahead, the side door that was their target was suddenly rimmed in red warning lights. The nighttime sentry chief was right on top of things . . . for all the good it would do him. Kanai's second shot arced lazily toward the door—slow enough for the antipersonnel motion sensors to pick up—

And the eaves directly above the door exploded into a lethal cloud of flechettes.

The tiny metal darts were still ricocheting off the patio flagstones when the two black-clad men flanking Kanai rose from cover and zigzagged off toward the mansion. On the roof-top a chain gun began to track; an instant later its first salvo went wild as the impact of Kanai's shot knocked it a couple of degrees off target. Beside the door a gunport slid open, and a scatter of flechettes sprayed at the running men. Uselessly, of course, as the few darts that managed to connect were stopped by their flexarmor. One of the attackers windmilled his arms, sending black throwing stars into the gunport. The barrel sagged as the *shuriken* found a target . . . and then the runners were at the door, one crouching beside it as the other slapped tiny shaped charges in an X pattern on the nearest window. With luck, Kanai's elimination of some of the door's automatic defenses would delude the mansion's defenders into expecting the main assault there.

The attackers dropped to the ground, and the window exploded with flashes.

It didn't shatter—the glasstic was too strong for that—but when the afterimages faded Kanai could see the honeycomb of cracks there. A few good whacks with a *nunchaku* would finish the job . . . and then only the inside defenders would be left.

Both attackers were on their feet now, flanking the window and flailing away at the glasstic with their *nunchaku*. Kanai loaded another pellet into his slingshot, trying to watch every-where at once for the inevitable counterattack.

His tingler gave first warning: *Bandits coming around north side*. A second later they were there: three of them, encased in heavy body armor, with flechette repeaters at the ready. Two came around the corner into military kneeling stances, their repeaters laying down an inaccurate but intimidating fire. The third stepped between them, a scud grenade clutched in his hand.

Amateurs. Behind his gas filter Kanai's lip twisted with contempt. Scud-grenade needles were a danger even to flexarmor at sufficiently point-blank range, and armored as they were the defenders were essentially invulnerable to the throwing stars and *nunchaku* of their attackers . . . and their blatant overconfidence was going to kill all three of them. The man with the grenade armed it and swung his arm back for an underhand throw—

And Kanai's tiny pellet slammed into his wrist.

Without hurting him, of course, through all that armor. But the impact was more than enough to knock the grenade from his casual grip and send it to the ground.

Kanai didn't see the thing go off; even at his distance he wasn't taking chances with scud needles against his goggles, and he kept his face pressed into the grass until the deadly sleet had spent itself against the trees around him. When he again looked up, all three armored defenders were lying motionless on the ground. Shifting his eyes to the broken window, he was just in time to see the second of the two black-clad men disappear inside the mansion.

Kanai: inside backup, his tingler signaled. Getting his feet under him, he sprinted across the lawn. The roof chain gun remained unfocused; those who should have been manning it were apparently busy elsewhere. Replacing his slingshot in its sheath as he ran, Kanai drew his *nunchaku* and prepared his mind and reflexes for the shift from long-range to close-in fighting.

But for the moment, at least, the fighting was over. Four bodies decorated the floor near the window, their weapons scattered about even more randomly. All four faces were familiar: street lice, the cheapest and most expendable part of Reger's organization. Put into the attackers' path for the sole purpose of slowing them down . . . which meant the real soldiers were farther in, waiting. Senses alert, Kanai headed inward.

To find the "real soldiers" hadn't done any better than their amateur counterparts. Kanai passed three more bodies, two of them still with deathgrips on their guns. All three had clearly been shooting from cover . . . and all three now carried *shuriken* in vital spots. Shifting his *nunchaku* to his left hand, Kanai drew out a pair of his own throwing stars— just in case—and continued on.

The sound of voices reached him half a hallway from the room where the trail ended. Conversational voices—calm, even, incongruous amid the carnage. Reaching the room, Kanai looked in.

It was a tableau he'd seen time after weary time before in the last few years. The two black-clad men stood at apparent ease a few meters from their middle-aged target victim, the five additional bodies silently staining the carpet around them showing their casual stance for the illusion it was. The attackers were always the same, the minor bodies might as well be; it was only the target victim who ever changed.

At least, Kanai thought, *this one isn't begging.*

Manx Reger wasn't begging. Standing by his bed, a dressing gown thrown haphazardly on, he spoke with the calm tones of a man who has already prepared himself for death. "So I'm overreaching myself, am I?" he was saying to the leftmost of the men confronting him. "Has it occurred to you, Bernhard, that *you* may be overreaching *your*self?"

"I do what the contract calls for, Reger," Bernhard told him coldly. "No more, no less. Right now my job is to tell you our client thinks you're eating too much of the black-market business in this territory."

"Your 'client,' eh? Sartan, I suppose? Again?"

Bernhard ignored the question. "So now I've told you. I suggest you do something about it." His hand curved in signal and both black-clad men began moving back.

A cautious frown creased Reger's forehead. "You mean . . . that's it?"

"I was told to cut back your ambitions," Bernhard said quietly. "How I do that is *my* choice. Though if I have to come back the results are likely to be more permanent."

"Ah. In other words, Sartan doesn't feel up to a full-scale war yet, is that it?" The older man snorted. "Well, let me return his favor with a little advice. No one's succeeded in fencing Denver up as his own private preserve for over two hundred years. Not in peacetime, not during the war, not in thirty years of Ryqril occupation. If Sartan thinks he can do it he's going to get himself buried—and if *you* get too closely tied to his muzzle you'll go the same way." He glanced at Kanai, and even across the room Kanai could see the aura of age around those eyes. With regular Idunine doses, Reger's middle-aged appearance meant nothing, of course, any more than Kanai's lithe body showed its own six decades. How old *was* Reger, anyway? Old enough to have been trying for control of Denver's underworld himself in the days before the Ryqril threat? Possibly. Maybe even probably.

Not that it mattered. The world had changed thirty years back, and it was Bernhard and Kanai who knew how to operate in it now. Reger and his kind were the dinosaurs, doomed to ultimate extinction.

"I'll give Sartan your words of wisdom," Bernhard told the older man, his tone lightly sarcastic. "Just don't make us come back."

Another hand signal passed, and Kanai headed back the way he'd come, ready to clear out any new threats Reger's men might have set up. But whatever firepower still existed in the mansion was apparently still too shaken to offer fresh resistance. The three black-clad men made their way back outside and into the woods surrounding Reger's now slightly damaged property. Kanai sensed, rather than saw, the four backups withdrawing with them, and all seven men arrived at their hidden cars at the same time.

"Well?" one of the backups asked.

"He'll fall into line," Bernhard said tiredly, pulling goggles and battle-hood off and massaging the bridge of his nose. "And once he does, all the little quarter-mark operations on this side of Denver should follow."

"At which point," someone else commented, "we'll have something real to play with."

"Or Sartan will," Bernhard said with just a hint of reproval. "*Sartan's* in charge of this, not us. Never forget that."

A minute later they were all heading toward the sprawling metropolis of Denver to the southeast. In the back seat, leaning against the right-hand door, Kanai stared moodily out the windshield as the first drops of rain began to fall. So the big consolidation scheme was working. The promise of a better future . . . and all they had to do to achieve it was continue to be the most elite strong-arm force the criminal world had ever known.

What a level, he thought, *for blackcollars to sink to.*

The universe seemed to agree with his assessment. Outside, the sky rained down bucketfuls of tears against the car. Tears for the shamed warriors.

Chapter 1

"The blackcollar forces are the elite warriors of this up-coming conflict of ours—the best chance the Terran Democratic Empire has of surviving the Ryqril war machine being launched against us."

For no particular reason the words flashed through Allen Caine's mind as he stood alone in the darkness. Words of hope, spoken originally by the TDE's chief military head at the first Special Forces Training Center commencement in 2416. The hope had been short-lived, of course. Two years later the war had begun: thirteen more and Earth itself had finally surrendered to the humiliation of Ryqril occupation troops and puppet governments.

And as for himself, Caine wasn't feeling especially elite at the moment. Nor, for that matter, much like a warrior.

So much for the wisdom of the past.

A faint scraping noise reached his ears, snapping his mind back to the immediate problem at hand. Somewhere between four and ten men—seven, he thought, from the sounds—were out there in the sparse woods, closing in on him with lasers and flechette guns at the ready. Against such firepower Caine's own *shuriken, nunchaku*, and slingshot didn't seem like a hell of a lot.

Especially considering his opponents weren't blind.

Automatically, before he could relax them, his eyes strained against the opaque goggles. *Damn you, Lathe, this is ridiculous*, he thought once. Taking a quiet breath, he forced his mind to relax and concentrate.

He had four of his opponents firmly placed: two ahead and to the right, one behind and also on his right, one dead ahead. The other three weren't so certain, but he at least knew they were somewhere to his left. Whether they knew exactly where he was or not wasn't clear; but it *was* clear some of them were getting too close for safety.

And blinded as he was, Caine's only hope was to take the initiative before they tripped over him.

Carefully, making no sound, he dipped his left hand into his thigh *shuriken* pouch and drew out a stack of five stars. He shifted one to his right hand, took a deep breath . . . and rose suddenly to his knees, hurling four of the stars rapid-fire at his known targets.

All four stars were away before the shout of discovery came from his left. Caine sent his fifth *shuriken* in the direction of that voice and dived into a forward roll just as a flechette gun opened up. The darts missed him completely, and the gun's sound gave him yet another target. Ending his roll on his knees, he scrabbled a *shuriken* from his belt pouch and threw it. Someone gurgled and Caine again hit the ground.

And froze, listening. The woods had gone silent. Had there in fact been only six, not seven, attackers?

Abruptly, Caine's tingler came on: *Bandit bearing twenty-five degrees, under cover.*

So there *was* a seventh man . . . but for the information to help him, Caine now needed to remember which way was north. Kinesthetic memory would have that, if he could relax his mind enough for the proper psychor technique to draw it out. There? . . . *there.* Twenty-five degrees east of that . . . there. Ten degrees left of dead-on. Sliding a finger under his right sleeve, Caine tapped out his own tingler message: *Specify bandit's cover.*

No response. Probably a small bush, Caine decided. Large trees seemed to be rare in this area, and a bush would at least provide the visual protection a sapling wouldn't.

Visual protection from a blind man. Though a thick enough bush would also provide some protection against the throwing stars, too. Caine was just reaching for the release strap of his slingshot when a sudden sound barely a meter away threw him into instant, violent reaction.

Ducking his head, he shoved off the forest mat into a flat somersault, rolling on his shoulders and kicking straight out at the unseen figure his ears had said was in front of him. His heels caught something solid, knocked it backward. He leaped after it, snatching his *nunchaku* from its hip sheath and swinging it toward the sound of the crash. The thirty-centimeter hardwood stick, swinging like a buzz saw from its plastic chain, connected with a hollow *thud* . . . and as Caine drew a three-pointed *shuriken* into a push-knife grip, a shrill whistle split the air. Caine slid off his goggles, blinking in the sudden sunlight, and looked down at his opponent as he got to his feet.

Rafe Skyler was a big man to begin with, and with the heavy armor he was wearing he looked positively monstrous. "I think I'm glad I couldn't see you," Caine told him. "You look like a giant sculpture of a beetle."

Skyler chuckled as he got easily to his feet. "A lesser man might take that as an insult," he commented, unsnapping his helmet and lifting it off for examination. On the top was a flaming-red mark a few centimeters across. "Good shot," he said approvingly. "Clean hit, with enough force to break even a Ryq's skull." Craning his neck, the big man looked down onto his chestplate and the twin red marks left there by Caine's heels. "Nice," he said.

"Of course," a voice behind Caine added, "ideally you shouldn't have let him get that close."

Caine turned, feeling the rush of mixed emotions that always, on some level, accompanied his interactions with Damon Lathe. A blackcollar commando commander—comsquare for short—doyen of the remaining blackcollars on Plinry, Lathe had saved Caine's life at least twice and had succeeded in pulling the younger man's first Resistance mission to success out of what had been wet ashes indeed.

On the other hand, he'd also lied to Caine on several occasions, sent him around the red-herring track more times than Caine cared to remember, and had virtually reduced him to pawn status on that same mission. And to top it off, for the past seven months Lathe had been the one running Caine through Plinry's brand-new floating blackcollar academy.

Which had included a *lot* of this brand of tooth-grinding test.

Stepping to Caine's side, Lathe glanced over Skyler's armor. "Not bad," he said. "You also got three fast kills and two slow ones with your *shuriken*. The last one, though, you nearly missed. Let's go to the lodge and run the tapes."

Skyler was looking upward. Caine followed his gaze, found the tiny black dot hovering far above. "Smile for Security's cameras," Skyler suggested.

Caine considered sending an obscene gesture instead, decided not to bother. Replacing his *shuriken* in its pouch, he followed Lathe back through the trees as, all around him, the "dead" returned to life to await the next victim.

It was really rather sobering to see the performance on tape.

Seated before the screen, his mind replaying his own memories as he watched, he listened to Lathe's running critique. ". . . here you lost half a second in the backward underhand throw. . . . Good roll, but he should by rights have nailed you on his next shot. . . . Skyler may have been too quiet to hear, but you should have sensed his approach. . . . Late, but a good takedown anyway."

The tape ended, and Caine uncurled his fists. "So what's the verdict?" he asked. "Are you graduating us now, or do I have to wait until the next time the *Novak* heads for Earth?"

Lathe set his elbows on the desk in front of him, fingering the ring he wore on the middle finger of his right hand as he gazed into Caine's face. Caine's eyes dropped to the ring: a silvery dragonhead, its batwing crest curving back over the knuckle, its ruby-red eyes proclaiming its owner to be a blackcollar comsquare. A symbol of ability, dedication, and sheer fighting power . . . and for Caine, a symbol too of what he intended to do with his new skills.

"You'd like to wear the dragon, wouldn't you?" Lathe asked into his thoughts.

"Not without earning it," Caine told him.

Lathe shrugged fractionally, his eyes still on Caine's. "We *could* grant you a special exception, provided we could find an unused ring to fit you."

"What good would *that* do?" Caine snorted. "I want to *be* a blackcollar, not just dress like one."

Lathe pursed his lips. "If we had any Backlash, you'd be the first to get it. You know that."

Caine nodded. Backlash—the code name for the drug that had been the heart of the whole blackcollar project. Given in a tailored dosage pattern, it permanently altered a man's neural chemistry, effectively doubling his speed and reflexes in combat situations. Backlash, and Backlash alone, had allowed the blackcollars to successfully pit their low-tech, low-profile weaponry against the more sophisticated Ryqril equipment and, in many cases, come out ahead. *Shuriken* and *nunchaku* passed detectors set for lasers and high-metal projectile guns without raising a ripple; Backlash speed and blackcollar marksmanship turned them into deadlier weapons than they had any right to be.

But there was no Backlash on Plinry, and no indication that it still existed anywhere else in the TDE . . . and if that was true, the first generation of blackcollars would also be the last.

Lathe was speaking again, and Caine snapped his attention

back to the blackcollar. "But without it, you and your team are about as ready as we can make you," the older man said. "So if you want to talk to Lepkowski about travel arrangements, this is the time to do so."

Caine licked his lips briefly. The moment he'd been aiming at for the past year . . . the moment when he would leave the relative safety of Plinry and strike out on his own against the Ryqril puppet government on Earth.

But there was no way he was going to show his private uncertainties before Lathe. "Good," he said briskly, getting to his feet. "Is the general still here?"

"He will be for another two hours. Then a shuttle's due to take him back up."

Caine nodded. "Okay. See you later."

General Avril Lepkowski's room at Hamner Lodge was small and sparsely furnished, as befit a man who'd spent perhaps a total of six days there in the past year. A cot, a desk and pair of chairs, a computer with scramble/code capability—brought down from one of the Nova-class warships Lathe and his blackcollars had dug out of decades-old storage from under the Ryqril collective snout a year earlier—and, of course, one of the ubiquitous "bug stompers" that seemed to sprout around the lodge and environs exactly like what their mushroom shapes suggested. Caine eyed the device dubiously as he entered the room. At the moment a good bug stomper was supposed to be proof against all known electronic monitoring devices, but that was bound to change someday. Unfortunately, no one would immediately know when that happened.

"Be with you in a minute, Caine," Lepkowski said, eyes on something tracking across his display. Nodding silently, Caine took the chair beside the desk, from which the screen was out of view. Whatever Lepkowski was working on, it was probably none of Caine's immediate business . . . and both Lathe and Lepkowski were very big on the compartmentalization of secrets. If you didn't need to know, you weren't told. And you didn't ask twice.

A minute later the older man sighed and leaned back in his chair. "Damn them all back to hell," he muttered.

"Trouble?" Caine asked.

"Yes, but so far only at the annoyance level." Lepkowski gestured at his screen. "The *Karachi*'s last intelligence sweep through the TDE indicates the war front with the Chryselli has shifted again, and the damn Ryqril convoy routes have changed accordingly. Means we're going to have to detour around Navarre and maybe New Morocco if we don't want to run into anything big.''

Caine grimaced. The huge Ryqril war machine which had overrun the TDE thirty years earlier was currently locked in combat with the Chryselli Homelands, and the legged furballs were giving the Ryqril a distinct run for their money. It was the only reason Lepkowski's three Novas were being allowed to wander around loose, in fact—the Ryqril simply couldn't afford the front-line ships and time it would take to chase them down. But that didn't mean a ship that just happened to bump into one of the Novas wouldn't take a shot at it. ''You going to have any trouble hitting Earth?''

Lepkowski shook his head. ''None at all—Earth's way off the convoy routes. I understand your team's riding with me.''

''News travels fast,'' Caine said. Of course, Lathe would have given Lepkowski advance notice of the team's graduation. ''Tell me, General, do you have any ideas about where military secrets on Earth might still be preserved?''

Lepkowski's eyebrows rose slightly. ''Any particular secrets you had in mind?''

Caine took a deep breath, suddenly afraid this was going to sound either stupid or boastful or both. ''As a matter of fact, yes,'' he said between stiff lips. ''I want to find the formula for Backlash. The blackcollar drug.''

If Lepkowski thought the goal ludicrous, it wasn't immediately evident. For a long moment the general eyed Caine in silence, his face giving away nothing. Then he twitched a shrug. ''Nothing like starting at the very top of the list. I suppose it's occurred to you that other people have undoubtedly gone on the same treasure hunt over the past thirty years, and that there's no evidence anyone's succeeded yet.''

The thought *had* crossed Caine's mind. Frequently. ''True. But maybe they were looking in the wrong place.''

''And you expect *me* to know the right places?''

''I know you were in charge of this sector before the Ryqril took it. Surely you knew most of the military safe drops on Earth and elsewhere.''

Lepkowski snorted, a wry smile touching his lips. ''Safe drop. I haven't heard that term in years. Your tutors had a definite military bias.''

''General Morris Kratochvil was one of them.''

"Kratochvil." The age lines around Lepkowski's eyes seemed to deepen. "A good man . . . No, Caine, the formula for Backlash wouldn't have been put in any safe drop. If it still exists, it'd have to be in one of the Seven Sisters."

Caine frowned. He'd heard that term before. . . . "Those were the seven top command/defense bases, weren't they? One per continent, roughly."

"Right." The general nodded. "Major secrets of all sorts would have been stored there. Unfortunately . . . well, maybe there's a way to check." Leaning forward again, he began working his keyboard. "We've got some orbital maps of Earth from our last flyby a few months back. Thirty years is a long time, but the force necessary to destroy one of the Sisters ought to have left some lingering scars."

Within a very few minutes that prediction was painfully borne out. Six of the seven spots Lepkowski pointed to were in the middle of either slowly eroding blast craters or unnaturally defoliated wildernesses. Or both.

The seventh . . .

"Almost completely untouched," Lepkowski murmured as he tried various image-enhancement programs and topographical reconstructions. "Incredible. How could they have missed it?"

"Where is the base, exactly?" Caine asked.

Lepkowski did something to the keyboard and a topographic overlay appeared on the orbital photo. "Here," he said, tapping a wide mountain peak. "Aegis Mountain, about thirty klicks west of Denver, North America. Major highway passes north of it here; the entrance opens onto it about *here*."

Caine stared hard at the image. No defoliation; certainly no obvious crater. "What are those things up there to the north?" he asked, pointing to a pair of slightly off-color patches.

"Uh . . ." Lepkowski tapped keys. "Neutron missile scars, I'd say. Probably from the war—they don't look recent."

"Could that be how the base was neutralized? Saturation neutron bombing?"

"No, Aegis had better shielding than that. But you're right—the base *was* neutralized somehow. The Ryqril surely wouldn't have left a fully manned and armed base sitting untouched on the doorstep of a major metro area."

"Maybe they didn't need to destroy it," Caine suggested. "Maybe they got inside and took it over."

"In which case *you* might as well scratch any plans to get in yourself." Lepkowski rubbed his chin. "Hard to believe, though. Once the base was locked down no one should have been able to get in without bringing the whole mountain down on top of himself."

Caine bit at his lip. "Maybe it was *un*locked, then. Surrendered to them."

Lepkowski was silent a long moment. Then he shook his head. "No, that doesn't sound right, either. Kratochvil wouldn't have given Aegis away. And neither would the local commander."

There was another pause. "So what's your end-line assessment?" Caine asked at last. "Is there any use in my looking for Backlash there?"

"Your chances are slim at best," Lepkowski said bluntly. "Whether Aegis is locked down, burned out, or up to its hangar level in Ryqril, your chances of getting in are almost nonexistent. Maybe with some help—but I don't even know what kind of help you could find in the area."

"I might," Caine said. "There were supposed to be some blackcollars working in the central continent somewhere. And my Resistance tutors also had limited contact with a North American group called Torch."

"Competent?"

Caine shrugged. "They were still around when I left, as far as I know. Real hard-wrapped fanatics, from what I heard—ready to do anything to overthrow the Ryqril."

Lepkowski shook his head. "I wouldn't go near them if I were you. Never trust fanatics any farther than you absolutely have to."

"Because they take stupid chances?"

"*And* because they'll turn on you in a second if you stray half a step off their personal version of the 'correct' way."

Caine hissed a breath between his teeth. "Well . . . is there any other place in the TDE where I'd have a better shot? What about Centauri A?"

"The blackcollar training center?" The general shook his head. "It's gone. Bombed so thoroughly the planet looks to be headed into an ice age. The Ryqril had had enough experience with blackcollars by then to know they sure as hell didn't want any more of them coming out of Centauri."

No, of course the Ryqril didn't want any more blackcollars. Caine had seen for himself just what blackcollars could do against the aliens and their loyalty-conditioned human allies . . . and the memories reminded him of exactly why he'd decided on this goal in the first place. "All right," he said slowly. "Then Aegis is it, I guess. Can you tell me anything about the base—layout, defenses, anything?"

Lepkowski eyed him. "I can give you a few generalities, but not much more." He tapped a spot on the photo. "The entrance is off the highway here. Leads back under the crest of the mountain, about three klicks away. The tunnel is wide enough for fighter aircraft, which would be rolled out onto the highway for launch."

"About how many of them were there?"

"Aircraft? I'd say a hundred at least, maybe more. But there won't be any of them left—they would all have been out attacking Ryqril landing craft and escorts at the end."

"None of the survivors would have had the proper codes to get back in?"

"There aren't any codes for opening a battle-sealed fortress from the outside," Lepkowski said flatly. "When I said no one could get in, I meant it. Unless the people inside open up, the place stays sealed. Well. Below the hangar level are eight personnel levels, plus one more with the fusion generators and gas turbine and fuel cell backups. Water from artesian wells dug to various depths, air through long ventilation tunnels with a dozen different filtration systems. Enough food, fuel, and spare parts to survive a good fifteen years. That's for the entire contingent of about two thousand officers and enlisted men, of course."

Caine shook his head in wonderment. "The place must be *huge*. Any emergency escape tunnels?"

"There would have been one, but don't count on using it. It would have been collapsed automatically after any survivors got out."

"Or collapsed manually by those still inside?"

"Point," Lepkowski admitted. "A small contingent *could* have survived in there this long. If they'd lost weapons capability during the last battle the Ryqril might have postponed dealing with them. . . . No. No, it doesn't make sense. They wouldn't have left a group of potential rebels locked up in a functional military base."

"Unless they don't know where the entrance is," Caine suggested suddenly. "If there were even a minor rock fall—"

"Except that anyone in Denver could have shown them where it was," Lepkowski put in dryly. "It wasn't exactly hidden or anything. In fact"—he peered at the display—"it looks to me like there's a small encampment right by the door now."

If there was, Caine's untrained eyes couldn't spot it. "A Ryqril checkpoint? Or just a group of cultists worshipping the dead base?"

"Don't laugh—it could easily be something that crazy." Lepkowski pointed to a spot a few kilometers west. "That town shows signs of habitation, too, despite the fact that the tunnel linking the highway through to Denver has clearly collapsed. I don't know about you, but *I* sure wouldn't want to live that isolated from everywhere else."

"Unless the Ryqril allow them aircars—yes, I know how likely that is. What about those ventilation tunnels you mentioned? Could someone get in that way?"

"Only if he had more lives than a litter of kittens. Those tunnels have at least eight types of sensors, hooked to three separate sets of active and passive defense systems. *Lethal* defense systems."

"After thirty years—"

"Some of them will be working for another century or two."

Caine pursed his lips. The whole thing was sounding less promising by the minute . . . and he might have said so if Lepkowski hadn't beaten him to it. "You know, Caine, the more I think about this the more I think the mission would be a dangerous waste of time. If the Ryqril haven't been able to get in, you won't be able to either; and if they *have* gotten in, you won't *want* to. Maybe you'd better go for something a little less ambitious."

Something a bit easier for beginners? Even if that wasn't what Lepkowski had meant, the thought was too much to ignore. "Thanks for the advice, sir," he said, perhaps a shade too stiffly. "But it's *my* time to waste. It can't hurt to just take a look."

Lepkowski shrugged. "It's your team and your mission. But you're totally insane to even consider it."

Caine had to smile at that one. "Any more than you are to zip around the TDE in that big flying target of yours? But let's keep my insanity our private secret, if you don't mind," he added, glancing automatically at the humming bug stomper. "Even my team isn't going to know the objective until they need to; I don't want anyone else knowing, either."

"Not even Lathe?"

"No. Compartmentalization of secrets, remember?"

Lepkowski's eyes bored into his. "It's hardly the same thing. Lathe is in charge here."

"*Here* he's in charge. Not on Earth."

For a moment the general gazed at him, a frown creasing his forehead. Then he shrugged. "I suppose I can understand how you feel. It *is* your first command, after all. Well . . . good luck. If there's anything else I can do to help, just let me know."

"Thank you, sir, but I think all we'll need from you now is safe passage to Earth. The rest will be up to us."

The rest will have *to be up to us*, Caine reflected as he returned to his own room. Any details about Denver that Lepkowski or the blackcollars might have once had would be at least thirty years out of date. His team would have to pick them up once they were down.

And hope that local Security was slow on the uptake.

Chapter 2

Seen from several kilometers up, the picture artificially enhanced six ways from center, Caine's blind-man test was still one hell of an impressive display. Prefect Jamus Galway, head of Plinry Security, ran the tape twice before turning to his aide. "Have the Ryqril seen a copy of this tape?" he asked.

Ragusin shrugged helplessly. "This tape and all the others. There's still no change in the order."

The order. No need to specify, of course. *Monitor all activities at the blackcollar training camp but do not attempt disruption.* Galway had appealed it twice, but the Ryqril had consistently turned him down, and the apparent foolishness of that position was beginning to get to him. Were the aliens so intimidated by those three Novas that they were willing to put up with a military school in occupied territory? A school run by *blackcollars*, for God's sake?

"It could be worse," Ragusin broke into his thoughts. "At least they're not turning out full blackcollars—the analysis shows Caine's reflexes are only a few percent better than when he began the training. Same range of improvement we've found with the other trainees."

Galway nodded. He knew all that, probably better than anyone else on Plinry. The training center had occupied far too many of his waking hours over the past few months, taking his attention away from other, more routine, security matters. There were reports on the rise of teenage gangs in Capstone's poorer sections which he'd barely had time to skim; details on the upgrading of the Hub's protective wall that he should be paying better attention to. And to be fair, as long as Lathe was turning out little more than unusually good guerrilla soldiers—and as long as Ryqril could keep tabs on both school and graduates—there really *was* little danger to either Plinry or the Ryqril Empire as a whole.

Or so the logic went. Galway didn't believe a word of it.

He ran the tape again. There was little data yet on such things, but Galway's gut feeling was that Caine had passed. "So Caine is finished here. Any idea when he'll be leaving? And with whom?"

"Only indications, but they're pretty positive ones," Ragusin said, shuffling a page out of the stack of paper he habitually carried around these days. "The *Novak*'s leaving in five days for a swing around his section of the TDE—stops at Hegira, Juniper, New Calais, Earth, Shiloh, Magna Graecia, Carno, and Bullhead. Presumably Caine will be aboard."

"Passengers?"

"They'll start with thirty businessmen from here, undoubtedly add and subtract en route. All ours have been checked out and seem legit."

Galway nodded sourly. Before Caine and his Novas only government officials and a handful of loyalty-conditioned businessmen had ever been permitted interstellar travel. Now, General Lepkowski's starships and the concessions he'd wangled out of the Ryqril had scrapped that policy—and turned Galway's security responsibilities from headache to nightmare. Lepkowski was hardly going to be content with ferrying petty entrepreneurs around the TDE, and Galway's office simply didn't have the manpower to weed out the spies, saboteurs, and weapons that would eventually begin pouring through the pipeline.

But again, there was nothing he could do about it. "All right." He sighed. "Potential teammates?"

"Only one probable set," Ragusin said. "Woody Pittman, Stef Braune, Doon Colvin, and Mal Alamzad. Almost all of Caine's team exercises have been with them."

The names were familiar: local Capstone kids, all four,

who'd gotten a head start in their guerrilla training through the secret martial arts classes the blackcollars had started seven years back. One name was familiar for another reason, as well. "What about the blackcollars themselves? Any chance Lathe would send one with Caine?"

"It's possible, I suppose, but there's no indication of anything like that. No indication, either, as to which planet Caine will be making for."

"Earth." Galway had no doubts on that score. Born, raised, and Resistance-educated in Europe on Earth, Caine would surely return home to begin his private war. Eight parsecs out of Galway's jurisdiction . . . which meant the prefect could file his report, watch Caine climb aboard the shuttle, and then put it all out of his mind.

Except that he couldn't. And he knew it.

Reaching to his intercom, he buzzed for the Blackcollar Monitor duty officer. "I want locations for four trainees," he said when the other answered. "Pittman, Braune, Colvin, and Alamzad."

There was a slight pause. "All four are at the Hamner Lodge camp, sir," the other reported. "Braune since five this morning, the other three since seven."

Galway glanced at his watch. Almost five now; they'd been there for fifteen and thirteen hours, respectively. If Lathe stuck to his usual scheduling pattern the kids would be heading back to Capstone soon. "Let me know immediately if any of those four or Caine comes out," he instructed the officer and broke the connection. "Ragusin," he said to his aide, "get two cars and drivers and meet me outside. We're bringing them in for a farewell chat."

"*All* of them, sir?" the other asked, moving toward the door.

"It'll be safer that way," Galway said. "Besides, I'd like to see up close how Caine's changed in the past seven months."

Ragusin nodded and left. Opening his desk drawer, Galway pulled out his laser and holster and strapped them on. If the trainees didn't want to come peaceably the weapon would be of only marginal use, but seeing how they reacted to the presence of armed Security men on their home territory might prove interesting.

Presumably the reaction would remain at nonlethal levels. But if not . . . well, that was something he needed to know, too.

*   *   *

Caine was in the lodge dining room, studying the orbital maps of Denver Lepkowski had run off for him, when Chelsey Jensen came in with the news.

"Galway wants *me*?" He frowned at the blackcollar, feeling his stomach tighten within him. "Why?"

Jensen ran two fingers through his blond hair. "All he'll say is that he wants to take you and your team into the Hub for some routine questions before you leave for Earth."

Caine grimaced. "Nothing like having secrets from the opposition, is there?"

Jensen shrugged. "Galway's always been good at reading minds," he said. "It's just one of the things we have to put up with."

"Yeah. Do you think I should go?"

"Up to you. But he's already got your team."

"Right," Caine said, getting to his feet. In the past year or so Jensen had developed almost an obsession with personal loyalty, and it wouldn't do at all for Caine to seem ready to abandon his teammates to the wolves. "Would you ask someone to take these to my room, please? No sense giving Security a head start on where we'll be dropping."

"Sure." Jensen accepted the stack. "Watch yourselves, and good luck."

Galway was standing beside one of two cars as Caine walked down the sloping dirt road to where the prefect had parked. The second car, he noted, had three of his new teammates in back and two men in Security gray-green in front. The fourth trainee sat in the back of Galway's car.

"Caine." Galway nodded as Caine walked up to him. "I presume Jensen told you what I wanted."

"Yes. And it'd better not take too long."

"I understand. Preparations to go offworld and all must have you pretty busy."

Caine suppressed a grimace. "More to the point, Lathe will take action if we're in the Hub too long."

"Two hours at the most," Galway said equably. "Shall we go?"

Seated beside Pittman, behind Galway and a Security driver, Caine maintained a cool silence through the sixteen-kilometer drive to the edge of Capstone, Plinry's capital city. The others did likewise; but as the cars began threading their way through the city streets toward the Hub, Galway half turned in his seat to send appraising looks at his two passengers. "You've both made remarkable progress these past few months," he commented. "That blind-man combat, especially, must be a real killer to get through, and you both did quite well on it."

Caine's hands, folded in his lap, curved into a blackcollar signal: *no noise*. Pittman made the proper interpretation and remained silent.

Ahead, the gray wall that marked the edge of the Hub had become visible, its brooding presence a symbol both of the Ryqril domination and—to Caine—of the limits to the aliens' power. Lathe's blackcollars had gotten over that wall once— gotten over it despite its sensors and automatic defenses and human guards. When the need arose, he knew, they'd get over it again.

The private pep talk helped. Caine found his heartbeat nearly normal as the metal-mesh gate closed behind them.

Galway turned around again. "I understand you're heading out in a few days," he said. "Any particular part of Earth you're making for?"

"Antarctica," Caine told him. "The Hollick-Kenyon Plateau, specifically. If you wanted to make small talk, we could have done that at the lodge."

"True, but there are other things we couldn't have handled there. New photos of you, for example, plus fingerprint and retinal patterns. For our records."

"And for export?"

Galway's lip twitched in a grim smile. "The Ryqril are very interested in you, Caine—in all of you," he amended, eying Pittman. "They just love to read about the progress you've been making."

Caine didn't reply.

The five trainees were taken one by one into the interrogation room Galway had set aside for the purpose. Each was fingerprinted, ret-shot, and photographed with quiet efficiency by Ragusin as Galway, for his part, kept up a steady stream of questions. Mostly, this worked out to be a monologue, a result the prefect had more or less expected from Caine and three of his teammates. With the proper stress analysis, answers to even innocuous questions could sometimes yield valuable information, and the standard approach was thus to ignore the interrogator as much as possible. Caine knew that, and Galway knew he knew it, and it made the whole exercise rather a waste of time . . . except that Galway expected the fifth interview to run somewhat differently than the first four had.

And he wasn't disappointed.

"You *are* leaving with the *Novak* in five days, aren't you?"

Seated at the ret-scan machine, lips tightly compressed, Woody Pittman nodded once. The gesture was rich in nonverbal emotion, and Galway felt a twinge of sympathy for the boy's position. But the prefect had a job to do, and his personal feelings about what the Ryqril had done to Pittman couldn't be allowed to get in the way. "I gather you're going to Earth. Any idea where?"

"North America," Pittman said. "We'll be riding the shuttle down toward Denver, but Caine said we'll be dropping off before it lands."

Galway called up a file map on the room's display and gave it a quick scan. A useless gesture; there were far too many targets in the Denver area that a spy or saboteur might find interesting. "Any idea whether your mission goal is in that area?" he asked. "Or could you just be staying in the area long enough to collect identification and lose any pursuit?"

Pittman shook his head. "Caine hasn't told us anything at all. *Nothing*; so you can quit trying to rephrase the question. He takes Lathe's lectures on secrecy very seriously."

Galway sighed. "Somehow, that doesn't surprise me." He thought a moment, watching as Pittman's face was photographed and, for good measure, layer-scan-printed as well. "Has Caine mentioned any special equipment? Or have you had any out-of-the-ordinary training?"

Again, Pittman shook his head. "There isn't a thing more I can tell you until we're on Earth, Galway. Maybe not even then."

"All right," Galway said, giving up. Pittman wasn't likely to be holding out on him, after all. Though with the boy's lack of loyalty-conditioning Galway could never be a hundred-percent sure of that. . . . "I'll set you up a contact in the Denver Security office—use the code name Postern to identify yourself when you call."

Pittman nodded and stood up. "Anything else?"

"Not right now. Good luck."

The boy's face twisted in a sardonic smile and he left the room, Galway catching a glimpse of the guard falling in beside him as the door swung shut. Sighing, he tapped the intercom. "Escort all the blackcollar trainees out of the Hub," he instructed the desk man.

"Caine'll want to be taken back to the lodge."

Galway snorted. "Tell him he can find his own way up there. We're not running an autocab service here."

"Yes, sir."

Galway signed off and turned his attention back to the map of Denver, peripherally aware that Ragusin had moved to look over his shoulder. "You see anything obvious?" he asked his aide.

"Not offhand," Ragusin admitted. "There's an awful lot there."

"My thoughts exactly. Well . . . why don't you go down and make sure Caine and company don't make any trouble on their way out. I'll head over to my office and give the Ryqril a call. Tell them another team's going to be hitting Earth soon."

It wasn't a pleasant duty; and for several long minutes after he'd signed off Galway stood at the large window beside his desk, gazing out at the Hub as he let the tension of that contact work itself out through trembling muscles. He didn't hate humanity's conquerors, of course; the loyalty-conditioning he'd undergone at the age of eighteen had permanently eliminated that emotional response to the Ryqril. But the conditioning didn't block fear . . . and Galway feared the rubber-skinned aliens more than anything in the universe. Not only for what they could do to him personally, but also for what they'd already shown themselves capable of doing to whole worlds.

To *his* world.

Lifting his eyes, Galway looked past Capstone's buildings to the Greenheart Mountains, where even thirty-six years after the Ryqril Groundfire attack the vegetation was still nowhere near its prewar lushness. Plinry had come close to dying in that attack, and it would be another generation at least before the planet could survive anything comparable.

And if the blackcollar training camp became too much of a threat to the Ryqril . . .

Galway shuddered. No, he couldn't simply pass on information about Caine to someone else and then forget about it. He had a highly vested interest in making sure every team Lathe and Lepkowski sent on its way was neutralized, and neutralized fast. Involuntarily, as if seeking one final cathartic shiver, his eyes slipped back to Capstone, and the Hub, and

the tall black wall rising like a truncated mountain from near
the center of the government section. The Ryqril Enclave.
The impregnable town-within-a-city-within-a-city from which
the real rulers of Plinry sent their orders to puppets like
Galway. The place where the decision to obliterate the
blackcollars—and perhaps the entire planet along with them—
might someday be made.

And all that stood between Plinry and that decision was a
competent Security prefect doing his job.

Turning away from the window, Galway stepped back to his
desk and, with fresh determination, got to work.

"Backlash."

Lathe said the word quietly, almost reverently, fingers
playing over the red-eyed dragonhead ring on his hand. Two
hours ago his ambitions had been of a small, comfortable
size; he'd felt himself lucky just to have a training center and
men of Caine's and Pittman's caliber with whom to work.
But if Backlash was once again available, there was suddenly
no limit to what he could accomplish. . . .

With an effort, he forced both mind and eyes back from the
visionary future to the reality of the man facing him. "What
are his chances? Really?"

Lepkowski shook his head. "I don't know," he told the
comsquare. "I'd bet heavily that the formula was in the Aegis
secrets file during the war. But after that point I can't even
hazard a guess. I suppose it could still be lying around in
there gathering dust—it's nothing the Ryqril would be especially interested in rooting out."

"Nor your average resistance team, either," Lathe mused.
"Even mainline military people might not realize how heavily
the blackcollar project hinged on the drug."

Lepkowski cocked an eyebrow. "Or else they simply didn't
think the blackcollars were worth bringing back."

Lathe smiled grimly. "Can't hurt my feelings *that* easily,
friend—I *like* being underestimated, remember?"

Lepkowski grinned in return, a smile of shared memories.
Then he sobered. "Caine won't like being interfered with,
you know."

"I sort of expected that." Lathe thought a moment. "Well,
we've got five days to come up with something clever."

"And remember that that something clever shouldn't inter-
fere with or compromise Project Christmas," the general
said.

"Oh, hell," Lathe muttered under his breath. Project Christmas had been in the works for so long he hadn't immediately made the—obvious, now—connection. "That *does* complicate everything, doesn't it?" he admitted. "Though in some ways it actually might work to our advantage. Well, we'll just have to make double-damn sure Christmas comes off without a hitch."

Lepkowski waved a hand. "We've been in worse spots with tighter tolerances—and as you say, we've *got* five days. Let's get to work, shall we?"

Chapter 3

One of the biggest problems Lepkowski and the Plinry blackcollars had faced with their year-old businessmen's shuttle, Caine knew, had been that of maintaining proper security while civilians were aboard the new starships. It wasn't a trivial matter; with the tool of loyalty-conditioning at Security's disposal, the government could theoretically slip saboteurs through even the finest screening procedures. The danger had eventually been at least minimized by completely sealing off a section of the *Novak* exclusively for civilian passenger use.

Which sounded rather cramped to most people . . . because most people didn't have any real feel for just how big the *Novak* really was.

Certainly Caine's four teammates didn't, expecting confinement to a special section of their own away from both crew and other passengers, neither of which knew of their presence. Caine had watched with secret amusement as they first learned what a "small private section" really meant. After the cramped homes most of them had grown up knowing in nongovernment Capstone—and the even tighter conditions at Hamner Lodge—the *Novak* was almost like a luxury vacation by comparison.

A vacation that ended three days out from Earth with the arrival of Lepkowski for their final briefing.

"The shuttle will be coming into Denver from the west, on

this vector,'' the general told them, indicating a path west by north over the Rockies on the detailed map he'd brought for them. ''Your drop pods will be jettisoned here, about twenty-five klicks from the edge of the mountains and civilization.''

''A bit of a stretch, isn't that?'' Stef Braune asked dubiously.

''We did nearly thirty on Argent,'' Caine told him. ''And that was without any tailwind assistance.''

''These *are* mountains, though,'' Doon Colvin pointed out. ''That means strong and often dangerous air currents to fight.''

''How dangerous?'' Caine asked. Unlike any of the others— including Caine—Colvin had had a lot of private experience with hang gliders.

Colvin shrugged. ''Depends on the mountains and the weather at the time. Could be a relatively minor annoyance or an immediate catastrophe or anything in between.''

Lepkowski and Caine exchanged glances. ''Can you drop any closer to the metro area?'' the general asked.

Caine shook his head. ''Too much of our path's going to be visible on Security's radar as it is. I want to be on the far side of these mountains *here* and *here* when we swing around to follow this road. We need to draw their first countermove to the wrong place if we're going to have time to lose ourselves in Denver before they realize their mistake.''

Alamzad cleared his throat. ''Not to push or anything, Caine, but as long as we're all together now anyway . . . how about breaking down and telling us just what we're supposed to do once we get there?''

Caine could feel Lepkowski's eyes on him. ''Sorry,'' he said, looking at each of his team as he spoke. ''But this is too important a mission to take any risks whatsoever with. It's not that I don't trust you,'' he added, ''but there's always a chance Security might snatch one of you . . . and even psychor conditioning techniques can be broken with the right kind of pressure.''

None of the four liked it—that much was obvious from their faces. But they accepted it without further argument.

Some of that same faith was also in evidence later on in a different part of the starship, but in this case the participants had a good deal more experience on which to base it. Seated together with his own four-man team, Lathe ran through the details of Caine's plan. ''. . . so *we'll* drop approximately three klicks back and one up from their drop point,'' he finished, marking the spot on his copy of Lepkowski's map.

"Colvin seemed to think we'd have some trouble with winds, but I don't see us having any choice."

"How about dropping from an entirely separate shuttle?" Chelsey Jensen suggested. "If we go first we could be on the ground near Caine's landing site and keep track of them that way."

"Doubt if Lepkowski could finagle loads well enough to justify two shuttles," Dawis Hawking said, shaking his head. "Besides, two obvious drops might stir up Security more than we can really afford."

"That's the clincher," Lathe agreed. "Security's used to us doing things one way now, and keeping the illusion that we're still following that pattern is the way to buy us some time."

"Which we're going to be on short enough rations of as it is," Rafe Skyler said with a shake of his head. "Lathe, this is about as crazy a scheme as I've ever seen you tackle. No matter *what* shape Aegis Mountain's in, Caine's got about zero chance in a thousand of getting inside. With or without us playing backstop for him."

Lathe shrugged. "Perhaps. All right—*probably*, even. But I don't think it's completely hopeless. Anything people can get out of other people can get into. It's largely a matter of locating those other people."

"And hoping the Ryqril haven't already set up shop in the base," Jensen murmured.

Hawking snorted gently. "It wouldn't be the first time blackcollars have planned to invade a Ryqril stronghold."

"Not even the first time this year," Jensen said archly. "That is, if Christmas is still on schedule."

"It is," Lathe said. "The point is that we've got an awful damn lot to gain if we *do* somehow manage to pull this off."

"Yes," the fifth blackcollar, Mordecai, said quietly, the first time he'd spoken since the meeting began. Lathe studied the other's dark face for a moment; but, characteristically, the small man added nothing more to his single word of agreement.

It was enough, though. Mordecai didn't talk much, but his support carried a lot of weight on a mission of this sort.

"Well, who wants to live forever, anyway?" Skyler shrugged. "Any idea what we can expect in the way of opposition?"

"The government center's here," Lathe told him, tapping a spot wedged between the southwestern edge of Denver proper and a ridge the computer had labeled Hogback. "Originally a separate town named Athena, apparently full of support personnel and families for Aegis during the war. It was a logical spot for the collies to set up shop, and they seem to have done so.''

"Where's the Ryqril section?" Hawking asked, frowning at the photo.

"Oddly enough, there doesn't seem to be one," Lathe said. "At least there's no separately fortified enclave within Athena."

"Which are two ways of saying the same thing," Skyler rumbled. "Bad sign, Lathe—if the cockroach spawn aren't there, they've got to be somewhere they consider safe."

"Such as Aegis Mountain?" Jensen suggested.

"Well, yes, the logic *does* seem to lead us that way," Lathe admitted. "But I'm not ready to carve it in stone quite yet. There may be other rat holes in the area the Ryqril have found and appropriated. We'll just have to wait and see."

That was, unfortunately, the bottom line for nearly everything about the mission. Still, Lathe had to admit they'd managed on a lot less up-front data on other missions. This time, at the very least, they knew their target city still existed.

And finally, it was time to go.

For Caine, it was with an odd feeling of displaced déjà vu that he followed Lepkowski to the hanger where the specially equipped shuttle was waiting: displaced, because the last time he'd been the greenest of Lathe's team, the one from whom the fine points of strategy and tactics had been withheld. This time—

This time *he* was the leader, the man in charge of it all. The man with both the authority *and* the responsibility for other men's lives. A sobering thought; but down deep he had to admit that it was exhilarating, as well.

The shuttle was a standard ground-to-orbit craft, with one important design difference. Attached to each side, at both fore and aft positions, were two pairs of drop pods, shaped like truncated cones three meters tall. Each pod would hold up to four men.

It was Braune who asked the obvious question as Lepkowski led the way toward the forward pair of pods. "What're the ones in back for?"

"Decoys," Lepkowski said over his shoulder. "We drop them a klick or two before yours go."

"Won't they draw more attention?" Pittman asked.

"If you're scope-visible at the time it's not going to make

any difference if we drop one pod or sixty.'' The general shook his head. "This way the enemy's response at least gets diluted a little.''

Inside, the pods were a maze of cables, straps, and bars. Caine settled himself into the starboard one with Pittman, Braune, and Alamzad, leaving Colvin to himself in the supply pod on the other side. "All set," he told Lepkowski after everyone was strapped into place. "Seal us up and let's get going.''

"Good luck," Lepkowski said . . . and then the thick door swung shut, plunging them into darkness.

The waiting's always the hardest part, Caine told himself; but in this case good management on someone's part had minimized that annoyance. Caine's eyes had barely adjusted to the faint glow of the pod's luminous instruments when he felt the subtle vibrations of someone boarding the shuttle . . . and then another, and another. The Earthbound passengers, heading groundside. Caine wondered briefly if they would face an angry Security grilling on arrival, but put that concern out of his mind. None of them were in any way connected with the impending illegal entry into Ryqril-owned territory, and Security wasn't likely to pick on them once that fact was established. Caine hoped not, anyway.

It was perhaps a quarter hour after the footfalls had ceased when the pod gave a jerk and Caine's stomach abruptly tried to climb up his esophagus. "Going down," Braune murmured in a conversational tone that almost succeeded in covering up his nervousness.

"Down but not out," Caine replied, eyes on the altimeter. The shuttle pilot, he knew, would be dropping the pods at five klicks . . . almost there . . .

A dull thud, more felt than heard, made him start against his straps before he realized it was the decoy pods breaking free. "Here we go," he told the others . . . and with a wrench they were suddenly in free fall.

Someone hissed something under his breath. A second later gravity returned with twin jolts as Caine popped the drogue and main chutes. "Get ready," he said as their flight smoothed again. "Five seconds to breakout . . . three, two, *one*—

He wrenched the control, and the pod's walls split from floor to ceiling, the floor disintegrated, and the four men were flung apart into the darkness as the wall sections they were strapped to caught the inrush of air and separated. Caine got a dizzying glimpse of stars above and black ground below; and then, with a snap of spring-loaded connectors and a hiss of compressed air, the pod section above him unfolded into a hang-glider wing. For a second he felt himself slipping sideways as the glider leveled itself, and then he was flying smoothly over the landscape far below.

His second experience with blackcollar drop pods. Eventually, he supposed, one got used to the ride.

Licking his lips briefly, he made a quick scan of the visible sky. Off to his left were two starless blotches that could be other gliders. "Report, Colvin," he said into the short-range mike curving along his cheek.

"I think I can see everyone," Colvin's voice came in his ear. "You're all below and ahead of me."

"UV beacons in turn," Caine ordered. "Pittman . . . Braune . . . Alamzad . . . me."

"Yeah, you're all more or less together," Colvin reported. "Zad, you don't seem very steady, though. You having trouble?"

"I don't know." Even through the radio Alamzad's tension was clearly audible. "Either I've got a loose connection somewhere or the damn wind direction keeps changing."

"It's the wind," Pittman put in. "I've got some of that, too, and you're closer in to the mountain than I am."

Mountain? Caine peered into the darkness. Sure enough, there was a sharp peak looming off to his right that he hadn't noticed before. Shielding from Security's radar, for sure, but as a sudden eddy current bucked his glider he began to wonder if the protection was going to be worth it. If the winds decreased their flight range badly enough—

"I'm going down!" Alamzad snapped abruptly. "A downdraft of some kind. Trying to pull up—"

"No!" Colvin barked before Caine could respond. "Ride it—pull up and you'll stall."

"Too late," Alamzad said with a hissing sigh of resignation. "I'm going down. Hope I can find a clearing or something."

For a long second Caine's mind seemed to freeze. Down in unknown territory, far from any sort of populace to disappear into. . . .

The moment passed, his Resistance and blackcollar training driving logic and calmness into his mind. "Alamzad, turn on your UV," he ordered. "Colvin, there should be a road somewhere nearby angling southeast into Denver. Can you see it?"

"Got it. Zad, goose your glider a little bit—if you can thread those two humps ahead of you, you'll at least land on a downslope in sight of the road."

"Okay," Alamzad said tightly. "Where do I go after I'm clear?"

"Follow the road southeast," Colvin told him. "It starts to switchback up through the mountains there, I think, and the farther up we get the less climbing we'll have to do. Caine, what should I do?"

"Get as far along the road as you can," Caine said. "Pittman and Braune, go with him. Try and stay together." Below, the faint purple glow of Alamzad's ultraviolet beacon had successfully cleared the mountain peaks and was weaving like a drunken moth as the other searched for a landing site. "Alamzad, there looks to be a gap in the trees east of you. If we can make it that far, we'll be fairly close to the road."

The significance of the pronoun wasn't lost on the others. "I'll stay with you," Pittman volunteered immediately. "Three men in mountainous territory are safer than two."

"Thanks, but no. You're as likely to end up in an even more inhospitable place. Besides, I want you three to have the supplies repacked for backpacking when we reach you."

A crash of breaking branches in their earphones stifled any further comments. Caine held his breath. . . . "I'm down," Alamzad said. "Afraid the glider's shot."

Caine let out his breath quietly. "They're of limited use on the ground anyway," he said. The other's UV was still glowing; turning carefully, Caine prepared to join him. "Get going, everyone—we'll meet you up the road. And go easy on radio usage."

"Good luck," Colvin said, and then there was silence. Licking his lips once, Caine set his teeth together and started down. They were definitely off to a great start.

Floating along on the strong breeze two kilometers above, Lathe listened long enough to confirm all of Caine's team had landed safely before switching back to the blackcollars' frequency. "Suggestions?" he asked.

"Not much choice, is there?" Jensen said. "We dump the silent backstop role and go get them out."

"Out of what?" Hawking countered. "About all we can do at this point is hold their hands as we all slog along together."

"Seems to me," Skyler rumbled, "that we need to either

help them get to Denver quickly, or else set up a diversion to pull Security off their backs while they find their own way there.''

Jensen snorted. "That'd be one double hell of a diversion. Even once they're all together they'll be a good twenty klicks from the edge of town.''

"Good point," Lathe agreed. The discussion had given him time to put his own thoughts in order and decide on their best course. "All right—transport it is. Let's make for civilization and see about borrowing a car.''

The radio went silent as the five blackcollars settled down to squeezing all the distance possible out of their hang gliders. Caine, Lathe had a sneaking suspicion, wasn't going to like this a bit, but injured pride was low on the priority list at the moment. Eyes scanning the blackness around him for the Security flyers that must surely be on their way, he steered toward the lights just beginning to show through gaps in the mountains. And hoped to hell he didn't fly into anything solid on the way.

Chapter 4

Civilization, in this case, was a small town nestled among the mountains flanking the road, separated from Denver itself by the massive eastern-slope peaks that ran right to the edge of that city. As Lathe had often found with mountain towns, this one had no clearly defined edge, its houses dribbling off into hills and brush in relatively isolated ones and twos.

It was near one of these more secluded residences that they came down, landing along a dirt road and ditching their gliders in the woods flanking it. "Now what?" Skyler asked after the supply packs had been sorted out. "We walk up to the door and ask to borrow an autocab hailer?''

"Something like that.'' Lights showed in three of the house's windows, Lathe noted, but no driveway guidelights were on. So the family probably wasn't expecting any company. "Mordecai, you're outside backup; Hawking, check for signs of a vehicle; Jensen, go watch the far end of the drive.''

With murmured acknowledgments the group split up. Skyler at his side and Mordecai a few paces behind, Lathe headed through the trees toward the lights. Something above to the west caught his eye, and he turned just as two distant blue-violet lights vanished behind some mountain. ''A mite slow on the uptake,'' Skyler murmured. ''Collies should've had patrol boats up there half an hour ago.''

''Maybe we took them by surprise,'' Lathe said, knowing full well how unlikely that was. Galway would have sent word of Caine's imminent arrival via a Ryqril Corsair, and the *Novak*'s multiplanet circle had taken nearly three times the four days in which a Corsair could have made the direct flight. ''Maybe they want to watch us for a while,'' he told Skyler. ''Try and see what Caine's up to before grabbing him. It wouldn't be the first time they'd tried that game.''

''And lost it,'' Skyler agreed. ''Well, lead on.''

The house was single-story, reasonably nice but probably no more than lower-middle-class if Plinry standards were at all applicable. The blackcollars could have broken in in any of a dozen ways, but Lathe preferred to try the polite approach first. Stepping up to the door, he knocked.

There was a short wait, during which time an entry light went on and a shadow passed over the inner side of the door's spyhole. Eventually, the door opened a crack and a man peered out. ''Yes?''

''Sorry to bother you,'' Lathe said, ''but we're lost and need some information.''

The man's eyes dropped briefly to the Plinry-style clothing hiding the blackcollars' flexarmor. ''Sorry,'' he said, his voice abruptly tight. ''I don't think there's anything I can—''

''I'm sorry, too,'' Lathe said, slipping the ends of his *nunchaku* into the gap. Simultaneously, Skyler leaned on the door; and a moment later the two blackcollars were inside.

''Don't be afraid,'' Lathe told the man, whose face had gone gray. Beyond him, sitting together in a conversation room, were a woman and small girl. The woman looked as terrified as her husband, the girl's face rapidly heading the same way. ''Really,'' Lathe assured them all. ''We aren't going to hurt you. All we need is some information''—he glanced at the man's clothes—''and something less conspicuous than what we're wearing. Is this everyone who's in the house?''

The woman caught her breath, but before anyone could speak Lathe's tingler came on: *Young man in back room— approaching with crossbow.*

Skyler's response was to drift toward the hallway exiting from the conversation room. The woman's eyes widened as they followed him. "Ask him to put down his crossbow and join us," Lathe told the father. "He's only going to get himself hurt."

The other licked his lips. "Sean?" he called, voice cracking a bit. "Better do as he—"

And with a karate-type shout, a teenager bounded into the room, crossbow leveled and tracking toward Lathe. He fired—

And the bolt dug itself into the rug a bare meter in front of him as Skyler's *nunchaku* snapped out and down onto the front of the weapon, knocking it toward the floor.

The boy froze, and for a handful of heartbeats the room was as silent as a tomb. Then Skyler stepped forward and plucked the weapon from Sean's nerveless fingers. "Aren't allowed firearms or lasers, I gather," he commented conversationally, examining the crossbow briefly before leaning it against the wall behind him. "Nice. Not really intended for close-range work, though."

"Blackcollars," the father whispered, his eyes on the *nunchaku* dangling casually from Skyler's hand. "You're *blackcollars.*"

"Don't make it sound like a crime," Lathe admonished him. "Now—"

"I'm sorry, sir—I'm *sorry*," the man all but gasped, almost cringing before the comsquare. "I didn't mean—that is— "

"Relax," Lathe told him, flicking a glance at Skyler. The other blackcollar shrugged minutely, Lathe's puzzlement mirrored on his own face. Over the years Lathe had seen a lot of reactions to him and his fellow blackcollars, but instant and abject terror was a new one. "All we want are some clothes, some transportable food if you've got it, and some maps."

"Maps?" The father blinked, surprise momentarily eclipsing the fear. "Why do you—? I'm sorry—of *course* we've got maps. They're, uh, in my desk—in there."

Lathe nodded permission and he sidled off, Skyler falling in quietly behind him. Shifting his attention to the others, Lathe tried a smile. "Relax. Please. We just need a few things, and then we'll be gone." He paused as his tingler again came on: *Two bicycles and snow-track vehicles in garage; no car.*

That was going to be inconvenient. Lathe eyed the teenager, still standing like a condemned man in the middle of the room. A bit shorter than Lathe, but otherwise about the same build. "Sean, go get me some of your clothes," he told the other. "A complete outfit, like you'd wear for a night on the town."

The boy gulped and hurried from the room, and Lathe returned his attention to the woman. "We're going to need a car," he told her. "Any idea who around here might have one?"

"We don't own a car," she whispered. "There aren't too many in town."

Pursing his lips, Lathe nodded and tapped at his tingler: *Jensen: locate central town lights?*

Visible. Estimate two klicks away. Small group half klick away.

Acknowledged. "What's the group of buildings half a kilometer down the road?" he asked the woman.

"It's just a marketing area," she said. "A couple of stores, a bar, a restaurant. Mostly for people traveling on the highway."

And a likely spot to find transportation. *Jensen, Hawking: head for half-klick lights; quiet scout of area; will rendezvous there.*

As the blackcollars acknowledged, Sean came back, his arms full of clothes. Lathe was busy trying them on when Skyler returned with the father and a fistful of paper. "Maps of Denver and some of the mountain areas, a two-year-old restaurant guide, and a five-year-old almanac," the big blackcollar reported. "Should at least give us a start."

"Good." Lathe glanced at the maps. Roads, city and town boundaries, some general business and commercial information—a good supplement to the topographic maps Lepkowski had provided. "I'm afraid we won't be able to return these," he told the father, sliding the papers into his pack. "But we *can* pay for them."

A frown creased the other's forehead. "I don't understand."

"I said we'd pay for what we're taking."

"No, I meant . . . surely you've got better maps than *these* old things."

Lathe frowned in turn . . . and suddenly a piece seemed to fall into place. "Skyler, see if you can find at least a coat or something that fits you. Go show him what you've got," he added to the father, putting an edge on his voice.

The other gulped and led Skyler away. Lathe regarded the mother thoughtfully. "You've seen other blackcollars in town, I take it?"

She shook her head quickly. "We haven't seen anything," she almost whispered. "No one. I mean, we're just working people around here."

Lathe pursed his lips and turned away. Lying through her teeth, obviously—telling him what she thought he wanted to hear. Given a little time, he could probably get past that to the truth, but time was a commodity in short supply just now.

Skyler and the father came back, the blackcollar wearing a nondescript coat over his Plinry clothing. "A little tight, but it covers well enough," he told Lathe, flexing his arms experimentally.

"It'll do," Lathe said. "You have any cash in the house?"

The father's lips twitched. Stepping to a small console/ desk in the conversation-room corner, he pulled a flat folder from the top drawer and withdrew a thin stack of familiar-looking bills. "My wallet's in the bedroom," he added, handing Lathe the banknotes.

"Don't bother," the comsquare said, examining one of the bills closely. TDE marks, just like the ones they'd brought from Plinry, but with an extra seal embossed on one side that identified its origin as the Phoenix printing office.

"Not going to work," Skyler murmured over his shoulder.

"Not unless we want to advertise just how far out of town we're from," Lathe agreed. "On to plan beta, I guess." He looked up at the father. "Afraid we'll have to take your cash after all. I trust this will cover everything."

The other caught the small box Lathe tossed him. His eyes widened momentarily as he saw the small diamond inside. "Yes— yes, this is more than enough. I—uh—thank you, sir."

"You will, of course, keep our visit quiet," the comsquare said.

"Oh, yes—of course we will."

"I hope so. For your sake." Turning, Lathe headed for the door.

The bar the mother had mentioned was at the upslope edge of the shopping area, its parking lot edged with trees. Jensen and Hawking were waiting in the shadows there when Lathe and the others joined them. "About twenty people in the bar—all male, I think," Jensen reported. "Of the four cars there, the one at the north end would probably be our best bet, the one next to it second best."

"Be a bit of a squeeze even with two," Skyler murmured.

"We can take all four if you want," Jensen said dryly. "Barman's a big harmer who looks like he's been in a fight or two—may have a weapon handy. The restaurant at the other end of the block's already closed for the night, and everything else seems empty."

"Communications?"

"Phone behind the bartender," Hawking said. "No obvious antenna anywhere, so it's probably a groundwire or optical-fiber connection to a central station. Easiest place to knock it out is inside."

"Though we *are* within running distance of other phones," Lathe pointed out.

"There's that, of course."

"Um. All right. Hawking, get busy on that car. You and Jensen will rendezvous with Caine while Skyler, Mordecai, and I take a good look inside and clear the tracks for you."

The car was of a type Hawking had never seen before, and it took him nearly five minutes to bypass its antitheft system and get it started. "Now what?" Skyler asked as the car purred off into the darkness.

"We try our famous smuggler impersonations and see if we can shake loose some kind of underground. Mordecai, you'll be backup out here."

Lathe had been in and out of bars since he'd turned eighteen, nearly forty years earlier, and he'd long since learned that it was the clientele—not the decor, stock, or planet—that distinguished the various types from one another. Skyler a step behind him, he headed toward the bar, throwing casual glances at the dark and sparsely occupied tables they passed among, and by the time he hooked an elbow over the stained ceramic counter, he'd made his assessment.

This wasn't the sort of bar where people came simply to enjoy themselves. The men openly eying the newcomers were hard, middle-aged working types, the late hour and almost tangible bitterness in the air suggesting they were unemployed. A place for being angry together, and a potentially fertile recruitment center for an anti-Ryqril underground.

The barman took his time stepping over to them. "Evening," he rumbled. "What'll you have?"

"Two glasses of your best beer," Lathe told him. "And have something yourself."

"Thanks," the other said indifferently. He stepped to a line of spigots in the back wall, drew three glasses. "Just passing through?" he asked as he set two of them on the bar.

A blunt question; it deserved an equally blunt answer. "Depends on how fast we find an interested buyer," Lathe told him, sipping at his glass. The beer was unexpectedly bitter. "You wouldn't happen to know anyone in the market for, shall we say, hard-to-get merchandise?"

The other's face didn't change. "Most business around here gets done in Denver."

"Ah." Reaching into his pocket, Lathe withdrew a small laser pistol, a rebuilt souvenir of the Terran-Ryqril war. "Sorry to have wasted your time, then," he said, turning the weapon over in his hands as if looking for imperfections in its dark gray finish. "I guess we'll be moving on."

He looked up. The barman's eyes were on the pistol, his mouth hanging slightly open. "Uh, well, now wait just a second. How many of those do you have?"

"Are you interested in buying?" Lathe countered.

The other licked his lips. "Not me personally, but I know someone who'll definitely want to talk to you. If you and your chaser want to take a seat I'll give him a call."

A setup? Possibly. But the barman didn't seem the Security type . . . and besides, Mordecai was outside. "Fine," he told the other. "He's got fifteen minutes." Slipping the laser pistol away, he nodded to Skyler, and together they headed to a back-wall table that offered a good view of both door and bar.

"Any bets as to who he's calling?" Skyler murmured, sipping at his beer.

Lathe looked at the barman, wrapped secretively around his phone. "Not Security, I'd say. On the other hand, he doesn't strike me as the fanatical type, either, and from what Caine told Lepkowski about Torch I wouldn't expect them to take anyone who wasn't frothing over with Noble Purpose."

"Maybe we've got two separate undergrounds operating here," Skyler suggested. "As well as a group of blackcollars."

Lathe smiled wryly. "I rather thought you'd pick up on that."

"What's to pick up? The family back there labeled us from the second I used my *nunchaku*, without even needing to see our flexarmor. They may not have had any direct contact with blackcollars before, but we haven't been consigned to ancient history, either.''

"Agreed. Which unfortunately leads to a disturbing question: why were they so terrified of us?''

Skyler chewed at his lip. "They were, weren't they? Worried about Security reprisals for aiding us?''

"Maybe.'' Conversation had returned to its earlier level in the bar, but several of the patrons still seemed to have half an eye on the blackcollars. ''This bar may not be as innocent as it seems—could be it caters largely to a certain type of traveler. The type that doesn't care much for strangers.''

Skyler shrugged. "If so, the smuggler routine should put us right at home here.''

"Maybe.''

They sat in silence for a few minutes, keeping a general eye on things and waiting for a signal from Mordecai. The fifteen minutes Lathe had allotted the barman were nearly up when the word finally came: *Big car arriving; five men inside . . . three approaching you.*

Acknowledged, Lathe sent. Hitching his chair a few centimeters back from the table, he surreptitiously drew a *shuriken* from his belt pouch and slipped it into the pocket where he'd put the laser pistol. Skyler, across the table, made his own preparations.

The three men walked into the bar as if they owned the place, and almost instantly all conversation again ceased. The barman nodded toward the blackcollars' table, and two of the men swaggered forward, leaving the third standing guard beside the door.

"Hear you've got some poison for sale,'' one of them said as he stopped a meter in front of Lathe. His partner took another few steps to hover behind Skyler.

"Poison?'' Lathe shook his head minutely. "Weapons.''

The other gave him a long, appraising look. "You *are* new at this, aren't you? 'Poison' is illegals, dimbo. Let's see it.''

Lathe didn't move. "You in the market to buy or just browsing?''

The second man growled something. "Don't push your luck or my patience,'' the first man told Lathe, his tone icy. One hand reached up to unfasten his coat, and the comsquare caught a glimpse of a compact pistol slung under his arm. "Let's see the merchandise.''

Lathe cocked an eyebrow and reached his right hand into his pocket. For a moment he froze there, as a gun magically appeared at Skyler's head. Then, moving with exaggerated caution, he drew the laser out by its barrel and held it out. "I've left the power pack out, of course," he said.

"Yeah, uh-huh." The other looked the weapon over for a moment. "How many you got?"

"How many you want?"

The man turned cold eyes on the blackcollar. "Twenty-five percent of your stock. For permission to sell the rest—and I'll throw in some helpful advice about doing business in this area."

"Oh?" Lathe eased his right hand up to smooth his beard, the *shuriken* he'd palmed biting gently into his skin. "That seems a bit high."

"Not really. Especially when you consider the price lets you keep your skin, too." Stepping back a pace, he drew his own pistol and leveled it at Lathe. "You got five seconds to make up your—"

The last word never made it out of his mouth—but most of his air did, as Lathe's foot snapped in a curving kick that knocked the gunhand aside and then buried itself in the man's abdomen. The other folded over and dropped to the floor as Lathe's *shuriken* flashed across the room to bury itself in the wall by the third man's head. The backup jerked violently in reaction and then stood perfectly still, his hand dropping empty from inside his coat.

A flicker at the edge of his vision made Lathe turn, just in time to see Skyler's knife bounce hilt-first off the barman's right forearm. The man bellowed, the short rifle he'd been holding clattering to the floor . . . and a deathly silence descended on the room.

Just as it had in the house up the road. And from the terror-frozen faces at the bar's other tables it was very likely for the same reason.

Standing up, Lathe retrieved his laser and his assailant's gun. Off to the side, Skyler was also on his feet, scooping up his knife and the barman's weapon. The man who'd been standing behind the big blackcollar, Lathe noted, was stretched out unconscious two meters back from Skyler's chair.

"That wasn't very polite," Lathe said to the first man, curled around himself on the floor where he'd fallen. Through the pain in his eyes Lathe could see a fading remnant of fear being replaced by resignation. "Pulling a—looks like a fle- chette or dart gun—on us. Skyler?"

"This one had a pellet scattergun," the other reported, hefting the barman's weapon. "Pellets may be paral-drugged."

Lathe eyed the man by the door. "Dump your gun onto the floor and come here."

The other obeyed instantly, moving in the jerky fashion of an unoiled automaton. "I'm sorry, sir—we didn't know it was *you* guys—Phelling just said—"

"That we were easy targets?"

"Oh, no, sir—just that you were selling in the boss's territory without his okay—"

"Shut up, Travis." The man at Lathe's feet spat between clenched teeth.

"Ignore him, Travis, this is very interesting," Skyler put in. "Just who *is* this boss of yours?"

Travis gulped but remained silent. Lathe switched his gaze to the barman. "What's his name, Phelling?"

The other shrugged slightly. "It's no secret—you could figure it out easily enough with a territory map. Manx Reger."

Lathe nodded, though the name didn't flip any switches. "And what's *your* excuse?"

Phelling spread his hands wide. "Look, all this is Mr. Reger's territory. You know how it works—part of the price for letting me run my place is to keep my eyes open."

"Uh-huh." Lathe's fingers sought out his tingler. *Mordecai: Clear out backup.*

Acknowledged.

"Well," Lathe told Phelling, "I suggest you be a bit less enthusiastic about joining in the fight next time. Let's go, Skyler."

The two blackcollars walked through the still-frozen tableau to the door, dropping their appropriated weapons there as Lathe pulled his *shuriken* out of the wall.

Mordecai was standing beside a large and well-polished car as they emerged into the parking lot, two vaguely crumpled figures sprawled beside him. "Any trouble?" Lathe asked.

"Hardly." Mordecai gestured to the car. "This thing's a rolling arsenal—a pair of scatterguns in the back seat and a long-range sniper's flechette rifle in the trunk. Are they Security?"

"No, they seem to be the local underground. The *wrong* underground, unfortunately." Lathe stooped to peer inside the car. Plenty of room for both themselves and part of Caine's team. "Might as well ride in comfort. You got the keys?"

Mordecai dangled them in reply.

*   *   *

They reached the site of Caine's forced landing fifteen minutes later . . . to find that while they'd been gone the universe had taken a hard left turn.

"What do you mean, *not here*?" Lathe fumed to Jensen. "They *have* to be here."

"All I know is that no one's replying to tingler signals," the other said, frustration evident in his voice. "Hawking's been driving up and down the road for ten minutes without drawing a single buzz in response."

"But—" Lathe broke off as their tinglers came on: *Glider located, four hundred meters west on road.*

They found Hawking in the bushes about five meters off the southern edge of the road. "Torn up some, but it's definitely Colvin's cargo glider."

"Any sign of the cargo pod itself?"

"Not yet. Maybe Colvin just pushed his range too far and crashed, but everyone was in good enough shape to hike it."

Lathe looked around. Behind them a tall bluff rose against the starry sky, directly back along the route the gliders had been tracking.

Jensen followed his gaze and his thoughts. "Could be they steered around it," he suggested. "A bit tricky, but possible."

"The road switchbacks upward on the other side of that bluff," Skyler pointed out. "That would have created some updrafts this direction. And Colvin *did* have more altitude than the others."

"Finding the other gliders might give us a better idea of what happened," Hawking added.

Lathe glanced west just as another blue-violet light appeared briefly between distant mountain peaks. "Unfortunately, we haven't got that much time," he said. "Whether Security's got them or not, we're going to need help finding them." *So much for giving Caine his grand illusion of independence*, the comsquare thought with a touch of bitterness. *I should have known better.*

"Help from whom?" Hawking asked. "Caine's mysterious Torch?"

"Maybe later—if they really exist. For now, I've got someone a bit more substantial in mind. Come on—we need to get back to the bar before it closes."

Chapter 5

Back on Plinry, Colvin knew, he would never live this down.

He'd made it over the mountain that had nailed Alamzad and was gliding above the road watching for the switchbacks with plenty of altitude to spare. And then that damn wind had come in out of nowhere and that bluff had shot up right in front of him, and he'd panicked.

Panicked. There was no other word for it. He'd frozen like an amateur, riding that wind dead-on for the bluff until there was no time to try to steer around it. By the time he'd been able to think again he had exactly two options: ram the mountain just above the second switchback, or try and fly over the damn thing. He'd almost made it, too . . . but *almost* never counted for anything.

And so now here he sat, all alone on top of the bluff with an injured bird and a heavy cargo pod and a wind that was trying to freeze his face off . . . and a massively bruised ego.

"Colvin?" Pittman's voice came anxiously in his ear. "You okay?"

"Sure," Colvin said, trying to sound casually hearty. *I meant to do that; of course I did.* Not fooling anybody but himself. "Where are you?"

Braune's voice cut in. "We're on the road around beyond the bluff you landed on—maybe a couple hundred meters past that last switchback curve. The road looks pretty level now for a while—shouldn't be too bad a hike."

"Though it'll probably get worse before it gets better," Pittman added. "What's the view like from up there?"

"Oh, terrific." It *was* a terrific view, too. The problem was that it was a terrific view of all the wrong things. To the southeast he could see that the road did indeed begin to climb again no more than a kilometer or two past the others' position; to the west he could see the blue-violet lights of searching aircraft circling the mountains a few kilometers away. The trajectory of the falling drop pods had temporarily

46

fooled them, but that wouldn't last long. Soon the search would widen, and picking up five men hiking along the road in the middle of nowhere would be child's play.

And as he gazed westward, he saw a flicker of light along the road.

Headlights.

It was a crazy idea—he *knew* it was a crazy idea—but for all that it was their best hope. The road passed beneath him twice in a sharp hairpin switchback turn before rounding the bluff to continue past Braune and Pittman. At their position the vehicle would be starting to pick up speed, but around the curves it would surely be going slowly enough to hijack.

If he could get down there fast enough.

He stood up, nearly losing his balance to the wind, and sent his hands on a quick inspection tour of his glider. Injured, sure, but not crippled. A few bent struts and a small rip or two in the wing, but nothing that couldn't handle a short flight. The cargo pod was the only problem, but if the gale whistling in his ears held up he'd have no problem launching even with that dragging along the runway.

The lights were moving closer, approaching the first pass beneath him, and for the first time Colvin could see that the headlights were backed up by a minor Christmas-tree display of amber running lights. The "car" was actually a large trailer truck—which opened up an entirely new possibility.

Wrestling the glider against the wind, he snapped into his harness and pushed off. For a second the pod dragged against the bare rock like an anchor, threatening to send him head-downward over the rim to the road below. Then it came free and he was airborne, fighting the eddy currents near the bluff as he came around in a tight circle. The truck was laboring along the upper part of the switchback now. Coming around behind and above it, he brought the glider's nose sharply up to kill his excess speed, and dropped squarely onto the top of the trailer.

And for a long second thought he was going to lose the whole thing. Even as he snatched out a knife and cut the pod loose, the truck rounded the top curve and the winds sweeping his perch abruptly changed. Ramming his knife hilt-deep into the trailer roof, he held on, fighting the bucking glider with his other hand until the pull eased enough for him to hit the harness release. The glider flew off into the darkness, and he was just trying to figure out how best to assault the cab when the truck rounded the curve and came to a tire-screeching stop at the side of the road.

Again, he managed to hold on. From ahead came the sound of doors opening, and suddenly he realized what was going on. The truckers had heard the thump of his landing and were coming back to investigate.

Pittman, Braune: Assistance needed NW on road, he signaled, flattening himself against the rooftop. Tackling two men single-handedly on opposite sides of a truck would be a tricky proposition, and the stakes were too high to risk botching it. Drawing his *nunchaku*, he eased to the left edge of the trailer and looked down.

To discover the driver examining the truck's axles was a woman.

Even in the faint backwash glow of her flashlight there was no doubt about that. Young-looking, reasonably petite—hardly the sort, somehow, that he would have expected to be driving such a monster on a tricky mountain road at night. But perhaps her companion was a man.

"Karen?" the driver called over the wind. "Anything?"

"Not on this side," a second female voice drifted back. "You?"

"Nope. What could it have been?"

Colvin recognized a cue when he heard it. Flipping his legs over the side, he dropped to the ground in front of the driver.

She jumped backward, eyes going wide. "What the hell— who are *you*?"

"Unexpected company—the thump you heard on your trailer," he said. "Sorry to interrupt your trip, but I'm afraid I need transportation to Denver." He raised his voice. "Karen? Come over to this side of the truck, please."

The driver's gaze dropped to the *nunchaku* in Colvin's hand. "Oh, God," she breathed. Eyes flicked over his shoulder. "Karen—*no!*"

And with the *crack* of a small projectile gun from behind him, something hard slammed into the center of Colvin's back.

His hidden flexarmor was equal to the attack, stopping the pellet and distributing its impact over a large part of his torso. An instant later reflexes had taken over, twisting him around on the balls of his feet into a low crouch and sending the *nunchaku* whipping through the air toward his assailant. He caught a glimpse of the woman pointing a pistol marksman-fashion from around the protection of the truck's front bumper before the spinning *nunchaku* forced her to duck back. The driver hadn't moved; leaping to her side, Colvin grabbed her arm and pulled her in front of him as he snatched a *shuriken* from his pouch. Karen's head and gun poked out from cover again—

"No, Karen, stop!" the driver almost screamed. "He's a *blackcollar*."

Karen paused, gun still pointed. "Let her go," she called to Colvin. "You can have the truck, but let her go first."

"I don't want the truck—just a ride to Denver," he called back. His tingler came on: *Distract her.* "I got caught out here without a car," he continued, raising his volume a bit, "and need to get to town. You were the first vehicle that came along—"

There was a sudden flurry of motion, and when it was over Braune and Pittman had the gun. And Karen.

They had the gear from the pod distributed into packs and stored in the trailer by the time Caine and Alamzad reached them. Colvin was standing guard at the rear doors as they approached. "There's room for all of us in the trailer," he reported. "Cargo's some kind of rock—unprocessed oil shale, they called it."

Caine nodded. "Good. Incidentally, Colvin, that was easily the most insane stunt I've ever heard of. Next time clear something like that with me *before* you do it, okay? Fine job, though." He nodded to the women sitting with their backs to the front tire under Braune's watchful gaze. "Now, who do we have here?"

"We haven't had full introductions yet. The dark-haired one's named Karen; she's the one who had the pistol."

"Well, we might as well be civil about this—and then get the hell out of here before Security finds us." Caine headed forward, nodded to Braune, and then gestured to the women. "Stand up, please," he told them. "Sorry to have disrupted your trip like this, but as my companion said we need transport to Denver. Your names are . . . ?"

"Karen Lindsay," the dark-haired woman said as they got to their feet. Unlike her companion, she seemed more watchful and angry than afraid. "This is Raina Dupre. If you want the truck, just take it and go."

Caine shook his head. "Afraid a missing truck would raise a little more official notice than we can afford right at the moment. You live together in Denver?"

"In a twoplex, yes," Lindsay answered. "With Raina's husband."

Caine turned his attention to Raina. "When does he expect you in?"

"He works nights." Her face seemd to sag, as if the possible reason for that question had just occurred to her. "He won't be back till seven. Please—you don't need to hurt us—"

"We're not *going* to hurt you," Caine interrupted her. "You—Ms. Lindsay—where are you taking the truck?"

"Coast Shipping," she told him. "It's in the northeast part of town, near the Seventy-two/Ninety-three crosspoint."

"All right," Caine said, pretending that that meant something to him. "Ms. Dupre, I'm afraid you'll have to stay in back with my men. I'm going to ride up front with your friend to make sure she doesn't try anything heroic."

Raina's mouth tightened, but it was Lindsay who spoke up. "Why not let *her* drive? I'm not afraid to be locked back there."

"Because I want to talk to you," Caine told her. "Come on—we need to get moving."

For the first kilometer or so they rode in silence, Caine watching out the windows as the truck wove in and out through the curves. At times the mountains would be little more than shadows at the edges of the headlight beams; then suddenly a jagged rock face would be rolling along bare meters from the side window. A small town flashed by, its sprinkling of lights wedged into what seemed to be little more than a wide spot in the road.

As yet no sign of Denver itself. *We almost had to walk all this*, Caine thought soberly. *Almost.*

The town disappeared to the rear, and beside him Lindsay cleared her throat. "I've heard a lot of stories about blackcollars," she said, "but never anything about them getting lost out in the mountains."

"Some of the things blackcollars do would amaze you," Caine told her, trying not to let his annoyance at the near disaster spill out onto her.

"I'm sure."

He pursed his lips, studying her face as best he could in the dim backwash of the headlights. A pleasant enough face; more to the immediate point, a face with spirit behind it. A spirit that reminded him strongly of some of the Radix resistance fighters he'd met on Argent. "Do you also hear stories about a group called Torch?" he asked.

There was no reaction he could detect. "Never heard of it," she said. "What sort of business is it in? Or shouldn't I ask?"

He shrugged. "It's not a secret. Presumably, they fight Ryqril."

She snorted. "Doesn't sound like a group blackcollars would be interested in."

"Then you don't know much about blackcollars. The schools around here don't go in for recent history?"

"I get all the recent history I need from the local news," she retorted.

Caine sighed quietly and gave up. Clearly, the government was slanting the news something fierce—and in retrospect, he should have expected that. If there were blackcollars operating anywhere within a thousand kilometers of Denver, the local Security office would be doing its damnedest to poison public opinion toward them.

Which meant that, for the near future at least, they were going to be completely on their own. "Let me see your ID," he said.

Lindsay dug out her wallet and tossed it into his lap. A card was set into a plastic window in the front, and with a penlight Caine gave it a quick once-over. Name, photo, address, physical description, company. "Company? They put *that* on IDs here?"

She threw him an odd look. "Of course—the companies *issue* the IDs. Where are you from, anyway?"

"Europe," Caine told her, choosing the simplest of the possible responses. "What do you mean, the companies issue them? Doesn't local Security handle that?"

"Not around here. This way, if they catch you without an ID they can toss you into the hamper right away for being a driftist."

"And then they have to try and figure out who you are?"

She shrugged. "They've *got* everyone's fingerprints and retina patterns on file. Or so they say." She risked another glance away from the road. "If you don't mind my saying so, you don't seem very well informed."

"We're new on the block." Careful to keep the beam out of her eyes, he ran his light over her clothing. Similar fabric to that of the team's Plinry clothing, at least in appearance and texture. But the cut, color pattern, and ornamentation were unacceptably different. "How far do you live from the place you'll be dropping off the truck?" he asked.

"A couple of kilometers."

"Which way?"

Her lip twitched. "We'll pass within a few blocks on our way in."

"Good." Another town, more spread out than the previous one, opened up to their right. "I want you to swing over to your house and let my men out. They'll stay there with your partner while you and I take the truck in."

"And you're going to pass yourself off as Raina? They'll be expecting her to be with me, you know."

"I'm counting on you to cover that one," he said, letting his voice chill a few degrees. "Remember, you'll be right in the middle of things if there's any trouble."

"You don't need to elaborate," she said, matching his tone.

"Good."

The town vanished behind them, and as the sheer cliff faces returned so did the earlier silence. Settling back in his seat, Caine unfolded one of Lepkowski's maps and set about figuring out where and when they would emerge from the mountains.

The scene at the warehouse turned out to be anticlimatic.

Only a single gateman was on duty at the entrance Lindsay drove the truck through, and he accepted without question her story that Raina had gotten sick at the last minute and that Caine was the best replacement she'd been able to scare up on short notice. The inside manager made them wait until he'd counted the sealed drums in the trailer, but Caine got the impression he was going through the prescribed motions purely out of long habit. Unprocessed oil shale, apparently, wasn't high on anyone's hijacking list.

They arrived via autocab at the truckers' twoplex a few minutes later, to find that Braune and Colvin had scouted out the immediate neighborhood while Pittman and Alamzad had similarly checked out the house itself. "Seems as secure as anything else we're likely to find grab-bag style," Pittman reported. "Zad's got the bug stomper set up, and we've keyed out the most likely approaches to the house."

"Escape routes?"

Braune snorted. "Nothing to make a hard copy of. If Security finds us we're in trouble, pure and simple."

Caine glanced across the room, where Raina and Lindsay were whispering together under Colvin's watchful gaze. "We'll try to relocate as soon as possible. What did you find in the way of clothes?"

"Geoff's things—that's Raina's husband—are really too big, but they fit well enough to pass casual muster. Nothing beyond that, though. We'll have to buy new outfits as soon as the stores open."

Caine looked at his watch, set before they left the *Novak* to local time. Three a.m. "Stores probably open sometime between eight and ten—we can check with the women. Braune, you and Colvin will take shopping detail; as soon as you can get back we'll start hunting for a new base."

"On foot?" Pittman asked.

Caine shrugged. "Ideally, no, but I don't think stealing a car at this point would be a particularly brilliant move."

"I'd like to scout around anyway, if I may," the other replied. "Maybe I can find a way to get something without drawing any attention."

Caine pursed his lips. It *would* be handy to have their own transport. "Well . . . all right, you can poke around for an hour or so. But only *after* we get proper clothes for you. You look suspicious enough as it is."

Pittman gave him a tight smile. "Yes, sir."

He turned away, stepping over to relieve Colvin's guard on the women. *A good man*, Caine thought, again glancing at his watch. Three-oh-five. Better set up a sleep rotation right away, he decided. The night had already been a busy one, and the morning was likely to be even worse.

Chapter 6

Three-ten a.m.

Galway dropped his wrist with its borrowed watch back into his lap and reached for his mug, feeling the long night's fatigue soaking into his muscles and brain. It was like an echo of the weary stakeouts from his early Security years, missing nothing of the tension and boredom he remembered from those long-ago vigils.

But at least here he didn't need to worry about sudden physical danger. Or so he'd been assured.

Raising his eyes from his mug, he scanned slowly across the bank of monitor screens set before him. Athena Security's situation room was about six times bigger than his own back in Capstone, with at least ten times as much sophisticated tracking and communications gear, and Athena's defenses were on a par with everything else in the government center. Even blackcollars would find this town and building impregnable—and Caine's team were *not* blackcollars.

The back of Galway's neck refused to be comforted. It continued to tingle its warning of imminent destruction.

A figure brushed by Galway's elbow and dropped into the chair beside him. General Paul Quinn, Athena Security chief. "Anything?" Galway asked.

"Not yet." Quinn's voice was stiff. "This is what we get for playing silly games."

Galway's jaw clenched momentarily. Quinn had been tacitly blaming him for the loss of Caine's team for the past two hours, and the prefect was getting roundly tired of it. "Yes, well, let's try to keep in mind that it was Prefect Donner's idea, not mine."

"Of course it was Donner's idea." Quinn snorted. "What the hell can he know about mountainous terrain out in Dallas? That whole area is optically flat—you could buzz around forever pretending not to find someone and still be able to read the stitch pattern on his shirt. Out here—well, hell, *he* doesn't care how much trouble it costs us."

Galway took a deep breath. "Look, General, Caine's not going to do anything tonight. Blackcollars aren't just some kind of mad berserkers—they're tactically oriented warriors, and Caine can't possibly have all the information he needs yet. Give Postern a chance to get clear and send a message."

"Postern, huh? Your trusted spy? Your *non-loyalty-conditioned* trusted spy?"

"He'll deliver. By noon tomorrow you'll have your surveillance teams back on Caine's shoulder."

Quinn snorted again. "We should have just grabbed them when they landed. I don't care *how* much psychor training Caine's had, we could have gotten what we wanted out of him."

Which was a thoroughly ridiculous statement, and Quinn

surely knew it. But Galway was tired of arguing. "What about that other set of drop pods? Anything on those?"

"Decoys," Quinn said shortly. "Thought I told you that earlier."

"What you told me was that in past drops—"

"Galway." Quinn swiveled to face him. "Let's get one thing clear from the start, okay? I didn't ask you to come here, I don't want you here, and if the Ryqril hadn't given me direct orders you wouldn't *be* here. You don't know the area, you don't know the city or its people, you don't know how we do things on this planet. You're here for one purpose, and one purpose only: to advise me on Caine and his troublemakers. When I want that advice I'll let you know. Clear?"

"Perfectly," Galway said through stiff lips, a hot flush creeping up his neck. Quinn turned and stalked off; turning back to the displays. Galway clenched his jaw and waited for the fury to subside.

It did so quickly. This wasn't a matter of pride or jurisdiction, whatever Quinn chose to believe. It was the potential survival of Plinry—and even if it killed him, he would give the general all the help against Caine that he could.

A good and noble resolution. Galway hoped he'd be able to hang onto it.

Kanai awoke on the first buzz from the phone, lying still for a half second as his senses flicked around his bedroom. He was alone, and all was secure. . . . On the third buzz he answered. "Yes?"

"Kanai, you krijing son of a delwart toad, what the krijing *hell* was that all about?"

"Vac it," Kanai snapped into the tirade. The voice was strained with fury, but recognizable enough. Manx Reger. "Back up and try it again, Reger—and try to be civil this time."

"Civil!" Reger spat. "You pull crap like this and you want me to be *civil*? I oughtta—"

"*What* crap? Reger, shut up and tell me what the hell you're *talking* about."

"Don't play cutesy with *me*, Kanai. You tell Bernhard that this time he's gone too far. Your krijing blackcollars have no business making trouble in my territory, damn you. I'm deducting the medical costs for my boys from Sartan's cut—*you* can figure out how to pay him back. *And* I want my car back, intact. You got that?"

"Reger—"

"And if you pull anything like this again, you'll have a full-scale war on your hands. Sartan can count on it."

"Reger, listen—"

The line went dead. Kanai stared at the phone for half a dozen heartbeats more before folding it back up, a hard knot beginning to form in his stomach. It was impossible—no blackcollars were out in northwest Denver making trouble for the hell of it.

At least none of Bernhard's team were.

Kanai thought about that for a long minute. Then, opening the phone, he punched for Bernhard's secure line.

The comsquare answered on the third buzz. "Yes?"

"Kanai. We've got new blackcollars in town."

A brief pause. "How do you know?"

Kanai recounted his one-sided conversation with Reger.

"Could this just be the setup for some kind of elaborate trap?" Bernhard asked when he'd finished. "He's been sulking ever since we slapped his nose a month ago."

"I doubt it. He's smart enough to pull something like that, but he doesn't strike me as being actor enough to foam-mouth that convincingly."

Bernhard hissed between his teeth. "Great. Just great. Where the hell could new blackcollars have come from? Never mind. Wherever they're from, we've got to track them down before they trigger a flash fire that'll crash everything. I'll alert the rest of the team, see if we can find a trail. Reger give any hint as to where they might have gone?"

"Only that they apparently took one of his cars to travel in." Kanai pursed his lips. "Bernhard, what chance they've been brought in by one of the other bosses as a counter to us?"

"And stumbled into Reger's territory by mistake?" Bernhard swore softly under his breath. "I hope to hell that's not it."

"Yeah. Well . . . we meeting at the usual place?"

"*We* are; *you* aren't. Whatever's going on, I don't want you away from the contact phone. New data could come in; the damn blackcollars themselves might even get your number and call."

"Okay." Kanai looked at his watch. Three-fifteen a.m. "The usual emergency comm setup?"

"Right. I'll check with you periodically for nonemergency news. Sit tight and watch your back."

"Sure. Good hunting."

Carefully Kanai folded the phone and replaced it on his nightstand. Just as carefully, he stepped to the window for a cautious look outside. Pure reflex, and faintly ridiculous besides—the sensor web around his house would have picked up any intruder long before he became visible.

Any normal intruder, that is. Could a blackcollar team circumvent the web?

Kanai shivered. Were the new blackcollars indeed merely another set of hired hands? Or could they still be fighting the Terran-Ryqril War? And if the latter, what would they think of the course Kanai and his fellows had taken?

It doesn't matter what they think, Kanai told himself fiercely . . . and knew it was a lie. To see his own self-disgust reflected back by the eyes of those who had not shamed themselves would be a humiliation he wasn't prepared to face.

If they came for him now, and offered him the choice, he wondered if he would have the nobility and the courage to perform the *seppuku* of his ancestors.

No one moved in the street outside. Letting the edge of the curtain fall, Kanai went to his closet and began to dress.

The bar closed at three a.m. sharp, and the half-dozen remaining customers had staggered out by three-oh-five. It was another half hour before the barman emerged, locked the door behind him, and trudged toward the single remaining car in the lot. Lathe let him get within two steps of the vehicle before rising from his concealment on its far side. "Good morning," he said conversationally. "You remember me, I trust."

The barman froze, and in the faint starlight Lathe could see the other's mouth working soundlessly. "I see you do," the comsquare nodded. "Phelling, wasn't it?"

Phelling finally got his vocal cords unstuck. "What do you want with me? I got nothing against you."

"Maybe we've got something against *you*," Skyler suggested, coming up on Phelling from behind. "You and this Reger character."

Phelling seemed to shrink. "Oh, sh—look, sir, I don't have anything to do with him—*really*."

"You just act as fingerman?" Lathe suggested.

"What? Hey, look, I *had* to call his people in when you came on with that smuggler slidetalk."

"Maybe," Skyler said darkly. "Maybe you were just looking forward to shooting down a couple of helpless strangers."

"No! No, I *swear*—"

"And at any rate," Skyler interrupted, "you're the only
one available to use as an object lesson."

Lathe gave that a few seconds to sink in. "Unless you want
to tell us where we can find Manx Reger, that is," he said.

Phelling turned wide eyes on the comsquare. "I *told* you—
I'm not part of his organization. If he's not home I don't
know where he could be. You've *gotta* believe me."

"No, we don't," Lathe said. "But for the moment we'll
settle for his home address."

Phelling opened his mouth, closed it again. "His . . .
home address? But . . . you've *been* there. I mean, you tore
up the place a month ago, didn't you?"

Lathe exchanged glances with Skyler. Their first positive
confirmation that there were indeed other blackcollars operating in Denver. Doing . . . what?

For the moment, the question would keep. "Let's just say
we've been out of touch with the other blackcollars in town,"
he told Phelling. "The hows and whys don't concern you.
What concerns you is that we want to talk to Reger and
you're going to show us the way."

Phelling had apparently gotten stuck half a statement back.
"You trying to get in touch with the other blackcollars—is
that it? Hell, that's easy. Their contact man Kanai goes to the
Shandygaff Bar in Central Denver on Tuesday nights to wait
for new business—"

"We'll get to them later," Lathe cut him off. "Right now,
all we want is Reger. Let's go."

Phelling licked his lips. "I . . . yeah, sure, I'll take you
there. Sure. The place isn't a secret."

"Good." Lathe sent a brief tingler message, and a minute
later Hawking drove their appropriated car into the lot. "Get
in," Lathe told Phelling as Skyler opened the front door.
"Let's have your keys first."

Wordlessly, the barman handed them over and climbed in,
Skyler getting in behind him. Lathe tossed Phelling's keys to
Mordecai as he and Jensen emerged from their backup concealment. "No memory slips, Phelling," the comsquare
warned, sliding in behind Hawking.

A minute later the two cars headed southeast into the night.

Chapter 7

When the cat's away, the ancient adage ran through Taurus Haven's mind, *the mice will play*.

The cat being Prefect Galway, of course. It was now just five days since the hidden 'port spotters had seen Galway sneak aboard a Ryqril Corsair and disappear into the sky. Bound for Earth, presumably, and certain to arrive before the *Novak*. If the collies there opted for the heavy-handed approach . . .

Haven put the thought firmly from his mind. The best way to help Lathe now, he knew, was to do his job properly. And to make sure the rest of the mice did theirs.

The other mice being Capstone's unemployed and increasingly frustrated youth . . . and Haven had to admit that this little mob scene Dayle Greene had set up was the finest peaceful demonstration Plinry had ever seen. The crowd gathered around the Hub's floodlit east gate numbered at least six hundred, perhaps one in ten holding a sign or lighted torch against the black of night. They were being quiet, for the most part, listening as their spokesman brandished their list of grievances and called on the guards lined up inside the mesh gate to come out and accept the paper.

None of the Security men had taken him up on the challenge. Nor, Haven thought as he studied the half-hidden faces behind the mesh, did any of them look as if they intended to.

His tingler came on: *Hammerschmidt approaching in car*. Haven grinned tightly and began working his way unobtrusively toward the front of the crowd. They'd read Hammerschmidt correctly, all right, down to the last decimal. Galway would never do anything so stupid as coming out of the Hub to face down a mob, but his second-in-command had always had more idiot pride than was good for him. Hammerschmidt would come out, all right; with luck he'd at least have enough brains to bring a carload of troops out with him.

The assistant prefect's car arrived at the gate a minute later, and a short but animated argument seemed to take place between Hammerschmidt and the guard captain. The captain apparently lost, and Hammerschmidt's driver maneuvered the car to point at the center of the gate. The mesh slid open just enough to pass the vehicle, closed immediately behind it. Capstone's Security men had had a mob get past the wall once before and were clearly not interested in repeating the experience.

The crowd seemed to shiver like a thing alive as the car rolled toward it. *Easy*, Haven cautioned. *Don't spook them.* But the crowd's leaders had been carefully coached, and no one moved as the vehicle came to a halt a few meters from the crowd's edge. The back doors opened and Hammerschmidt and a laser-armed Security man stepped out, the latter gripping his weapon tightly. "All right," Hammerschmidt bellowed. "What the hell do you slime think you're doing?"

He was answered by the deep-throated *twang* of a large catapult a block south. All Security eyes jerked toward the sound, just in time to see a load of loose garbage arc neatly over the wall into the Hub. Trash-throwing had become a popular pastime among Capstone's youth in the past few days, a deliberate thumb in Security's eye. And from Hammerschmidt's expression, it looked as though he'd about had enough of it. "Over there!" he'd snapped, pointing south as he scrambled back into the car. The other man joined him and the driver started to swing around—

And the crowd surged forward. An instant later the car was surrounded by a solid wall of shouting people.

The buildings around them lit up with flickers of light, and screams of pain mixed with those of anger as the gate guards opened up with their lasers. Set at low power, Haven hoped, but he had no time to worry about it. He was in position now, directly behind two of the blackcollars' trainees, who were pounding flat-palmed on Hammerschmidt's window and screaming at the top of their lungs. A better distraction Haven couldn't have asked for. Ducking down, he wove through the gap the trainees had formed between their legs and slid onto his back under the car.

It was a cramped fit, but Haven had practiced on mock-ups at the lodge and his motions were quick and sure. Pulling the quick-release package on his belt, he spilled onto the pavement six "question marks"—fifteen-centimeter hooks with thermite self-welding connectors at the ends. He grabbed two, tore off the safety covers, and touched them firmly to the car's frame about shoulder width apart. There was a sharp

hiss as the primer ignited, and abruptly the narrow space
under the car flickered with blue-white light. Haven held the
hooks steady for the three or four seconds it took for the fire to
burn down. Then, scooping up two more, he wiggled down
toward the rear of the car and implanted them a meter behind
the first set. The screams of the burn victims were getting
louder, he noted uneasily, and through the pavement he could
feel the pounding of feet as the crowd peeled itself open before
the laser beams. If the car was freed too soon . . .

The flames died and Haven moved forward again, stripping
the last two question marks and jamming them into the outer
parts of the frame. The running feet had become a stampede
now, and looking toward the gate he could see occasional
glimpses of the wall as his human screen melted away into
the darkness.

The last two question marks burned out. They would need
another few seconds to solidify properly, but Haven couldn't
afford to wait. Hiking up on his elbows, he eased his upper
arms snugly into the first set of hooks. His legs went into the
second set; and even as he grabbed the third set with his
hands the car jerked into motion, swerving around toward the
gate. Gritting his teeth, Haven pressed against the frame,
hoping to hell the bodywork overhang and shadow would
give him adequate concealment.

The car darted through the gate and skidded to a halt,
jamming Haven's arms painfully against their supports. For a
moment Hammerschmidt and the captain conversed—Hammerschmidt's voice was too muffled for Haven to understand, but
he sounded furious—and then the car was in motion again,
heading through the largely residential outer parts of the Hub
toward the official buildings near the center. For another
kilometer or two there would be virtually no other traffic,
which meant that here was where Haven had to get off.

He had his opportunity at the next corner as the car stopped
to let some cross traffic pass. He wriggled out of the hooks
and eased slightly to the side where he would be safe from
both wheels and the rear set of question marks. Flattening
himself against the pavement, he mentally crossed his fingers
. . . and the car drove off, leaving him lying safely in the
middle of the road.

Fortunately, no one else was coming; equally fortunately,
Hammerschmidt's driver apparently wasn't watching his mir-
rors. Haven lay motionless until the car had cleared another
block, then sprinted for the cover of the nearest building.

There he took a moment to orient himself and listen for signs he'd been observed. Keeping to shadows as much as possible, he headed down the empty streets back toward the wall.

The distant *twang* of another catapult shot and the nearer *splock* of newly arrived garbage came right on schedule and gave him his final bearings. The trash had made it two full blocks inside the wall—the trash, and the tightly wrapped backpack that had gone over with it. Stepping carefully, Haven retrieved the heavy bundle, stripping off the filthy covering and settling the pack onto his shoulders as he faded back into the shadows. Faint cries reached his ears from distant parts of the wall—the multiple demonstrations that should, for the next hour, hold Security's attention outward.

He had just that long to reach his objective.

The objective was the Agriculture/Resources building, and he made it in just over forty minutes.

Made it to the outside, at least. It took him another ten minutes to scale two floors, find a window that could be opened without leaving any traces, and climb eight flights of steps to the roof.

The stairs ended in a large equipment shed that also contained the building's elevator machinery and a handful of neatly racked maintenance tools. Sliding his pack onto the floor, Haven took a quick look around and then stepped out the shed door onto the roof proper. A couple of blocks away the Security building—not surprisingly—still showed lights; beyond that the flitting lights of spotters indicated Hammerschmidt had finally gotten annoyed enough to call in his air power. But none of the spotters were close enough to bother him. Moving cautiously anyway, Haven went to the corner of the shed and looked around it.

Barely a block away, the black wall of the Ryqril Enclave rose brooding into the sky.

The Chimney, the blackcollars privately called it, and it was as different from the Hub's gray walls in its defensive philosophy as could be imagined. The Hub's wall, rich in sensors and induction fields, was designed to detect intruders and attacks, relying mainly on human forces to counter any such threat. The Ryqril had no such humanitarian pretenses: their wall was deliberately designed to kill. Haven let his eyes trace along the nearest of the slightly inward-sloping edges to the heavy laser mounted atop the structure. Sensor-aimed and -fired, the lasers were reputed to have line-of-sight antiair capability, and all four firing together were thought capable of taking out small craft in low space orbit. Aimed down along the wall, they wouldn't have the least bit of trouble vaporizing a mere human being.

The Ryqril took their own safety very seriously.

Haven returned to the shed and rummaged in his pack, and a minute later was back outside with his sniper's slingshot, a small flat case, and a set of light-amp binoculars strapped around his face. Through the binoculars the wall-mounted laser looked even meaner, its heavy-duty gimbal platform and sensor cones adding a cold efficiency to the picture. The blackcollars hadn't been able to sneak anyone into the work parties who'd built the wall thirty years back, but they'd watched carefully from afar as the lasers were being mounted, and Haven knew that throwing anything substantial at the laser or its sensors would be an invitation to a brief round of target practice.

However . . .

Setting the slingshot brace against his left forearm, Haven opened the flat box and drew out a marble-sized sphere with the consistency of soft putty. He loaded it into the sling and drew back to fire, and as he did so it occurred to him that if he survived it this mission would likely cost him a bout with cancer somewhere down the line. But it was hardly worth worrying about at the moment. Aiming carefully, he let fly.

A good shot; possibly even a great one. At high power, the binoculars showed the pellet—now badly deformed—sticking just at the juncture of the metal laser base and the ceramic wall. Directly over one of the electronic feeds from the autotarget mechanism.

Which line, if Hawking knew what he was talking about, was now being slowly degraded by the radiation from the chunk of plutonium embedded in the putty. Whether it would damage the system sufficiently over the next week or so was a separate question, of course. Hawking hadn't known the answer to that one.

But at least his threshold for the Chimney's motion sensors had apparently been correct. No alarms hooted into the night, no Ryqril on foot or in Corsairs came to see who was shooting things at their precious hideaway. Haven considered sending a second chunk of poison to join the first, decided against it, and retreated back into the shed. Tomorrow night would be soon enough to continue the attack.

He spent the rest of the night erecting a false wall behind

the elevator machinery, making it from a cloth hanging that
was stiffened and color-camouflaged with one of the last cans
of chameleon dye in the blackcollars' arsenal. Moving his
gear inside the cubbyhole, he got his airpad inflated and set
up for what might be a long stretch of housekeeping. By the
time the elevators began bringing the building's employees to
their jobs, he was fast asleep.

Project Christmas had begun.

Chapter 8

Geoff Dupre arrived home precisely at seven o'clock, and
to Caine, at least, he was something of a surprise. Raina's
description of his job as a computer systems troubleshooter
for the city's vast water retrieval network had somehow led
Caine to expect a large yet quiet, intellectual man. He was
unprepared for the spirited off-key singing interspersed with
tuneless whistling from the hulk who came through the back
door. Came through the door, and froze at the sight of five
oddly dressed strangers grouped around his wife and friend.

"Your wife's unhurt," Caine said into the suddenly brittle
silence. "We're only going to be here a few more hours, and
as long as you behave there's nothing to be afraid of."

Dupre sent his gaze to each of the team in turn, then locked
eyes with Caine. "Who are you?" he asked, his voice deep
but surprisingly calm. "What do you want?"

Raina broke in before Caine could answer. "They're
blackcollars, Geoff. They hijacked our truck out on Seventy-
two— "

"Just hitched a ride, actually," Lindsay put in. "Caine
here let me deliver the truck intact."

"Probably only to avoid stirring up attention." Dupre
snorted.

"And also because we're not here to steal," Caine told
him. "Whatever we need from you, we'll pay for it."

Dupre considered that. "May I sit down?"

Caine waved him to a sturdy-looking chair. The other
lowered himself into it and again looked around the group.

"Idunine must be cheap wherever you come from," he commented. "All right, then. What *do* you want from us?"

"For the moment, just shelter," Caine said. "And perhaps some information. Did you fight in the war?"

Dupre shook his head. "I have vague memories of it, but I was only three when it ended."

"Father? Older relatives? You know *anyone* who fought?"

A frown creased Dupre's forehead. "Not in Denver. My father lives in Sprinfielma, out near the east coast. No one talks about the war much here. At least not to me."

Caine pursed his lips. "Are there any veterans' groups you know about? Aboveboard or otherwise? The phone directory doesn't list anything obvious."

Dupre shrugged his massive shoulders. "I don't know about anything like that."

Dead end. If Aegis Mountain's emergency escape route had not, in fact, been collapsed when the base went silent, one of the men who'd been stationed there might be able to show them to its exit. But only if that hypothetical person could be found.

The others were looking at him expectantly. "I guess we'll have to find the old vets ourselves, then," he said, trying to sound confident. "In the meantime"—his eyes flicked to Braune and Colvin—"you two'd better get started. You have money?"

Colvin nodded. Their Plinry marks, Caine had quickly discovered, wouldn't pass as local currency, and he'd had to appropriate all the cash Raina and Lindsay had had on hand. It wasn't a lot, but it would do at least for the clothing they needed. After that . . . well, they'd simply have to get creative. "Off you go, then," he told the other two. "Watch yourselves."

They left. "I expect we'll be out of your lives by tonight," Caine told Lindsay and the Dupres. "Sooner if we can manage it."

"You expect us to believe that?" Dupre asked quietly. "We aren't stupid, you know. We know what blackcollars are like."

"They're not from Denver, Geoff." Lindsay spoke up unexpectedly in Caine's support. "I don't think they're like . . . the stories we've heard."

Dupre looked at her, then back at Caine. "Maybe not," he allowed, dropping his eyes with a slight shrug.

And in that instant Caine knew the big man had made his

decision. Sometime in the next few minutes, Dupre was going to make a break for it.

It was a situation they'd discussed frequently in their classes, and Lathe had given them exactly two choices as to a response: block the attempt before it started, or defeat the attempt and thus plant a psychological block against a second try.

And in this case the choice was clear. They couldn't simply tie everyone up for the next few hours, and Caine knew he wouldn't be able to concentrate on the hideout search if he was worried about the skeleton guard he would be leaving behind. Besides, a little fear might slow the inevitable phone call to Security when they pulled out for good.

"May I have a drink of water?" Dupre asked.

Caine focused on him. The big man's concept of a casual expression didn't even begin to camouflage the determination beneath it. "Sure," Caine told him, forcing unconcern into his own voice. "Raina, would you get it for him?"

Silently, she got to her feet and disappeared into the kitchen, Pittman stepping to the doorway to watch her. The sound of running water; and then she was back, carrying two tall tumblers. "I brought one for you, too, Karen," she said in a voice that trembled only slightly. Husband and wife were clearly on the same wavelength. She handed the two glasses to Dupre, started to reseat herself. Caine tensed, noting peripherally that his teammates were also ready—

And Dupre leaped to his feet, hurling the water at Alamzad and Pittman as he charged toward Caine.

Pittman ducked under the airborne wave, while Alamzad merely raised his arm to protect his eyes—and that was all Caine saw before Dupre, swinging the tumblers like short clubs, was on him.

For all his size, the man wasn't much of a fighter. Caine's right foot snapped upward between Dupre's waving arms to connect squarely with his solar plexus. The other *whuffed* with the blow, but his momentum kept him coming. Caine brought the foot down to his right, pivoting on his left foot into a crouch that left nothing in the path of Dupre's charge except an outstretched leg at trip height. Dupre hit it full force as Caine assisted him over with a left backfist under the shoulder blade. The big man slammed to the floor and lay still.

In the silence Caine heard a frustrated-sounding sob from the kitchen. He took a step toward the doorway as Pittman escorted a slump-shouldered Raina from the room. "Tried for the phone," he explained to Caine as the woman returned to her chair.

Caine glanced into the kitchen. The phone was lying open on the counter with about half its cord still attached. Embedded in the wall, near the rest of the cord, was a *shuriken*.

Dupre had gotten to his knees now, holding his stomach. "Go sit down," Caine told him shortly. "Next time it'll hurt a lot more."

"Next time you decide to beat on him, you mean?" Lindsay growled.

Caine turned to face her. "He brought that on himself."

"Don't give me that," she snapped. "You were ready for him—you *knew* he was going to try that."

"So?" Alamzad put in. "*We* didn't make him act like an idiot."

Lindsay kept her eyes on Caine. "You could have tied him up. Or even just warned him before he did anything."

But he would have eventually tried it anyway, Caine almost said. But the words caught somewhere between his throat and the almost tangible contempt radiating from Lindsay's face. The decision *had* been the right one, but no argument would ever convince her of that.

For a while, he'd thought they were slowly winning her to their side. She'd almost believed they were different, and in five seconds all that had been lost. A potential ally was once more an enemy.

He waited until Dupre was seated with the others and then retrieved the water glasses and returned them to the kitchen. Pulling on his flexarmor gloves to protect his hands, he began working Pittman's *shuriken* out of the wall. A simple enough job; with luck, he ought to be able to finish it without fouling something else up.

Manx Reger's estate was at the end of the long road that stretched southward from the main highway toward a set of tree-covered ridges that formed part of Denver's western boundary. Large houses on large lots were sprinkled to either side of the road—a gauntlet, Lathe saw, that wasn't nearly as innocent as it looked. At least twice he caught glimpses of watchers at various windows as he and Jensen drove up the road in their borrowed tow truck—watchers almost certainly on Reger's payroll. Presumably they had guns, as well, and the comsquare mentally crossed off the road as a possible exit route if this whole thing fizzled.

The estate itself was surrounded by a decorative fence: tall, obviously electrified, and impressive as hell in the early-morning sunlight. It was also probably highly effective at keeping stray rabbits off the grounds. Easing the truck to a halt before the gate, Lathe shook his head at the arrangement. Presumably Reger had motion sensors and laser-scan trackers in the woods inside the fence, but the fence itself was still pitiful.

As, to some extent, were the two men who came out of cover beside the gate to confront the new arrivals. They were out in the open, their shoulder-slung machine pistols poorly hidden beneath their coats, and Lathe could have taken both before they could possibly have gotten their weapons clear. Expendables; and they were damned lucky Lathe didn't need to expend them at the moment. Rubbing his palms on his borrowed yellow coveralls, Lathe settled his mind into his role and waited passively as the guards stepped up to the truck.

"Yeah?" the first said, glancing back at the car on the tow truck's sling as he came up to Lathe's window. If he recognized the car as the one appropriated earlier that morning, he didn't show it.

"Got a delivery," Lathe told him, jerking a thumb back toward the car. "Man told me to deliver it and a message here."

The other guard had gone back to give the car a brief inspection. "Okay," the first said. "Lower it down; we'll get it inside."

Lathe nodded at Jensen, seated beside him in an identical coverall, and the second blackcollar jumped out and disappeared toward the rear. "I also got a message I'm supposed to deliver to Mr. Reger. Personally, he said."

"I'll take it."

"He said *personally*," Lathe insisted.

"I don't give a damn," the guard growled. "I'm not getting Mr. Reger up at this hour for some stupid message."

Lathe licked his lips. "Look, uh . . . the guy didn't seem like the sort to double-up on, if you know what I mean. If I don't do this right—look, I'm not up this early 'cause I *want* to be. They came storming in—"

"*They?*" the guard interrupted.

"Yeah—three of 'em, dressed in black suits, just like the old blackcollar demos. Anyway—"

And the guard finally made the connection. "Barky! Check the plates. Is that the car Winner lost tonight?"

"Yeah," the other called back. "Looks clean enough."

"Yeah, maybe." His eyes shifted back to Lathe as he fumbled out a phone. "You get a good look at these guys?"

"Well . . . good enough, I guess."

"Okay. Sit tight." The guard backed a few steps, muttering into the phone. Jensen returned to his seat; a minute later the guard finished his conversation and climbed up onto the step beside Lathe's window. "Okay, we're going up to the house," he said, swinging his weapon into sight—a flechette scattergun, Lathe noted—and resting its muzzle against the windowsill. "Either of you got any weapons, drop 'em out the window now. The driveway sensors pick something up, I'll shred you."

Lathe shrank away from the barrel beside him. "No, no—we don't need guns. I just handle a tow truck—"

"*Move* it," the other snarled.

Ahead, the gate was opening. Keeping his movements jerky, as befit a highly nervous man, Lathe started the truck forward.

The driveway was a long, winding one that passed back into the hills, the trees giving way eventually to elaborately sculpted yards and gardens surrounding a large house. Not exactly the estate of a multimillionaire, Lathe decided, but certainly no hovel, either. Reger would do, provided the man chose to cooperate.

A half-dozen armed men were lined up by the mansion's front door as they approached. Their guide stopped the truck fifty meters back and made them walk the rest of the way. "You, stay here," one of the housemen told Jensen. "You"—this to Lathe—"come with me."

Another four guards joined them inside the carved wood door, and together they walked in silence down a richly carpeted hallway. Three turns later they reached a large study lit solely by a desk lamp swiveled to point at the door. Behind the glare, a dressing-gowned man was visible.

"You got a message for me?" the man asked coolly as Lathe and his escort stepped into the room.

"You Mr. Reger?" Lathe asked, eyes flicking about the room. Hidden gunport in the wall over Reger's left shoulder, a second in the wall to his right. Useless at the moment, unless

Reger was willing to cut down five of his own men along with Lathe. Which he might be perfectly willing to do, of course.

"I am," Reger answered with elaboration.

"Okay." Lathe shifted feet the way a simple man might under such abnormal circumstances, his hand clutching briefly at his right wrist and the tingler concealed there. *Ten seconds.* "The guy said your men were pretty amateurish and that you might like to hire some real fighters for a change."

"Why, you—" one of the guards snarled, jabbing Lathe's side with his snubnose rifle.

And Lathe moved.

It was doubtful that any of the guards ever figured out precisely what happened to them in that first second. Lathe's left arm swung at the gun barrel digging into his ribs, wrenching it from the owner's grip as a reflexive shot shattered the quiet of the room. Jamming the captured gun back into its owner's abdomen, Lathe simultaneously threw a hooking kick at the man on his immediate right, then swung the gun like a club at a third man's face. The other ducked, his shot going wild, and then the blackcollar was on him with a three-punch combination that took him out of the fight for good. Behind him, the last two guards fired, but Lathe was already out of the way, flat on the floor with his legs sweeping his attackers' out from under them. Both men crashed to the floor; and with a jab behind the ear of each to keep them quiet, Lathe finished his roll back to one knee with another captured fle-chette rifle in hand. A quick burst to each of the hidden gunports, and the muzzle came to rest lined up on the man behind the desk.

Reger hadn't moved. "Well?" he asked calmly.

"Well what?" Lathe said. "As I said, your men are amateurs."

Reger's eyes dropped briefly to the rifle. "You intend to use that on me?"

"Not really. Consider it a conversation piece." Lowering the gun to the floor, Lathe rose to his feet.

"Good. You might take a look at the gunports you shot, then."

Frowning, Lathe did so. The dark wood was unmarked. "Blanks?"

Reger nodded. "I couldn't take the risk you'd be hurt. I see now how unlikely that was. Excuse me." He leaned over slightly. "Stretcher team to my office," he said. "Five injured. Should I send another team to the front door?'' he added to Lathe.

"Probably ought to." The comsquare tapped his tingler: *Okay. Jensen?*

Okay. In control. "Make that definite. And better have everyone else leave him alone out there."

"Of course." Reger gave the orders, then leaned back in his chair and regarded Lathe thoughtfully. "After all, we can't start off by fighting with our new allies, can we?"

Lathe cocked his head. "Allies?"

Reger's eyebrows lifted slightly. "You suggested we might want to hire real fighters. I presume that's you."

The comsquare nodded, studying the other for a moment. Something about the man seemed wrong, somehow, behind that concealing light. "I must say, you're a cool one. When did you place us?"

Reger waved a negligent hand. "Oh, right from the beginning. The road out there isn't as innocent as it seems—I have watchers and sensors all along it. And of course my men got a good look at you at the bar."

"So why did you let us in?"

"Curiosity. Blackcollars out for vengeance or destruction wouldn't simply come walking up the front walk like you did. I thought it might be interesting to see what you wanted."

"It could have been fatal," Lathe told him bluntly. "Even with the gimmicked guns."

"You weren't carrying any of your *shuriken* or *nunchaku* weapons." Reger shrugged again. "And I took some other precautions."

Lathe frowned . . . and suddenly understood. Reaching down, he picked up the rifle again and lobbed it gently over the desk.

Reger didn't move as the weapon arched neatly through his chest and chair and clattered to the floor behind.

"My congratulations," Lathe said. "An exceptionally good hologram. I didn't know they could be made that realistic."

"All sleight-of-hand," the other said modestly. "The light in your eyes is the key—even this one has the usual flat look when you see it under normal conditions. But most of the visitors I use it for don't have the time to be that observant."

Lathe nodded. "So what happens now?"

Reger folded his arms across his chest. "We discuss business, of course. Why don't you start by telling me exactly what you want here. —Ah."

The "ah" was for the arrival of the medical team. Lathe watched them closely, half expecting them to suddenly sprout guns and attack. But they merely loaded the casualties onto stretchers and carted them off.

"You were saying . . . ?" Reger's image said when they were gone.

"We need information," Lathe told him. "I'm guessing you have the connections to get it for us."

"I see. And in return you offer what?"

"That's negotiable. I realize that blackcollars-for-hire is probably a new concept for you, but we have a number of specialties you might find useful."

Reger's face didn't acknowledge the delicate probe. "From what my men said and implied, I take it you haven't been in town long."

"About seven hours now," Lathe admitted.

"From . . . ?"

"Plinry."

That got a raised eyebrow. "Indeed. Off the shuttle that came in from orbit?"

"More or less."

"Which means that along with information, you also need protection. Security exists in large part to hunt down people like you."

"With the paying off of informers part of their yearly budget?" Lathe asked pointedly.

Surprisingly, Reger smiled. "You really *are* uninformed. Do you know who I am?"

Lathe pursed his lips. "You're Manx Reger, who collects a share of smuggling operations in this area. I gather there's more."

"A great deal more. I own nearly every illegal operation from Arvada west to the mountains, and a fair amount of the legal stuff as well. My yearly income is in the three-quarter-million-mark range, my total assets probably five million. What the hell can Security offer me that'll make it worth turning you in?"

"I suppose that depends on what you want us to do for you?"

For a moment Reger was silent. "Yes, it does," he conceded. "Okay. Let's start with what exactly this information is that you need."

"We weren't the only team that dropped from that shuttle," Lathe told him. "The other group's gone to ground, and we need to find them."

"Didn't you have signals or a rendezvous place picked out? I'd have thought—"

"They don't know we came with them."

Reger snorted, shook his head. "Damn pretzel thinking'll get you every time. So you want them found, but not brought in or tipped off?"

"Right—*and* I don't want Security to get a sniff of them, either. Your people have the finesse for something like that?"

"Enough of them do. I've been in this business a long time, blackcollar. I know how to find people I can trust."

"I hope so, for your sake," Lathe told him grimly, "because any unravelings will come back here to spawn."

Reger gazed at him a moment. "Let's get one thing straight from the top," he said coldly. "I don't react well to threats. Not yours, not anyone else's. You ask, you deal—you don't threaten. All right?"

"Fine," Lathe said. "As long as we've got a clear understanding. Now, let's discuss your half of the trade."

"Yes." Reger stroked his lip thoughtfully, his eyes drifting to the side wall and the hidden gunport there. "You caught the Judas holes pretty quickly earlier. You always that good at finding stray openings?"

"Some of us are better at it than others. You need someone infiltrated?"

"No—quite the opposite." Reger waved his hand in an all-encompassing sweep. "You've seen my home and grounds, at least in passing. What do you think of its security?"

Lathe shrugged. "I'd have to take an in-depth look. Good security is never visible on the surface."

"True. All right, then, here's the deal. I'll find your stray team and offer you shelter if you'll upgrade my security system. *Totally* upgrade. When you're through, *no* one is to get in here without my knowing about it."

Lathe returned the other's gaze steadily, trying not to show any reaction. It was a far more ethically acceptable bargain than he'd expected to have to make, all things considered. And yet, the oddness of it was setting off quiet alarms in the back of his mind. A man with Reger's resources shouldn't need to hire blackcollars to fence his yard for him.

Unless he was trying to keep out *other* blackcollars. Such as those Lathe and Skyler had been mistaken for. Whose existence Reger had blatantly avoided mentioning.

"All right, it's a deal," the comsquare said. Whatever the undercurrent was he was sensing, he needed time to track it down, and this was the simplest way to buy a few days. "We'll need complete specs on the system you've got now, plus layouts of house and grounds, power and water systems, and other odds and ends we'll think of as we go along."

"You'll have them," Reger said. "How many of you are there?"

"Enough," Lathe replied. "You probably won't see more than three of us at any one time."

"If you're staying here—"

"Not all of us will be. You're too far from central Denver for this to be a practical base."

He'd expected Reger to object, but the other merely shrugged. "Fine. I trust you'll accept local clothing, money, and IDs?"

"Certainly. At the moment, though, we need to return the tow truck and these coveralls before their owner misses them."

Reger smiled. "Of course. We don't want any extra attention drawn this way, do we? I take it you'll return for your money and clothing before you head into Denver?"

"We'll be back within the hour," Lathe promised. "And I'll leave two men here to start on your security system at that time. For the moment we'll all use my name as a pass with your gateman."

"And that is—?"

"Comsquare Damon Lathe, Blackcollar Forces. Temporarily at your service."

Reger smiled again. But it was a tighter smile than before, and it was accompanied by a slight shiver.

They rendezvoused outside the still-closed service station after the tow truck and coveralls were back in place. Or, rather, four of them did. "Where's Hawking?" Lathe asked.

"I left him outside the road into Reger's little subdivision to watch for interesting traffic," Skyler told him. "Reger bought it?"

"It *and* us. And our part of the deal is to secure his house for him."

"Oh?" Skyler cocked an eyebrow. "Against whom?"

"He skimmed around that part, but there's only one real possibility."

Skyler glanced back at Phelling's car, where the barman

was peacefully sleeping off the drug they'd given him. "The blackcollars Phelling mentioned."

"Whom he also implied were for hire," Lathe reminded him.

Jensen's eyes flashed with contempt. "Blackcollars for hire. He'd better have been wrong."

"Maybe they're just runing a mission with the mercenary bit as cover," Hawking pointed out. "Especially given that Reger apparently can't buy them out himself."

"Possible," Lathe agreed. "He certainly isn't dying to talk about them—I dropped one or two conversational gambits around the topic that he totally ignored. He may be hoping we'll get his job done before we find out we're working against other blackcollars." Lathe looked at Jensen. "I want you and Hawking to start work on the project as soon as we get back there. Do a good job, but leave a keyhole from due west to the house in case Reger tries to pull something backhanded. The rest of us will take the supplies he's offering and set up a safe house in central Denver. Then tonight . . ." He hesitated.

"It's only Monday," Mordecai reminded him quietly.

"I know," Lathe said. "But I think we'll give the Shandygaff Bar a try anyway. If this blackcollar contact man Kanai isn't there, maybe someone will know where we can find him."

"Are we in that tearing a hurry?" Skyler asked.

Lathe glanced at Jensen. "If Reger and the blackcollars are on opposite sides of the fence, we need to find out which side *we* should be on. And we have to do so before Reger's men find Caine."

Chapter 9

It was nearly ten when Colvin and Braune returned with the team's new clothes. Pittman, still keen on trying to find transportation, headed out alone shortly afterward on that errand. Privately, Caine considered it a likely waste of time, but was willing to let him indulge it for a short while, anyway. Leaving his own house-hunting route with Colvin and Braune so that Pittman would be able to catch up later, Caine and Alamzad headed out.

And ran straight into delayed culture shock.

Caine had been raised in Grenoble, Europe, and his Resistance tutors had exposed him to even larger cities during his training. But none of that had prepared him for Denver at full blast.

It was incredibly crowded, for starters—crowded not only with pedestrians but also with all kinds of vehicles. Caine had seen traffic of such ferocity only once before, in the government sector of New Geneva. Alamzad, born on Plinry after its fall to the Ryqril, was clearly and thoroughly dazzled by it all.

The pedestrians they passed among were almost as bad a shock as the cars. The young people, especially, showed an incredible range of clothing style and demeanor, in sharp contrast to the drab outfits and almost universal sullenness Caine had always noticed in the teenagers of Capstone.

But perhaps strongest of all was the sense of antiquity that gradually grew as they wandered about the city. Denver felt *old*, its years somehow permeating even the newest of its buildings. Like an old man being kept physically young by Idunine, Caine thought once—and that realization prompted bitter comparisons. Plinry had been nearly destroyed by the Ryqril; on the other side of Earth, old Geneva was a blackened ruin.

Denver had hardly been touched. And Caine found himself resenting the city its good fortune.

They had been searching for nearly two hours without finding any place that had the combination of accessibility, safety, and space Caine was looking for when a familiar voice called to them. A familiar voice, from a distinctly unfamiliar car. A minute later he and Alamzad were inside.

"Where did you get this?" Caine asked Pittman, looking around the aged but neat interior.

"I bought it," Pittman told him, voice tight with tension. Fighting the local traffic was clearly taking its toll. "I found a place that resells cars the owners don't want anymore. You have any luck out here?"

"Not so far." Caine shook his head. "What'd you use for money? One of our diamonds?"

"Indirectly. There was a jewelry store a block from this

place, so I went there first, sold the diamond, and then went back and talked the car dealer down to that amount of cash."

"What did he say when you didn't have an ID?" Alamzad put in.

"He didn't ask for one. I get the feeling cash on the counter bypasses a lot of official regulations around here."

They reached a corner and turned right. "Where are we going?" Caine asked.

"I passed an old house on the way here that looked promising," Pittman said. "As long as you haven't found anything, I thought it'd be worth a closer look."

Then suggest it—don't decide it. With an effort, Caine swallowed the words unsaid. Command discipline and individual initiative, Lathe had often warned, could easily become mutually exclusive. The best blackcollar comsquares worked hard to walk that thin line.

And in this case, it paid off. The house Pittman took them to was perfect.

"Probably been abandoned for months," Caine guessed, eying the broken windows, darkened gaps in the siding, and wild hedges gradually taking over the small front yard. "Wonder why it hasn't been torn down."

"A lot of the houses along here aren't in much better shape," Alamzad pointed out. "Could be no one's noticed."

"Maybe." Caine grunted. "Let's go inside."

The front door was locked, but not seriously so. Alamzad got it open while Caine and Pittman, the latter waving an official-looking note stick, stood near the sidewalk making house-inspection-type comments for the benefit of anyone watching. Inside, the house was in slightly better shape, though Caine had doubts about the stairs to the second floor, and in ten minutes he was satisfied. "Some blackout covers for the windows and I think we'll have it," he told the others. "Let's go get Braune and Colvin and load the gear into the car. We'll move in after dark tonight when we won't be so conspicuous."

"What do we do in the meantime?" Pittman asked as they locked up and went back to the car. "Try and hunt up the vets you want?"

"Or look for Torch?" Alamzad added.

Torch. Fanatics. Caine's lip twitched as he remembered Lepkowski's warning about such allies. But at least now he understood why the local resistance had gone that way. If Denver was at all representative, North America hadn't suf-

fered from the war nearly as much as Europe had, and with
life under the Ryqril essentially business as usual, there was
little incentive for ordinary citizens to get interested in their
overthrow. "I think just looking around would be a waste of
time," he told the others. "We'll need to attract their attention, and that'll take preparation. For now I think it'd make
more sense to go take a look at our target."

"Our target?" Pittman asked, his voice oddly tight as he
slid into the driver's seat and gripped the wheel.

"Well, the place we need to get into, anyway," Caine amplified. "Let's get moving; we've got a long day yet ahead
of us."

The satellite image of Denver skittered across the display
screen in a standard scan pattern: northwest corner working
down to southeast corner, then kicking back to the top again.
"Damn it all," General Quinn ground out between clenched
teeth. "Damn and damn and *damn*."

That makes number eight, Galway added to his mental
tally, being careful to sit perfectly still in his chair. The mood
Quinn was in now, even the slightest hint that Galway was
about to speak might trigger a preemptive explosion. He'd
argued strongly against Quinn's plan to put a tracer aboard
the car they'd given Pittman, pointing out that Caine would
surely go over the vehicle with a bug stomper at his earliest
opportunity. The satellite-detectable infrared-reflective paint
around the edge of the car's roof had been a reasonable compromise . . . except that the satellite had now completely lost
the damn thing eight times since Pittman had driven it away.

A motion caught the edge of Galway's eye: a foolhardy
aide venturing into blast range with a sheaf of papers.
"General?"

"What?" Quinn growled, eyes still on the display.

"I have the analysis of Postern's first stop this morning."

"Go on."

"Assuming he didn't park more than two blocks from his
objective, it's eighty-two percent probable that he did indeed
go to 7821 North Wadsworth. Two of the three people at the
twoplex there—Raina Dupre and Karen Lindsay—brought in
a truckload of oil shale from the Miniver depot late last
night."

"Um. Yeah, that would have come down Seventy-two. The
timing work for Caine to have hitched a ride with them?"

Galway cleared his throat. "If you'll remember, sir—"

"I know what he *told* you, Galway," the other cut him off. "I'll run my own checks, if you don't mind."

Galway pursed his lips and shut up.

"I've got someone checking on that now," the aide said. "Background dump shows nothing that would indicate subversive leanings by any of the three. Probability that the rendezvous was somehow prearranged is below point one percent."

"Keep digging. Double-check all relatives and previous employers for any connection to Torch. And put a couple of men in the immediate neighborhood, just in case we need a fast reaction."

"Yes, sir." The other turned and left.

Fat lot of good two men'll be against Caine, Galway thought. But something else Quinn had said . . . "I thought Torch was supposed to be dead," he ventured.

"It is," Quinn said. "Haven't heard from them in five years—haven't seen any of their leaders for nearly that long. Doesn't mean a damn thing when you're dealing with fanatics."

Galway grimaced with painful memory. Plinry's blackcollars, apparently harmless for thirty years . . . until the right opportunity came along.

"There!" Quinn barked, jerking forward to jab a finger at the display. The view had stabilized, and in the middle, centered within a red circle, was a tiny white rectangle. "Adams? You on it?"

"Yes, sir," one of the techs across the room replied. "Feeding the LockTight program now."

"It'd better work," Quinn warned darkly.

"It should," the other said.

"Then we've got you, Caine," the general muttered under his breath. "We've got you for good."

Galway exhaled carefully, the knot in his stomach slowly relaxing. The gamble was finally working. "Looks like they're leaving the city," he commented. "What's out there they might be interested in?"

"You name it." With his tracking system functional again, Quinn was almost civil. "There are at least a dozen targets in the mountains, depending on how ambitious Caine feels. Everything from oil-shale miners to Aegis Mountain itself. Pity your spy hasn't been able to find that out."

"He will," Galway replied. Aegis Mountain. The name had figured prominently in the orientation files the prefect had been skimming for the past few days—a symbol, he'd thought more than once, for Denver as a whole. Surely Caine wouldn't even *consider* tackling the place.

Or would he?

On the display the marked car was still heading west. Galway gave Quinn a sideways look, wondering whether or not he should share his sudden intuition that Aegis was Caine's target. *Not*, he decided. Quinn would surely reject the suggestion out of hand, and would then be that much slower to come around if Caine made a move in that direction. No, for the moment it would be better to just watch and be ready. Besides, it was *Lathe*, not Caine, who was the real miracle worker, and Lathe was eight long parsecs away. They could afford to give the enemy some extra rope.

Settling back, he turned his full attention to the satellite view. And tried to ignore the vague tightness in his gut.

Chapter 10

The road into the mountains was as twisted as the one the previous night had been, but at least Pittman got to drive it in full daylight. Traffic, though still heavier than the average Plinry driver would be used to, was greatly reduced from its city levels, with seldom more than one other car or truck visible at any given moment. Except for the occasional short tunnels, with their oddly unnerving pitch-darkness, Caine found himself almost relaxing as they wove in and out of the mountains toward the spot he'd chosen for their jump-off point.

They reached it about half an hour after leaving Denver: a wide part of the road with a small stream lapping through a rocky creekbed alongside the pavement. Past the stream to the south, foothill-sized mountains rose again.

"But you can see what looks like a smaller creek feeding into this one from between the hills," Caine told the others, tracing it on the aerial map. "We should be able to backtrack it to about *here*, then head straight south and get a good look at the Aegis Mountain entrance from this ridge."

"Risky," Braune said doubtfully. "If the settlement there

belongs to either Ryqril or Security they won't take kindly to visitors."

"Which is why we watch out for sensors and tripwires and whatever," Caine said. "Remember, the ridge is over a klick away from the settlement—chances are good Security won't have any real antipersonnel stuff at that distance."

"The Ryqril might," Colvin pointed out. "If it's within line of sight, they watch it."

"So we keep our heads down," Pittman said impatiently. "Come on—the afternoon's getting away from us. If we're going to go, let's *go*."

Caine nodded. "Right. Pittman, get the car started while we move the emergency packs across the stream. Drive over there, behind those bushes, and we'll put a camouflage net over it."

The operation took five minutes. Five minutes after that they were out of sight of the road, walking single-file along the creekbed Caine had chosen.

Considering what the terrain had looked like from the road, the trek was surprisingly easy. The creek was clearly of the intermittent type; just as clearly, it was at one of its low points. For a meter or more on either side the gurgling water was bordered by wide, flat stones which offered sure footing without any of the surprises the patches of grass beyond them might have hidden. Beyond the grasses the tall, thin pine trees began, their dead lower branches mute testimony to the precarious hold the flora had in these relatively dry hills, and more than once Caine thought about the millions of people living bare kilometers away in Denver and the tremendous feat it must be to supply enough water for such a metropolis. Directly above them, the sky was an incredibly deep blue. Beautiful but potentially lethal: if Security had spotter aircraft monitoring this approach to Aegis Mountain, their view downward would be equally good.

But for the first kilometer, anyway, no one came blasting out of the sky at them. In fact, as far as the evidence of their eyes could prove, they might easily have been on a completely uncharted planet.

It was at the end of the kilometer that they reached the iron gate straddling the streambed.

"I'd say offhand we now know their attitude toward company over there," Colvin said tightly as Caine and Alamzad examined the rusty metal.

"I don't think this is something Security put up," Alamzad

disagreed, touching the mesh gingerly. "Looks pretty old, and it hasn't been maintained very well. No sensors I can find, either."

Caine looked up at the slopes angling down to the stream. "Just a simple barbed-wire fence leading off from it, too. Probably somebody's old estate line, with the fence to discourage hikers. Maybe even dates to before the war."

"It's not *that* old." Alamzad shook his head. "Ten to twenty years at the most, I'd guess."

Which meant someone could conceivably still be living in the area. Caine took a quick three-sixty of the area, wondering with a twinge of uneasiness whether they were being watched. "If anyone challenges us, we're hikers out for an afternoon's walk," he instructed the others. "Try to keep your shirts fastened all the way up so the flexarmor doesn't show, and keep all weapons out of sight unless absolutely necessary. Clear?"

There were muttered assents. "Up and over?" Colvin asked, nodding at the gate.

"We'll go upslope a ways instead and go over the fence." Caine pointed, glancing at the blue sky overhead. "It's about time to head overland anyway . . . and suddenly I don't care much for this open creekbed."

It wasn't nearly as easy as it had looked. The slopes bordering the creek seemed to be composed mainly of loose soil and looser rock, and climbing them was an awkward and noisy operation. The trees dotting the region, far from being a help, were actually much more of a hindrance, and Alamzad narrowly escaped a bad fall when he snatched at one of the dead lower branches for support and had it snap off in his hand.

But again luck was with them, and they made it up to the first ridge without either injury or—as far as they could tell—attracting any unwanted attention. Caine hoped that kind of luck would hold out; he'd seldom seen terrain that combined such high travel difficulty with such low combat cover. If it came to a fight, their hidden flexarmor was almost literally all the protection they would have.

The continued on up. Fortunately, with the first ridge behind them the slopes became gentle enough to be handled without any serious risk of falling. The computer-generated contour lines superimposed on his map, Caine quickly discovered, couldn't be taken too literally, and after traversing a couple of rough patches unnecessarily he gave up and reordered the team from vertical to horizontal formation. Spread twenty meters apart across the hill, staying in contact via tingler, they were able to find the easiest routes upward more quickly.

An hour after leaving the road, they were there.

The final hill wasn't much more than a gentle hump on the surrounding terrain, and they took it in a cautious crawl with senses alert for guards and alarms. As with the rest of the trip, though, they made it through apparently undetected; and as they reached the hilltop, Caine raised his head cautiously and peered through the grass and trees at the Ryqril base below.

There was, unfortunately, no question at all of the ownership. Ryqril design permeated the place: the not-quite-geodesic-dome construction of both the main buildings and the smaller barracks units; the spindly sensor tower with its gently rotating metal/power-detector dishes; and above all the heavy black laser cannons mounted at the corners of the camp's perimeter, line-of-sight death for anything the detectors chose to label as a threat.

A dry lump settled into Caine's throat as he thought about that. Easing his head back down out of line-of-sight range, he gestured the others to take a look. They did so, in equally cautious turn. Then, huddling closely together against the still existing danger of sound sensors, they discussed the situation.

"So much for the direct approach," Colvin whispered with a grimace. "You suppose the town a few klicks west is theirs, too?"

"Has to be," Pittman said. "That base down there can't hold more than fifty to a hundred Ryqril, and they'd want at least three times that many to keep an eye on a city the size of Denver."

"And this isn't nearly secure enough for a full-fledged Ryqril enclave, anyway," Braune put in.

Alamzad snorted gently, but nodded. "Four multigig autolasers would sure as hell make *me* feel secure—yeah, yeah, I know how they are."

"Paranoids," Braune murmured. "All of Aegis Mountain to protect them, and they need lasers too."

Caine shook his head. "They're not in Aegis," he said. "At least not in the base proper."

Braune frowned at him. "What do you mean? The outer door is gone—you can see that from here."

"The outer door wouldn't have been that hard to crack,"

Caine told him. "It's the barriers farther in that would give them trouble. But look at the placement of the lasers down there—they're set up to defend the encampment, not the tunnel entrance. Ergo, they haven't got anything to speak of in the tunnel itself."

Alamzad eased up for a second look. "You're right," he agreed, settling back into the group. "Which means what we've got here is nothing more than a task force trying to get into Aegis without destroying it."

"Wonder why they're bothering," Colvin murmured. "Their technology level is essentially the same as ours."

"Probably better—they won the war, after all," was Braune's dry rejoinder. "Maybe there's something specific in there they want."

"Why not? There's apparently something in there *we* want," Pittman added, cocking an eyebrow at Caine.

"Yes, well, I think we've seen enough," Caine said, evading the other's unvoiced question. A kilometer from a Ryqril base was no place to discuss their mission. "We know the Ryqril haven't gotten in the front door, and that we're not going to. Let's see if we can round it out as a perfect day by getting out of here without being caught."

The first hundred meters back down the hill were the most nerve-racking—more so than even the approach had been, as the thought of those lasers below added an extra dollop of caution to their crawling technique. But again, they might have been forest deer for all the notice they attracted, and within a few minutes they were heading back down the slopes toward the stream and their car.

The return trip took longer than the approach had. The inexact contours on the map and Caine's attempts to find an easier route conspired to shift them farther to the east than he'd intended, and by the time he realized his error they were already committed to what was becoming a very tricky slope indeed.

"Any idea where we are?" Pittman asked as they began working their way through a patch of small cacti around a steep-sided bluff.

"The road should be that way," Alamzad said before Caine could answer. "No real way we can miss it—it cuts directly across our path. The real question is how far we are from where we left the car."

"Not far at all," Caine told them, tapping the map. "If I'm right, the road is right around the bluff here—"

"And about four hundred meters down?" Colvin put in dryly.

"Something like that," Caine admitted. "But we'll come down right at the mouth of the creek we followed on our way up, if that makes you feel better."

"Shh!" Braune hissed suddenly. "I hear another car."

Not just another car, Caine realized as they all strained their ears, but another car on the stones beside the road . . . on the stones, and coasting to a halt.

There was no need for orders. Simultaneously, all five spread apart on the steep hillside into a loose stalking pattern, pulling sniper's slingshots from their packs as they did so. Whoever was down there, they'd found the team's car.

Five minutes of cautious movement brought them within sight of the scene, and if it wasn't as bad as Caine had feared, it was bad enough. A second car was pulled up to the bushes a dozen meters behind theirs, and three men were busy stripping off the camouflage netting. A fourth man was walking guard around the area, a compact machine pistol of some kind cradled in his arms. Flechettes or slugs, probably, but either way clearly not one of Security's standard snub-nosed laser rifles. Whoever the intruders were, at least they weren't Security.

The team continued down the mountain, Braune and Pittman in the lead giving information on path and cover to the others via tingler. Below, the intruders had gotten the net off and began a thorough examination of their find. The supplies in the trunk seemed to surprise them, and there were a couple of intense discussions followed by uneasy glances at the surrounding hills. That was fine with Caine; the longer they took to make up their minds as to what they'd stumbled on, the better his chances of making sure they didn't keep it.

The intruders apparently had the same thought, and it took them only a couple of minutes to decide to take their new acquisition and run. But even as one of them twisted pretzel-fashion under the control panel and began the task of bypassing the starter lock, Caine's men reached position, and with only a few seconds' worth of rustling brush to warn them, the strangers were suddenly faced with a backpack-laden hiker strolling into sight.

"Hold it!" the man with the machine pistol snapped, swinging the weapon around to cover the newcomer. "What do you want?"

Caine froze, letting his mouth fall open with apparent shock. "Hey—take it easy, huh?"

One of the others stepped forward. "This your car?" he asked, gesturing toward it.

"No, hell no." Caine shook his head vigorously. "No, I'm just out for a hike. Uh—meeting someone upstream a ways in half an hour.

"Sure you are." The second man glanced back at the two by the car, who'd halted their own activities at Caine's approach. "Move our stuff to his car—it'll be better for the drop. Let's have the keys," he added, turning back to Caine.

"The keys? But I told you, it's not mine."

The other snorted with disgust and strode forward. Stepping behind Caine, he pulled off the backpack—

And with a crack like a stick on a ripe melon, the man with the machine pistol toppled backward, his weapon flying into the grass behind him.

The two at the car gaped . . . and Caine took a half-step backward to drive his elbow into his frisker's stomach. Two more punches and a kick and the other fell and curled around himself to the ground.

"Don't try it," Caine advised the others, turning back to them. One did anyway; he collapsed from a second slingshot bull's-eye halfway to the machine pistol. "I warned you," Caine said, retrieving the weapon himself and waving it toward the last man. "Now, suppose you tell me just who the hell you are and what you wanted with—"

He broke off as his tingler abruptly signaled: *Car approaching from west.* He took a step to the side to get a better look—just in time to see the car skid onto the stones beside the road and discharge a half-dozen uniformed Security men.

It was so unexpected that Caine was caught completely flatfooted. But his opponent wasn't. "He tried to steal my car!" he shouted to them, jabbing a finger at Caine . . . and the laser rifles swung up in response.

There was only one thing Caine could do, and he did it without hesitation. The gun in his hands was surprisingly noisy as it drained its clip in the Security men's general direction, scattering them as they dove for the ground. Laser bursts filled the air; dropping the gun, Caine sprinted back toward the mountains and the limited cover of the bushes on the lower slopes. There was a shout from behind him, and a new series of shots scorched at his shirt as he hit the ground and turned around.

The Security men were on their feet again. Or rather, four of the six were, and as Caine watched, two of the four flipped over backward as the snipers on the hillside found them.

Abruptly, the landscape in front of Caine's eyes exploded with light. Twisting around, Caine tucked his head to his chest, letting his back take the brunt of the attack. A shot found him, painfully hot even through the flexarmor—a second brushed his leg—and abruptly, the attack ceased.

Cautiously, he raised his head again. The Security men had joined their companions on the ground—alive or dead, he couldn't tell. Behind him, he could hear the crashing of bushes and tree branches as the rest of his team abandoned stealth for speed. And at their car—

Caine ducked involuntarily as, with a sleet of thrown gravel, their car spun around and raced for the road. "Damn!" he spat, jumping to his feet and hurling a *shuriken* toward the nearest tire with all the power he could muster. But the clouds of dust and wild fishtailing worked against him, and over the noise he heard a *thunk* as the star hit somewhere in the car's bodywork.

"What the *hell*?" Pittman panted from behind him.

"I guess he was farther along at getting it started than I thought," Caine said grimly. All their supplies, everything but the emergency packs they had with them—all of it gone. *Damn!* "Come on," he said as the others came up, "let's get moving. If Security doesn't have reinforcements already on the way, they will soon."

"Which car do we take?" Braune asked, already moving to obey.

"Both," Caine told him. "You and me in the Security car, everyone else in the other. Pittman, you drive. And you go first—we may need to pretend that we're chasing you."

Both sets of keys were in the appropriate starter locks, and half a minute later they were roaring down the road back toward Denver. "What do we do if Security sends more cars or aircraft against us?" Braune asked, his voice studiously casual. "It's a fair distance back to Denver."

"True." Caine's lips felt dry. "But remember that they've presumably got some distance to come, too. The guys in this car were probably just patrolling and happened upon a suspicious group near—"

A blare from the car's radio interrupted them. "Car Em-Jay Forty-six, what is your mark-fourteen? Repeat, your mark-fourteen?"

"What the hell is a mark-fourteen?" Braune muttered.

"*I* don't know," Caine shot back. "Situation code, probably." Gritting his teeth, he pulled the slender microphone from its clip. "Car Em-Jay Forty-six," he said, hoping the noise of tires on pavement would disguise his voice enough to get by. "Tailing possible smuggling suspects east on one-one-nine. Request all units stay clear of area to avoid spooking them."

A new voice came on the line. "Do you require air backup, Em-Jay Forty-six?"

"Negative," Caine said.

"What happened with the mark-twenty-one?"

The confrontation by the road? "No problems," Caine said, feeling sweat gathering on his forehead. The longer this conversation went on, the better the chance he'd say something so far out of normal parlance that they'd tumble to the charade.

"Okay. Mark-four, Em-Jay Forty-six. Stay on it."

"Smugglers?" Braune asked as Caine replaced the mike.

"Best I could come up with on the spur of the moment," Caine told him. "I'm not at all sure he bought it, though. Better signal the others to watch for company."

Braune nodded and reached for his tingler.

They'd covered perhaps half of the thirty kilometers back when the reaction finally came.

It came from both air and ground, and was clearly more than simply a routine check. Rounding a gentle curve, Caine caught a glimpse of a Security car parked sideways three hundred meters ahead, directly in front of one of the short tunnels straddling this part of the road. Simultaneously, an armed spotter swooped down to pace them a few meters up.

"Have Pittman drop back; I'm passing," Caine snapped to Braune, swinging into the other lane and leaning hard on the accelerator. Once, Lathe had demonstrated that Security cars on the planet Argent were routinely built tough; Caine hoped to hell that pattern held here, too.

Ahead, the Security men grouped behind their car suddenly realized what he was intending, and laser flashes lanced ineffectively out as they tried to fire while dashing madly for cover. Caine aimed toward the rear of the blocking car and braced himself . . . and with a horrendous crash they were past and into the relative safety of the tunnel.

"Signal the others to pull over," he told Braune, confirming via mirror that the second car had successfully followed them through the ruined roadblock. "When we get out, check the trunk and see if we've got anything heavy enough to take out that spotter."

A moment later the cars were side by side in the darkness. "We've got to lose that air cover," he told the others through their side window as Braune rummaged in the Security car's trunk. "If I remember the road properly, there's another tunnel coming up maybe four hundred meters past this one. Somewhere in that open area or in the next tunnel, we've got to take out that spotter. Suggestions?"

Before anyone could answer, the tunnel lit up with laser light. "Spotter's reported we're still in here," Alamzad said tightly. "We're going to be up to our necks in Security men in a minute if we don't get moving."

"Yeah. Braune? Anything?"

"Couple of standard laser rifles," the other reported, lifting them out. "Nothing that'll take out an aircraft."

"Not easily, anyway," Caine gritted. "Alamzad—did you get a good look at that spotter? It looked like a standard prewar TDE design to me."

"Yeah," Alamzad agreed. "A Hap-Kien Two-oh-something, I think. Heavy shielding on sides and belly for laser defense."

"Has it got any weaknesses?" Pittman put in.

Alamzad shrugged helplessly as another burst of laser fire flicked at them. "All I can think of are the two intake grates on top, just beside the canopy. If we can get a clear shot at those, we might be able to disable the thing."

"Close enough," Caine said. "All right, here's what we'll do—and we'll hope whoever it is has normal reflexes. Get your gloves, battle-hoods, and goggles on while I talk."

He outlined his plan briefly, cut off all attempts at protest, and in a fresh flurry of laser blasts they piled into the cars and spun off toward the end of the tunnel.

Caine, alone in the now battered Security car, took the lead, leaning on the accelerator as hard as the unfamiliar road would permit. The end of the tunnel rushed toward him—he was out in the fading sunlight again—

And the waiting spotter shot across his path.

He ignored the obvious warning, pushing his speed up a bit more. The road made a gentle curve to the right through a jagged cut in the mountain; ahead, the mouth of the next tunnel became visible—

And abruptly his left arm was awash in laser fire.

Another warning, clearly; the shirt blackened but the flexarmor beneath it took the blast without trouble. Gritting his teeth, Caine kept going, hoping they wouldn't switch intensities before he reached the relative safety of the tunnel. Behind him, the mirror showed their second car had made it around the curve and was gaining on him. Caine let his car swerve a bit, hoping to hold the spotter's attention a few seconds longer.

The laser beam cut off as the pilot pulled out of his collision course with the mountain ahead, and in almost the same instant the darkness of the tunnel snapped closed about Caine.

The knife blade flickered with reflected light in his peripheral vision as he sprang it from its forearm sheath and leaned over as far as he could without losing control of the car. The accelerator was of the piezoelectric pressure type; jabbing the tip of the blade into the center console, Caine wedged the haft onto the plate. The car's speed faltered, then stabilized as he got the brace in position. Straightening up, he glanced out the side window to see the other car had caught up and was pacing his a meter away. Ahead, the tunnel exit was growing larger, barely a handful of seconds away. Pulling out a *shuriken*, Caine wedged it into the gap between steering wheel and column. Then, in a single motion, he swung open his door and jumped.

Braune and Colvin, in the front and rear seats on that side of the other car, were ready. Caine's outstretched arms came in through the open window and were caught instantly by the two men. Bracing his feet against the side of the car, Caine clenched his teeth as Pittman tromped on the brakes. The Security car shot on ahead into the sunlight . . . and as Pittman brought them to a skidding halt the tunnel echoed to the sounds of a thunderous crash.

Pittman and Alamzad were out their side of the car before Caine and his human anchors could disengage themselves, racing toward the tunnel mouth with their appropriated laser rifles at the ready. Caine and the others followed, to discover that the spotter pilot did indeed have normal reflexes.

The Security car had shot off the road to the right, crashing through the barrier and down the cliff to the creek below. The pilot, perhaps startled thoughtless by the apparent accident, had followed it down and was just coming to a hovering stop overhead.

Leaving its upper side exposed to the road above.

And the beams from the two lasers lanced out together, striking the intake vents dead on.

They took barely half a second of the fire before the pilot jumped the spotter out of position like a scalded bat. But the action was too late, and even as he brought the spotter around toward the road it was clear he was starting to lose altitude. His lasers fired once, too low, and then he gave up, and a moment later the spotter came to rest beside the ruined Security car.

Caine licked his lips briefly, arms trembling with reaction. A certifiably crazy stunt . . . but it had worked. "Let's get out of here," he told the others, as calmly as he could. "He may have enough range even in these mountains to whistle up reinforcements."

Apparently he didn't. Fifteen uneventful minutes later, they were once again within the teeming anonymity of Denver.

Chapter 11

Quinn set the phone down and turned to Galway with an expression that was just short of murderous. "I trust you're satisfied now," he bit out. "That brings us up to two deaths from that fiasco—a second man's just died from brain hemorrhaging. And for *nothing*."

Galway forced himself to return the general's glare steadily. "Would you rather have left them stuck out there with no transportation?" he asked.

Quinn snorted. "So instead we have them running around Denver in an untrackable vehicle. Great. Just great."

"It's not *my* fault that someone tried to steal their car," Galway said stiffly. "It's also not my fault Caine got back at the wrong moment. I could point out that if your men had bothered to make a surveillance pass first they would have seen that Caine had things under control and could have just kept going with no one the wiser."

"Oh, right." Quinn was heavily sarcastic. "And I suppose if the central router had been omniscient we could have saved the wrecked car and spotter, too."

Galway sighed. "We *both* assumed it was the others in the stolen Security car, General—don't try to push all that off onto my shoulders."

"Why not? You're the one who claims to know these bastards—why the hell didn't you recognize Caine's voice?"

"What difference would that have made? Really? All right, suppose I *had* realized it was Caine's team in those two cars. He knows that Security dispatchers aren't stupid enough to fall for such a simple charade—he'd have been suspicious as hell if we hadn't made some reasonable response. All right, so we've temporarily lost them. So what? As long as Postern is alive and unsuspected, we're still on top of things."

Quinn snorted and turned away, stomping over to where the monitor duty officer was still tracking the marked car. Galway took a deep breath and went the other direction, to the situation room's main communications board. The officer there looked up with a face that was studiously neutral. "Yes, sir?"

"What have you got on the three people Caine's team took out?" Galway asked.

The other shrugged. "Smugglers, it appears, though we won't know exactly what they were smuggling until we get their car back—maybe not even then if they were on their way to a drop when they stopped. It's nothing particularly unusual—Denver's a sewer sludge of criminal types."

Galway pursed his lips. Smugglers. Caine had mentioned smugglers when he talked to the dispatcher on that wild ride back to Denver. Had he simply pulled that out of the air, or had he had time to interrogate the failed car thieves before the Security team blundered onto the scene? Though he couldn't see offhand what difference it made either way.

Aegis Mountain.

Galway shivered. So he'd been right about Caine's target—the team's afternoon trip virtually assured that. There was nothing else in that area that could possibly be of interest to the commandos.

Unless . . .

"Are there any private residences out in those mountains?" he asked the Security man slowly.

The other's eyebrows lifted slightly. "I can't imagine the Ryqril letting anyone live that close to their base," he said.

"Neither can I. Check it out anyway."

"Yes, sir." Swiveling around to his board, the officer logged the request with the appropriate research unit. "Unless it's urgent, Prefect, you probably won't get anything on this until morning," he pointed out. "Do you want me to tag it as a priority?"

Galway hesitated. "No, don't bother. Morning should be soon enough."

Especially since anything like a priority tag would be likely to attract Quinn's attention. Galway had had enough of that for one day. Besides, whatever Caine was up to, he still couldn't be ready yet to make his move. And unmarked car or not, Postern was still there to betray them.

Still, it wouldn't hurt to hang around for another hour or so. Just in case something came through.

Seen from space, nighttime Denver looked even more alive and active than its daytime incarnation had, and for the umpteenth time since Quinn had left for the night Galway found himself staring bemusedly at the steady flow of pinprick lights that marked the city's incredible traffic density. Now and again his eyes flicked to the locator circle in the southeast that marked where Caine's stolen car was sitting. There had been a second locator circle once, but it had vanished soon after Caine had entered the traffic pattern of the city. It wasn't likely to reappear, unfortunately.

"Prefect Galway?"

Galway started, realizing with some embarrassment that he'd dozed off. He looked up as Colonel Poirot, the man in charge of Denver's night watch, sat down beside him. "Yes, what is it? Have you found Caine's new car?"

Poirot shook his head. "No chance now, really. The satellites had him until about halfway through Golden, but we just couldn't keep track of him once the traffic got too thick."

Galway sighed. "Yeah. I suppose I was hoping we could get enough high-resolution stills that we could trace through them. By hand if necessary."

"You've already seen the highest-resolution we've got, I'm afraid." The colonel exhaled with frustration. "You know, before the war we had satellites that could count the eggs on a picnic table. I'll never understand why the Ryqril didn't replace them."

"Because satellite tranmissions can always be tapped into," Galway told him. "The Ryqril don't like the chance that someone else might be monitoring their movements. Well . . . what good news *did* you bring me?"

"Good news is a rarity around here tonight," Poirot said

dryly. "This little gem came in a few minutes ago: the Ryqril have picked up a small ship skulking around a few million klicks out."

"What?" Galway took the proffered report, scanned it quickly. Scout-ship-sized, possibly left behind by the *Novak*. Presumed purpose: observation and/or rescue. "Are they going to send a Corsair to investigate?" he asked, handing the paper back.

"For the moment, apparently not. The ship certainly can't come any closer without triggering alerts all over the planet; by the same token the Ryqril can't get something out there without spooking it."

At which point it would simply swing around through hyperspace and take up its vigil elsewhere, forcing the Ryqril to waste time locating it again. Galway understood the logic, but that didn't mean he had to like it. "Postern didn't say anything about a ship," he muttered. "I wonder just how many other cards Caine's got stashed up his sleeves."

The colonel gave a little shrug and shook his head. "I wouldn't even want to guess."

"Nothing come in yet about possible residents near Aegis Mountain?"

"No—and if it hasn't come through by now it's not going to until the day shift comes back on. Research must have higher-priority work to do at the moment."

Galway nodded. "I suppose I might as well pack it in for the night, then."

"Good idea. I hope you have better dreams than the rest of us do."

Poirot stood up and moved off, and after a few moments Galway levered himself out of his chair. There really wasn't anything else he could do at the moment. And with Caine's trip to analyze tomorrow, to say nothing of studying whatever was available on the mysterious ship out there, the morning's work was already promising to be hectic.

He paused at the door, an odd thought pricking at his mind. Possible misdirection regarding Aegis, the efficient action against the Security forces, a seemingly accidental encounter that had just *happened* to dump the marked car—the whole thing was starting to feel familiar. Uncomfortably familiar, in fact.

But that sort of thing was Lathe's trademark. And Lathe wasn't here this time. Couldn't possibly be here.

On the other hand, it wouldn't hurt to take a few hours in the morning and sift through the intelligence files for the past few days. Just to see if anyone had spotted any new strangers in the city . . . and had lived to report it.

Chapter 12

The Shandygaff Bar turned out to be a large, elegant-looking place smack in the middle of a pedestrian mall near the center of Denver. On the face of it that shouldn't have been surprising—any city with as much wealth as this one had would hardly scrimp on its entertainment—but Lathe had still been prepared more for the sort of hole-in-the-wall roll joint he'd known on Plinry.

Skyler, apparently, had had similar expectations. "Looks fancy," he commented as they approached the door. "Think they'll let us in?"

"I don't think we're offering them a choice." Lathe gave the area one last scan, confirmed Mordecai was in his pre-planned backup position off by one of the benches, and pulled open the door.

Inside, all was dim lights, bland music, and the quiet drone of conversation. An anteroom led into the main area, which, except for an open space at one end containing a traditional wooden bar, was divided up into a honeycomb of booths, each wrapped in translucent privacy plastic. "Designed for quiet chats," Skyler murmured as they paused at the main room's threshold. "How do we go about finding him—go to each booth and knock?"

"May I help you?" a female voice asked from behind them.

Lathe turned to see a coatroom counter he hadn't noticed, half hidden back in a corner of the anteroom. The woman there was young and far too heavily made up. "We're looking for a man named Kanai," he told her.

"I believe tomorrow is the night Mr. Kanai usually does business here," she said.

"So we've heard. Would it be possible to get in touch with him before that?"

"Most anything is possible here," a new voice chimed in; and a small, thin man in formal wear glided in from the main room.

Lathe glanced back at the woman, taking a quick reading of her expression. Familiarity, quiet dislike, perhaps a touch of contempt. "Are you in charge here?" he asked, turning back to face the man.

The other smiled, an oily sort of expression. "I manage the Shandygaff, yes," he said. "As well as other things. You're looking for Kanai, correct? Business or personal?"

"A little of both," Lathe told him.

"Are you representing someone? He'll want to know."

"Then he can ask us himself, can't he?"

The little man's smile slipped a fraction. "We play by certain rules here, *sir*" he said, leaning not quite insolently on the last word. "And the first rule is that to conduct business here you first identify yourself."

Lathe gazed at him thoughtfully. "And if we don't?"

The other raised a finger and two walking hulks silently moved in from the main room to flank him. Above their formal wear, their impassive faces showed the evidence of innumerable fights. "You can leave peacefully," the little man said, "or in pain."

Slowly, deliberately, Lathe brought his left fist chest-high, covering it with his right hand. The little man's body went rigid as the red-eyed dragonhead ring caught the dim light. "Call Kanai," Lathe instructed him quietly. "I think he'll be willing to see us."

A handful of the nearest booths in the convoluted floor pattern had openings which faced the door. Lathe and Skyler let a waiter take them to one of those, ordered a beer apiece, and settled down to wait.

"We're sure spending a lot of time on this mission hanging around bars," Skyler noted as they waited for their detox tablets to neutralize any potential drugs in their drinks. "You think he'll come alone?"

Lathe shrugged. "That *is* the question, isn't it? It may depend on how deeply they're involved with the criminal element in town."

"That barman—Phelling—talked about them drumming up

business here. Could be the local criminals keep them informed on potential collie targets.''

"You really believe that?"

Skyler smiled lopsidedly. "Probably not. Though if they've really quit the war to become mercenaries they're taking an awful risk on Jensen's righteous indignation.''

"We'll save that threat for our trump card," Lathe said dryly.

"Right."

Conversation lagged, and Lathe took the opportunity to study their booth and its surroundings. From the shoulders up they were shielded from the rest of the room only by the privacy plastic—which, while not even remotely bulletproof, at least fogged images enough to make aiming difficult. The booth's seatback was thick enough to provide a somewhat better shield, though again its strength was dubious. The table itself bothered him more. Thick and heavy, it was bolted solidly to the floor via a metallic central stem. An immediate and formidable obstacle to a fast exit from the booth, should such a move become necessary. He was surreptitiously testing the strength of its connectors when Skyler cleared his throat. "I believe this is our company arriving now."

Lathe looked up. Moving toward them from the anteroom was a slim oriental man. He stepped to the edge of their privacy shield, glanced at Skyler, then turned his attention to Lathe. "I'm Lonato Kanai," he said, raising right hand to left shoulder in formal blackcollar salute. His dragonhead had the vertically slit eyes of an ordinary commando.

"Comsquare Damon Lathe," Lathe said, returning the salute. "Commando Rafe Skyler. Sit down."

Kanai did so, something in his face and movements suggesting wariness. "I suppose we might as well dispense with the obvious question of where you came from," he said, "and go right to the important one: why are you here?"

"Here in Denver or here in the Shandygaff?" Lathe asked. Kanai smiled faintly. "Either, or both."

"We hear you're for hire. We want some details."

The smile vanished. "We handle . . . difficult jobs for our clients," he said, his voice oddly stiff. "Penetration, goods recovery, intelligence—"

"Against whom?" Skyler interrupted.

Kanai's lip twitched. "Against whomever the client wants."

"Government targets?" Skyler persisted. "Rival criminal bosses? Or just ordinary citizens who get out of line?"

Kanai's brow darkened. "We don't touch the ordinary citizens," he growled. "Ever. Only those in charge."

"The government?" Lathe asked.

"The government isn't in charge in Denver," Kanai snorted. "The roachmen keep pretty much to Athena while the parasites run the city."

"Parasites like Manx Reger?"

"Like him and a dozen more. He's furious with you for whatever you did to his men this morning, incidentally. You'd better stay clear of northwestern Denver."

"I'll keep that in mind," Lathe said. "Why doesn't the government do something about these organizations?"

Kanai eyed him. "You *are* new here. The roachmen don't do anything because they can't. Organized crime was entrenched in Denver long before the war, and it would cost billions to eradicate it."

"And the people as a whole can't do anything?"

"The people generally accept it." Kanai shrugged. "You have to understand that the bosses here are parasites but not bloodsuckers. They want long-term profits, not a dead city. Their payment scale runs lower even than the roachmen's taxes—which in turn are lower here than in a lot of other areas because there aren't as many official government services. In exchange the bosses provide protection for their clients, certain financial services, and other benefits. It really *does* qualify as an invisible government—and at ten percent or less of their income most people consider it a fair bargain."

"Reger's men were charging twenty-five percent," Skyler murmured.

"Spot-market rates," Kanai said. "Must have thought you were outsiders trying to move in."

"How long has this system been running?" Lathe asked.

"Openly, since the end of the war. Covertly, probably a lot longer. As I said, the people here generally accept the situation."

"Like they accept the Ryqril," Skyler said. "No wonder Torch can only draw the lunatic fringe."

"Torch?" Kanai's eyes narrowed. "Have you been in contact with them?"

"Not yet. But we've heard stories about them."

Kanai relaxed again. "Oh. Well, your stories are old ones, I'm afraid. Torch disappeared about five years ago. I thought for a minute they'd come back."

"Destroyed?"

"If so, it was done with remarkable finesse. We had some slight contact with them, and as far as we could tell they simply up and vanished."

Lathe stroked his dragonhead gently. "You were working with them before that?"

Kanai shifted slightly in his seat. "Not working, exactly. We occasionally exchanged information, but they were too radical for our taste."

"They believed in outmoded stuff like overthrowing the Ryqril?" Skyler asked coldly.

Kanai returned the other's gaze steadily, but there was tension around his mouth. "I know what you're thinking," he told Skyler quietly. "But you're wrong. We haven't given up the fight, just switched tactics. When the time is right, we'll make our move."

"Glad to hear it," Lathe said. "Because the time *is* right."

"Meaning?"

"Meaning we're on an important mission here, and we're calling on your squad to assist us."

Kanai stared at him—a long, measuring stare rich with conflicting emotions. "You'll need to talk directly to our doyen about that," he said at last.

"Fine. Where is he?"

Abruptly, Kanai twitched a smile. "At the moment, he's out looking for *you*." He glanced at his watch. "At any rate, I doubt he'd be willing to meet on such short notice."

"You did so."

"I'm the contact man," he said simply. "It's my job to be both visible and available. The rest of us can't afford that kind of exposure."

Lathe pursed his lips; but that *was* the only way a guerrilla force survived. "All right, then. Where and when?"

"Tomorrow night at nine, here," Kanai said. "I'll either bring him or else take you to him."

"Fair enough." Lathe stood up, Skyler following suit.

"It might help," Kanai said, "if I could tell him what exactly you want from us."

Lathe looked down at him, considering. The other had a point; but on the other hand the comsquare had no intention of saying anything important in a place like this. "For starters," he said, picking his words carefully, "I want the names and current locations of high-ranking military people who were stationed in the area during the war."

"Um." Kanai frowned thoughtfully. "That's a pretty big

order. I don't know of anyone higher than colonel who's still here.''

"A colonel might work. Just do what you can."

"All right." Slowly, Kanai got to his feet. "Comsquare . . . I have to be honest with you. Denver—and our position in the power structure here—is very stable. You're an intrusion, and an unknown one at that, and there may be some who won't like the risk you bring.''

"Are you telling us your doyen might betray us?" Skyler asked.

"No, of course not. But he might decline to help you."

Lathe pursed his lips. "Let's face that possibility when we get there, all right?"

"Yes, sir." Kanai looked as if he wanted to say something more. But he merely nodded. "Tomorrow at nine, then. Good night."

Lathe nodded back and left the table, Skyler falling into step beside him. "What do you think?" the big man murmured.

"Rusty but willing," Lathe told him. "Let's hope his comsquare is equally tired of being a hired thug.''

The little man and his two cohorts were nowhere in sight as the blackcollars crossed into the anteroom. The coatcheck woman was still at her window, though, and she looked up as they approached. "I saw Mr. Kanai come in a short time ago," she said.

"We had our talk," Lathe nodded.

She smiled. "I hope it was productive."

Something about the way she said that . . . and abruptly Lathe realized what it was. "I hope so, too," he said. "You work here every night?"

"Five nights a week, till three a.m."

"You handle anything besides coats?" he asked with a wink.

She seemed taken aback. "Sometimes they need an extra waitress.''

"I was thinking more on the personal level." Lathe shrugged. "Never mind. We can go elsewhere for female companionship."

A look that was almost disgust crossed her face before she could cover it. "Good night, sir," she said, dropping her eyes from his gaze.

They left the building and headed west across the mall. Though it was nearly eleven o'clock, most of the stores lining the area were still open, and the pedestrian traffic was correspondingly heavy. "Interesting," Skyler murmured, nodding to one of the shops. "High-class places, notice—jewelry stores, restaurants, import shops. You suppose the Shandy-gaff's a common meeting place because each of these places is owned by a different boss?"

"So that if anyone starts trouble, one of his own places is likely to get trashed in the process?" Lathe shrugged. "Makes sense. We'll ask Kanai about it sometime."

"Yeah." Skyler cleared his throat. "Incidentally, you mind telling me what that business with the coatcheck lady was all about?"

"Not at all. You notice anything out of character about her?"

"Aside from not mentioning her other second job is backup gun in case of trouble?" Skyler shrugged. "I don't know. She seemed maybe a shade too nosy about our talk with Kanai, but maybe she backs up the little guy in that post, too."

"Possibly. But I'm referring more to the fact that she's just about the first regular person we've met in this town who wasn't scared spitless of us."

"Mm. Interesting. Of course, she sees a lot of Kanai and his friends . . . but so does Mr. Charm, and he folded as fast as Reger's harmers did. Implication is she knows more about blackcollars generally than can be learned from the local representatives?"

"That was my thought. Hence the leering-soldier-in-search-of-random-female gambit."

"Totally out of character for you."

"For me and most blackcollars I've known, too," Lathe said. "And you saw how she reacted."

"Surprised," the other said thoughtfully. "Almost disillu-sioned, even. So you're right—she *does* know a fair amount about blackcollars. Government spy?"

"Could be. Laissez-faire attitude or not, I can't see them *or* the Ryqril failing to keep an eye on such an obvious meeting place as the Shandygaff. But she could just as easily be a war veteran who worked with the Aegis Mountain blackcollar contingent." He shrugged. "Or even a member of Torch."

"You think they're still around?"

"I don't believe in fanatics deciding overnight to roll over and quit. Beyond that I haven't even got a guess as to what they've done with themselves. But any way you slice it, that woman bears watching."

Skyler nodded. "Agreed."

They'd reached the edge of the mall now and the quiet business-section street where they'd parked their car. They got in and waited, and a few minutes later Mordecai joined them. "Well?" Lathe inquired.

"Just one," the small man said indifferently. "Big harmer in fancy dress. Not very professional."

"Probably never had to tail blackcollars before," Skyler said dryly, starting the engine.

Pulling away from the curb, they headed off into the night.

Chapter 13

Caine had expected Security to make another snatch at them before they finished tracing the carefully convoluted route to their new hideout house; failing that, the next most likely scenario was that the enemy would launch a predawn raid. He was therefore more than a little surprised to awake the next morning with sunlight streaming in through the dirty windows and not a single Security man in sight outside them.

"Now what?" Braune asked when they'd breakfasted as best they could on what rations they'd had in their emergency packs.

"First step is to try and replace the stuff we lost with the car," Caine told them. "We still have one diamond left, so buying food and clothes should be easy enough. The more specialized equipment, unfortunately, is going to be another problem entirely. The bug stomper alone is probably irreplaceable now, and the spare weapons and explosives aren't going to be a lot easier."

"What exactly were we going to use the explosives for, if it's not still a secret?" Alamzad asked. "We certainly weren't going to blast our way into Aegis Mountain with those firecrackers."

"No, of course not," Caine said. "But at this point it would be nice to attract Torch's attention. To do that we need to make some noise, and to do *that* properly we need explosives."

"Okay." Colvin shrugged. "So who around here would have explosives on hand?"

"And who wouldn't also have six layers of security wrapped around it," Pittman added dryly.

"That's the real problem," Caine agreed. "Any suggestions?"

"Construction companies," Braune said promptly. "With the rate of growth Denver shows, there's bound to be a lot of building and demolition work going on around here."

"We could presumably follow a construction truck back to its headquarters from a site," Pittman said. "Of course, that would mean tailing in broad daylight in a car that Security may have a good ident on."

"So what we'd really like is a night worker who's at least marginally connected with explosives," Caine said, an idea clicking into place. "That remind you of anyone?"

There was a short pause. "You mean Geoff Dupre?" Colvin hazarded. "But he works for the city water department, doesn't he?"

"For the city water retrieval network, specifically," Alamzad corrected him. "And any system that has that much underground piping will use a hell of a lot of explosives."

"Only if they're constantly upgrading or expanding the system," Braune said doubtfully. "Routine maintenance wouldn't require anything big."

"We don't need anything big, either, if all we're looking for is noisemakers," Caine pointed out. "Besides, it occurs to me that there's another good reason to check out the retrieval network. The majority of the pipelines were presumably laid before the war, and some of them *may* travel under Athena. If so, the government's cozy little fortress city may not be quite as secure as they think."

Colvin smiled, almost wickedly. "What an intriguing thought. I hope you're right."

"We'll find out tonight," Caine told him. "Right now, we'll concentrate on replacing our lost living supplies and getting caught up on our rest. This may be our last chance to take it easy for a long time."

With the attempted tailing from the Shandygaff in mind, Lathe elected to take a cautious, roundabout route to Reger's estate, and it was therefore after nine in the morning by the time he drove down the long road to the main gate. The guards passed him with considerably more respect than those the previous day had shown, and a few minutes later he was at the house.

Reger—in the flesh this time—was waiting for him just inside the door. "Comsquare Lathe," he said in greeting, his voice barely audible over the din of hammers, saws, and drills that seemed to fill the house. "I think I may have some news for you about your missing companions. If you'll come with me . . . ?"

They set off through a maze of drop cloths, scaffolding, and busy men. Directing the whole operation was Jensen; exchanging "all's well" hand signals with him, Lathe continued on. Reger, it appeared, was deadly serious about transforming his estate into a fortress.

"There was a disturbance just off of Route One-nineteen yesterday afternoon," Reger said when they were seated in his office, its soundproofing holding most of the noise outside at bay. "A group of smug-runners on their way to a drop stopped to check out a camouflaged car and were crunched for their curiosity. One of them got away with the car while losing his own, this after Security somehow got mixed up in it. The runner aborted the planned pickup and ditched the car as soon as he could, but not before grabbing the stuff in the trunk." Reaching into his middle drawer, Reger withdrew a small three-pointed *shuriken* and handed it across the desk. "One of yours?"

Lathe nodded, picking it up for closer examination. "It's a nonstandard shape we teach them to carry as an emergency push-knife. How did you get hold of it?"

Reger smiled grimly. "As I said, the guys were runners. They work for someone I know in south Denver."

"Who was kind enough to volunteer the information and the *shuriken*?"

Reger shrugged. "We traded." He didn't elaborate.

"So where is Caine now?"

"We don't actually know. I've sent a description of their new car to my people, so ideally we'd have him in a day or two. Of course, since Security may also have an ident on the car, your friends might ditch the thing as fast as they can."

"Which brings us back to square one," Lathe said with a grimace.

"It might." Reger paused. "There's one other item that you might find interesting. Before the runner ditched the car, he gave it a quick once-over . . . and in the process found out it was marked."

"Um."

Reger gave him a keen look. "That's all you can say? 'Um'? That means Security's been on to Caine since before he got that car, possibly since he landed here."

"Security's been on to us before." Lathe shrugged. "Their usual problem is that they'd rather have information than bodies, and to get it they have to let us run relatively loose."

"There are a whole spectrum of drugs—"

"None of which is especially effective against the psychor training we give our people," Lathe told him. "Let me worry about Security; you worry about finding Caine. And I'd like to get the rest of his equipment back from your runner friend, too, if I can."

"That should be possible." Reger had a sour look on his face. "You know, Comsquare, you strike me as someone who might well be playing two of the corners of this triangle. If you are, be advised right now that I have no intention of being pulled into whatever mess you're trying to make."

"Our deal is perfectly well defined," Lathe said coolly. "You find Caine; we redo your defenses. To be perfectly honest, I don't trust *you* all that far, either."

Reger smiled thinly. "As long as we understand each other."

"Good. Then I'd like to have that description of Caine's new car, and then go see my other man, Hawking."

Reger handed over a piece of paper. "Hawking's out on the perimeter looking over the sensor line," he said. "You want a guide?"

"No, I'll find him," Lathe said, getting to his feet. "Just make sure your guards know I'm going to be out there. I don't want to have to hurt anyone."

Reger nodded. He was speaking into his intercom as Lathe left.

He found Hawking sitting in the lower branches of a gnarled tree, drilling holes into the trunk. "You building him a full sensor wedge?" he asked as Hawking dropped back to the ground.

"More or less," the other said. "I can see how the local blackcollar force got in before—the primary-line tolerances allow for slow-foot infiltration. I'm setting up a sequential-event trigger system to try and plug that hole."

"Sounds good."

"And you were right about the raid being recent," Hawking continued. "Jensen found some *shuriken* and flechette marks under a fresh topcoating in the walls near Reger's bedroom when he was tearing everything up."

Lathe glanced back in the direction of the house. "What exactly is Jensen building back there, anyway?"

"A full-fledged death-house gauntlet," Hawking said, shaking his head. "Hidden escape doors, scud-net drop ceiling panels—the works. *His* idea, incidentally, not Reger's. And if you ask me, he's just a little too enthusiastic about the whole project."

Lathe pursed his lips. "He's had that hard edge ever since Argent. I'm hoping it'll fade with time, but for now we'll just have to keep an eye on him."

"Yeah." Hawking rubbed his chin. "Did you find the local blackcollars, by the way?"

"Their contact man, yes. We're allegedly meeting their doyen tonight."

"You don't sound thrilled by the prospect."

Lathe grimaced. "It looks very much like they've turned their backs completely on the war. I don't know if we can rekindle them enough to get any help. And if not . . . well, we'll just have to make do with Reger."

"I'm not sure how far Reger wants to get into the war, either."

"He *is* beginning to wonder whether we're worth the risk of bringing Security down on him," Lathe agreed soberly. "I suppose that means we'll just have to keep raising the ante on him."

"How?"

"I don't know yet. But I'm sure we can find a way to keep his interest."

"Well, don't push him too hard," Hawking warned. "Beneath that mild exterior there's a tough old man."

"But also a smart one who recognizes a good deal when he hears one. If we need more help from him I'll be sure it's genuinely worth his while."

"A good philosophy," Hawking said dryly. "Remember it when you talk to the other blackcollars tonight."

"Right. I'll be in touch. And keep an eye on Jensen."

"Ridiculous." Quinn snorted, tossing the paper aside.

Galway took a deep breath, all his preparation for the general's expected reaction threatening to evaporate before

the surge of anger within him. "It's from your own agent—
your own *loyalty-conditioned* agent—at the Shandygaff—"

"I can read," Quinn cut him off harshly. "I also know that
anyone can walk into a bar wearing a dragonhead ring.
Doesn't even prove they were blackcollars, let alone Lathe
and Skyler."

"The descriptions fit," Galway persisted. "And as for
them not being blackcollars, don't you think this Kanai
would've taken violent exception to their right to wear those
rings?"

"Kanai wouldn't lift a finger if the guy had money and a
job for him," Quinn said with contempt.

Underestimating Denver's blackcollars. A shiver went up
Galway's spine as he remembered what that attitude had once
cost him. "It would be easy enough to settle the question,"
he told Quinn. "Call your agent in and ask for identification
of my photos."

"No," Quinn said flatly. "Bringing agents in can jeopar-
dize their anonymity, and someone in that good a position is
too valuable to risk. Ditto for calling or sending the photos
over by messenger. I don't want any of my men even to go
near the Shandygaff."

"That's absurd," Galway snapped, fed up in spite of
himself. "Don't you send men in even occasionally to check
out the bar?"

Quinn turned an icy glare onto the prefect. "No, we don't,"
he said. "The Shandygaff polices itself, and we keep our
hands strictly off."

"So that the criminal bosses can meet and make their deals
in comfort?" Galway snorted.

"And can settle their business with words instead of open
warfare on the streets. I warned you once that you don't
understand how things are done in Denver, Galway. Now I
suggest you quit trying to meddle and content yourself with
providing information on Caine—when you're asked for it."

Galway clamped his teeth tightly over the retort that wanted
to come out. "As you wish," he said stiffly. Turning, he
stalked out of Quinn's office. *It's out of my hands,* he told
himself as he headed down the hall to his own cubicle.
Whatever happens is on Quinn's head alone.

Except that there was no guarantee the Ryqril would see it
that way.

And then Plinry would suffer.

Damn it all. No, he couldn't leave Quinn to sink or swim

on his own . . . but fortunately he didn't have to. Security men were barred from the Shandygaff, fine—but Galway wasn't technically a Security man in this jurisdiction. And a private citizen could go anywhere he damn well pleased.

For a moment he gazed out his window to the city beyond. Legal technicalities or not, he'd still be smart to wait until Quinn had left for the day before making his sortie. The general usually didn't close up shop before seven, sometimes as late as eight-thirty. Still, that was all right—the Shandygaff was open until three.

His phone buzzed. "Galway here," he answered it."

"Jastrow, sir—research," the man at the other end identified himself. "We've got something on your request of last night, Prefect. It turns out there *is* someone living in the area you demarcated for us: Ivas Trendor, who used to be Security prefect for North America before they moved the central office from here down to Dallas. He's got a self-sufficient seven-room cabin up there and about thirty hectares of land behind an old barbed wire fence. Apparently lives pretty much like a hermit."

"Is he still active in Security matters?"

"I don't think so, sir. I've never heard of him coming in for any reason."

Galway chewed his lip. "How long was he involved with Security?"

"Oh, since the end of the war at least. He was made prefect in—uh—2440, nine years after the Ryqril came. Retired six years ago, in 2455."

A retired Security prefect, who presumably knew a lot about the war and the immediate aftermath. Postern had said that Caine was trying to locate veterans' organizations. Coincidence? "Does this Trendor have any guards at his place?" he asked slowly.

"Ah—I really don't know, sir. I can check and get back to you."

"Do that. I'll be here until early evening at least."

He broke the connection with a muttered curse. So Caine's trip yesterday could very well have had nothing at all to do with Aegis Mountain. Nothing directly, at least. Former Prefect Trendor might still be a minor stop on the way to that final goal; at the moment the whole thing was still too murky to trace that far into it.

As murky as if Lathe was directing it personally.

Galway took a deep breath. *Patience*, he told himself.

Tonight he'd settle that point once and for all. Until then, it might be a good idea to search the files for everything that was known about the local blackcollars. If Quinn foolishly insisted on underestimating them, that was no reason Galway had to, too.

Chapter 14

Geoff Dupre pulled out of his driveway a few minutes before nine, headlights cutting twin cones through the light mist that had sprung up in the past hour. Caine let him get a block away, then nodded to Braune. "Let's go."

"Right," the other said. Pulling smoothly away from the curb, he gave a leisurely chase.

Dupre was easy to follow. Braune stayed one to two blocks behind him as they headed northwest, drifting farther back as the traffic thinned and the buildings of Denver were replaced by trees and hills. Caine kept a close watch for signs that Security had identified their car, but as far as he could tell that danger hadn't yet materialized. If so, splitting the team might turn out to have been a bad decision, especially if he and Braune ran into more opposition than he expected. But getting all five of them caught in the same car would be a disaster; and Security still might tumble to them before the night was up. Better that three of the team were out of the opposition's immediate reach on this one.

The small office-type building Dupre eventually parked his car beside was situated between two large hills that hid it from Denver proper. Cutting across one end of the parking lot was a half-buried pipeline that disappeared into the foliage upslope; surrounding the whole area was a tall fence with sensor clusters mounted at each corner and over the single gate. Inside the fence, flanking the gate and drive, was a one-man guard shelter.

"Now what?" Braune asked as they drove toward the gate.

"It's too late to stop—we'd look suspicious."

"Agreed." Caine pursed his lips, eyes taking in the details as he thought. With civilian clothing over their flexarmor they should be able to approach the gate attendant without panicking anyone. Breaking in was out of the question—the sensors were surely good enough to spot that and relay an alarm to the nearest Security post. But something more subtle might get by the defenses. "I wish we'd brought Alamzad," he commented. "He might be able to give us a better reading on those sensors. Well, let's go ahead and try the old bureaucratic confusion approach. You have your Special Services ID?"

"Sure."

"Okay. Play off my cues."

They rolled to a stop in front of the gate. Caine stepped out of the car and walked briskly over to the guard shelter. The guard himself, a middle-aged man in a loose uniform, had emerged by the time Caine reached him. "Yes?" he asked, squinting a bit against the car's headlights.

"Inspector Craig Nielson, Special Services," Caine said, holding his ID against the fence for the other's scrutiny. It was an impressive card, with two seals and three signatures and some of the best etched-gold trim the Plinry blackcollars had ever turned out. The fact that it had nothing to do with any actual government agency was almost irrelevant—it *looked* official, and for many people that would be enough. Caine held his breath, hoping the guard was one of those.

Almost, but not quite. "Yes, *sir*," he said, his tone abruptly respectful. "I'm afraid I'll have to run your prints and retina pattern through the Athena link, though, before you can come in."

"Of course, of course," Caine said, mindful of the sensors overhead. They might not be continuously monitored, or even contain audio pickups at all, but he couldn't take the chance. "Just hurry it up."

"Yes, sir. If you'll slide that ID through here, this will only take a minute."

Caine passed the card through the indicated gap in the fence and the guard stepped into his shelter. Half seen through the doorway, he busied himself with a compact terminal, and Caine forced his muscles to relax. If Hawking had gimmicked the card properly . . .

He had. "Uh, sir?" the guard said, frowning as he stepped back to the fence. "I can't seem to get the prints to read."

"Damn," Caine muttered with proper irritation. "I've told them and *told* them the alignment's off—half the readers on the continent won't pick the pattern up. Do you have another machine?''

"No, sir, but I've got a direct scanner right here. We can just bypass the ID entirely.''

"Sure, sure, just get on with it," Caine said, waving a hand impatiently. The guard leaned into his shelter and the gate slid open half a meter. Caine stepped through and joined the guard, eyes flicking once to the other's belt holster. A paral-dart gun, by its size, and it presented a safer alternative to the nerve punch Caine had planned.

"Right here, sir," the guard said, gesturing into the shelter. Caine brushed past him, and as the guard leaned in behind him, he turned back and jabbed two fingers into the older man's solar plexus.

The guard's mouth popped open, a strangled *unh* the only sound to escape. Caine's right hand shifted to a steadying grip on the other's arm, his left deftly sliding the pistol from its holster and pressing its muzzle against the guard's thigh. A quiet burp, a reflexive jerk of the leg, and a second later the man went limp. Caine was ready; palming the gun and shifting to a two-handed grip, he swung the guard smoothly around and into a chair that took up most of the shelter's rear. Hitting the switch that opened the gate, he dropped the pistol into his pocket and then took a couple of seconds to make sure the guard was well enough braced and balanced to remain upright. Braune had the car through by the time he'd finished; closing the gate again, Caine got back in the vehicle for the hundred-meter drive to the building.

They parked just off the main door and headed inside. From the relative emptiness of the parking lot, Caine guessed that the graveyard shift was run by a fractional staff. If they were careful, they might pull this off without running into anyone who would ask awkward questions.

The entry foyer was lit but deserted, as was the hallway beyond its double doors. Caine and Braune padded quietly past a row of closed office doors, turned a corner—

And came face to face with Geoff Dupre.

The big man stopped with a jerk, the steaming cup in his hand sloshing dangerously. "You!" he half whispered.

"No noise," Caine warned, letting the other see the *shuriken* in his hand. "We aren't going to hurt anyone unless you make that necessary. Understand?"

Dupre licked his lips. "What do you want?"

"Take us to your office first. No sense in standing around out here."

In silence Dupre led them down the hall to a cluttered room near the building's center. An open interior door showed several men working at a line of consoles beneath a computerized wall map alive with spidery lines. Braune caught Caine's eye and nodded fractionally toward the room before closing the door and positioning himself beside it. Caine closed the hallway door and gestured Dupre to his desk chair. The big man hesitated, then sat down. "Well?" he asked, almost belligerently.

Caine regarded him coolly. "You have a real talent for getting your courage up at the wrong times," he told the other. "Where do you store the explosives in this building?"

Dupre's mouth twitched. "Explosives?"

"Things that go bang," Braune supplied. "You use them in digging new aqueducts for the water system, remember?"

Dupre flicked a glance in Braune's direction, then looked back at Caine. "There aren't any real explosives here. All that stuff is kept in the operations warehouse."

"What *have* you got here?"

"Nothing really except some primer caps that we sometimes send down the pipes to clear out blockages. They're not very powerful."

"They'll do for a start," Caine said. "Where are they?"

"What're you going to do with them?" Dupre asked.

"Clear out some blockages of our own. Where are they?"

For a moment Dupre seemed ready to argue the point further. Then his eyes dropped to the star in Caine's hand and he sighed. "They're in the basement storeroom."

"Good. Braune, go with him and get a box or two."

They left. Caine waited until the sounds of their footsteps had faded down the hall, then stepped to the inner door and cracked it open. Four men, backs to him, were working at the consoles. Pulling the paral-dart pistol from his pocket, Caine eased into the room, eyes darting around for anyone he might have missed seeing. Then he lined up the gun on the farthest man and squeezed the trigger.

Five seconds later all four were sprawled in their seats, fully conscious but unable to move. Stepping to the consoles, Caine gave them a quick scan and settled down to work. By the time Braune and Dupre came looking for him he had found a complete map of the water retrieval system and was halfway through printing a copy. "Any trouble?" he asked

Braune, eying the long, flat box cradled under the other's arm.

Braune shook his head. "But we'd better get moving," he said, glancing at the sprawled figures. "There are at least another five to ten people wandering around the building."

"Right. Almost ready." Caine looked at Dupre, who was staring at his paralyzed colleagues with a mixture of horror and fascination. "Dupre, I'm afraid you're going to have to join them," he told the man, drawing the paral-dart gun from his pocket once more. "Lie down and get comfortable."

Dupre's jaw tightened visibly, but he obeyed without argument. Caine sent a cluster of paral-dart needles into the man's shoulder and then, after a moment's hesitation, returned the gun to his pocket. The gun's unfired shots would tell them later which of the plethora of paralyzing drugs was being used locally, a bit of knowledge that would be crucial if they ever needed to counteract its effects themselves. Virtually all antidotes to paralyte drugs were highly toxic unless the corresponding drug was already in the bloodstream.

A minute later the last of Caine's requested maps was finished, and he and Braune began their withdrawal. Luck was with them; they saw no one as they made their way down the corridors, out to their car, and across the lot to the fence. The guard's eyes held impotent rage as Caine opened the gate and rejoined Braune. Leaving the gate open, they drove off into the night.

The same woman as on the previous night was sitting in the coatcheck window when Lathe and Skyler came into the Shandygaff bar, her makeup still far too heavy for Lathe's taste. "Good evening," he nodded to her, gesturing toward the main room. "Mr. Charm in tonight?"

"Who?" she frowned.

"The short lad with the itchy palms and the mobile guardhouses," Skyler amplified.

"Oh—Mr. Nash. The guardhouses' names are Briller and Chong, if you're interested." She cocked her head. "What did you do to Chong last night, by the way?"

"Who, us?" Lathe asked innocently.

She studied him for a moment, then shrugged slightly. "It doesn't matter, I guess. All three are here tonight, if you really care, wandering around inside somewhere. And, uh, Mr. Kanai is also here. Shall I have a waiter take you to him?"

"We'll find him," Lathe assured her. On his wrist, his tingler came to life as Skyler covertly tapped out a message: *Kanai: Lathe and Skyler are here.*

Kanai; Bernhard's with me. Come back; booth four, seventy-five degrees from entrypoint.

"Talk to you later," Lathe said to the girl. Skyler was already through the door; lengthening his stride, the comsquare caught up. Angling to the right, they headed through the tables until they spotted Kanai.

"Good evening," Kanai said as they slid into the booth. "May I present Commando Jorgen Bernhard. Comsquare Damon Lathe; Commando Rafe Skyler."

Bernhard nodded in turn, his eyes cool. "From . . . ?"

"Most recently, Plinry," Lathe told him.

The other's eyebrows rose at that, but if he was overly impressed he hid it well. "I see. A long way from home, then. All the more reason why you need our help."

" 'Need' may be too strong a word," Lathe said. "But we certainly could use it."

"You're pretty confident for a couple of strangers who don't even know how this city operates," Bernhard returned. "You need our help, all right. The only real question is whether or not you're worth risking our position over."

"Kanai said the same thing," Lathe said. "If you're trying to inflate your fee, consider the point made."

A tight smile flicked across Bernhard's face. "If you're expecting me to take offense, you're wasting your time. I've been insulted by people far more skilled at it than you." He folded his hands into a double fist on the table in front of him, his dragonhead ring glinting as he did so. "Let's get down to business. You want a list of high-ranking military people who were here during the war, correct?"

Lathe nodded. "More specifically, I'm interested in those people who were with the Aegis Mountain contingent."

Bernhard's face didn't change, but for just a second his clenched hands seemed to tighten. "Why Aegis?" he asked carefully.

"Why not? It was the major installation in this part of the continent, so it's reasonable to assume the top of the cut would have been assigned there."

Bernhard snorted. "Don't. We had as many dimbos at all levels as any other base I've seen."

"Ah—so *you* were in Aegis, too," Lathe said. "Good. You'll know who the best people were, then."

Bernhard's face hardened. "Sure. They're the ones who stayed behind to run the krijing machines when the gas attack began and the rest of us ran like geldings."

"Gas attack?" Skyler frowned. "Aegis was supposed to be proof against that sort of thing."

"It was," Bernhard said quietly, eyes focused somewhere else. "We think a neutron warhead must have cracked a fault line and taken out the gas sensor and filtration system in one of the ventilation tunnels. By the time the interior environment sensors let us know the gas was coming in, it was too late."

"Someone should have noticed the ventilation sensors weren't registering—" Skyler began.

"I know that!" Bernhard snapped. "We were busy fighting an invasion at the time."

He stopped abruptly, and for a moment the only sound in the booth was the muffled background hum from the rest of the room. "Sorry," he muttered at last. "It still hurts, sometimes."

Lathe nodded. "We've all got memories like that. So . . . you ran interference for the evacuation?"

"Such as it was." Bernhard shook his head. "I don't know what the idiot in charge thought he was doing—if the gas was seeping into the base, he should've realized the air outside would be rancid with the stuff. Even with the masks enough got into most people's skin to affect them. I don't think more than fifty out of the eight hundred we got out lived more than six months afterward."

Skyler grunted. "Sounds like Denver itself was damn lucky."

"It was a pretty heavy gas," Kanai said. "Stayed in the valleys around Aegis for the most part. But you're right—the Ryqril could easily have destroyed the city if they'd wanted to."

Lathe shifted his eyes to the oriental. "Were you in the base, too?"

Kanai shook his head. "I was on bodyguard duty in Athena. They were using us a lot for guard and civilian-control work at the end."

"Really?" Skyler asked, cocking an eyebrow. "Seems a waste of talent."

"What else were they going to do with us?" Bernhard returned sourly. "The war was lost, pure and simple. Why save us for guerrilla activity that would never take place when they had the immediate problem of crowd control?" He snorted and swore under his breath.

Lathe felt his own jaw tighten in sympathetic response. The Plinry blackcollars had taken their own share of contempt after the war from a populace who understood neither their abilities nor their limitations. But the military people of Aegis and Denver ought to have had more sense. "I know how you feel," he said to Bernhard. "You just have to keep remembering that it's that selfsame underestimation that's let us survive this long in enemy territory."

Bernhard regarded him coolly. "Maybe that's how *you* survived, Comsquare, but we got tired of being mistaken for sheep long ago. Everyone in Denver knows what blackcollars are and what we can do."

"Including the government?" Skyler asked.

"Of course."

"And they let you alone?"

Bernhard's eyes dropped briefly to the table. "We have what you might call an unwritten nonaggression pact with them," he said. "We don't hit government targets, and they don't bother us."

Lathe stroked his dragonhead ring. "That includes Ryqril targets, too, I suppose?"

"Yes, though given that the base outside Aegis and the town a couple of klicks farther on are the only sizable ones in the area, that's hardly a major consideration."

"Interesting. I presume you remember the oath you took when you were given that ring?"

Bernhard looked back up, his eyes blazing into Lathe's. "The war is *over*, Lathe. Over and done with, and we *lost*. What comes now is survival, by any means available. I don't need your permission or your approval, and I damn well don't want your quixotic preachments. My force can't do anything against the Ryqril, and I'm not going to throw their lives away to satisfy some outdated notion of honor. Understood?"

"Understood," Lathe said evenly. "So are you going to take my job or not?"

Bernhard inhaled deeply, the anger fading from his face as he did so. "You'll get your list of names, sure. And then you'll get out of Denver."

Lathe raised his eyebrows. "Or else?"

"Consider it our fee. And I mean it."

"I'm sure you do. Understand in turn that we're not leaving until our mission's completed."

"That mission being something that'll get Security all stirred up, I suppose?" Bernhard said sourly.

Lathe smiled. "Join us and find out."

Kanai stirred in his seat, and Bernhard sent a glance in his direction. "I'll have the list for you tomorrow night," he told Lathe. "Be here at eight."

"How about a different meeting place?" Skyler suggested. "This one's getting a bit stale."

"You're too easily jaded." Bernhard snorted. "Aesthetics apart, the Shandygaff's the safest rendezvous around. Anywhere else in the city we'd be in someone's territory, and there could be trouble. I'm sure you'd like to avoid that."

"Doesn't bother *us*—we're leaving this town soon, remember?" Skyler said. "But if you're worried about it, why don't we go somewhere in Sartan's territory?"

For a split second the corners of Bernhard's mouth tightened. "What do you know about Sartan?" he asked carefully.

"Only that you've done a lot of work for him." Skyler shrugged. "I assumed you'd have free rein in his part of town."

"Um. Well, as it happens, Sartan hasn't got any real territory of his own. Yet. You have any real objections against the Shandygaff?"

Kanai cleared his throat. "I believe a possible objection has just arrived."

Lathe knew better than to turn and look; but Skyler would have a view of the anteroom area. "Skyler?"

"One of the mobile guardhouses," the other reported. "Probably Chong—the way he's favoring his right arm suggests he's the one Mordecai took out last night. The other one, Briller, seems to be hovering back in the anteroom."

"Both will be armed," Kanai said. "You wearing flex-armor?"

Lathe nodded. "So much for neutral territory."

"I saw Chong when he limped back in last night," Kanai said. "One of the rules here is that you don't pick on the bar's enforcers." He slid his legs out from under the table and stood up. "Let me see if I can placate them—the last thing you want is to draw attention to yourselves with a fight."

"Remind him we can get rougher than last night if we have to," Lathe told him.

Kanai nodded and headed across the room. Lathe watched him stop in front of Chong, took a quick reading of the bigger

man's body language, and reached two fingers under his right
sleeve. *Mordecai: Report.*

*Man loitering near entrance; suggest lookout. No evidence
of massive Security presence.*

So charming Mr. Nash had decided to handle this without
official involvement. That was one plus, anyway. "How
many men besides Briller and Chong does Nash have?" he
asked Bernhard.

"Half a dozen regulars, more on short call," the other
said, eyes starting to darken.

"You look perturbed," Skyler said.

Bernhard's gaze stayed on Chong and Kanai. "You assume
Nash is after you. He could just as easily be after *me*."

Lathe thought about that for a moment. Unlikely, but not
impossible. "You have any backup men outside?"

"Unfortunately, no," Bernhard said grimly. "I didn't expect it to be necessary. You have anybody besides the one?"

"No, but don't let that worry you." *Mordecai: Possible
encirclement in progress. Scan for outside troops.*

Troops identified, was the prompt response. *Four, including doorway lookout. Inadequate visual support.*

In other words, Nash's men weren't in solid visual contact
with each other, which meant they could be taken out quietly
one by one. "Amateurs," Skyler said and snorted.

"That's fine with me," Lathe said. *Mordecai: Clear gauntlet quietly. Minimal force.*

Acknowledged.

"It's been a long time since I've heard the old tingler
codes," Bernhard mused. "Brings back memories. . . . You
think he'll be able to do the job alone?"

"If they don't spot him, easily. If they do, we'll just have
to start punching from this side without him. Chong's wearing an earphone—if he twitches, we move."

"But no killing," Bernhard warned. "You kill someone
here and the whole city'll be after you."

"If we weren't worried about killing," Lathe said pa-
tiently, "we'd have been out of here three minutes ago."

"Just wanted to remind you." Bernhard grunted. "Looks
like Kanai's not getting through."

Lathe focused on the distant conversation. Chong hadn't
budged, but his expression now resembled a thundercloud and
his right hand had taken up residence in a side pocket.
"Negotiations do seem to be breaking down," he agreed.
"No back door, I suppose?"

"If there were, I'd have suggested it three minutes ago," Bernhard retorted. "There's nothing we can use. No windows, either."

"Your basic firetrap," Skyler said. "Can we assume that there are a lot of important people in here tonight? People Nash and company would hesitate to damage?"

"Chong'll roast over a slow fire if he shoots anyone but us," Bernhard said flatly. "But he's a damn good shot, and this table is fastened pretty solidly to the floor. We'll never even get our legs out from under it before he gets one or more of us."

"Only if he can see what he's shooting at. Lathe?"

"Probably our best approach," Lathe agreed. "Main switches are to the right of the door; emergency lights high on the wall behind you, Bernhard, and near the back of the room on my side."

"There's one over the main switches, too," Skyler pointed out.

"That one goes last—it'll be shining right into Chong's eyes when it comes on." Lathe tapped at his trigger: *Mordecai: Stand by for fast break. Kanai: three-count, then distract Chong to right.* Sliding two *shuriken* into his hands, Lathe set his feet . . . and as Kanai's left hand twitched toward the anteroom he moved.

His first star spun across the room to bury itself in the wall just above the light switches. There was a sputtering flash of shorted circuits, and the room's soft glow was abruptly replaced by the harsh floodlights of the emergency system. Shouts of surprise and anger, Chong's bellow louder than any of them—and Lathe was out of the booth, diving flat to open up Skyler's line of fire, then rolling up on one knee to send his second *shuriken* over the booths toward the emergency light box in the rear. Peripherally, he caught a glimpse of Bernhard swinging out his side of the booth; a second later the light back that way winked out in a tinkle of glass. Even as he spun around to the door the last of the backups yielded to Skyler's *shuriken* and the room was plunged into darkness.

Almost. From the anteroom a pool of light was spilling through the doorway, silhouetting Chong neatly against the opening. Possibly the big man's mind was still trying to catch up; if so, it never had sufficient time to do so. Skyler's knife flickered just once as it bounced hilt-first off Chong's forehead, dropping the man where he stood. One down, one—or more—to go. Lathe sprinted forward, skirting the pool of light and flattening himself by the doorway.

He needn't have bothered. Briller, folded up fetal-style on the floor, had already lost all interest in the proceedings. Across the room Kanai, *shuriken* at the ready, was easing the outer door open for a quick look. Sidling around the doorframe into the anteroom, Lathe looked for the coatcheck girl.

If she was, indeed, the Shandygaff's backup gun, she wasn't doing her job. She stood upright at her window, empty hands folded almost primly on the sill; her expression behind all the makeup showed simple interest, with no anger or fear accompanying it. She looked at Lathe as he entered, nodded toward Chong. "Is he dead?" she asked.

"Not if I know Skyler," he replied, squatting to retrieve his teammate's knife. "He avoids killing even more than the rest of us. Ryqril excepted, of course."

"They'll get you before you take five steps outside, you know."

"I doubt it." Bernhard and Skyler slipped into the anteroom; Lathe tossed the latter his knife and reached for his tingler. *Mordecai: Report.*

Lookout approaching door. Others neutralized.

Lathe cocked an eyebrow at Skyler, who nodded and stepped to the door. He exchanged low words with Kanai—and abruptly flung the door wide, hurled his knife, and slammed the panel shut. A single splintering impact shook the thick wood, followed by silence. Skyler eased the door open a crack just as Mordecai's message came: *All clear.*

"I suggest you two fade while you can," Lathe told Bernhard as he stepped to Skyler's side. "But first give me a way to contact you tomorrow."

"Just call in a message for me here," Kanai spoke up. "We can discuss a rendezvous point then."

Halfway out the door, Lathe looked back at him. "Call you *here*?"

Kanai met his gaze evenly. "I'm the contact man. It's my job to be here."

"What about Nash?"

"I can handle him. Just go."

Lathe flicked a glance over Kanai's shoulder at the coatcheck girl, then nodded. "Tomorrow night," he said, and ducked out the door.

Skyler was waiting for him a short way down the sidewalk. "Let's get moving," he urged as Lathe joined him. "The other customers might eventually take exception to being left in the dark.''

They set off quickly across the mall toward the sidestreet where they'd parked their car. "A fairly profitable evening, as these things go," Skyler remarked as they walked. "If nothing else, we at least found out that Bernhard's team can still fight."

"We learned a lot more than that," Lathe said. "We know the Ryqril have a center *outside* Aegis Mountain—which suggests that they at least, are still locked out."

"Hmm. So the gas-attack survivors locked the place down before they died. Maybe that's why the commander sent so many of his people out—didn't want anyone around who might consider opening up in exchange for an antidote."

"That's my guess," Lathe said, glancing behind them. No tails tonight, apparently. Hardly surprising. "Could be one of the reasons Bernhard resents having been sent out with the cattle drive, too. Probably feels it was a slight on his integrity. That, or else his current life-style has rubbed blisters on his conscience."

"Kanai certainly has blisters on his," Skyler agreed. "Given that, you think Bernhard will come through with a useful list?"

"I don't know, but it doesn't matter anymore. We've already found our native guide."

There was a pause. "You're not serious," Skyler said at last.

"Why not? A blackcollar would certainly have made sure he knew all the ways in and out of a base he was assigned to."

"You'll forgive me if I doubt Bernhard's enthusiasm for such a project."

Lathe sighed. "He'll help us. Willingly or otherwise, he'll get us in. It's all a matter of finding the lever that'll move him."

"And of surviving his reaction to its use."

"There's that, of course," Lathe said. "There's always that."

The chaos lasted at a low level for quite a while after the brief battle, and the lights remained off even longer. Eventually the Shandygaff's employees finished getting their portable lanterns set up and a seething Mr. Nash got them working on the damaged wiring. The exodus of the angrier customers slowed to a trickle and stopped, leaving a remnant of the hardier and less impatient behind.

Seated alone at his small table, Galway sipped his drink and contemplated the tightening of his stomach muscles. Lathe and Skyler. On Earth, in Denver . . . and with the local blackcollars already signed on as allies. The files had said Bernhard's team always left government targets strictly alone— but Galway had seen for himself just how fast "harmless" blackcollars could turn.

Plinry's history was about to repeat itself in Denver. Galway could only hope Quinn still had time to start taking all of this seriously.

Chapter 15

From the government section of New Geneva to the Hub in Plinry's Capstone, Caine had seen a fair number of fortress cities, but even so Athena was unique. Nestled against the ridges of the Hogback to the west, with Green Mountain rising above it to the north, it didn't *look* like a fortress city, for one thing. Its simple mesh fence and spotlighted outer perimeter were almost throwbacks to an earlier age before sophisticated sensors and automated defenses. True, the fence was topped by a sensor ring, but the weaponry to back the sensors up was conspicuous by its absence. So much so, Caine thought at one point, that a sufficiently naive attacker might actually think the place an easy target.

Until and unless he noticed the dark buildings squatting on top of Green Mountain. . . .

"Ready," Alamzad murmured, breaking into his train of thought.

Caine brought his attention back. The three makeshift catapults were indeed ready, their elastic stretched taut against the braces dug into the building roof on which the four men were standing. "Looks good," he said. "You think they'll have time to explode before the lasers up there get them?"

Alamzad shrugged. "We'll see soon enough. But I think

we wrapped enough ablator around the primers to give them a chance.''

Caine nodded. It almost didn't matter—laser fire above Athena would attract almost as much attention as laser fire plus explosions. But the extra sound effects would be a nice added touch. "Okay—load 'em up," he said, reaching to his tingler. *Braune: Any attention from unfriendlies?*

Negative, came the reply, and Caine let a smile twitch across his lips. They'd returned from the water retrieval station to find Pittman and Colvin with a trophy of their own: a set of license plates and registration transponder borrowed for the night from a vehicle parked a few blocks from their hideout. Transplanted onto their own car, the camouflage should throw Security off the scent, at least for the rest of the night.

"All set," Alamzad reported, his face briefly illuminated by a flicker of flame. "Delay cords lit—we've got five minutes to grab some distance."

The cords burned through exactly six and a half minutes later, and from five blocks away they watched as the tiny payloads arced through the air and were met in flight by bright lines of laser fire from the top of the mountain. Three miniature bombs per sling—nine total in the salvo—and at least four of them managed to make little *cracks* before dissipating into clouds of component atoms.

"That's it," Caine said as the brief light show ended. "Let's get home before they send out spotters looking for someone to blame."

"You think they're even going to notice?" Colvin asked.

"I would if I were in charge," Caine told him. "And anyway, we don't really care if Security pays any attention to us at this point."

"As long as Torch does," Pittman murmured.

"Right. If it doesn't work, we'll just have to try something more noticeable."

The lasers had lit up the night sky while Galway was returning from the Shandygaff, and he'd half expected to find death, chaos, and a ruined entrance gate on his arrival. But that fear, at least, was quickly laid to rest; except for the beefed-up guard contingent at the gate everything looked the same as when he'd left that evening. But he'd been a Security prefect too long to expect that surface calm to extend to the situation room, too; and in that he turned out to be right.

What he wouldn't have predicted was that Quinn would also be there.

"We found three of these on the roof, right where the ballistic backtrack put them," someone was reporting via the communications board as Galway entered. The screen showed a catapultlike contraption being carefully examined by two more Security men.

"Any evidence of remote control or delay fuses?" Quinn asked.

"Some ash that may have been from time-delay rope," the man said. "We won't know for sure until it's been analyzed."

Quinn glanced up at Galway, returned his attention to the screen. "Make damn sure they aren't booby-trapped and then bring them in."

"Yes, sir."

Quinn turned to a man hovering at his shoulder. "Anything further on the water-station break-in?" he asked.

"They were definitely Caine and Braune," the man said, handing the general a piece of paper. "Positive identification from everyone who saw them. They made off with a box of fifty AK-29 primer caps, rated strength point zero two each. Not much more than small firecrackers."

"I think we can assume they have more than holiday noisemaking in mind for them," Quinn said icily. "Feed that report down to analysis and have them find out whether or not that's the strength of the bombs that were launched over Athena half an hour ago."

The man gulped. "Yes, sir," he said, and hurried away.

"Idiot," Quinn muttered, turning to face Galway for the first time. "Noise wake you up?"

Galway shook his head. "I was still up, out at the Shandy-gaff Bar."

"I told you that place was off-limits."

"They're here, General. Lathe and Skyler at least—and judging by the carnage outside, I'd say at least two more came with them."

Quinn hissed between his teeth. "I ought to have your skin on a rack for going there against orders. No chance you're wrong, I suppose."

"Hardly. And there's more. Two of your local blackcollars helped them punch their way out."

Quinn's eyes narrowed. "The blackcollars *helped* them? Didn't just fail to stop them, I mean?"

"Helped and a half. One of them was Kanai—the one your

files say is contact man for the group—and he not only provided diversion but also cleaned out the bar's backup man.''

"They'll roast him alive.'' Quinn shook his head. "He goes there every week—Nash'll have his head for something like that.''

I warned you about underestimating your blackcollars. The words bounced around Galway's brain, but he left them unsaid. Having to admit his error would be humiliating enough for a man like Quinn without being reminded that Galway had been right all along. "Should I get those pictures of Lathe and the others copied for general distribution now?'' he asked instead.

Quinn focused on him. "What could Lathe have offered them that they'd risk shaking up the Shandygaff for?'' he asked.

Galway frowned. "What do you mean? There's no need for deals. Lathe has the authority to bring the group back to full combat status—''

"Nonsense. I *know* these people, Galway—and they are *not* going to start fighting a thirty-year-old war again. No, Lathe's made a deal with them, and the only question is what the payoff is.''

Galway took a deep breath. "General, I don't mean to question your knowledge of the city and its people, but isn't it possible that Kanai and his people have been lying low waiting for just this sort of opportunity?''

"Opportunity for what? You haven't yet even come up with a plausible mission for Caine, let alone one he'd need Lathe along for.''

"I've filed reports—''

"I said *plausible* missions.'' Quinn snorted. "Getting into Aegis Mountain hardly qualifies as such.''

With an effort Galway held his temper. "All right, then; what do *you* propose be done at this point?''

"We're going to find Caine.'' Quinn's tone was grim. "This Postern scheme of yours has obviously failed—whether because he's defected or because they're on to him.''

"He wouldn't defect—''

"Spare me your unfounded opinions. Postern has failed— and as of tonight Caine's moved up out of the simple nuisance category. Whatever he's got planned, he's started work on it in earnest, and I'm tired of sitting around waiting for phone calls. As of right now I'm shifting the hunt for him onto full priority status. We're going to get that car he took out of the mountains, and we're going to check out all reports of stolen vehicles in case he's decided to switch cars. And when we find him, we're going to bring him in."

"You do and Prefect Donner will have your scalp," Galway snapped, his control breaking at last. "That's if the Ryqril don't get to you first."

"You let *me* deal with Donner and the Ryqril," Quinn returned. "However you sold them this swampland deed, I'm going to get it overturned."

Galway bit down on the inside of his cheek, fighting his frustration down to a manageable level. Quinn could afford the luxury of a personality feud; he, Galway, couldn't. Plinry's survival was hanging from the wire here. "Would you at least agree to discuss this with Prefect Donner before you take any burned-bridge action against Caine?" he asked.

Quinn seemed to measure him with his eyes. "No promises," he said at last. "We'll see how much work it is to find him first."

"Do you want Lathe's picture circulated in the meantime?"

"I'd like to stick with one group at a time, if you don't mind. Besides, we can find Lathe anytime we need to—he's teamed up with Kanai, remember?" Quinn glanced at his watch. "Tomorrow's likely to be a busy day. I suggest you go get some sleep."

It was clearly a dismissal. "Yes, sir. I'll talk with you in the morning, then."

Turning, Galway stalked out the door. He'd had as much of Quinn as he could stand for the moment, anyway . . . and whether the general knew it or not, he was right.

Tomorrow *was* going to be a busy day.

Chapter 16

The alarm's twitter snapped Kanai out of a troubled sleep, and almost before he was fully awake he had rolled out of bed, *shuriken* pouch in hand. The window was intact, the door to the rest of the house still closed. Taking a deep breath, he eased over to the window and cracked the shade away from the wall.

It was perhaps half an hour before dawn, judging by the faint glow starting to compete with the haze of city lights to the east. Traffic was practically nonexistent at this hour; parked cars lined both sides of the street, none showing any lights. Touching a hidden wall switch, Kanai shifted a section of the glass to infrared sensitivity. Nothing—all the cars within view had apparently been parked there for several hours. But the alarm had been triggered from that side of the house. . . . He was just about to step to his monitor for a complete area scan when a lone figure came into view, striding purposefully along the walk toward his front door.

Lathe, was his first instinctive guess; but another second's observation eliminated that possibility. The man's walk showed none of a blackcollar's feline grace; his obvious glances to left and right were a far cry from the more subtle awareness of his surroundings that was the blackcollar norm.

Which meant it wasn't one of Kanai's teammates, either. And at this hour of the morning, it sure as hell wasn't a casual visitor.

He stepped to his room monitor, keyed for a center-walk view with light amplification. It would be another couple of seconds before the man would be close enough for a good look; reaching to his bedside, Kanai scooped up his robe and the *nunchaku* hidden under the pillow. Eyes on the monitor, he got the robe on . . . and swore under his breath.

The man walking up to his door was General Quinn.

The doorbell rang twice in close succession; impatience personified mechanically. Jamming his *nunchaku* into the robe sash, Kanai reset his alarms and headed for the door.

"General," he said coolly as he unlocked the reinforced panel and swung it open. "You're up rather early."

Quinn didn't bother with even the forms of politeness. "Kanai," he growled, brushing past the blackcollar and into the living room. "You putting them up here?" he added, glancing around him.

"Putting who up?"

"Don't play innocent," Quinn snarled, turning back to face him. "You know who—Comsquare Damon Lathe and his pack of troublemakers, that's who."

Kanai felt his stomach tighten, consciously relaxed it. "They're not here. Sorry to disappoint you."

Quinn grunted. "What do they want here?"

"What business is it of yours what our clients want?" Kanai countered.

"Don't insult my intelligence, Kanai. These aren't ordinary money-slicers renting you to cut other money-slicers' throats—these are guerrilla soldiers who want to rekindle the war. If I were you, I'd be thinking about what something like that would do to my cozy arrangement here in Denver."

"Meaning?"

"Meaning that if you and Bernhard rock the boat too hard it's going to sink with you aboard it." Quinn smiled sardonically. "Do I detect a grain of surprise at Bernhard's name? Thought we didn't know who your leader was, did you? Believe me, Kanai, we know just about everything there is to know about your team—you can't run around the way you have for so many years without scattering a lot of lint along the way."

"Perhaps," Kanai said as calmly as he could. "You might find it expensive to try and get more than just information, though."

"Sure we would—why else do you think we've put up with you this long? But we *could* do it, if we had to."

Kanai nodded. "All right, consider the point made. If that's all you came for, you can go now."

Quinn ignored the offer. Pulling a photo from his pocket, he flipped it through the air toward Kanai. "Ever seen this man before?" he asked.

The blackcollar caught the photo, looked at it. "No. Should I have?"

"Name's Allen Caine. Has Lathe mentioned him to you?"

"Again, no. What's he done that has you so interested in him?"

"In other words, how much do we know? Forget it. But as long as we're on the subject of information, what exactly are you doing for Lathe and what's he paying for it?"

Kanai cocked an eyebrow. "As someone here just said, forget it. You've about worn out your welcome, Quinn."

Casually, the general looked around the room. "You've got a nice place, Kanai," he said. "A real nice place. A lot nicer than the interrogation cells in Athena; a damn sight nicer than a box underground." He brought his gaze back to Kanai. "Take some good advice and stay away from Lathe."

"Or else?" Kanai said softly.

"Or else," Quinn replied. "Consider it a threat or a warning, I don't care which. But believe it." With one last glance around the room, he walked past Kanai to the front door. A moment later he was gone . . . and the blackcollar spun and threw, his pent-up frustration burying his *shuriken* center-deep in the far living-room wall. The thud of its impact was a thunderclap in the silent house, its sound almost covering up the ancient Japanese curse he spat in the same direction.

"The cabin should be just over this next rise," the pilot told Galway, easing the small spotter craft between a pair of tall pines. "Sorry about the ground-scratching here, but I have to stay low because of the Ryqril base over to the south—their lasers recognize their own aircraft, but I've never gotten a really airtight guarantee that we get the same courtesy."

"Fine by me," Galway said, swallowing. "I'd just as soon show up unvaporized myself."

The pilot grinned and gave his full attention back to his flying. Galway kept his eyes on the landscape ahead and tried to relax, and a minute later they were there.

To find that the term "cabin" hardly did the place justice. "Mansion" was a far more appropriate term—a single story, rustic-walled millionaire's hideaway. The lump in Galway's throat grew another size, and it was all he could do to keep from ordering the pilot to lift and get him the hell back to Athena where he belonged. But the aircraft was already crunching down onto the forest mat, and at the cabin doorway he could see the owner watching him.

He stepped out almost before the craft was fully stabilized, walking over to the cabin with artificial confidence. "I'm Jamus Galway," he identified himself as he approached the man. "I called from Athena this morning. You *are* Prefect Ivas Trendor . . . ?"

"Former prefect," the older man said curtly. "Long since retired. Come in, Galway."

He led the way to a living room the size of Galway's entire Capstone apartment and gestured to a feather-plait couch. "This had better be as important as you claimed," he warned as he took a matching chair across a glow-pit from the couch. "I have even less interest in getting involved in Denver's Security programs than Quinn has in my doing so. I presume you didn't tell him you were coming?"

"No, sir, but as I mentioned this morning I'm essentially a free agent—"

"Which also thrills Quinn right down to the marrow, I expect."

"Ah—I think that's a fair statement, sir. But I felt I had to see you because I've come across information that indicates you may be in danger."

Trendor's eyebrows lifted with polite skepticism. "You'll forgive me if I tell you that's ridiculous," he said. "Why would anyone want to hurt me?"

Galway shrugged uncomfortably. "I can't say for sure, sir. But I looked up the record of your tenure as Security prefect, and—well, it occurred to me that it might have made you some enemies."

Trendor's expression didn't change. "I make no apologies for what I did, Galway," he said coldly. "Denver was at flashpoint—it could have gone up like a strat nuke practically overnight. I kept it together, and if it cost a few lives, so be it. Better to decapitate a few radical organizations than watch the whole thing go up in flames."

A slight shiver went up Galway's back. In principle he agreed . . . but the way Trendor said it made it sound decidedly cold-blooded. "Yes, sir," he said, allowing the older man to take that any way he wished. "The records certainly indicate you were successful in keeping the peace. But there may still be people who resent what you did back then."

"I suppose that's possible." Trendor shrugged. "Though I don't know why anyone would wait this long to do something about it."

"I don't know, either, sir . . . unless it's because the right people for the job have just arrived. I don't know if you've heard, but the reason I'm here on Earth is that an offworld blackcollar force has just arrived in Denver."

Trendor's eyes narrowed, and he seemed to sit up straighter in his seat. "I think you'd better start from the beginning," he said quietly.

Galway did so, describing Caine's team and its still-secret mission, the trip into the mountains and its proximity to Trendor's own home, and the unexpected arrival of Lathe on the scene. "And you think these blackcollars, out of touch with Earth for over thirty years, would want to seek me out for some sort of delayed retribution?" the former prefect asked when he'd finished.

"Unfortunately, they *haven't* been entirely out of touch," Galway shook his head. "General Lepkowski and their three Novas have made several trips to Earth in the past year, and it's conceivable they received intelligence during one of those flybys that caused them to latch on to you for God only knows what reason.''

Trendor stroked his chin thoughtfully. "You said Caine had asked specifically about old war veterans. You think that fireworks display over Athena last night was designed to attract their attention?''

"I don't see what else it could have been. Does his asking about the vets mean anything to you?''

"It might." Trendor stood up and wandered over to the picture window at the south end of the room. "Some of the groups I quashed had a high percentage of war vets in them. Could be he's trying to reactivate one of them with some new blood.''

Galway thought about that. With the last of the resistance groups, Torch, apparently gone the way of the others, Caine could indeed be trying to start his own. Certainly he would accomplish a lot more with that kind of support behind him. "Possible," he admitted. "But then I don't understand exactly how you fit in.''

Trendor smiled grimly. "I can think of at least two ways. Once, I knew a lot of the vets, both inside and outside the subversive groups. He may think that I could be persuaded to give him enough names to get started on his recruitment drive. Or else"—he snorted—"I'm to be another way to attract their attention.''

Assassination of a former Security prefect. Galway licked his lips. But it would certainly do the job. Nowhere in the records had he ever seen a case of political murder by blackcollars, but there was a first time for anything. "I think, sir," he said quietly, "that you should consider moving back to Athena, at least for the time being.''

"No," Trendor said flatly, his eyes still on the wooded hills outside his window. "I've earned my home and my peace out here, and I'm not giving it up for anyone—I don't care if there are a hundred blackcollars gunning for me. Let them come—I'll blow them all to hell and back.''

Galway grimaced, wondering fleetingly whether refusal to face reality was a requisite for Security positions in this city. "They're more likely to blow *you* away, sir—and you know it.''

"Are they now?" Trendor snorted contemptuously, turning back to face the other. "Well, let me tell you something, Galway. I killed a few blackcollars, too, when I was in charge of things around here. And I'm damned if I'm going to start running from them now.''

Galway took a deep breath. "In that case, sir, I respectfully suggest that you should at least request some additional security around here. Some perimeter guards, at the very least—perhaps a full sensor/defense network as well.''

Trendor didn't reply for several heartbeats, his eyes drifting back to the window. Then he sighed. "Because if I don't, I'll be handing Caine an easy victory and making things tougher for Quinn, right?'' he said at last. "I suppose you're right. Damn it all—if Quinn wasn't so loose-wired about crunching dissension, people like Caine wouldn't show up within a hundred kilometers of Denver.''

Galway swallowed. For the first time since he'd read the records of that period, the almost casual carnage of Trendor's reign was beginning to sound believable. "With your permission, then,'' he said, "I'll head back to Denver and start making arrangements with General Quinn's office.''

"What size guard contingent did you have in mind?'' Trendor asked as the two men headed for the door.

"I thought perhaps a three-tiered force of sixty or seventy men—''

"You thought *what*? Don't be ridiculous, Galway. Give me ten men and to hell with layering. All outside guards are for is to slow down the attack and give me some advance warning, anyway—you know that.''

"Yes, sir,'' Galway said, resorting again to the most neutral tone possible. "Then for electronic surveillance equipment—''

"There's enough of that around the area already,'' Trendor interrupted. "You just get me my ten men, give them lasers and comms and a sandwich apiece, and we'll let it go at that.''

Quietly, Galway admitted defeat. He'd done his duty; if Trendor refused to accept his advice, there was nothing more he could do. "As you wish, sir. Thank you for your time . . . and I hope I'm wrong about what Caine's up to.''

"You probably are,'' Trendor agreed. "But somebody's got to do the unnecessary worrying, don't they?''

The spotter aircraft was halfway back to Athena before the hot flush finally receded from Galway's cheeks.

The preliminary reports on the midnight catapult attack had arrived while Quinn was downstairs at lunch, and with the meal churning in his stomach he read them over twice. Probability ninety-four percent that the explosives used were the same strength as those stolen from the water reclamation center earlier that evening; probability less than fifteen percent that that theft had involved inside help.

The hell with probabilities, Quinn snarled to himself, jabbing at his intercom. "Yes, General?" his aide answered.

"I want this Geoff Dupre brought in for questioning," he told the other. "Bring in his wife, too, and their housemate—that Karen Lindsay woman. Have interrogation prepare a full-spectrum for them."

"Yes, sir," the other answered. "Do you want the surveillance on their house lifted once they're here?"

"No—Caine may decide to drop by, and if he does I want someone there to follow him."

"Yes, sir. Oh, General, there's a message just coming in for you from one of the search squads."

Quinn tapped the proper switch. "Quinn here."

"Abramson, sir," the voice came, brisk and self-satisfied as all hell. "We've *got* him, General—we've found Caine's stolen car, parked right out in the open on the sixteen-hundred block of Rialto Avenue."

Quinn felt his lips curl back from his teeth in a tight smile. "Any sign of Caine or his men?"

"Not yet, sir, but we've been holding back as far out of sight as possible, per your instructions."

"Continue doing so—I'll have backup units there in five minutes. Under no circumstances are you to move in or confront any of them until we've got the net solidly in place—you understand? Pass that on to any other units already in the area—I'll have the skin off of any man who spooks them."

"Understood, General. They won't get away."

That's for damn well sure. Quinn cut off the connection, punching for tactical command. At last—at long and bloody last—they had him. By nightfall at the latest Caine would be in a cell; by midnight, psychor training or no psychor training, they'd know just what the hell he was doing in Denver.

And half the pleasure of this was going to be seeing the look on Galway's face when they brought him in to see the prisoners.

Tactical command answered, and Quinn began issuing orders.

Chapter 17

It was nearly three in the afternoon, and Lathe was idly searching his maps for a secondary escape route from the Shandygaff, when Jensen arrived with the news.

"Where?" he asked the other as Skyler and Mordecai joined them from other parts of the safe house.

"Over on Rialto Avenue, Reger said—sixteen hundred block," Jensen told them. "Looks abandoned, but I doubt Caine's dumped it this soon."

"No, he'd hold on to it as long as possible," Lathe agreed, stroking his dragonhead ring gently. "Having lost his original car, the only way to get a replacement would be to steal one, and Security would be bound to notice something that obvious."

"So what now?" Skyler asked. "We go pick him up, dust him off, and set him back on his feet?"

"I'd like to avoid that," Lathe said. "Besides the question of putting Caine's nose out of joint, there're certain advantages of running two independent groups. But we sure as hell are going to get our eyetracks back on him. Jensen, are you mobile, or did someone drop you off?"

"I've got one of Reger's vans—I was coming into the city to pick up some new equipment anyway when the word came through from his people."

"All right. I'd like you to come in convoy with us, if you can spare the time. We may need the van for surveillance purposes, depending on what cover's available in that neighborhood." Lathe glanced at Skyler and Mordecai, wondering whether he really needed to drag both of them out there for what was likely to be a simple reconnaissance probe. But this was enemy territory, and he'd hate to run into trouble with his backups unavailable. "You two can come along—the fresh air will do you good," he told them. "Jensen, you lead the way."

Lathe had long since resigned himself to the fact that he would never really become comfortable with Denver's horrendous traffic level, but as Skyler guided the car through the

mess he found it was becoming possible for him to ignore the
whizzing vehicles and concentrate on the buildings and pedestrians beyond them. Denver was easily the most prosperous
city he'd seen since the war, and it was with a mixture of
envy and determination that he gazed around them. *Someday
Plinry will be like this, too,* he promised himself silently.
Without the Ryqril, if at all possible.

"Makes you wonder what kind of deal the city's leaders
struck with the Ryqril after the war, doesn't it?" Skyler
commented, waving a hand toward the unscarred landscape.
"They sure as hell didn't go down fighting."

Lathe shrugged. "Maybe they decided it was futile to do
so. Plinry would've given in a lot faster if we hadn't been all
hell-bent ourselves on keeping a guerrilla war going. Anyway, look on the bright side—if they'd made the Ryqril
scorch the city there wouldn't have been nearly as large a
populace here for us to blend into."

"There's that, of course," Skyler admitted. "Though I
don't suppose—"

He broke off as their tinglers came on; *Lathe: Note quiet
Security position at right curb.*

Frowning, Lathe took a careful look as they passed. It was
a surveillance team, all right: a parked car with four men
sitting in it trying to look inconspicuous. "Maybe it's a
stakeout by one of the raft of criminal organizations in town,"
Skyler suggested.

"They're Security." Mordecai was quietly positive. "Backup
position off on the left now—there. Standard unimaginative
Security placement."

"It's standard because it makes sense," Lathe pointed out.
But a small knot was beginning to form in the pit of his
stomach. "Skyler, turn left up here," he directed, fingers
finding his tingler. *Jensen: Continue straight; rendezvous in
three blocks. Watch for stakeout positions; estimate enemy
strength.*

Acknowledged. Battle conditions?

Lathe hesitated. *Prebattle. Soft probe only.*

"Damn them to hell," Skyler muttered. "I hope we're not
too late."

"Me too." Lathe leaned against the edge of his window,
trying to get a view of the sky above them. "Mordecai, check
out your side. Any suspicious aircraft up there?"

There was a short pause. "I see something that might be a
spotter lazing around—it's too high to tell for sure."

Lathe pursed his lips and returned his attention to the street. If the spotters were still hanging that far back, chances were Security wasn't ready to make its move quite yet. "I'd say we still have some time," he told the others. "Let's get a fast strength estimate and rejoin Jensen. And try to figure out how the hell we're going to pull Caine out of here."

"Once we actually find them," Skyler murmured.

"There's that, of course."

Ten minutes later they had their estimate: something close to a hundred Security men and perhaps fifteen or twenty vehicles. Not counting whatever backup troops might be riding in the three aircraft they'd spotted circling the area.

"On the more hopeful side," Lathe said as they squatted in the back of Jensen's parked van, "Security seems to have a better pinpoint on Caine's location, probably from checking city records on abandoned houses in the area. If we can key out the net's structure, we may be able to get that information ourselves." He shrugged. "Then comes the fun part. Any suggestions on where and how we cut our way out of this one?"

"We find the sleepiest-looking carload and punch through there," Skyler offered. "Fast and clean, and not until we've got Caine's team in motion."

"The problem being that with this much invested in the primary net, they'll certainly have some insurance backup primed and ready to move," Lathe pointed out. "Ideally, what we'd like is to get a look at Security's operational map."

"Well, why not?" Jensen said, an odd edge to his voice. "The spotters up there have to have copies—let's get one down and look at it."

Lathe regarded him thoughtfully. "Interesting idea. Tell me, you think you'd be able to fly one of those things?"

"Sure. An airlift makes the most sense, anyway. I was wondering when you'd get around to it."

"Yeah. Well . . ." Lathe thought for a moment. "All right, let's try it. First step is to find the spotters' ground-support vehicle—they're bound to have something like that around for tight communications. Mordecai, you come in the van with me; you two follow in the car."

They found the unmarked van four blocks away, sitting at the far end of an office building's parking lot. A flying ambulance sat resting on its landing skids a few meters away;

between and around the two vehicles were nine plain-dressed but obvious Security men.

"Signal Skyler and Jensen for slingshot backcover," Lathe told Mordecai as he pulled their van into the lot and drove toward the Security force. "You and I will handle primary assault if and when needed; we'll try the soft approach first."

"Got it." Mordecai busied himself with his tingler.

Two of the Security men, paral-dart pistols at the ready, stepped over to them as Lathe brought the van to a stop near the group. One opened his mouth to speak; Lathe beat him to the punch. "Where's your officer?" the comsquare snapped, striding between the pair of them toward the van. "Who's in charge of this unit?" he called in a louder voice as the two would-be challengers scrambled to catch up with him.

"I'm Major Garret," a middle-aged man said, stepping down from the open van door and taking a step forward. "Who are you and what do you want?"

Lathe pulled a card from his pocket and handed it over. "Captain Hari—Special Services," he identified himself. "We've got some unexpected trouble back there. This guy Caine's apparently gotten a lock on our command and tactical frequencies—"

"He's *what*?" The major looked up from the ID card, his frown deepening. "That's impossible. We've got full-spectrum scramble-freq lock codes running here, coupled with—"

"Don't argue with *me*," Lathe cut him off. "*I* don't know how the hell he's doing it. All I know—and all *you* need to know—is what we're going to do about it." He nodded toward the van. "I want you to call the spotters down one at a time so I can clue them in on this. Then they'll go back up and behave exactly as if nothing was happening. With luck we'll be able to lull Caine into thinking he knows our every move while we move some units into new positions."

The major fingered the ID thoughtfully. "What do the spotters have to do with it?"

"They'll see what's happening below, of course," Lathe explained in a tone of strained patience. "We don't want them broadcasting the news that some of our units are out of their proper positions, now, do we?"

Garret pursed his lips, then half turned toward the van door. "Harris—call Spotter Three down here. Tell them . . ." He hesitated.

"Tell them we're adding on an extra observer," Lathe supplied.

"Good enough," Garret said. "Do it, Harris." He turned back to Lathe. "Now. Just what the hell is this Special Services, anyway?"

Lathe let a faintly disgusted look cross his face. "We're a brand-new unit working directly out of the Security prefect's office—started four months ago. Don't you read your daily reports?"

"Sure do, but I never saw any mention of any special units," the other returned. "I'm going to have to verify this with Athena, Captain, before I can take any orders from you."

And by now Spotter Three would be on its way down with a catbird view of any trouble that might erupt. At all costs they had to make sure it saw nothing suspicious. "Do whatever you have to, but do it fast," Lathe told the major, waving a hand impatiently. The motion concealed his hand signal to Mordecai; out of the corner of his eye he saw the small man take a casual step toward the open van door. "Caine'll be making his move to break out as soon as he thinks he's got the net figured out, and we have to have the gaps plugged by then."

"Right." Garret turned back to the van, stepped past Mordecai to climb inside.

"Where the hell is that spotter?" Lathe growled, lifting his gaze to the sky. Peripherally, he saw the outside men shift their own attention upward in automatic response . . . saw Mordecai slip silently into the van behind Garret. "*There* it is. Come *on*, you jelly-heads—*move* it," he snarled toward the descending craft.

Because he was listening for it, he heard the muffled *umph* from inside the van.

The spotter settled down to the pavement beside the van, the pilot popping his side door and leaning out. "What's going on?" he asked. "I don't need another observer—"

"Change in plans," Lathe snapped, giving the aircraft's interior a quick once-over. A single observer, seated next to the pilot; rear compartment empty of backup soldiers but big enough—barely—for the crowd they'd need to stuff in there. Perfect. "We've got some communication-leakage problems," he continued, gesturing Jensen over from the blackcollars' van, "and we're replacing your man with a specialist. Get out," he added, shifting his eyes to the observer.

"Now *wait* a second," the pilot protested as his companion obediently popped his own door. Jensen was already on that side, offering a hand with the harness release. "My orders came directly from General Quinn's office—"

"*What the hell?*"

Lathe caught just a glimpse of one of the Security men gaping into the open van door, his hand scrabbling for his pistol—and then the comsquare jabbed stiffened fingers into the pilot's throat.

The man gagged, folding over his controls as Lathe hit the harness release and hauled him bodily out of the aircraft. On the other side Jensen similarly took the observer out of the fight; turning, Lathe found Mordecai had exploded from the Security van and was cutting a deadly swath through the remaining men with his hands and feet. All around them, the remaining defenders scrambled to bring their weapons to bear, confusion as to the most immediate target slowing their response. Snatching a pair of *shuriken* from behind his belt, Lathe sent them spinning into the farthest of the defenders. A nearer man, suddenly seeming to notice him, swung around and fired; Lathe dropped under the cluster of paral-darts even as Jensen's *shuriken* blurred over the spotter to end that particular threat. Lathe rolled into a crouch, sent two more *shuriken* into the melee, and watched yet another man drop as Skyler opened up from the van with his slingshot.

In seconds, it was all over.

"Dump them in the ambulance," Lathe ordered the others, hoisting the nearest man up into a shoulder carry. "Jensen, get that thing into the air right away—I'll keep in touch with you from the Security van."

"Right." Jensen slid into the spotter and closed the doors. A moment later the gravs flared with blue-violet light and the craft headed smoothly into the sky.

"I hope he doesn't do anything stupid," Skyler said. "Maybe I should've gone with him."

"I need you here," Lathe said shortly.

They soon had the casualties out of sight in the ambulance. "And now a quick look at the maps to find out where Caine is?" Skyler suggested.

"Right," Lathe said, glancing back toward the street. Ever since the fight had started, he'd been halfway braced for reinforcements to come swooping down on them; but either none of the Denverites walking and driving a hundred meters away had noticed the fracas or else they'd chosen not to get involved by reporting it. He'd seen the same thing happen in other cities, both during the war and immediately after it, and while it still struck him as an odd reaction he'd long since learned to accept and make use of it. "You go ahead," he told Skyler. "Mordecai, come take a quick look at the ambulance cockpit with me."

It was a somewhat smaller compartment than the equivalent space in the spotter aircraft had been. "You going to try and take this one, too?" Mordecai asked.

"Not right away," Lathe answered, trying to move one of the seats away from the back of the cockpit. "You ever had any experience flying something like this? Never mind; it doesn't look like there's any way in from the main compartment anyway."

Mordecai looked, grunted agreement. "You have something specific in mind, or just gathering gleanings?"

"A little of both." Lathe glanced at the controls once more and backed out of the cockpit. "Well, that's for another day. Let's see how Skyler's doing."

The big blackcollar had the information ready by the time they joined him in the Security van. "The net's clearly centered on this block right here," he told them, jabbing a finger down onto the map. "This number here might be an address, but I wouldn't count too heavily on that."

"Fortunately, we don't have to," Lathe said. "All right; here's the plan."

He outlined it for them, and a few minutes later they all left the lot: Lathe in the Security van, Mordecai in the car, and Skyler driving the second van. Skyler headed south as Mordecai and Lathe set out toward the target zone, signaling periodically with their tinglers. They were almost to the block Skyler had pinpointed when a response finally came.

Identify yourselves.

Lathe breathed a sigh of relief. *This is Lathe,* he sent. *Danger/emergency—Security net encircling you. Escape must be immediate.*

There was a short pause. *Lathe: Prove identity.*

"Damn," the consquare snorted under his breath. *Code signal four follows: gamma ray, cluster charge, hammer throw. Respond.*

Incense, Carno fandragon, operant. Why are you here?

Danger emergency. Location?

The reply was almost grudging; clearly, the blackcollars' unexpected appearance still had Caine off-balance. *1822 Renforth.*

Half a block down. *Come out now; get in northbound blue van. Mordecai: Take forward ram position.*

Acknowledged.

He was almost to the house now, and for a long moment he thought Caine would miss the pickup. But the younger man was merely playing tight on the timing: as the van drew abreast of the walkway, the front door suddenly opened and the five men sprinted out toward the street. Lathe had the side door sprung before they were halfway there, and in five seconds flat they were all aboard.

"Get yourselves braced," Lathe snapped at them, stomping on the accelerator. Ahead, Mordecai's car had emerged from the next street to lead the way; from the van's radio a slow flurry of commotion was beginning to flood in as the Security watchers belatedly realized something unscheduled was happening. At the next intersection four plain-dressed men scrambled out of their parked car, bringing laser rifles to bear—and dived out of the way as Mordecai put on a burst of speed and did his best to run them down.

Beside Lathe, a figure slid into the van's other front seat. Caine. "What can I do?" he asked tightly.

"Grab the mike and punch in Combat Freq One," Lathe told him, fighting the steering wheel as he rescattered the Security men. "Jensen's up there in a spotter—tell him to put down in the parking lot we just left."

"Got it." Caine busied himself with the radio, and Lathe risked a glance in the mirror at the rest of the team. Still rattled, but adjusting rapidly enough. "Full combat garb," he ordered them. "The next group may get some shots off at us. Braune, signal Mordecai to make for the lot we just left."

"Yes, sir," Braune said, pausing with battle-hood halfway in place to tap at his tingler.

The radio pinged, and a familiar voice came on. "Jensen acknowledging. Sit tight—I'm going to take out some of the opposition first."

"What does he mean by that?" Caine asked.

Lathe consciously relaxed his jaw. "I'm not sure," he admitted. "He may be going to buzz some of the positions closest to the rendezvous point before landing."

Without warning, a flash of light erupted from the next corner. Lathe ducked reflexively as part of the van's front blistered into a cloud of vaporized surfacing; and an instant later the vehicle tilted sideways as the left front tire blew with the heat of a second shot. "Hang on!" Lathe snapped, twisting the wheel hard. The tire would surely be equipped with an inner travel rim, but if the laser fire had damaged that too, they could well wind up taking the last couple of blocks on foot.

Ahead, Mordecai's car slowed fractionally at the hidden gunner's street and the blackcollar's left arm whipped outward through the open window. Whether the *shuriken* found its target or not Lathe didn't know, but the van passed the intersection without drawing any more fire.

They were barely a block away from the parking lot when the thunder of an explosion nearly shook them off the road.

Lathe's first, horrible thought was that Jensen had crashed his spotter. But seconds later they turned the next corner and saw the other's apparently undamaged aircraft settle onto the parking lot. Mordecai pulled over to let the van pass ahead of it into the lot, then turned sharply to bring his car to a halt sideways across the opening. In the mirror Lathe saw a pair of Security cars in hot pursuit; Mordecai sent a flight of *shuriken* in their general direction and then turned and sprinted for the spotter. Stomping on the brake, Lathe swung open his door and leaped out as the van screeched to a halt. "Everyone into the spotter!" he snapped over his shoulder.

They hurried to obey. Beyond the running Mordecai, the Security cars had also stopped and were beginning to discharge armed men. Lathe sent a *shuriken* toward the crowd and then pulled his slingshot from under his tunic and unfolded the forearm brace.

"Here," Caine said from beside him, pressing a tiny cylinder into his hand. The younger man, Lathe saw, also had his slingshot ready, another of the objects in his hand. "It's a primer cap," he explained, and fired it over Mordecai's head.

As a serious explosive device, the primer cap was a joke; as a creator of chaos, it was absolutely perfect. The Security men scattered as Caine's and then Lathe's projectiles blew up in their midst, laser rifles forgotten in the scramble for cover. The two men kept up the barrage until Mordecai had passed them, then turned and sprinted after him. Seconds later, squeezed together like small fish with the rest of Caine's group, they were airborne.

"Any place in particular we headed for?" Jensen asked casually over his shoulder.

"Head south to where the expressway starts—Skyler's supposed to wait for us there," Lathe told him, trying without success to get a look out of one of the cockpit windows.

"And watch your back—the other spotters will be on top of us any second now."

"Unlikely," Jensen said, shaking his head, "seeing as I knocked both of them out of the sky a few minutes ago."

"You did *what?*" Alamzad gasped.

"Forced them down. Rammed their rear stabilizer assemblies, to be specific—this design has always had a glass tail. One of them crashed trying to chase me on manual. The other had more sense and settled for an emergency landing."

"My God," Pittman muttered. "You could have been *killed*."

Jensen shrugged. "It's not dangerous when you know what you're doing."

Across Caine's shoulder, Lathe caught Mordecai's eyes. The other grimaced slightly, shook his head in disbelief. Lathe twitched his own head in agreement.

They reached the expressway a minute or two later, setting down just off the road where Skyler's van was waiting. "Everyone out," Lathe ordered, scanning the sky quickly as he trotted toward the van. Nothing—Jensen's quick air victory had apparently caught Security by surprise.

"They'll have backups in the air any minute now," Jensen reminded him as the comsquare climbed into the seat beside Skyler.

"Right," Lathe said. "Let's get out of here, Skyler."

"The safe house?" the other asked, pulling out into a gap in the traffic flow.

"I think a little extra distance would be appropriate," Lathe answered. "Let's make it Reger's house. He's got a right to see how his end of the bargain came out, anyway."

Skyler nodded, and silence descended on the crowded van. Behind and above, ground and air Security forces converged on the downed spotter to begin a long and futile search.

Chapter 18

Quinn finished his brief conversation and replaced the phone onto his desk, hand trembling—with anger or frustration; Galway couldn't tell which—as he did so. "Well?" Galway asked, fighting to keep his own anger under control. "Any traces at all of them?"

"No, but we're not giving up yet," the general growled. "We've got the car they abandoned—belongs to a building company in northwest Denver—and we're checking to see how they got hold of it."

Galway snorted. "In other words, you haven't got a clue as to where they've vanished. And aren't likely to get one anytime soon, either."

"Look, Galway—"

"No, *you* look, General," Galway cut him off. "I told you not to move against Caine—I told you time and again that the best chance we were likely to get was already planted in the group. But you wouldn't listen—and now you may have blasted the whole thing to hell."

"*Have* I, now," Quinn shot back. "Then tell me, if you would, why your precious Postern didn't tell us Lathe was here. Huh? Answer me *that*."

"I don't know. My guess is that Lathe didn't bother to tell them he was going to come along."

"Oh, really?" Quinn's voice dripped sarcasm. "He just forgot to mention it or something?"

"Or something, yes. You might recall I *did* ask you to confirm that the first set of drop pods really were just decoys—playing off other people's assumptions is one of Lathe's specialties. Well, he also likes playing his games tight to his chest, and he may have decided to keep his presence here secret in case one of Caine's team got captured."

"Except that you also said once that interrogating them wouldn't gain us anything," Quinn growled. "I wish you'd keep your damn stories straight."

Galway took a deep breath. "Of course Caine's teammates

144

aren't likely to break. That doesn't mean Lathe wouldn't hedge his bets anyway." He waved a hand in disgust. "And believe it or not, that might have worked to our advantage once. If Lathe didn't want Caine to know he was here—and we could have confirmed that was the case as soon as Postern made his next contact—then he would have been reluctant to expose himself to Caine by coming to his aid unless there were some immediate danger. We could have kept a full-scale surveillance on Caine without any risk of having the watchers taken out."

"Until the timing suited them, anyway." Quinn grimaced. "Well, it's all academic now. They're together, they know we're on to them, and it's going to be a race now as to whether they can finish whatever they're up to before we find them again. I don't suppose you've come up with any more ideas on that score?"

"You've already heard them: some kind of assault on the Ryqril's Aegis Mountain base, or an attack on former Prefect Trendor."

"Neither of which makes any sense." Quinn shook his head. "Especially with Lathe and a full blackcollar team now taking an interest in it. Blackcollars aren't likely to waste their time on something that isn't difficult, important, *and* feasible."

He fell silent, and Galway fought down the urge to once again explain the logic behind an assassination attempt on Trendor. Clearly, Quinn wasn't stupid—he couldn't have risen to such a high position if he was—but he'd just as clearly created a mental block to anything Galway might have to say, whether it had any value or not. *I shouldn't have come*, the prefect thought bitterly. *Maybe he'd have done a better job of this if he hadn't somehow gotten it into his head that he had to show me up.*

Then again, maybe he wouldn't have. Quinn was, after all, successor and possibly protégé to Prefect Trendor, and Trendor hadn't struck Galway either as a man of great intellect or finesse.

But then, neither had many of the Security officials he'd met on Argent during Lathe's mission there, something he'd been too busy at the time to notice. Was Galway's ability to follow these tangled threads of logic *that* far out of the ordinary? Or could it be that Quinn simply had so much firepower and manpower at his disposal that he'd never needed to outthink his opponents?

"The hell with it," Quinn muttered, breaking the silence. "There's no way we're going to figure out Lathe's plan in time, so we're just going to have to take him out of the game."

"You just tried that," Galway reminded him.

"Yeah, well, this time we're going to do it right." The general jabbed a finger in Galway's direction. "He's still got to get to Kanai for that list of veterans, right? Well, to do that he's got to contact the Shandygaff Bar—and when he does, we'll have him."

"What, use a phone signal tracer?" Galway shook his head. "Come on, General—don't you think Lathe's just a little too smart to fall for that?"

"What else is he going to do—go there personally?" Quinn retorted. "Hardly. Not after what they pulled on him there last night."

"Unless he *expects* everyone to reason that way," Galway suggested slowly. "And in that case he might do just that."

Quinn paused, a battle clearly going on behind his eyes. "Well . . . maybe," he conceded at last, and Galway could sense how much the admission was costing him. "You think I should put a Security cordon around the bar, then, as well as trace the phone lines?"

"I frankly don't think a cordon would work, sir," Galway said. "You saw how easily he identified the plain-dressed units out there today—blackcollars have a knack for spotting Security troops. I think you'd do better to try and use people he'll be expecting to see at the Shandygaff anyway."

"Chong and Briller?" Quinn pulled at his lip. "Interesting. May be worth a try—they'd certainly be keen for another round with him."

"You could feed a tip to them via your informer that Lathe's going to show," Galway suggested. "They probably can't actually stop him, but they may be able to slow him down enough for you to get an aircar full of troops there in time."

"The bosses won't like that part," Quinn growled. "Especially if their mall stores are damaged in the process."

"You weren't there last night," Galway said grimly. "They were more furious at what could have happened to their own skins in there. I don't think they'd make more than token noises over a successful attempt to cage the man responsible for the fight."

"A 'successful' attempt, you say?" Quinn said with sudden coolness. "Well, rest assured, Galway—this one *will* damn well be successful."

"Yes, sir." Galway sighed, a heavy weight seeming to settle onto his back. For a minute the frustrating rift between him and Quinn had shown signs of closing . . . but now, for no real reason, they were suddenly back at odds again. "If I can do anything to help, General—"

"I think you've done all you need to," Quinn cut him off. "You might want to stop by the situation room later, though, and watch us nail your blackcollar comsquare." Picking up a report, the general slid it into his reader.

Getting up, Galway headed silently for the door.

"You're not serious," Reger's voice said from the doorway.

Lathe swiveled in his chair to see the other standing just inside the living room, a disbelieving frown on his face. "You shouldn't sneak up on people like that," the comsquare said reproachfully, though all five blackcollars had heard the other's approach. "What aren't we serious about?"

"Don't play innocent," Reger growled. "You barely escape from a Security noose this afternoon, and now you're proposing to go put your heads back into it? What kind of a fool do you take Quinn for, anyway?"

"An unimaginative one, for starters," Skyler said dryly from the lounge chair where he was stretched out. "Chances are he'll reason it exactly the same way you just did, that we're far too intelligent to try something that stupid."

Reger snorted. "The hell with what *chances are*—and to hell with Quinn, for that matter, because you've got a damn sight more trouble than just him. I've been hearing foammouthing from all over the city today over what you dimbos pulled last night in the Shandygaff. You go back there and Nash'll hang your skins out to dry, while the customers stand up and applaud."

"Including the blackcollars?" Lathe asked mildly.

Reger broke off, and something twitched in his cheek. "What's that supposed to mean?" he asked cautiously.

"Oh, I don't know—just sort of a conversation opener. I thought you might want to explain why you've carefully avoided mentioning the existence of other blackcollars in Denver."

Reger was silent for a moment. "I won't insult your intelligence by inventing some excuse," he said at last. "I didn't mention them because I thought you might automatically take their side of things in the power struggle going on in the city.''

"Their side, and Sartan's?''

"You've actually *met* Sartan?'' Reger asked, cocking an eyebrow. "What's he like?''

"No, no one's introduced us yet.'' Lathe shook his head. "Can I assume this confession means that you've laid any fears about us to rest?''

"At the moment, frankly, I don't seem to have any choice,'' Reger admitted. "If you and Bernhard are setting up an elaborate trap for me, I've yet to see through it. Until and unless I do I have to accept or reject you on faith alone.''

"Basically the same position we're in, you'll notice,'' Lathe said. "As it happens, I have no intention of getting us involved in your private little intrigues, on Bernhard's side or anyone else's. We're here to do a job, and I fully intend to get the hell out of here once we've done it. Until then, we still owe you a fortress for your help in finding Caine, and we're going to keep our part of that bargain.''

"And if it helps your nerves any,'' Hawking said from across the room, "we knew there were other blackcollars in town well before we struck our deal with you. You only *thought* you were keeping information from us, and we're pretty used to that.''

Reger smiled lopsidedly. "Thank you,'' he said with a trace of sarcasm. "Now if we can get back to the original subject, what the hell do you think you can accomplish by going to the Shandygaff?''

Lathe shrugged. "We meet Kanai, as we promised. We perhaps get a little closer to the key we need to finish our mission, one way or another. And if the cards fall right, we might even pick up another ally.''

Reger snorted. "As trustworthy as Kanai and Bernhard?''

"And as trustworthy as you,'' Lathe said bluntly. "You can take your pick.''

The older man eyed him in silence for a long moment. Then, turning, he left the room. "Hell of a way to run a circus,'' Skyler murmured.

"Agreed, but untrustworthy allies are all we're likely to get in this town,'' Lathe said. There was another footstep at the door, and he turned to see Caine enter the room. "How's your team doing?'' he asked the younger man.

"Resting,'' Caine said, an odd stiffness in his voice. "I

think this is the safest they've felt since we landed, and they're taking advantage of it.''

"Just as long as they don't come to feel *too* safe here," the comsquare said dryly. "We should be all right for a few hours, though, at the very least. Was there something in particular you wanted?"

Caine hesitated. "I'd like to have a private word with you, Comsquare, if I may."

"Sure," Lathe agreed, getting to his feet. They'd been at Reger's now for nearly two hours, and he'd been wondering when Caine would finally get around to this confrontation. "Let's go out back and see how Hawking's tracking placements look."

They walked in silence until they were out of the house and heading across the sculpted lawn. "You're not going to make this easy, are you?" Caine asked at last.

Lathe shrugged. "If you have a complaint against a superior, it's up to you to bring it to his attention."

"Even when he knows perfectly well what it is?" Caine countered.

"Even then. It's standard military etiquette and procedure— besides which, sometimes you're wrong about the officer's knowing about your grievance."

"Not in this case, though."

"No," Lathe admitted.

They walked another few steps before Caine spoke again. "I'd like an explanation, if you've got one."

"In its simplest form, I thought we might be needed."

Caine snorted. "If we're that incompetent, why did you graduate us in the first place?"

Lathe pursed his lips. "This may come as a rude shock, but the blackcollar school on Plinry isn't designed to create indestructible superwarriors. It's designed to turn out reasonably competent guerrilla fighters in reasonably quick time. Period. You've been granted no particular immunity from enemy attacks or unexpected changes in climate or even lapses in tactical logic. The mean survival time in enemy territory of a team like yours is probably measured in weeks or even days."

"So what's our *real* purpose? To make the government waste time and resources chasing us down?"

Lathe winced at the bitterness in the other's voice. "To be blunt, at some level the answer is yes. Of course we don't *want* any of you to be captured, but the only way to avoid that entirely is not to send anyone out in the first place.''

''And as you've so often reminded us, this is war.''

Lathe sighed. ''Yes. I remind myself as often as I remind you, if that helps any. I've lost a lot of friends to this war over the years, you know. If I could find a rationale that I could live with for giving it up, I'd probably have done so long ago.''

Caine was silent for a long minute. ''I'm trying very hard to be mad at you,'' he said at last, ''but you're not making *that* easy, either. Maybe because I've seen what it's like now to send my own men on missions they might not come back from.''

''It'll be worse the first time you actually lose one of them.''

''Yeah. I've already come closer than I like.'' Caine paused. ''So . . . asking the question nicely this time, why are you here? Really?''

Lathe shrugged. ''On the most noble level, because your mission sounded like something that would make an incredible contribution to the war effort if it succeeded. On the most petty personal level . . .'' He hesitated. ''It looked like the only chance I'd ever have of retiring from the war someday.''

He hadn't expected Caine to understand, at least not immediately; but to his mild surprise, the younger man nodded. ''A chance to finally lay the burden onto the next generation's shoulders. Is that it?''

''Basically,'' Lathe said. ''And as I said, the mean life of a guerrilla team in hostile territory is short. With two teams working together, the odds are considerably better.''

''So why didn't you simply come right out and invite yourselves along? Why the backshadow skulking routine?''

''Well . . . frankly, I hoped to avoid having this conversation. It was supposed to be *your* mission, and I knew you'd resent anything that looked like interference from me.'' There was another reason, but for the moment it was best that Caine didn't know that one. He'd be furious when he found out, but there was nothing the comsquare could really do about that.

''So what happens now? Organizationally, I mean?''

Lathe brought his mind back from Project Christmas to the subject at hand. ''That's entirely up to you. If you want, we'll fade back into the shadows, play backstop if and when you need it, and otherwise let you run the show. Alternatively, you can add us to your team, and we'll do our best to carry out your orders.''

Caine snorted. ''Oh, that would be a new classic, wouldn't it? Blackcollars taking orders from recruits. What's the third alternative? There *is* a third one, isn't there?''

Lathe pursed his lips. ''I take over. Pure and simple.''

''I thought that would be it.'' Caine stopped, turning to look behind him at Reger's mansion. ''So what would you do if you were me?'' he asked the comsquare. ''Maintain the role of leader whatever the cost, or lose face before your teammates by meekly turning over command to someone else?''

''If I were also your age? Probably the former. At *my* age, and with the experience that goes with it, I'd say to hell with face. The mission is what counts.''

''And of course you'd also counsel taking the advice of the experts in any given field, wouldn't you?''

Lathe glanced at Caine, caught the wisp of a smile on the other's face. ''Yes, I suppose I would,'' he admitted.

Slowly, the younger man nodded his head. ''I've been afraid ever since we left Plinry of looking weak as a leader,'' he said softly. ''I'd never done anything like this before. But I think I'm even more afraid of looking like a fool . . . and throwing away the best leadership available for my team would be a foolish thing to do.'' He hissed a sigh between his teeth. ''All right, Comsquare. I hereby officially offer my command to you.''

''I accept,'' Lathe said, but he could see the tight lines gathered around Caine's mouth. It would be a long time before the younger man would be happy with that decision. If he ever truly was. ''Let's get back inside and let the others know. We've still got a lot of planning to do before we head out to the Shandygaff tonight.''

''You're really going through with that?''

Lathe nodded. ''I'm afraid it's a gamble we have to take. Time is running out, and we've got to find a lever to pry out the information we need. One way or another, we start building that lever tonight.''

Chapter 19

Honor.

The word echoed over and over again through Kanai's mind as he sat alone at his booth in the Shandygaff. A five-letter curse; a two-syllable question which had no answer. *Honor. Honor. Honorhonorhonor—*

Stop it! Shaking his head violently, he snapped the mental loop. The philosophy of his ancestors wouldn't help him now, either as a source of advice or as a refuge from action. What was about to happen was taking place in Denver in the year 2461; and he, Kanai, was the man who would have to live with his decision . . . or would have to die with it.

Across the room, Briller was talking quietly with one of Nash's other henchmen near the doorway to the bar's anteroom. The tip had come down about two hours ago, as nearly as Kanai's reading of events could place it, and for almost an hour now they'd been poised and ready. An obvious sucker trap . . . and it wasn't hard to guess who it was for.

Damn you, Lathe, he snarled once to himself. *I told you to call me here. Not to come in person.*

And come he would—Kanai had no doubt of that. The news of Security's bungled net operation was all over town, and if Quinn didn't know any better than to try a standard net on blackcollars, he *did* have enough brains to set up those horribly expensive tracers on all of the bar's fiber-op phone lines. And Lathe, of course, would know enough to anticipate that.

If only Kanai had thought to give the comsquare his home phone number. But Quinn almost certainly had that line monitored by now, as well. So Lathe would come to the Shandygaff in person. And would walk right into Briller's trap.

So where did Kanai's loyalty lie? With Bernhard and the rest of the team? In that case, honor required him to merely sit here and allow Lathe to fight on his own, to win or lose as his skill and the universe allowed. If Kanai declined to assist

152

him further, perhaps the strains between Bernhard's team and the rest of the city could yet be smoothed over.

But if there was indeed a higher loyalty Kanai was being called to . . .

Chong slipped inside the main room, conferred briefly with Briller. Once, their eyes flicked to Kanai in his booth; and then Chong headed back through the anteroom to the troops Nash had stationed outside. They were keeping an eye on him, all right, the bar's enforcers and the Security spy both. Watching to see which path Kanai would take: that of life, or that of suicide.

Or rather, that of life or that of *seppuku*.

And put that way, there was really no doubt as to which path was the honorable one. Kanai was a blackcollar, first and foremost, and to allow another blackcollar to go unaided to his death would be a betrayal of everything he knew to be right. And if the attempt cost him his life, he would at least be able to face his ancestors without that added shame tarnishing his soul.

But before he died he would claim a single personal satisfaction: he would eliminate the triple-damned Security agent who had placed him in this position. He'd deduced the other's identity long ago, but until now it had been a matter of complete indifference to him how Quinn kept track of Denver's shadow government. But no longer. It would be his final gift to Bernhard's team, and perhaps the most fitting response he could make to Quinn's insulting invasion of his home this morning.

He was easing a *shuriken* out of his belt pouch, concentrating on keeping his movements invisible to those watching him, when his tingler suddenly came on.

He froze as the message came through: *Kanai: Lathe and Skyler approaching Shandygaff. Safety level?*

"Damn," he breathed viciously. Tingler frequencies were unusual ones, and the short range of the devices made them hard to tap into, but Nash and his people undoubtedly had something set up for the occasion. Probably they had no real knowledge of blackcollar combat codes, but the very existence of a message told them all they really needed to know.

And indeed Briller had already reacted, drawing his pistol from his pocket and holding the weapon muzzle-up by his cheek. His eyes sought out and met Kanai's in silent warning.

Kanai met his gaze coolly . . . and deliberately reached to his tingler. *Lathe: Trap/encirclement in area. Escape imperative.*

Acknowledged. What about you?

There was no time for a reply as Briller belatedly swung his gun down and brought it to bear. Dropping sideways onto the seat, Kanai rolled to the floor beneath his table as Briller's flechette shattered the privacy plastic behind him. There were yelps of surprise and anger from the nearer patrons as the big enforcer corrected his aim and fired again. Under the table, Kanai curled into a fetal position with his back to his opponent, letting the flexarmor beneath his shirt absorb the blow and deflect the shot. The projectiles couldn't penetrate the tough material, but on the other hand the sheer kick of the shots and the flexarmor's stiffening action as it spread the impact around could throw off his own counterattack, possibly fatally. The timing here had to be precise.

Another flechette ricocheted off his back . . . and Kanai made his move.

He rolled onto his back, left hand sending a *shuriken* spinning in Briller's direction. It was a lousy shot from a lousy position and it missed completely, but it served its purpose of forcing Briller to break off his own attack and duck. In the momentary breathing space, Kanai tucked his legs to his chest and kicked up as hard as he could at the table towering over him. With a splintering of torn wood, the fastenings holding the slab of wood to its center post broke, and the tabletop flipped over to rest on its edge against the metal column.

Landing there just in time to catch Briller's next shot squarely on its polished surface.

Briller must have realized at that moment that he was dead, but he made a game try of it anyway. By the time Kanai had his battle-hood and gloves on and had poked his head over his impromptu shield, the big enforcer had sidled around the edge of the room toward the massive bar, trying to get a shot around Kanai's tabletop without simultaneously exposing himself to the blackcollar's *shuriken*.

But now that his head and hands were protected, Kanai had little to fear from the other's gun—or from anyone else's, as a shot glanced off his shoulder from behind him. Twisting, he spun a *shuriken* off in that direction, then turned back to send another star toward Briller. The big man spat in pain as the *shuriken* caught him in the right shoulder; he emptied his gun in blind fury. Kanai ducked out from his shelter and sprinted through the hailstorm toward the anteroom.

He'd expected a larger reception committee to be lying in

wait in the anteroom, and was therefore vaguely surprised to find only two people there. "Kanai!" Nash snarled toward him, swinging his flechette pistol around to center on the blackcollar's stomach.

"Give it up, Nash," Kanai told him, eyes flicking over the little man's shoulder to the coatcheck girl and the tiny pistol in her hand. Paral-dart gun, probably—more useless against him than even the flechette pistols. "Your quarry's been warned," he continued, drawing out a *shuriken*. "He's probably half a klick away by now."

"And you're the one who warned him, I suppose?" Nash bit out. "Damn you, Kanai—"

"Sorry about this, lady," Kanai said to the coatcheck girl. He raised his *shuriken*—

And then everything happened at once.

Across the room the door slammed open and a pair of black-clad men leaped in. Simultaneously, a brilliant flash lit up the room from behind Kanai and a chunk of wall by the door exploded into superheated vapor and brick fragments. Kanai spun around, just in time to see Nash's "flechette" gun blaze a second laser blast toward the intruders. "Watch it!" he snapped reflexively. The disguised laser swung in his direction—

And there was the *chaft* of an airgun, and Nash collapsed to the floor, his last shot burning a black groove in the rug in front of him.

"Nice shooting," Lathe said, breathing a bit heavily. "Does this mean you've officially joined our side?"

Kanai turned as the coatcheck girl lowered her pistol, her expression simultaneously furious and scared. "Damn you, you dimbos," she snapped at Lathe and his companion, a blackcollar Kanai didn't recognize. "What did you think you were doing, coming back here? Nash's lice are all over the mall, just waiting for you."

"Oh, we know," Lathe said, glancing into the bar itself. "We came in to talk to Kanai . . . and to see whose side *you* were on."

"I'm on *my* side—no one else's," she bit out. "Damn you, anyway, for doing this to me."

"If we can talk about this somewhere else," Kanai put in, eyeing the main room doorway, "they'll be pulling themselves together in there anytime now. You mind getting the hell out of here?"

"You coming with us?" Lathe's companion asked the woman, raising an eyebrow.

"What choice do I have?" she growled, gesturing sharply at the prone figure of Nash. "If I don't, he'll have me strapped over a firepit the minute he wakes up."

"Oh, well, that's easy enough to fix," Kanai said. His *shuriken* was still in his hand; raising it, he hurled it down squarely into the little man's throat.

The woman inhaled sharply. "You—"

"He was a Security spy, and I was going to kill him anyway," Kanai told her calmly. "All right—your job's safe again. *Now* can we get out of here?"

But Lathe was still looking at the woman. "Your choice," he said.

For a second more she eyed them in silent indecision. Then she gave a sharp nod. "Back here." She motioned to them, stepping back from the counter. "There's a hidden trapdoor back here, leads a few blocks away—"

She broke off to fire a burst of paral-darts through the doorway. "The company's getting restless," Lathe agreed, taking a long step and vaulting over the counter. "Let's go."

The other blackcollar followed; with a deep breath and underlying misgivings, Kanai joined them. The girl pushed aside a rack of coats and sent a hard kick against the wall there, and a small square of flooring popped up a millimeter or two. A knife appeared in her hand, and she pried the square up, revealing a handle. She tugged, and the tiling around the handle cracked into a rectangular shape and lifted up. "Down the stairs and along the tunnel," she instructed, gesturing. "I need to grab a couple of things and then set up the self-destruct."

"Right." Lathe's fingers found his tingler: *Backup: Pull out. Escaping via rathole. Rendezvous at point beta.*

Acknowledged.

Kanai took another deep breath and followed Lathe down the stairway. He hoped to hell the comsquare knew what he was doing.

The stairway led a dozen meters beneath Denver's streets to a complex and ancient-feeling warren of ceramic-walled tunnels. With the blackcollars' penlights throwing odd reflections from the frequent puddles of stagnant water underfoot, they traveled along in silence, all of them apparently aware that Security could conceivably have scattered audio sensors in the tunnels.

The woman was clearly familiar with the territory, guiding them through the maze without hesitation. Fifteen minutes later they came to a more modern-looking metal ladder disappearing upward through a broken section of roof. The woman headed up, and a minute later they were all standing around a dimly lit basement smelling strongly of mildew and neglect.

"Sorry about the mess," she apologized, stepping to a rickety set of stairs and shining Lathe's light briefly onto a white square set into the wall there. "We should be safe here for a while—long enough for Security to shift the search somewhere else, anyway."

Kanai moved to her side, glanced up the stairs at the closed door there, then flashed his own light on the white plate. Fifteen or twenty barely visible black threads were set into it, leading off in all different directions. "What's this?" he asked.

"Passive intruder alert," the woman told him. "The monofilaments are anchored upstairs to doors and windows and whatnot. If anyone comes in, the thread is pulled out of the plate. Looks like no one else has been by here since the last time I was in. Not surprising."

"Interesting system," Lathe commented, removing his flexarmor battle-hood. "Sounds like the sort of thing that an organization with more ingenuity than funds would come up with."

She gave the comsquare a long look, but then shrugged. "You're right on that one. Being the last surviving member of a resistance group is hardly a money-making proposition—and we were never exactly rich even at our strongest."

"Your group being . . . ?"

"Torch, of course. What else?"

Chapter 20

Her name was Anne Silcox, and she wasn't anything like what Caine had expected.

Outwardly, she didn't seem especially out of the ordinary. Her voice and manner of speech were normal enough, her face and body language tense but under reasonable control. Nowhere was there any obvious display of the holy fire Caine would have looked to find in a member of such an avowedly fanatical group.

But then he'd already learned a lot on this mission about discrepancies between theory and reality.

"I wish I knew what happened to the rest of them." Silcox shook her head. Her eyes made their fourth quick search of the unfurnished living room, as if she wasn't ready yet to put complete faith in Lathe's assurances about the safe house's security. "I was only seventeen when they disappeared, and hardly in the inner circle. All I know is that it wasn't something unexpected, because they set me up in the Shandygaff specifically to keep an eye on things in the absence of better information sources." Her eyes flicked from Lathe's face to Caine's and Hawking's, then settled onto Kanai's. It was a tendency Caine had already noted in her, perhaps a need to connect with the familiar in such an unfamiliar situation.

Beside Caine, Lathe shifted in his seat. "That's not much to go on," he told her. "Do you know anything about their contacts here—communications with the criminal hierarchy, perhaps?"

Her eyes were still on Kanai. "All I know is that they occasionally had doings with blackcollars—both the ones here and some from other areas. Kanai could probably tell you more about that."

Lathe shifted his own gaze to Kanai. "You never mentioned other blackcollars."

The other shrugged. "I've heard reports, mostly through Torch, of other teams operating east and south of here, but I've never met any of them. You have to remember that

long-distance travel is pretty severely restricted. As to deal-
ings with the crime lords, if Torch did any of that I never
heard about it. Frankly, I doubt it—their goals wouldn't mesh
very well.''

Lathe nodded thoughtfully. ''Perhaps. I presume Bernhard
handled your contacts with Torch—do you know whether or
not he was in touch with them at the time Anne says they
closed up shop?''

''Possible, but I don't know. Bernhard isn't big on telling
us everything he knows.''

''Occupational hazard,'' Caine murmured.

If Lathe heard the remark he didn't show it. ''Did Torch
have any standard records caches?'' he asked Silcox. ''Hard
copies, computer files, even a dummy program on someone
else's machine? *Anything* that might give us a clue as to what
happened to them?''

She shook her head. ''All I was was a walking eavesdrop
in the Shandygaff. No one would have trusted me with stuff
like that.''

''All right, then,'' Lathe said. ''Let's switch to exactly
what you've learned in the last five years. Any idea when the
Ryqril started taking such an active interest in Aegis Mountain? Surely they haven't been trying to break in since the war
ended.''

''No, that's been a recent development,'' she said. ''I
started hearing rumors about it a year ago from smug-runners
who were annoyed at how the extra security around there was
interfering with their runs westward.''

''The same time we snoggered them out of the Novas,''
Hawking pointed out. ''Maybe they decided they needed to
play catch-up again.''

''What's that supposed to mean?'' Caine asked.

''Means they're hoping to find more of our technology to
steal,'' Lathe said. ''Makes sense, I suppose. There could
very well be something left in Aegis they didn't get elsewhere
from us after the war—''

''Wait a second,'' Caine cut in. ''Why should they care
about the thirty-year-old technology of a race they've already
beaten?''

Lathe turned a strange frown on him. ''You're serious?''
the comsquare asked. ''How did your teachers miss *that*
one?''

''Maybe I was absent that day,'' Caine returned archly. ''If
it's not a state secret . . . ?''

"The Ryqril are technological imbeciles," Lathe told him. "That's a literal, medical term—no insult implied. The whole race is incapable of creating new technology on their own beyond a fairly low level. It's probably the main driving force beyond their constant attempts to conquer their neighbors, in fact—it's one of the few ways they've got to advance their technological level."

Caine stared at him. It was such an unbelievable statement . . . and yet, now that it was in front of him, a lot of other things began to make sense. The gamble the Ryqril on Argent had taken—and ultimately lost—of trying to beat the black-collars to the hidden Novas was suddenly a lot less foolish than it'd seemed to him at the time. With their forces bogged down in a standoff with the Chryselli, an influx of new weaponry could have made a real difference in that war. "I gather," he said slowly, "that's why Security is still using the old-style aircraft and equipment designs that we know how to deal with."

Lathe nodded, the frown still on his face. "It's risky, certainly, but even when you know how to disable an aircraft, that doesn't mean you can pull it off in actual practice. The Ryqril can copy any technology they can steal, of course, so they're not stuck using the actual thirty-year-old crates."

"You really didn't know?" Hawking broke in. "It was common knowledge among the TDE hierarchy even before the main conflict started."

"There was a lot my teachers seemed to forget," Caine told him, trying to keep the bitterness from his voice. Once again, the Resistance leaders he'd trusted so fully had withheld important information from him, and while this one didn't hurt as badly as the first of those revelations had, back on Argent, it hurt enough.

"Maybe they simply forgot to mention it," Kanai suggested hesitantly. "Or else the information was lost somehow—"

"No," Caine said flatly. "They kept it from me on purpose. After all, I was being trained to hate the Ryqril—why tell me anything that might make their actions understandable?"

Kanai fell silent. Hawking busied himself studying a corner of the room, and even Lathe looked uncomfortable. Turning to Silcox, Caine saw to his annoyance that even her expression had softened a bit.

And the last thing he wanted right now was sympathy from

a stranger. "You were telling us about the Ryqril and Aegis Mountain," he reminded her tartly.

Her face went back to neutral. "As I said, they're apparently trying to get in without bringing the mountain down on top of them—and from what I hear, that's not going to be an easy trick."

Lathe nodded. "It'll be loaded with doomsdays all the way down the tunnel. All right—change of subject. How was the rest of Torch supposed to contact you when and if they came back to Denver?"

She shrugged. "They'd send someone to the Shandygaff or call me at home, I guess. It's not just crime bosses that go to the bar, you know."

Lathe exchanged glances with Hawking, and it wasn't hard for Caine to read their thoughts: Silcox wasn't going to be a lot of help. "Well, I think both home and the bar are going to be off-limits to you from now on," the comsquare told her. "If you like, you can stay here—we've got other safe houses we can use." He stood up.

"Wait a second," Silcox said, scrambling to her feet as well. "That's *it*? I get you out of the Shandygaff, blow my cover there to hell and gone, and you're just going to say goodbye? The hell you are. Whatever you're involved in here, you've just hired yourself a new recruit."

"Look, I appreciate the offer, but—"

"But nothing," she said, and for the first time Caine caught a glimpse of the fire buried beneath the ashes. "Just because I'm young doesn't mean I don't know what I'm doing. I'm good with a gun, I can scrounge anything you could possibly want—probably better than Kanai here can— and even without Torch I know how to get good information from anywhere in town."

Lathe sighed and shook his head. "I'm sorry, but to be brutally honest you're as likely to get in our way as you are to help us. And we already have our own information sources, thanks."

"Maybe, maybe not," she shot back. "From what I hear you lost a couple of your outriders already."

"A couple of what?" Hawking asked as he and the others followed Lathe toward the door.

"Your informants and helpers. The people who ferried Caine out of the mountains and got you your explosives."

Caine froze in midstride. "What? Who? What are their names?"

Silcox cocked an eyebrow. "You mean you didn't know? Well, well."

"Who are they?"

She seemed taken aback by Caine's explosion. "Geoff and Raina Dupre and Karen Lindsay. Security took them in for questioning this afternoon."

A cold hand closed around Caine's stomach, and he mouthed a silent curse. He'd hoped to convince them someday that he and his team were people they could trust; instead he'd gotten them arrested. "Lathe, we've got to get them out."

"What do they know?" the comsquare asked quietly.

"About the mission? Nothing at all. But I got them into this mess, and it's my responsibility to get them out."

Lathe studied him for a long moment, shifted his gaze to Silcox. "Are they associated with Torch in any way? Or with any other resistance group?"

"The names aren't familiar," she said.

"It's nothing like that," Caine said impatiently. "They're just ordinary people that I got snarled up in this."

Slowly, Lathe shook his head. "I'm sorry, Caine, but I don't think it would be feasible. Getting into Athena at all, let alone pulling anyone out, would be a major undertaking. We simply don't have the resources or the time. I'm sorry."

Caine stared at him, unable to believe his ears. "Lathe, we're not talking about blackcollars here, or even soldiers who went into action knowing the risks. These are *civilians*—people who happened to be at the wrong place at the wrong time. We can't just abandon them."

"We have no choice," Lathe said flatly.

For a long moment the two men locked eyes. Then, blinking sudden moisture from his eyes, Caine turned away. He couldn't, in all honesty, argue with the logic, but that didn't make the decision easier to bear.

The blackcollar forces are the elite warriors of this upcoming conflict. . . . The ancient words echoed in his mind, sounding more than ever like a hollow mockery.

It was Silcox who eventually broke the silence. "Well?"

"I suppose you've made your point," Lathe said dryly. The annoyance of civilians caught in the grinder was obviously already forgotten. "All right. Temporarily, anyway, you're hired. You can still use this house as HQ; we'll drop by periodically to get whatever information you've picked up."

Her eyes were steady on him. "You won't just walk off and forget me, will you?"

Lathe shook his head. "We'll be in touch. In the meantime . . ." He shifted his eyes to Kanai. "The night's still young, and we haven't had our talk with Bernhard. Shall we go?"

Chapter 21

The sounds of the riot south of the Hub had faded out of Haven's hearing nearly an hour previously, and he finally felt safe in taking a cautious look outside his rooftop hideaway. There was, unfortunately, no direct way to know whether or not Kelly O'Hara had made it inside the Hub safely—using even tinglers this close to the Ryqril Enclave would likely be a quick form of suicide. But there might be a more indirect method available. . . .

There were no aircraft flitting around the night sky as he took a careful look outside the elevator shed. Stepping out onto the roof, he moved to the corner of the structure and raised his light-amp binoculars for a leisurely sweep of the surrounding rooftops. Nothing moved anywhere.

Still, that wasn't unexpected. O'Hara might have arrived ahead of their loose schedule and have already battened down for the night, or he might still be on his way. Easing his face around the corner, Haven focused on the Chimney, concentrating on the area by the nearest laser as he jumped the binoculars to full power.

Five of the distorted pellets were visible there, clustered tightly together beneath the laser mount: four of his own and one more courtesy of Tardy Spadafora a couple of buildings down. Over at the Chimney's next corner, he knew, Spadafora would have put three more pellets on top of the laser's electronics, too. O'Hara would also be concentrating on that weapon when and if he made it through.

Haven's stomach growled, reminding him that he'd been on short rations for nearly a week now and hadn't eaten even that much yet today. For a moment he debated whether or not to go ahead and shoot tonight's pellet over at the Chimney, as long as he was out here anyway, or whether he should go back inside and eat first. Hunger, and common sense, won out; the kind of hairbreadth marksmanship this type of shooting required could be seriously affected by rumbles from the gut. Easing back around the edge of the shed, he went back inside and behind his false wall.

Chapter 22

The night breezes whispered through the pines crowding together on the slopes, sending a faintly tangy aroma wafting through the air. Shifting his grip on his snub-nosed laser rifle, Miro Marcovich sniffed at the odors as he pushed up his infrared goggles and sent a lingering look at the stars blazing down between the shadowy trees. The night sky was never visible like this from Athena or Denver, with all that background light washing it out, and more than once tonight he'd found himself wishing he could just settle back against a tree trunk and enjoy the view. But he was on duty, and neither his loyalty-conditioning nor his pride as a Security officer would let him shirk that responsibility. Sliding the goggles back into place, he continued scanning the dimly lit forest for intruders.

Intruders that almost certainly weren't there. Prefect Galway's theory had been thoroughly hashed around by the guards hustled onto duty out here, and the general consensus was that no one in his right mind would travel eight parsecs just to assassinate an old, retired Security prefect.

Though Marcovich had to admit that if anyone *was* going to do something that crazy, Trendor was certainly the target to go for. A shiver ran down his spine as he thought about the stories of Trendor's activities in Denver at the end of the war. Most of the tales he discounted, knowing full well the characteristic growth/mutation curve for rumors. But some of those stories were tied to his own family history, and those he knew to be true to the last detail. His own presence in the Security force, in fact, was due entirely to Trendor's warped sense of values—not satisfied with merely interrogating and executing those rebels he managed to take alive, the prefect had also insisted on loyalty-conditioning all of their children. Taking from the rebels, in effect, the last thing they could call their own.

Marcovich could still remember his father's face the morning after his own conditioning had been completed—the look of horror that had grown there as Trendor explained with macabre satisfaction what had been done to his five-year-old boy. It was the last time Marcovich had seen his father before the execution, and in the years since then he'd often lain awake at night trying in vain to find a better memory of him to cling to. For a long time he'd tried to hate Trendor, even after he'd learned just how futile such a mental exercise was. On an intellectual level, he could easily list reasons for such hatred, but the emotions that could turn that logic into concrete action were simply not there. And were impossible to invoke.

And it had taken him years longer to come to grips with the fact that that impossibility—as well as the accompanying inability to hate himself for such apparent weakness—wasn't anything he should blame himself for.

Off to the side something moved among the dead leaves.

Someone trying to sneak in past him? Marcovich took a careful breath, pretending he hadn't heard the sound. All he had to do was continue on, and the invader would go safely by, and within minutes Trendor would be dead.

He spun abruptly, swinging his laser up into position as the slaved infrared floodlight fastened to a branch a dozen meters away turned with him. The squeeze of a switch on his rifle and the landscape beyond his goggles lit up like day.

In the center of the view, a squirrel poked around for nuts, oblivious of both the invisible light and the lethal weapon aimed at him.

Marcovich snorted with both released tension and amusement and shut off the flood. Almost immediately the calls began coming in on his earphone from the other perimeter guards, all of whom would have seen the sudden light. Marcovich calmed them down, and within a few minutes the watchful silence had again descended on the area. *For men who don't believe anyone's coming*, he thought wryly, *they're sure jumpy enough.*

But then, staying a bit jumpy was how one remained alive in this business.

And so Marcovich would stay jumpy, too. Drawbacks and all, life was still reasonably worth living . . . and besides, it would be a damned shame to get himself killed on such a glorious night.

Throwing one last look at the stars, he continued on his rounds.

"I trust," Lathe commented dryly, glancing around the comfortable living room, "that this place is more secure than the last one we tried talking in."

Bernhard didn't bother to smile. "It's safe enough," he said, eyes flicking briefly to Caine. "More of your team?"

"Allen Caine," Lathe introduced him. "In charge of a separate commando team, temporarily under my command." This was no time to split hairs, especially when Bernhard didn't need the details in the first place. "You have a list for me?"

"Not much of one," Bernhard said. He paused, and something unreadable briefly touched his face. "You really *have* made Security mad at you, haven't you?"

"That used to be one of the things blackcollars did best," Lathe said mildly. "Is this sudden revelation the result of something new, or are you just now catching up on the day's events?"

"If I were you I'd be less flip about it," Bernhard returned sourly. He jerked his head in Caine's direction. "Especially with civilians in tow."

Caine stirred, but at Lathe's hand signal subsided. The comsquare had rather expected Bernhard to notice the lack of a dragonhead ring on the younger man's hand, but even so the other's reaction seemed oddly vehement. "He's had full training," Lathe said. "He knows what he's doing."

"For all the good that'll do him." Bernhard exhaled loudly, and with a glance at Kanai drew an envelope from his pocket. "All right, here's your list. There are all of five names on it, none of them higher than major. Sorry, but it was the best I could do."

Lathe took the envelope and slid it inside his tunic, combat senses abruptly flaring with the realization that something here was off-key. Bernhard's movements, his voice, his attitude—even on the basis of their single Shandygaff meeting, Lathe could sense the other's tension and his effort to keep it hidden.

His tingler . . . but if Bernhard had drawn them into a trap, alerting Hawking and Skyler outside would bring down the net in double-quick time. "I don't suppose," he said, mainly to cover his own reaction, "that there's any inducement we could offer you to join our side?"

Bernhard's lip quirked, almost invisibly. But enough. "No," he said shortly. "Okay, I've handled my end of the bargain. What about yours?"

"You mean leaving Denver?" Lathe waved a hand, other hand curving into a brief hand signal that he hoped only Caine would notice: *possible danger*. "I'm sorry; but as I told you before, we have a mission here. Until it's completed we can't leave."

"And that goes for the 'civilians,' too," Caine added tartly. "Maybe you don't realize it, Bernhard, but this is actually *my* mission—Lathe and his blackcollars are only along for muscle and advice." He glowered at both Bernhard and Kanai and then turned to Lathe. "Apparently these two feel even more strongly about letting strangers into your exclusive little private club than you do—and far be it from me to butt in where I'm not wanted. Whenever you're finished talking, I'll be waiting in the car. Doing the *real* planning for our next move." Turning his back on them, he opened the door and stomped outside, closing it behind him.

"Krijing toad-face," Bernhard muttered after him. "If that's the best you could come up with, Lathe, you sure as hell aren't going to last much longer around here."

Lathe shrugged. "He's a little hotheaded, but reasonably competent," he said. With luck, Bernhard would never learn just how competent Caine really was. Now the trick would be to stall off any attack until the blackcollars outside had been alerted. "But you see now why I want to have some more people like you behind me."

Bernhard took a deep breath and looked him straight in the eye. "You're dead, Lathe. All of you are—you simply don't know it yet. Security has the edge in numbers, technology, and time, and there's just no way to fight it. We came to an agreement with them a long time ago, but I don't think there's any way at this point for you to do the same. Even if you were willing to. You're dead—and I'm not going down with you. Will you try to get that through your head?"

"If you insist." And Lathe's combat senses were starting to scream at him. "I'll be in touch," he said, moving toward the door.

Beside Bernhard, Kanai stirred. "Comsquare . . . 755-3984-581. That's my home phone number, if you need anything. It'll probably be tapped, though."

Lathe nodded, mildly surprised and instantly suspicious. But if there was betrayal in the information it wasn't visible in Kanai's eyes. "Taps are easy enough to work around. Thanks."

The attack didn't come as he hurried down the walk to where they'd parked their car. Nor did it come as he drove around the block, picking up Skyler and Hawking and Caine. As they passed block after block of normal traffic, Lathe finally was forced to admit that they'd just escaped from a nonexistent trap.

"So when are you going to tell us what that was all about?" Skyler asked casually as they headed north toward Reger's home. "Just keeping us in practice?"

Lathe shook his head slowly. "I caught something off-key from Bernhard, but apparently I misread him. I thought perhaps Security had already gotten in with an offer he couldn't turn down."

"Such as his skin for ours?" Skyler suggested. "That would be all we'd need."

"Actually, I think it's inevitable," Lathe told him. He was banking on it, in fact, though for the moment it didn't seem advisable to tell the others that. "But apparently that's still somewhere down the line."

"But you weren't wrong about Bernhard," Caine said slowly. "I felt something wrong, too."

Lathe shrugged. "Well, let's not let it worry us. For the moment, anyway, he can't touch us."

"Well?" Kanai asked quietly when the sound of Lathe's car had faded into the night.

"Well what?" Bernhard retorted, his face unreadable.

"Come on, Bernhard—we know each other too well for games like this. Something's wrong. What?"

Bernhard held out for a few more seconds, then gave in as Kanai had known he would. "I had a visitor at home this evening just before I came here," he said with a sigh. "One guess as to who."

Something cold crawled up Kanai's back. "It wouldn't have been General Quinn, by any chance?"

"You got it. Just walked right in off the street, bold as a *khassq*-class Ryq. I didn't even know he had me located— and if he's got me centered, he's got all of us. I couldn't believe it."

Kanai nodded. "He dropped in on me like that, too, wanting information on Lathe. Whatever they're up to, Security's sure worked up over it.''

"Yeah," Bernhard growled. "Well . . .''

"So what'd Quinn have to say? Aside from threatening us if we help Lathe, that is?''

Bernhard's mouth quirked. "It seems to have gotten worse since he talked to you. He's decided that our leaving Lathe alone isn't going to be good enough.''

Kanai stared, the muscles of his throat tightening. "No.''

"Yes." Bernhard nodded heavily. "No choice, Kanai. As of an hour ago we're officially on the Security payroll.''

"We can't do it," Kanai insisted stubbornly. "Bernhard, we can't betray another blackcollar team in cold blood—''

"You think *I* like it?" the other shot back. "I'm a black-collar, too, in case you've forgotten. We have no choice, dammit. Our own survival's at stake here—our survival, against bringing down a little sooner a team that's doomed anyway.''

Kanai took a deep breath. "I don't give a damn," he said between clenched teeth. "I'm not going to be a party to this. Quinn can go straight to hell—and if you do his snake work you can go with him.''

Anger flushed Bernhard's face. But the emotion quickly vanished, to be replaced by weariness. "I understand your feelings, Kanai. I wish to hell myself this wasn't necessary. But it is. You don't have to help, but I at least need you to stand out of the way.''

Kanai hesitated. To say no, to break all ties with Bernhard once and for all, to cross over and ally himself with Lathe . . . but he knew down deep it was all just wordplay. He'd fought too long at Bernhard's side, shared too much history with him and the others. "All right.'' He sighed. "I'll stay clear. I hope you realize he's not going to be an easy target.''

"I agree." Bernhard's eyes searched Kanai's face. "But his allies may not be quite as tough or slippery. Where is she?''

"Who? The Shandygaff woman?" Kanai's lip twisted in contempt. "So you're giving up already on the bull and instead going after the calf?''

"If what she did in the bar is any indication, she hardly qualifies as a calf," Bernhard replied dryly. "Would you rather some friend of the late Mr. Nash finds her?—and he had a lot of very nasty friends.''

"They don't even know where to look.''

"You know better than that. Eventually someone will get to her. And . . . well, I've seen some of the ritual executions that've been done in this town. I guarantee you don't want her to go that way."

No, Kanai didn't, and once more he found himself in a no-win situation. Honor—what did honor demand here?

But for once he couldn't even rationalize an answer to that question. Perhaps because honor had no meaning to a man who'd betrayed himself and others so often.

And was about to do so again. "She's alone in a house about a mile north of the Shandygaff," he said, giving up. "Some place Lathe set up." He supplied the address. "I suppose you'll immediately turn her over to Quinn?"

"I don't know. I'll try to get permission for us to question her ourselves first."

"But if you don't learn anything, you'll let him have her. Sure—I understand."

"Kanai—"

Silently, Kanai turned his back and walked out, suddenly feeling the need for solitude. Solitude, and cleaner air.

Chapter 23

They took her at dawn the next morning—Bernhard and two of his men, entering the house with a silence and speed that had her before she could get to her gun. Hawking, watching from a safe place, was too far away to go her aid and therefore didn't even try, which probably saved his life minutes later when the Security forces appeared to take her from the blackcollars.

"*Damn* them," Caine snarled, squeezing one of Reger's expensive handmade mugs viciously with both hands. "We shouldn't have let her stay there alone. Dammit, Lathe, why didn't you let us bring her back here, anyway?"

"Because we didn't know if we could trust her," was the comsquare's even reply. Caine glared at him—how could he take this so damned calmly? He opened his mouth to speak, but Pittman beat him to it.

"Didn't her actions at the Shandygaff prove anything?" the other youth demanded. "She risked her life to save yours."

"Not really—we could have taken Nash ourselves." Lathe shrugged slightly. "And you ought to know by now how easily something like that can be staged."

"Maybe this part's been staged, too," Alamzad suggested. "Or is that ridiculous?" he added as Pittman sent him an astonished look.

"Not out of the question, actually," Lathe said. "But I don't see this Security office as being that subtle. No, I think it was the real thing."

"So Bernhard and Kanai have gone over the line," Skyler said, almost as to himself. "You were right about Bernhard, Lathe—just a bit premature. I suppose the next question is what we do about it. If anything."

"Can't we go into Athena and get her out?" Colvin asked. "I mean, she has now pretty well proved herself, hasn't she?"

"Only in a negative way," Hawking said dryly.

"Besides, we're not in the rescuing business this time around," Caine told Colvin, throwing a baleful glare at Lathe. "Our mission's apparently the only important thing on the list, and there's nothing in the schedule for caring about Anne or anyone else."

Lathe cleared his throat as Colvin started to protest. "Actually, I think that we're going to have to make an exception on this one," the comsquare said.

Caine stared at him, unable to believe the other's reversal . . . and a nasty suspicion began to grow within him. "Oh—I see now," he said bitterly. "When it's people whose deaths are going to be on *my* conscience, it's one of those things I have to learn to live with. When it's someone on *your* conscience, we do something about it. Is that it?"

Lathe returned his gaze evenly . . . and only then did Caine notice the tightness around the comsquare's eyes. "It's nothing like that," the other grated, "and if you'll turn your glands down for a minute so you can think straight you'll understand that the cases are entirely different. The truckers aren't connected with anything subversive—us or Torch or anyone else. A simple, nondamaging interrogation will establish that, and they'll be released forthwith. Anne Silcox is something else entirely, and whatever she knows about Torch will eventually be drawn out—and it's *not* likely to be easy on her.''

"Though it doesn't sound like Security will get a hell of a lot from her," Hawking put in. "And what little she knows is five years out of date, besides."

"True," Lathe said. "But we can't take the chance some of it might still be useful." He looked at Caine. "Do you follow the argument? I don't want you thinking there's anything personal about this."

Caine consciously unclenched his jaw. "I suppose so," he said grudgingly. "So . . . how do we go about it?"

"I've got some ideas," the comsquare said, sweeping his gaze around the room at all of them. "Jensen, find Reger and get a couple of vans from him. You, Colvin, and Alamzad will get to work reinforcing the bodywork and frame, particularly the front. Hawking, did you get that supply of paral-dart antidote Reger promised us?"

Hawking nodded. "He delivered both that and the darts themselves yesterday evening. The belly-bomb will take a few more hours to put together, but I can probably have it ready by noon. The limpet mines and special *nunchaku* are already finished."

Lathe nodded. "Good. That'll be your project for the day, then."

"Belly-bomb?" Caine frowned. "What's a belly-bomb? And what were you rigging up mines and special weapons for?"

"I'll tell you later," the comsquare said briefly. "Mordecai, you'll take Caine and Braune into Denver to pick up some high-temp ablation paste to coat the vans with—Reger can tell you which businesses in town may have some stashed away. Skyler and I will meanwhile work out the details and contingencies. Pittman, you'll assist us in that."

"Me?" Pittman asked, sounding startled. "I mean—why me?"

"Because you're the one who's left," Lathe said reasonably. "Besides which, you'll be driving one of the vans and I'll need to know exactly what you can and cannot do with one of the things."

Pittman seemed to straighten in his seat. "I can do anything the van itself can take," he said with a touch of pride.

"Good." Lathe glanced around the room. "Let's get busy. I don't know if Torch gave its members any psychor training, but I doubt Anne can hold out for too many hours. If we're going to spring her, it has to be tonight.''

The detention cells and interrogation rooms took up most of the Security building's fifth floor, only a single row of offices along the northern end not devoted directly to that purpose. Galway took the elevator up from the fourth floor— the only way in or out of the level—and headed down the hallway, an odd shiver running up his back. This was possibly the most secure place in Athena, but he couldn't help recalling that the interrogation rooms in Millaire on Argent had been along a hallway very similar to this one.

And he'd nearly died while sitting in one of those rooms.

Two of the interrogation cells near the end of the hallway showed the glowlights that signaled occupation, but only one had guards posted outside. Reasonable enough—most everyone else had agreed hours ago that the two trucker women were totally harmless. The sole reason anyone was still questioning them was that Quinn had ordered it done. Galway grimaced in mild disgust, but at the moment he had far more urgent things on his mind than Quinn's treatment of innocent civilians. ''The general inside?'' he asked the guards as they saluted him.

''Yes, sir,'' one of them said. ''He probably won't be there much longer, though—the interrogators don't like outside people present while they're working. Distracts the prisoner sometimes.''

Galway tried to imagine Quinn being thrown out of his own interrogation room by underlings, but the picture was as unlikely as it was satisfying. ''Tell him I want to see him *immediately* when he's finished,'' he instructed them. ''I'll be at the guard lounge down the hall.''

''Yes, sir.''

From the sounds filtering down the hallway, Quinn emerged from the interrrogation room about three minutes later, but it was nearly ten before he condescended to wander down to where Galway was waiting. ''You wanted to see me?'' he asked, not bothering to sit down.

Galway nodded. ''First of all, how's the interrogation going?'' he asked.

Quinn's face darkened a bit. ''Slowly. She's got a high degree of tolerance—some sort of mental conditioning, they think. But it's only a matter of time. I trust you aren't bothering me just to ask *that*.''

"Not at all," Galway said. Pulling the phone across the table, he drew a cassette from his tunic and slid it into the reader. "I came to warn you that your time with her is in danger of being cut short."

"What the hell are you talking about?" Quinn growled.

"This is a phone coversation I had fifteen minutes ago." Galway tapped the switch, and his own voice abruptly came over the speaker.

Galway: "Galway here. What is it, Postern?"

Postern: "Look, I've only got a few minutes—this is the first chance I've had to get to a phone without any of the others around. Lathe and the other blackcollars are planning to—"

Galway: "Speaking of Lathe, why didn't you tell me before you left Plinry that he was coming along?"

Postern: "Because I didn't *know* about it, that's why. Will you shut up and listen? Lathe's planning to break that Torch woman, Anne Silcox, out of there tonight."

Groping blindly with one hand, Quinn pulled a chair over and sat down next to Galway, face contorted with an expression that might have been either anger or intense concentration. Probably a combination of both.

Galway: "That's ridiculous. Athena's far too well guarded for them to even get into the city, let alone into the Security building."

Postern: "Maybe. But Lathe's going to try it—and if I were you, I wouldn't be too sure he can't pull it off. I only know a little of his plan, but I can tell you *he* sure as hell is confident he can do it."

Galway: "All right, settle down. What exactly do you know?"

Postern: "Only that he's preparing a couple of vans with laser protection and armor reinforcing and he's been talking to me about how to do high-speed sideways crabbing moves without turning them over. I think he's planning to just ram the fence at a guard station and hope that the lasers are programmed not to fire when they're in danger of wiping out a Security post as well as an intruder."

"He's wrong on that one," Quinn muttered, half to himself. "Any vehicle trying to ram the gate . . ."

Galway: "Even if that gets him into Athena—"

Postern: "Look, Galway, don't argue with *me*—it's not *my* plan. If you want to assume he can't do it, fine—sit back and watch."

Galway: "All right, just relax. Can you tell me where you're staying?"

Postern: "Ah—not really. I rode there in a closed van, and I'm not really sure of the location or address. Besides, you raid the place and *I'm* likely to get killed, too."

Galway: "Take it easy—we're not *that* stupid, you know. Can you tell me anything about the route Lathe plans to take to Athena?"

Postern: "Not really, but I know the final approach to the fence will be along New Hampden Avenue. Look, I've got to go."

Galway: "First tell me what numbers we're talking about. How many blackcollars does Lathe have with him?"

Postern: "I've only seen four: Skyler, Mordecai, Hawking, and Jensen. But hell, he could have a whole combat force lurking around somewhere for all I know."

Galway: "Yeah, well, I doubt that—he only had a pair of drop pods to work with. You said two vans?"

Postern: "Right—one's red and brown, the other's dark yellow. And for God's sake take it easy if you try anything—I'll be driving one of the damn things."

Galway: "Don't worry, we'll be trying to take all of you alive. One last thing—any idea yet of what your actual mission is?"

Postern: "Caine's been hinting that it involves getting into Aegis Mountain, but I don't know whether to believe him. Jensen's just come out of the store—I gotta go."

The tape ended. Quinn drew a long breath, all his earlier annoyance gone. "Damn," he said, very softly. "Damn. Well . . . did you do an analysis on it?"

Galway nodded. "A quick one—the lab's running it more thoroughly now. He was calling from a booth in northwestern Denver. I opted not to send men there, and it's probably a good thing I didn't. Jensen would've spotted them for sure, and I don't think taking him alone would've been worth losing Postern's ear into the rest of the group."

Quinn shrugged in agreement or acceptance; Galway wasn't sure which. "Stress analysis?"

"He's worried and nervous—that much is obvious even without the analysis. He also lied about not knowing where they were holed up. Aside from that, everything else seems to be true.''

"Or at least he *thinks* it is." Quinn frowned at the phone. "Ridiculous. Completely ridiculous. Lathe can't *possibly* get in here."

"He got out of the Rialto Street trap," Galway reminded him softly, aware of the thin line he was treading. If he pushed Quinn too hard, the general might very well get his back up and refuse to take action just to spite him, and they'd be forced to find out the hard way just what Lathe had in mind. "I presume you've read my reports of the Plinry and Argent actions, too—"

"All right, you don't need to hammer it to death," Quinn snapped. "Besides, if we let them crash the fence and get vaporized we'll never find out what the hell they think they're going to find in Aegis Mountain—if Postern wasn't lying about that too. Unless you think the Ryqril would rather just let them commit suicide?"

"As a matter of fact," Galway said, ignoring the other's sarcastic tone, "the Ryqril have already sent authorization for us to try and capture them. I think they must have a tap into your communications systems."

Quinn glowered; and despite his dislike for the man Galway felt a twinge of sympathy for him. Security work was difficult enough without the alien overlords continually watching over your shoulder. "Well, good," the general growled. "At last they're giving up on this stupid Postern game. I'll get some units in position along New Hampden right away, set up a pincer and see if the idiots can hang on to them this time. Come on—you might as well be there, too. Just in case we need a quick identification."

And in case you need someone else there to share the blame? Galway wondered as they headed back down the hallway toward the elevators. But it didn't really matter. This time the element of surprise would be on Security's side . . . and *this* time Lathe was going to lose.

Guaranteed.

"Well?" Lathe asked Skyler as the latter entered the room and closed the door quietly behind him.

"He's got one, all right," the other said. "A beautiful high-power laser that we can tie a modulator into and that'll punch a bell-clear signal all the way out to the scout ship. Assuming it's still at one of its specified positions, of course."

"It will be," Lathe assured him. "Great—that means we won't have to find the one that Security'll have tied into their Athena headquarters. One less item to worry about. I presume we won't have any trouble getting to the laser?"

"Depends entirely on how big a mess you're willing to leave of Reger's men," Skyler told him. "Considering that the man's still our ally, I'm not sure we really want to antagonize him at this point."

"In other words, you think I should ask permission to use his laser," Lathe said dryly. "I suppose you're right. But it'll probably cost us."

"Why? Reger's not using the laser himself—oh. Right. If Security manages to track the pulses he risks losing it entirely to them."

"Not certain, but possible enough to make him queasy. Well, I'll go talk to him. I think I know how to swing the deal."

"And you don't want to talk about it, of course."

"Not right now. Bug stompers all over this house, but you know how I am."

"Don't I ever." Skyler hesitated. "Lathe . . . if we *can* use his laser, one of the major reasons for this Athena thing is suddenly gone. You sure you really want to go through with it? There are a hell of a lot of ways it can go wrong, you know, and I'm not sure the potential gain is worth it anymore."

"If you mean Anne Silcox, you're right," the comsquare agreed. "But there's no way we're going to convince Bernhard to help us find a way into Aegis without a lever of some kind, and this is our best chance to get that lever."

"And if he really *can't* get us in?"

Lathe shrugged. "Then we've lost it. Pure and simple. But I've got a very strong hunch that he can."

"I hope you're right. About that and everything else." Skyler scowled, an unusual expression for him. "What with us skating along here and Haven and Greene running that damn fool Project Christmas back on Plinry, I've got just about my fill of marginal operations at the moment."

Lathe smiled. "Come on, Skyler. Have I ever let you down?"

"No—and that's what's worrying me. So far you've won everything but the damn war itself. Eventually, you're going to have to lose one."

"Who says? Come on—I'll buy you a drink from Reger's private cellar. That'll cheer you up. And then you can go talk to Caine's team chock full of confidence while I brace Reger about his laser."

Chapter 24

The sun was low in the western sky as the two vans headed out from Reger's fortress home, driving north along the deceptively peaceful road to the eastward highway before turning south toward the heart of Denver proper. Seated on the floor in the back of the lead vehicle, Caine found himself fingering his *nunchaku* and slingshot restlessly, trying without any real success to project a confidence he didn't feel. It was a wasted effort: Colvin and Alamzad, seated across from him, were far too nervous themselves to pay any attention, while Mordecai, presumably privy to more of the details of Lathe's plan than Caine had been, didn't seem to need any reassurance. Though maybe that was just Mordecai.

Licking his lips for the half-millionth time, Caine slid off his flexarmor gloves and rubbed at his eyes. "Goggles down," Mordecai said quietly over his shoulder from the front seat. "And gloves back on. This is a combat zone."

"Right." Caine obeyed, wondering how the hell blackcollars developed such good back-of-the-head eyesight.

Behind the wheel, Pittman shifted in his seat. "This should be New Hampdon coming up now," he told the blackcollar sitting beside him. "Do I turn onto it, or pull over and wait for the others?"

"Turn," Mordecai said. "There's at least a klick to go before we reach the fence—plenty of time for Lathe to close the gap."

"Okay." The van curved smoothly around the corner, and Caine craned his neck to get a look ahead through the windshield. There were few things more unnerving, he'd long ago decided, than heading into danger without even being able to see what was coming.

Across the van, Alamzad cleared his throat. "Assuming we get through the fence without bringing the lasers down on us, do we have any actual idea where Security will have Silcox hidden?"

"Security building, of course," Mordecai said briefly. "Don't worry—it should be easy to find."

"Right—it's the one that'll have all the troops around it shooting at us," Colvin put in.

"And a rooftop landing pad," Mordecai told him. "There'll only be a couple of buildings like that, even in Athena—"

He broke off as their tinglers came on: *Security spotters to either side; break off operation.*

Mordecai swore gently under his breath. "Take the next right, Pittman," he ordered. "We'll circle around north and regroup with the other—"

And abruptly, the van's windows blazed with light.

The vehicle slammed to a halt, tumbling Caine and the other two up against the seats. For a single, horrible heartbeat Caine thought they'd taken a direct antiaircraft laser bolt, but even as he scrambled into a crouch his senses caught up enough to realize that the metal walls weren't melting around them and that the air inside the van was hot but not scalding. "What—?"

"Laser shots at the engine and tires," Mordecai snapped back. The blackcollar was already out of his restraints and grappling with an apparently heat-warped door. "Everyone out—we'll have a better chance outside."

Caine launched himself toward the van's rear doors, hitting the release lever and shoving them open in the same motion. He leaped out, hands coming up with a ready pair of *shuriken* . . . and froze in disbelief.

Facing the van from both sides of the street, half hidden behind a quick-foam barricade, were at least fifty Security men, lasers pointed and ready. Lathe's van had skidded to a crabbing halt a few meters behind theirs; beyond it Caine could see another barrier blocking movement in that direction. Reflexively, he hurled his *shuriken* anyway, but the taste of defeat was already welling up like vomit in his mouth. The game was over, and from the size and preparation of the force arrayed against them, it was obvious they'd been primed and ready.

Reger had betrayed them.

"You can't escape," an amplified voice boomed from somewhere, its point of origin lost among the echoes from the surrounding buildings. "This is General Quinn, Lathe. Raise your hands and surrender—all of you—or we'll burn you where you stand. Look up if you don't believe we can do it."

Caine risked a glance upward. Hovering perhaps a hundred

meters above them was a long, shark-shaped aircraft, reflected grav light showing the weapons pods on either side of its fuselage. The firepower that had taken out their vans . . . and could just as thoroughly take them out as well.

Tactics, strategies, contingencies—all his training seemed to swirl together into a useless, half-gelled mess. Behind him, he could sense Colvin and Alamzad crouching just inside the van's doors, waiting for a lead they could follow. Waiting for him to take action.

And he couldn't. There was nothing he could think of to do that wouldn't mean their instant death.

His first command . . . and he'd failed.

From around the van a quiet voice broke into his anguish. "Do as the man says, Caine," Mordecai said. "But don't give up hope."

Swallowing hard, Caine slowly lifted his hands over his head.

The man in charge of the operation was, at least, no fool. Neither the men at the barricades nor the fighter overhead made the slightest move until all ten of their prisoners were out in the open. Only then did a new group of Security men step forward, several of them lugging pairs of heavy-duty mag-lock forearm shackles. A lump rose in Caine's throat at the sight of the shackles . . . a lump of déjà vu and the painful realization that this time, at least, history would not be repeating itself.

And then the group came close enough for faces to be distinguished . . . and the mag-lock shackles were suddenly forgotten. "Galway!" Caine gasped.

"Caine." The perfect nodded gravely. His eyes swept the group, found Lathe; but it was another man who brushed by him and faced the comsquare.

"Comsquare Lathe, I'm General Quinn," the other said in a grimly satisfied voice. "You're hereby informed that the agreement between General Lepkowski and the Ryqril is no longer in force, at least insofar as you and your men here are concerned. You are in open rebellion against the Ryqril Empire and its authorized government, and are therefore subject to imprisonment and appropriate punishment for your actions—"

"Spare us the official speech, General," Lathe cut him off. His voice was calm enough, but Caine sensed a hint of steel beneath it.

Apparently the general did, too, and for a moment his

triumphant expression slipped a bit. But he recovered quickly. "I see that bravado remains part of a blackcollar's arsenal." He sneered. "I suggest you don't bother trying to impress me with your stoicism. From now on, *I'm* the one who decides your fate, and I've always found a particular satisfaction in breaking people who pretend they can't be broken."

"No," Mordecai said quietly. "You're wrong."

All eyes turned to the small blackcollar. "Wrong about what?" Quinn demanded.

"That you decide our fate," Mordecai told him calmly . . . but there was something about his face that sent a shiver down Caine's back. "You have only the power we grant you. I choose not to give you any at all."

Quinn inhaled sharply, perhaps suddenly understanding what was coming. "Guards!" he snapped.

But too late. Mordecai's right hand was a blur as it swung upward at his face beneath the goggles. Caine caught a faint flicker of light on metal . . . and even as the Security men belatedly surged forward Mordecai collapsed in a heap on the ground.

"Medic team!" Quinn shouted back toward the barricades. "The rest of you—get those shackles on them. This might be a trick."

Caine tensed, watching Lathe out of the corner of his eye for the signal that would mean taking action. But no signal had come by the time the massive shackles had been fastened around his forearms. Lathe, in fact, seemed almost in shock by what Mordecai had done . . . and slowly Caine came to the dark realization that this wasn't a ruse after all.

"Well?" Quinn snorted impatiently as the medic crouched by Mordecai's still form, instruments humming softly.

"Paralyte shock," the other said, drawing out a hypo and tugging at the mag-lock shackles enclosing Mordecai's arms. "Get these off him, someone—I have to give him a shot."

"No chance he's faking?" Galway put in as one of the Security men moved to obey.

"None at all. Yes, all the way off. Thanks." Pulling off the blackcollar's right glove, the medic jabbed his wrist with the hypo. "We've got to get him to the hospital immediately, General—I've got him stabilized, but that won't last long. He's taken an overdose of a paralyte drug, like getting shot repeatedly by a paral-dart pistol."

"So counteract it," Quinn growled. "We've got antidote—"

"But there's no way to tell out here which specific drug

he's taken," the medic interrupted him. "All the antidotes are poison unless the corresponding paralyte is already in the system. Injecting the wrong antidote would kill him almost instantly."

Quinn grimaced, but nodded curtly. "All right, get the ambulance here, then. I'm damned if I'm going to let him get away from me." He turned to the others. "The rest of you move over toward that barrier while we wait for the transport."

"Just a minute," Pittman said hesitantly, stepping over toward the group around Mordecai. The Security men let him pass—

And it was only then that Caine realized with a shock that the other's arms hadn't been shackled. "Pittman?" he asked. "What—?"

"I'm sorry, Caine," Pittman said, his voice low, his eyes avoiding contact. "Galway, Mordecai's carrying a cassette you'll want to have."

"Pittman!" Colvin gasped. "You lousy, *stinking* traitor. Why in the name of hell—?"

"Because I had no choice!" Pittman snapped tautly over his shoulder as he knelt down beside Mordecai's still form. "None at all. If you damn me, damn the Ryqril, too—they're the ones who did this to me." His hand reached under the civilian shirt hiding Mordecai's flexarmor, emerged with a small cassette.

"Yeah, I'll damn the Ryqril, all right," Colvin snarled, taking a step forward before the Security men at his side stopped him. "But whatever money they offered you that you couldn't resist—"

"*Shut up!*" Pittman yelled, jumping to his feet and spinning around. The hand gripping the cassette arched over his shoulder to throw—

Galway stepped in front of him, deftly plucking the cassette away. "Settle down, Pittman," he said, and even through his own haze of agonized disbelief Caine could hear something like regret in the prefect's voice. "It's over now. It's all over."

"Only for now," Lathe said softly. His voice was almost calm . . . but there was death in his eyes. "Only for now. But there'll be another reckoning, Pittman. I swear it."

Overhead, a shadow caught Caine's eye: the flying ambulance had arrived. It settled to the pavement next to Mordecai as the paramed inside flung open the rear doors and rolled a stretcher out to the waiting Security men. "You three—get in there with him," Quinn instructed a knot of guards as Mordecai was lifted inside.

"But then there won't be room for me," the medic protested.

"You've already said there's nothing you can do for him out here, haven't you?" the general retorted. "So ride in front. You'll be there in five minutes anyway."

The medic grimaced, but apparently knew better than to argue. He got in beside the pilot as the Security men and parameds squeezed in with Mordecai and closed the rear doors. The ambulance lifted into the night sky, and Quinn turned his attention back to the rest of them. "I trust none of you will be foolish enough to try anything so unnecessarily melodramatic," he said, almost conversationally.

"Don't worry," Lathe told him, still in that same soft voice. "None of us is going to die until we've taken care of you."

"I'm sure," Quinn said. "Lieutenant, call in the transports. And instruct the interrogation department to prepare for fresh subjects."

Numbly, Caine let himself be led over to the barricade. Pittman a traitor, Mordecai near death . . . and Lathe captured. What would come next he didn't know, but it almost didn't even matter.

For Caine, the universe had already been shattered beyond repair.

Chapter 25

It was a curious sensation, Mordecai thought, to be helpless.

Curious, and thoroughly unpleasant. Every small motion of the ambulance made him feel in danger of sliding off the stretcher, even though he knew they'd strapped him securely in place. Overhead, the dome light had been dimmed, for which he was thankful: with his eyes paralyzed open the glare could have quickly become painful. It would have been nice to be able to see the city below, but his head was pointed straight up and all his peripheral vision could pick up was reflections of the ambulance's own interior from the side windows.

About all he could do was listen. And he did.

"Easy as breezy, wasn't it?" one of the Security guards remarked from beside him. "I guess blackcollars aren't so tough to handle when you know they're coming."

"All guerrilla forces are like that," another responded. "They're long on nerve and short on numbers, and once you get them pinned down they fold."

"Yeah, well, I wouldn't get too confident if I was you," the paramed put in. "I helped treat some of the guys that came in after the Rialto Street fiasco—"

"Watch your mouth," the first Security man growled.

"A fiasco's a fiasco," the paramed insisted. "And these same blackcollars did a complete medical run-through on them."

"Yeah, but they could *move* then," someone said, and Mordecai sensed dimly that he'd been poked hard in the chest. "This one's not—"

"Hey, what's that?" the third Security man interrupted. An arm reached over Mordecai's face to his chest, reappeared with a small, flat disk. "Didn't you guys search him?"

" 'Course we did—got all his stuff right back there in that bag. How the hell did we miss something so—"

And with a *crack!* of released gas pressure, the belly-bomb disintegrated into a cloud of flying needles.

Exquisite pain jabbed into Mordecai's cheeks, and he tensed, dimly aware that for the first time since injecting himself with paralyte he *could* tense. A tingling sensation flooded his system, as, around him, the startled oaths and shouts of the others came to an abrupt halt. Muscles trembling slightly, he fumbled at the straps holding him down and managed to release the clasps. Taking a deep breath, he sat up and looked around him.

His four companions sat slumped in their seats, faces contorted in death into surprise or horror, depending, Mordecai supposed, on whether or not they'd realized in time what had been done to them. For his own part, he could sympathize most with the outrage clearly visible on the face of one of the Security men. Paralyte antidotes had been deliberately designed to be lethal so as to prevent potential targets from doping themselves up with antidote before being shot; it was unlikely the creators of that policy had ever realized how it could be used against them.

The trembling in his muscles was fading now, as was the stinging in his cheeks. Reaching to the lighting control board, he killed the lights in the compartment and looked out the windows, trying to get his bearings. They were over Athena now, clearly, and his inner ear told him they were starting to descend as well. Only a couple of minutes left. Pressing against the window, he searched quickly for the rooftop landing pads that would mark the hospital and—with luck— the Security building.

There . . . there . . . and there. Three of them. One was directly ahead, almost certainly the hospital, and he quickly scanned the other two buildings for clues as to which would be Security. The plainer ten-story one, he decided; the taller and fancier one would probably be the central government building. A tempting target for one of his limpet mines, per- haps even for some more serious attention if they happened to wind up with a little extra time. Fixing the locations of both in his mind, he turned in the darkness to the dead Security man nearest his height and build and began to strip off his uniform.

The ambulance cushioned to a landing on the hospital roof, and almost before it was down the medic was out and running toward the rear. Mordecai had the doors open by the time he arrived and was industriously grappling with the back end of the stretcher. ''Get the other end,'' he snapped to the medic. The other got a foot up into the compartment—

And folded over as Mordecai jabbed him in the belly.

The blackcollar gave him a surreptitious push to aid his momentum into the compartment, his attention on the four orderlies who'd abruptly burst from the observation corridor alongside the landing pad, shoving a gurney ahead of them as they hurried toward the ambulance. Easy to take out; but someone else might be watching the proceedings from else- where along that corridor, and he couldn't afford to trigger the alarm too soon. Fleetingly, he wished Lathe had opted to take this part of the plan himself—the comsquare was so much better at this kind of deception.

''Hurry up!'' he called to the orderlies, tugging the stretcher half out of the ambulance. ''We're going to need more help right away.''

''What the *hell*?'' one of them gasped, peering inside at the unmoving bodies. ''We were told only *one* casualty—''

''You were told wrong,'' Mordecai snapped. ''Come *on*— get moving.''

Three of them raced back into the corridor for more gurneys. The other helped load the stretcher—and the blanket-swathed Security man Mordecai had loaded onto it—onto the gurney and headed inside with it. The medic was starting to recover from the stomach jab; with everyone else temporarily out of eyeshot, Mordecai took the opportunity to lean into the ambulance and knock him out more thoroughly. He'd just completed that task when the pilot finally finished his shutdown procedure and strode back to see what was going on.

"What the hell?" he gasped, staring at the view inside.

"He had a doomsday gas bomb," Mordecai growled. "I was the only one who got to the oxygen in time."

The man hissed between his teeth and took a quick step back from the open door. "Damn," he muttered. "What kind of gas—*hey*! You're—"

Taking a long step toward him, Mordecai slammed a reverse roundhouse kick to the side of the pilot's head. The man went down without a sound. Mordecai was starting to scoop up the unconscious form when the corridor door behind him banged open. "Hey, you!" a voice shouted. "What was that—?"

Most people, Mordecai had learned long ago, didn't expect to be attacked while they were still talking, and he was on the three orderlies before they knew what was happening. Five punches later they were sprawled on the rooftop with the pilot.

Carefully, he scanned the windows in the corridor for any witnesses. No faces showed that he could see. Jogging forward to the cockpit, he opened the door and peered inside at the control panel. It was, fortunately, just like the one he and Lathe had looked at briefly the day before. With another quick glance at the corridor windows, he slid into the cockpit and gingerly took the controls.

He brought the gravs to life first, making sure they were set in neutral mode. Flipping on the autopilot, he keyed in a high-speed course due east. The gravs glowed brighter and the ambulance began to lift, and as he hopped out he reached in to flick off the aircraft's running lights before slamming the door closed. A dark mass barely visible behind the gravs' violet glow, it headed off across the city.

Slipping through the doorway into the still-deserted corridor, he looked about for the elevator. Somewhere on the street down there, he'd have to find a car to steal.

*   *   *

The transport was just making its approach to the Security building when word came through of the runaway ambulance.

"What do you mean, stolen?" Galway growled. "How could it have been stolen?"

"I don't know, sir." The transport's copilot shook his head. "But the hospital says they didn't send it out, and it isn't answering its radio. Wait a moment—there's more coming through. . . . They've found the pilot unconscious on the hospital landing pad, General."

Beside Galway, Quinn swore bitterly. "Damn that stupid medic. Is the ambulance still within range of the Green Mountain lasers, lieutenant?"

"No, sir, it's well outside the Athena perimeter now, heading east across Denver."

"What did you mean about the medic?" Galway frowned.

"Isn't it obvious?" Quinn snorted. "He must have gotten a telemetry reading from the hospital and found out what antidote to give Mordecai. And then given it."

"Galway?" Pittman called from across the cockpit aisle. "What's going on?"

The prefect turned to look at him. "It looks like Mordecai's managed to make a break for it," he told the youth. "He's stolen his ambulance and is heading to somewhere in Denver."

Pittman's eyes widened, and for a moment his lips moved wordlessly. "Oh, no," he breathed at last. "Oh, hell. Galway—General Quinn—you've got to protect me. You've *got* to. I've earned that much, damn it—"

"Protect you from what?" Quinn cut in. "Mordecai's to ground and gone by now—he sure as hell isn't coming back *here*."

"Maybe," Pittman said, eyes darting around as the transport set down on the rooftop pad. "But maybe not. He may just have gone for reinforcements."

"What reinforcements?" Quinn scoffed. But his eyes had narrowed. "Some remnant of Torch? Or someone else?"

Pittman shook his head. "I don't know who . . . but Lathe was pretty damn pleased they'd come over to our side. Those are his own words."

Quinn glanced at Galway, cocked an eyebrow. "You know these delwort toads, Galway," he said. "What sort of group would they be likely to link up with?"

"Hey, can we deal with the important things first?" Pittman put in before Galway could speak. "Like my safety? I want to be someplace where Mordecai can't get to me if he comes back in. I mean it, Galway—and you people owe me.''

Quinn sniffed in obvious contempt. "Your blackcollar training doesn't seem to have supplied you with much in the way of a backbone, does it?''

"Maybe I've seen Mordecai in action more often than you have,'' Pittman shot back. "Is there anywhere in the cell-block that would be safe?''

"We could lock you into solitary,'' Quinn suggested, shifting his gaze outside. The transport's side door was disgorging prisoners and guards now, and the general watched closely as the line disappeared through the armored door into the building. Galway held his breath, but no one made any trouble.

"No—no cell.'' Pittman shook his head. "At least not a locked one. I want to be able to get out if there's any trouble.''

"Well, then, just what the hell *do* you—''

"What about the emergency bunker, General?'' Galway cut in. "It's three levels underground, Pittman, with only one entrance, and it's designed to withstand a concerted enemy attack.''

"Wait a minute, Galway,'' Quinn growled, unfastening his restraints and stepping to the cockpit door. "That bunker isn't a hotel, you know.''

"How far away from the others is this bunker, Galway?'' Pittman asked.

"Shut up, Postern,'' Quinn snapped. "I've got orders to work with you, but I don't have to like you—and to be honest, traitors like you make me want to vomit. So I'll tell you this just once: you give me even half a reason to do so and I'll let Lathe weld your mouth shut. You can't stay in the bunker, but there's a lounge off the situation room you can cower in if you want.''

Pittman bristled. "I don't especially care for you, either, Quinn, if it comes to that. But there's a lot more I can tell you about Lathe and his men—stuff I'm pretty sure you and the Ryqril would like to know. I can't tell it to you if I'm dead. So if you want to explain to the damn cockroaches how you let Mordecai get to me—''

"All right—all *right*,'' Quinn said with an exasperated snort. "Anything to get rid of you. Galway, take him down to the lounge and tuck him in. If you can spare a moment later, we'll be processing the prisoners.'' Without waiting for an answer he opened the cockpit door and jumped out.

"Understood," Galway muttered after him, jaw tightening at the sarcasm. Pittman's paranoia wasn't *his* fault, after all. "Come on, Pittman, move it."

"How hard is it to get off the detention level, anyway?" the youth asked as they stepped out onto the roof. "I'm not just being fussy, Galway—I've *seen* these guys in action."

"They'll be on the fifth level; you'll be two levels underground," the prefect growled, starting to get fed up with Pittman himself. "There's a single elevator off the fifth level, which opens out only onto the fourth floor. The elevators off the fourth floor are then half the building away, and the entire level is guard barracks. Give Quinn a little credit for sense, okay? There really isn't any way they can get out without getting killed."

"Okay," Pittman murmured, and with that finally subsided.

They made the rest of the trip in silence, a quiet that, oddly enough, matched the building as a whole. Even during the night shift Galway had never seen the place quite as deserted as this, and he found it a bit unnerving until he realized that virtually all the troops at Quinn's disposal were either up with the prisoners or still out in Denver clearing up the aftermath of that operation.

The lounge was empty when they arrived, the handful of men who might be there clearly occupied elsewhere. "There's a luncheon pantry over here, and drinks in the cooler here," Galway said, pointing them out. "No beds, but the couch over there will do if you get tired enough. The situation room is through that door. Stay out of it if you don't want Quinn to yell at you again."

"I understand." Pittman took a deep breath, let it out. "I expect you've got some important torturing to attend to, so I suppose you'd better go."

"You're welcome," Galway said dryly. Turning, he stepped through the door and headed back toward the elevator.

Chapter 26

The unmarked van pulled to a halt by the Security building and a half-dozen men climbed out, laughing and chattering as they shouldered their laser rifles and walked up the steps to the glasstic-enclosed foyer. Seated across the street in his parked car, Mordecai watched closely through the windows as they passed the duty officer at his desk and lined up in front of a reinforced door at the reception room's back wall. Each did something to a small upright console; the machine's response each time was to open the door. Within a minute all six men had vanished through it, leaving the desk man alone.

Leaning back against the seat cushions, Mordecai considered. An ID check, presumably. Not completely unreasonable, even in such a supposedly secure place as Athena, but it was going to complicate things. He had an ID, of course—the dead Security man from whom he'd obtained the uniform had kept his in a breast pocket clearly designed for the purpose—and if all the machine cared about was the card itself, Mordecai was home free. If the program was also checking the bearer's fingerprints and retinal patterns . . .

Mordecai pursed his lips, searching his memory. No, that was probably unlikely—and if the thing was really being that thorough, it was doing so damn quickly. Odds were good that it was only checking the cards, and that would be easy enough to handle.

Presumably. He'd find out for sure in a minute.

The duty officer glanced up as he entered, nodded briefly, and returned his attention to his display. Mordecai nodded in return and strode briskly past him toward the rear door. Chances were good that Security men from both day and night shifts had been called up for this operation, and if the blackcollar behaved as if he belonged here anyone he met would probably assume the unfamiliar face simply belonged to someone on another crew.

Assuming, of course, that they hadn't paid close attention to the photos Galway had surely circulated.

The console by the door was indeed as simple as he'd hoped, apparently nothing more than a scan screen and a reset button. But there was always the potential for surprises. Palming a *shuriken* in his free hand, he pressed his stolen ID against the screen and held his breath.

There was a quiet beep, and the door ahead opened—and as he started through he noticed a display that hadn't been visible from the car outside. Three columns of names filled the screen, their positions shifting subtly as one more was added.

Which meant he'd been worried about nothing. Safe, fat, and sassy here in the middle of Athena, the Security bigtops evidently hadn't even considered the possibility of unauthorized entry. All they cared about was knowing who was on duty and available in the building and who wasn't.

Smiling tightly, Mordecai stepped through the door. So much for both enemy preparedness and blackcollar overcaution.

Beyond the door, a handful of people moved briskly along on unknown errands. Glancing once at his watch, Mordecai joined them, matching their businesslike air as best he could.

The situation room was considerably larger than Pittman had expected it to be, and for a long minute he just stood in the lounge doorway and gazed around at it. Four men were currently on duty, splitting their attention between a large overview screen of Denver, a bank of screens that looked to be from mobile units, a long panel that evidently handled voice-only communications from the field, and a second bank of screens that showed nothing but hallways and small rooms.

Hallways, small rooms, and a fair number of Security uniforms.

"You got the general's permission to be here?" one of the Security men said as Pittman moved toward the latter bank of displays.

Pittman nodded toward the screens. "That the detention level?" he asked.

"Yeah," the other said briefly, getting up and walking over to him. "Let's see your authorization."

"I don't have any, but Galway said I could wait in the lounge next door," Pittman said, his attention still on the displays. "You keeping a good eye on those guys?"

The Security man snorted. "Oh—right. You're Postern, aren't you? The informer."

Pittman's jaw tightened momentarily. He was getting tired

of the contempt that always seemed to accompany that identification. "Yes," he acknowledged shortly. "You haven't
answered my question."

One of the other officers snickered, swiveling his chair
lazily toward Pittman. "Worried they'll come down and pay
you a visit, are you? Maybe you should go back to the lounge
and hide under the couch."

Pittman sent a cold look in his direction, then turned back
to the original speaker. "Well?"

The Security man sighed. "Look, kid, there's really nothing to worry about. Your friends are harmless—they've been
searched, they're surrounded by guards, and in a few minutes
they'll all be locked away. I don't care how good blackcollars
are, they can't be very dangerous inside little steel cubes."

"Hey!" one of the others called from the first display
bank. "They've remote-forced the ambulance down—no one
in it."

"Oh, hell," one of the others murmured. "Quinn's not
going to like this one."

"Get Marsala and Abrams tied in," Pittman's challenger
instructed, striding over to the display bank and frowning at
one of the screens. "We'll want a fast diagnostic telemetry
set up, see if the thing's been on autopilot since leaving or
whether someone could have bailed out en route."

"Oh, come on," a third man put in, joining the others.
"We've had it under surveillance practically the whole time."

The discussion continued, and for the moment Pittman was
forgotten. Giving the detention display bank one final scan,
he returned to the lounge, closing the door behind him. As it
had been since he first arrived, the room was deserted; crossing it, he slipped out the far door and headed down a hallway
toward the elevator.

Already the building was beginning to fill up as more and
more Security troops filtered in from the aftermath of the
capture. Pittman shared the elevator with three men in combat
garb who were apparently on their way upstairs after checking
their heavy weapons into the building's armory. All three
gave Pittman a quick once-over, and though they remained
silent he could sense that they knew who he was. Gritting his
teeth, he got off at ground level, letting them continue to the
fourth-floor barracks on their own.

Six heavily armed men were waiting by the elevators, laser
rifles slung over their shoulders, obviously headed for the
armory. Pittman gave them a wide berth, eying the rifles

longingly, and began looking around for the building's front entrance. It turned out to be only a single turn and a dozen meters ahead, and was as secure-looking as he had expected. A small display set into the wall beside the door showed the view from the duty officer's desk; a single Security man was briefly visible as he passed the desk and headed for the door. No one else was in sight; all seemed perfectly quiet.

For a moment Pittman paused, wondering if he ought to head out into the lobby for a moment and talk to the desk officer. But everything appeared to be adequately under control out there. Which meant it was now time for the *real* test: to find out just how secure Quinn's fifth-floor cells really were. Turning, he headed back toward the elevators.

Elevators, and the lobbies where people gathered to wait for them, had a unique sound profile about them, and it was child's play to recognize that the place he sought was just down the hall from the entrance door. Senses alert, Mordecai headed off in the proper direction . . . but he'd barely taken five steps when he realized that the clothing of the man walking away ahead of him was familiar. The clothing, as well as the posture and the walk.

Pittman.

The blackcollar's lip twitched in a grim smile as he slowed his pace to avoid overtaking. Pittman didn't turn around, but continued around the next corner without pausing. A group of armed Security men were waiting for the elevator there, and for a moment Mordecai considered jumping them and getting himself a little extra firepower. But prudence won out, and instead he took up a casual position against the wall near the corner, staying well back from the others. Hanging his head in a posture of thought that would both discourage idle conversation and mask his features a bit, he waited.

Two of the elevators arrived almost simultaneously. "Going up?" Pittman called into the one nearest him. "I need to get to four."

"It's headed *down*, stupid—read the arrow," one of the armed Security men growled at him before anyone inside could reply. Shouldering past Pittman, he and the other four stepped into the car. The door closed; muttering something under his breath, Pittman stepped into the other elevator. Mordecai waited until it, too, was on its way before moving forward and punching the up button. He didn't know exactly

where Pittman was headed, but odds were that it was somewhere he wanted to be, too.

Another elevator arrived within the minute, and he stepped
inside with the two Security men already there. The fourth-
level button had been pushed; stepping to a back corner, the
blackcollar rubbed his lip thoughtfully and began the quiet
psychological preparation for combat.

The door opened. He let the others leave first, then stepped
out himself and looked around . . . and realized with a shock
that he'd walked into a massive trap.

Combat reflexes flared; but even as his hand twitched
toward his concealed *nunchaku* his brain caught up with that
first impression and he noticed that the dozen gray-green
uniforms weren't converging on him—were not, in fact, even
paying any attention to him. Carefully, he let his hand drop
back to his side and gave the bustling Security men another,
closer, look. Casual conversations, body language that spoke
of unconcern.

Level four was a Security barracks.

Great. Just great. Well, it could have been worse. Licking
his lips briefly, the blackcollar tried to look inconspicuous as
he looked around for Pittman. The other wasn't hard to find,
striding down the hall to Mordecai's right as if he owned the
place. The blackcollar set off after him, again making sure not
to get too close.

The hall was a long one, and at its end was a desk with a
Security duty officer and—surprisingly—a single elevator.
The implications were clear enough . . . and with almost a
sense of relief Mordecai realized the difficult part was over
and the fighting was about to begin. The only way to get to
Lathe and the others would be via that elevator—and the ID
machine he could see on the duty officer's desk was sure as
hell not going to be simply taking roll call.

He picked up his pace, and was within earshot when
Pittman reached the desk. "I want to go up and see General
Quinn," the younger man announced to the duty officer. "Do
I just get in the elevator there, or do you need to check me
through first?"

"Neither," the Security man said tartly. "Only authorized
personnel are allowed on the detention level, and you're not
one of them."

"That's ridiculous," Pittman said. "Galway said I could
come up here if I wanted to—"

"Galway's not in charge here, Postern—and if I were you,

I wouldn't keep using his name to try and slide your way into
places where you're not wanted.''

"Now *look*, you—''

Quietly, Mordecai slipped past the argument and gave the
elevator door a quick once-over. Armored, certainly, and
with no visible controls. Probably operated from the duty
desk after IDs and authorizations had been properly checked.
The blackcollar turned back, scanning the desk for anything
that looked like a panel; saw a touch plate by the officer's
right knee—

"Hey!'' the desk man half turned to glare at Mordecai.
"What the hell do you think you're doing? Get back here and
check through—''

And abruptly recognition flared in his eyes. "My *God*—''
he gasped.

Mordecai lifted his eyes a fraction, caught Pittman's.

And the younger man leaned over the desk to jab stiffened
fingers into the Security man's throat.

With a strangled choke the officer slumped in his seat.
Glancing over Pittman's shoulder, Mordecai stepped to the
stunned man's side. "ID,'' he said quietly to Pittman. "Upper left pocket.''

"Any reaction?'' Pittman asked as his fingers dug into the
pocket and emerged with the card.

"Not yet,'' Mordecai said, still watching over the other's
shoulder. But that wouldn't last long, he knew. At the moment Pittman's body was hiding the duty officer from view of
the milling Security men farther down the hall, but that would
change as soon as they made for the elevator. "This is the
only way to the cells?''

Pittman nodded. He had the ID pressed against the reader
screen now and was trying to maneuver the officer's hand
onto the fingerprint plate. "The only monitor station I know
of is down in the situation room, and it's not getting that
much attention.''

Mordecai grunted. The officer, his wind starting to come
back, was attempting to struggle. The blackcollar took a
moment to punch him at the base of the skull and he went
limp again. "We'll be taking out the cameras right away,
anyway. You have your battle-hood and gloves?''

Pittman grimaced. "No—I couldn't come up with a good
enough reason to keep them. They may be up where the
others' gear is stored, though, in a room just down the hall

from the elevator. I saw some of the stuff being put away on the monitors when I was downstairs.''

"Any real firepower up there, or just paral-dart guns?''

"All I saw the guards carrying was the latter, but that room looked like it doubled as a small armory. Sorry, but I couldn't find a quiet way into the big one downstairs.''

"We wouldn't have wanted a laser in the elevator, anyway—elevators and stairwells have the nasty habit of carrying resonance detonators for the purpose of destroying captured weapons. Okay—ready?''

"Ready.''

Pittman pushed the READ button, holding the officer's hand steady on the plate. Simultaneously, Mordecai heaved the man straight up out of his chair, turning the head to face the retina scanner. Bracing the limp body against his chest, he pried open the eyelids with thumb and forefinger and held his breath.

There was a beep, and something that sounded like a relay clicking. "Elevator,'' Mordecai murmured, dropping the officer back into his chair and reaching for the touch plate under the desktop. Behind him, the doors slid open; a moment later they closed again with both men aboard.

"How long?'' Pittman asked. There was a slight quaver in his voice—the first Mordecai had heard since this whole thing started.

"Till they catch on?'' The blackcollar shrugged, digging out his spare *shuriken* pouch and pressing it into the youth's hand. "Not very. That's why your first job upstairs will be to disable the elevator. Quietly, if possible—I'd like a few minutes to get the lay of the land before I hit the place.''

"I'll try.''

The doors opened, and Mordecai strode out, eyes darting everywhere. The long hallway dead-ended at the elevator, he saw, a duty desk like the one downstairs positioned a few meters in front of it. A potentially good spot to defend the elevator from, once the officer seated there was eliminated. Ahead, several doors opened out into the hallway, one of them with the heavy look of armor reinforcement. Beside it was another guard station; and with a rush of adrenaline-fueled recklessness, the blackcollar passed the duty desk and stepped boldly up to the Security man at the armory. "You got the blackcollar equipment inside?'' he asked gruffly.

"Yeah,'' the other said, looking up.

"Get it all out, fast,'' Mordecai growled, half turning to

peer down the hall. "We've got a report that some of the *nunchaku* are loaded with explosives—the general wants 'em out of there before they blow and take the whole armory out."

"Krij it—weren't the damn things bomb-sniffed?" the other muttered, reaching under his desk. But even as he lowered his eyes, his brain caught up with him and his expression twitched . . . and when his hand came back into sight it was holding a paral-dart pistol. "All right, you—"

Spinning a hundred and eighty degrees, Mordecai bent at the waist and snapped his right foot out in a back kick toward the other's head. The pistol went off with the *crack* of compressed air, the needles washing over Mordecai's back and legs. He spun back around, hand poised to grab the gun if necessary, but between the kick and the ricochets from Mordecai's flexarmor, the officer was down for the duration.

And down the hall, the alarms began blaring.

"Damn," Mordecai muttered as he leaped over the desk. From the elevator end of the hall there was a shout, and he glanced over to see the duty officer collapse over his desk, a *shuriken* protruding from his temple. Ignoring the sounds starting to come from the other end of the hall, Mordecai snatched his battle-hood and gloves from his tunic and got them on, studying the controls for the armory door as he did so. It looked like the same system as they'd found downstairs at the elevator, with a proper ID check all that was required for access.

At least until someone downstairs sealed the door by remote control.

A splatter of needles bounced off his goggles and battle-hood, and he looked up to see four Security men racing like kamikazes directly toward him. "Cameras!" he snapped.

"Already taken out," Pittman shouted from behind him.

"Good," Mordecai called back. "Get over here when it's clear." A new wave of needles washed over him, and with a convulsive leap, the blackcollar cleared the desk and landed in front of his attackers, *nunchaku* lashing out.

Three more seconds and the men were scattered broken around him. Someone down the hall stepped imprudently into view and started shooting. Mordecai sent him crashing to the floor with a spinning *shuriken* as Pittman slid to cover at the desk behind him. "I've got the elevator locked up here," the youth reported, breathing a bit heavily. "I got both cameras I could see pointed this direction."

"Good." Mordecai jerked his head toward the armory door. "Same trick as downstairs—get busy. I'll try to keep the collies away from you while I spring the others."

"Right. Good luck."

"You too." *Nunchaku* and *shuriken* at the ready, Mordecai sprinted down the hallway.

Chapter 27

Hatred, Lathe and the others had continually warned their trainees, was a subtle poison that did the hater more harm than it did his victim. Caine knew that, agreed with the philosophy behind it . . . and yet, when it came down to the wire, he found all the logic in the universe didn't do him a damn bit of good.

He hated General Quinn. Hated the man with a passion. And more than that, felt good about hating him.

It wasn't just the fact that the general had beaten them—wasn't even the fact that he'd beaten them so decisively. Instead, it was the increasingly apparent fact that the bastard was determined to gloat over his victory.

Somehow, Caine had always expected to be treated with some measure of respect when he finally lost to the enemy. Quinn, obviously, was determined not to give him even that much.

Was in fact even going out of his way to twist the knife. Seated across the conference room from Caine and three of the blackcollars, an uncomfortable-looking Galway beside him, he turned his monologue once again to the subject he'd already talked to death: Pittman and his treachery.

"He wasn't just recently suborned, you know," the general said, crossing his legs casually as he sent his gaze around at the four prisoners facing him. "He's been your double agent for, what, six months now, Galway?"

Galway shrugged. "Something like that," he said. Unlike Quinn, the prefect didn't seem to be getting any special pleasure out of this.

"He's been very useful, too," Quinn said, "and not only

regarding this mission. We'll be able to take that snake school of yours apart as soon as we debrief him fully and get a squad of commandos out to Plinry.''

Caine bit down hard on his tongue, knowing full well that that was the kind of reaction Quinn was looking for but not giving a damn. The cameras in the room would be recording all their expressions and body language for later analysis, and he knew he should be sitting as passively as Lathe, Skyler, and Jensen beside him. But he couldn't. He'd trained with Pittman, had worked side by side with him, had risked his life with him . . . and the realization that he'd been so wrong about the other's character was more than he could bear.

"Of course," Quinn went on offhandedly, "the Ryqril might consider leaving your people alone for a while if we knew what your mission here was—keep their paperwork and records clean, you know. It had to do with Aegis Mountain, didn't it?"

"Why don't you go to hell?" Lathe suggested conversationally. "You're just wasting our time here, Quinn, and you know it. We're not giving anything away free, and your chances of getting it without our cooperation range from slim to zero."

Quinn snorted. "And you're of course sticking to your ridiculous offer of information for the release of your teammates? Don't make me laugh, Lathe."

The comsquare shrugged. "Suit yourself. So, Galway: enjoying your visit to the homeworld?"

The prefect remained silent, and Caine shifted his eyes from the two seated officials to the knot of three Security guards lounging four meters away by the room's door. Standing there with no special alertness—no lasers or other heavy weaponry, their paral-dart pistols still in their holsters—it was a breakout begging to happen. And Caine could almost cry with frustration . . . because as vulnerable as the guards looked, they might as well have been in an armored bunker a klick away. Seated naked on bolted-down chairs, hands cuffed behind their backs and ankles hobbled by twenty centimeters of chain, he and the blackcollars were about as helpless as Caine could imagine being. About the only other thing Quinn could have done would have been to chain them bodily to their chairs, and it was slowly becoming apparent that the general's failure to do that was, along with the sloppy guard arrangement, a deliberate touch designed to tantalize his prisoners.

Caine didn't know about the others, but for him the gambit certainly worked. And it made him hate the bastard even more.

Lost in his own thoughts, he was startled when Galway abruptly got to his feet. "If you'll excuse me, General," the prefect said, "I'd like to get back to the situation room, see if there's any word on Mordecai."

"Sit down, Galway," Quinn said coldly. "You've spent a lot of your time here foam-mouthing about how these blackcollars of yours were unstoppable and unbreakable. Well, you were wrong about the first, and you're damn well going to watch while I prove you wrong about the second, too."

Skyler stirred, his ankle hobbles clinking as he did so. "You make friends wherever you go, don't you, Quinn?" he said dryly. "You know, I'll bet that if I walked over there and started beating your head in, half your subordinates would line up outside that door to buy tickets to the show."

Quinn glowered at him. "Perhaps we ought to experiment—but with *you* as the subject. What do you think of th—"

The last word was cut off by the abrupt blaring of alarm horns outside in the hallway. "What the hell?" Quinn snarled, turning to look at the door. "Sergeant, find out what's going on out there."

"Yes, sir." One of the guards reached for the door—

It happened so quickly that if Caine's eyes hadn't already turned back to the blackcollars he would have missed it completely. Without warning, Skyler suddenly dropped out of his chair onto his back, knees tucked tightly against his chest. Almost before he'd even hit the floor, Jensen was also in motion, throwing himself full-length onto the big blackcollar as if attacking him. He landed with his belly on Skyler's feet—

And with a convulsive shove, Skyler kicked the other over his head to crash into the knot of guards.

The Security men didn't have a chance. Bound hand and foot and without any balance to speak of, Jensen still tore into them like a tiger into sheep. His head, knees, and feet became blurs as he knocked the guards to the floor, jabbing them to death with short but vicious blows even as they struggled impotently to escape.

A motion to his right caught Caine's eye, and he turned to see Lathe similarly sprawled over Quinn and Galway, holding them down as Skyler rolled over to assist him. Breaking his paralysis, Caine got to his feet and hopped over to where

Jensen was levering himself to a kneeling position. "Check their pockets for the key to these things," the blackcollar instructed, already searching one of the limp forms himself. Swallowing, shame at his own inaction hot on his cheeks, Caine obeyed.

"Got it," Skyler announced. "Right where you'd expect— didn't trust anyone but yourself with the key, did you, General?"

"Damn—you," Quinn managed, the sound muffled by his own arm pinned across his mouth. "You'll never get off this floor alive."

"Really? I've heard that song before." Releasing his restraints, Skyler freed Lathe and then tossed the keys across to Caine.

"What's going on?" Caine asked, twisting around to pick up the keys and setting to work on Jensen's wrist cuffs. An uncomfortable suspicion was starting to set in. "Is that Mordecai running amok out there?"

"Mordecai and Pittman both," Lathe told him, fastening his former restraints securely around Quinn. "At least—"

"*Pittman?*" Caine gasped. Across the room Galway inhaled sharply. "But Quinn said—"

"Oh, come on, Caine," Skyler chided mildly as he fastened Galway's ankles to one of the chairs. "You know better than to take a collie's word for anything, don't you? How's it look out there, Jensen?"

Jensen had opened the door a crack and was peering out cautiously. "All the activity's around the corner down there, near the elevator. If we hurry, we ought to be able to surprise the collies with a rear-action sortie." Squatting down, he started to strip the uniform from one of the guards.

"Good," Lathe nodded. "Just make sure Mordecai doesn't get you in the process." He turned back to Quinn. "You'll forgive us if we take leave of your hospitality," he said, reaching down to draw the general's paral-dart pistol from its holster. "Pleasant dreams, and better luck next time."

"You won't get out of here alive," Quinn spat, his face contorted with fury . . . and then the burst of needles caught him in the chest and he slumped in his chair.

"Lathe," Galway said as the comsquare turned to him. "If you're not lying—if Pittman's really on your side—"

"I know," Lathe said. "One way or another, it'll all be over soon."

Galway hissed between clenched teeth, his expression a

mirror of emotions too convoluted for Caine to unravel. Then Lathe's pistol cracked and the prefect joined Quinn in helplessness.

A minute later the former prisoners were outside in the hall. "Let's get at them," Lathe said briskly, "and hope Mordecai got the armory open before they sealed it from downstairs. We'll need what's inside some of the *nunchaku* if we're going to get out of here."

Caine took a deep breath. "Whatever you've got in mind, I hate it already."

The comsquare almost smiled. "As it happens, Caine, the hard part is actually over. Help me make sure all the cameras and microphones are disabled and I'll tell you all about it."

"Well?" Major Eberly O'Dae demanded.

The man at the monitor bank shrugged helplessly. "I'm sorry, Major, but without vision and audio there's no way to tell for sure what's happening up there. All I can say is that there's no more running going on anymore—people are still walking around, but no one's running."

O'Dae cursed under his breath. So the fighting was over—or else had gone to a stalemate siege—and there was no way to tell which side was on top. Though it unfortunately wasn't too hard to make a good guess.

And General Quinn was square in the middle of it.

"You're sure they got into the armory?" he asked, wishing an instant later that he'd kept his mouth shut. It was at least the third time he'd asked that same question, and the others were bound to notice that.

There was a general shuffling of feet around the situation room, and the man at the monitors threw him an odd look before answering. "Yes, sir, quite certain. They haven't been fired yet, but the power-pack readings show several of the laser rifles have definitely been moved from the armory to other parts of the floor."

"The fact the lasers haven't been fired probably means the blackcollars are in control," someone murmured from the side.

"I'd figured that out, thank you," O'Dae growled. *When you don't need a senior officer,* he thought bitterly, *they're always right there on top of you.* Colonel Poirot was supposed to be on his way, but until he got here O'Dae was in charge of this mess, and he knew full well he was out of his depth.

"Major! Got something now," the man at the monitor announced abruptly. "Laser fire . . . about fifteen meters down the hall from—ah-ha." He looked up. "They're trying to burn through the wall by the main elevator bank, the ones that bypass five."

O'Dae felt a flood of relief. "Oh, they are, are they?" he said, and someone else snickered. The steel protecting those elevator shafts was specially reinforced against just this trick; the prisoners could fire all night and most of the next day without breaking through.

Which meant that O'Dae was off the hook. However long it took Poirot to get here, he could now afford to simply sit back and wait until then. The blackcollars weren't going anywhere—

"Major!"

O'Dae turned and looked over the crowd to the man at the audio comm panel. "Yes, what is it?"

"Explosion outside the Central Municipal Building, sir— the night guards there say the door's been blown."

"What?" O'Dae shoved through the others to the panel, stomach churning with fresh tension. The Central Muni held a lot of records, more than a few of them top-classified. Not to mention several pieces of equipment that were well-nigh irreplaceable. "Anyone trying to get in?"

"Not yet—at least they don't think so," the other said, shaking his head. "But they want some backup, fast."

"No kidding. Captain! Get a double squad over there, on the slider."

"Yes, sir." The officer left the situation room at a dead run.

O'Dae took a ragged breath, but he'd barely let it out before the man beside him swore. "Damn it. Major—another blast, this one near the spotter hangar."

O'Dae stared, hardly believing it. "What the hell—that was *near* the hangar, Corporal? Not *in*?"

"Report says near, sir. But it could be just a diversion."

The major grimaced as that thought penetrated the tension surrounding his mind and then split, amoeba-style, into two equally nasty possibilities. A diversion as prelude to an attack on Athena's air power? Or a diversion designed to empty the Security building itself of troops? It could be either . . . and the real hell of it was that it didn't matter. He *had* to send reinforcements to those other buildings, just in case. Which meant he could likely have a skeleton crew available here if the blackcollars tired of their attack on the elevators and tried to simply fight their way out.

And there was only one way he could think of to prevent that. If the blackcollars were indeed relying on allies skulking around Athena to set up their escape for them, the last thing he could afford was to allow them control of the timetable. "Lieutenant Baker, what's the situation with the elevator to five?" he called to the man at the detention monitors.

"Uh . . . we've got the override set up, Major," the other reported. "The blackcollars can't use it to get down."

"I was thinking more of our using it to get *up*," O'Dae growled. "Are the spotters up and in place?"

"One hovering in view of each side of the building. They can't see much, though—they're keeping their distance."

Cowards. Still, as long as they prevented anyone from sliding out a window on a rope, it didn't much matter how far back they were. "Still no response from the gas flood system, I take it?"

"No, sir. I think they must have disabled it at the same time they took out the cameras."

O'Dae grimaced. He'd been holding out hope that someone had just left a switch turned off in the control room or something. And without the floor's remote defenses to rely on, there was only one way to preempt any escape attempt. "Order the commando squad to get ready," he told the other. "I'll lead the first wave in myself."

The man's lip twitched, but he nodded. "Yes, sir. Do you want the medics along with them?"

"No—stretcher teams will be called up when a given area's clear, but the medics themselves will wait in the infirmary. We're going to have a lot of casualties to take care of, and I don't want to risk any of the medics too close to the fighting."

"Yes, sir." The other paused, listening. "All right, Major; the squad's ready anytime. Armed, armored, and they've been shown pictures of all the blackcollars up there. Including Mordecai and Pittman."

"Good." O'Dae sure as hell didn't want one or more of the blackcollars donning Security uniforms and walking blithely out through the front door. "We'll attack as soon as I get up there."

The elevator slowed, came to a stop. "Get ready," O'Dae murmured, his voice sounding oddly hollow as it echoed inside his armored faceplate. The door slid open, and he threw himself out of the car to land in kneeling position three meters down the hallway, laser rifle raised and ready.

Anticlimax. No laser beams lanced out, no one hurled any of those damned throwing stars at them, no one even looked out of any of the rooms or cross corridors to see what was happening. In fact, if it hadn't been for the bodies scattered down the hallway, it would have been easy to believe nothing at all had happened here.

The motionless, unnaturally twisted bodies. O'Dae looked once, then turned his eyes quickly away, stomach churning inside him. "O'Dae to monitor," he called into his mike. "Laser fire still going on down by the elevator shaft?"

"Negative, sir," the reply came in his ear. "Lasers have stopped firing and have been moved . . . looks like to the southeastern corner of the floor."

The safe room, of course. O'Dae's lip twisted into a grim smile. Yes, the blackcollars would have the brains to hole up there when their timetable was disrupted—nowhere else on five could hold out against laser fire for long.

Which meant O'Dae's hunch had been correct—they *were* expecting to be rescued. "Double the guard on the building's entrances," he ordered into his mike. "An assault could come at any time."

"Yes, sir. Is it clear enough to send litter teams up there?"

O'Dae scanned the hall once more. "Yeah, go ahead and send the first team up—second commando wave can follow them."

"Acknowledged."

Though at the moment it was still an open question as to whether or not the casualties were beyond the medics' help. "Harison, Peters—check this group for survivors," O'Dae ordered, gesturing around them. "Tag anyone who's alive for the stretchers. The rest of you'll come with me down the hall and make sure they haven't left a rear guard to ambush us."

Carefully, he set off, his men flanking him. The first two rooms they checked were empty, the third had two bodies lying in it . . . and the fourth had a survivor.

He was just getting gingerly to his knees, hands cradling his head, as they entered. "Who—? Oh, God, you're here," he said hoarsely.

O'Dae stepped forward and caught the man's arm as he started to weave again, helped him into a sitting position. "How do you feel?" he asked, eyes darting briefly to the sloppily tied bandage covering the back and side of the other's head and the blood that was still dribbling out from beneath it.

"Lousy," the other groaned. "Dizzy. I got the bleeding stopped . . . must have fainted again. Can I sit down?"

O'Dae started to tell him he *was* sitting, thought better of it. "Why don't you lie down instead?" he suggested. "The stretchers'll be here in a minute to take you downstairs."

"Okay," the other sighed. Already he was beginning to fade again. Beside him lay the medkit he'd apparently managed to get down from the wall; bunching up another of the kit's bandages, O'Dae made a pillow for the other's head and laid him down on it. Almost as an afterthought, he took a moment to study the other's face. Young, smooth, almost feminine—a fresh recruit, probably, or else someone whose family could buy more Idunine than they either needed or deserved. . . .

Resolutely, O'Dae turned his eyes away. Whoever he was, he definitely wasn't one of the blackcollars. "What are you all standing around here for?" he snapped at the rest of the squad grouped around him. "Let's get back to business."

They stepped back into the hall and continued on their cautious way. Behind them, barely audible through their armor, came a noise, and O'Dae turned around as a stretcher team emerged from the elevator and moved to the first of the crumpled bodies. "One in here, too," he called to them, pointing toward the room he'd just left. Their officer waved in acknowledgment, and O'Dae turned away with an odd feeling of relief. Hunting escaped prisoners could be highly unpleasant duty, especially if there was shooting to be done, but he would take it over stretcher carrying any day of the month. At least with prisoner hunting it was the enemy who usually got hurt, not his fellow Security men.

And some of the enemy *were* going to be hurt tonight. O'Dae was going to make damn sure of that.

Gripping his laser tighter, he hurried to catch up with his men as, behind him, the second wave of commandos arrived.

Chapter 28

Galway's head had fallen forward in such a way that the door was out of his sight, and his first clue that the rescuers were at hand was the tingle of a needle in his arm as paraldrug antidote was injected. "We'll have you out of here in a minute, sir," someone murmured in his ear. "Please be as quiet as possible—we think the blackcollars are holed up in the safe room across the hall, and we don't want them to know we're here until we're ready to blow them out of there."

"Ungh," Galway grunted in acknowledgment. Making noise wasn't likely to be a problem for at least a few more minutes; his tongue still felt like a long-dead animal.

Quinn was apparently made of sterner stuff. "Damn them all," the general ground out hoarsely. "Damn them—damn that Pittman, especially. Who's that—Major O'Dae? What's the situation, Major?"

"Not too bad, sir—I think they've outsmarted themselves." The major whispered a quick summary of events both inside and outside the Security building. Galway listened with half an ear, most of his attention on getting his muscles going again after nearly a half hour of paralysis. Still, if the major was reading things correctly, the situation did indeed seem to be under control at the moment.

A circumstance that struck him as suspiciously odd.

". . . we've taken fifteen injured men downstairs to the infirmary already—mostly head wounds, I gather, from what I could see of the bloodstains. Haven't had a report from down there lately, but most of the casualties apparently had good heartbeats, so my guess is they're doing all right—"

"Yes, fine," Quinn broke in, swearing under his breath as he gingerly massaged his calf muscles. "Never mind the wounded for now. You're sure the blackcollars are in the safe room?"

"We've been over the entire floor, General," O'Dae assured him. "There's nowhere else they could be."

"Could they have disguised themselves as Security men and gone down with your litter teams?" Galway asked, forcing the words out past his still-wooden tongue.

"No, sir," O'Dae said, sounding both confident and a little indignant. "No one but the injured have left the floor—we've made damn sure of that."

"Then perhaps—"

"And they *were* injured, all of them," O'Dae added, "unless you're suggesting the blackcollars cracked their own skulls for blood to dab themselves with."

"You *did* have medics up here making sure it was real blood, then?" Galway persisted, something in him unwilling to let go of it.

"I'm sure they did," Quinn cut in before O'Dae could reply. "Where the hell would they get fake blood from, anyway? Give my people a *little* credit, Galway—they're not stupid. All right. Major—how do you intend to blast the bastards out?"

"Uh . . . I've got two heavy laser cannon coming up from the emergency bunker, sir," O'Dae said, sounding suddenly doubtful. "Sir . . . we didn't actually have medics on the scene here—we just loaded the wounded on stretchers and took them down to the infirmary. Maybe we'd better check and make sure—"

"Make sure about what?" Quinn snarled. "That they weren't blackcollars in disguise? You *said* you looked at all their faces, didn't you?"

"Well . . . yes, sir. But if they could somehow have smuggled in fake blood . . . couldn't they have had disguise kits, too?"

"Oh, hell," Galway muttered as an unpleasant tremor twisted his gut. "General . . . the whole setup for our ambush came from Pittman."

"Hell!" Quinn barked suddenly into the hush. "Bloody, krijing *hell*! Major—guard team to the infirmary. *Now*. And alert the exit guards to watch for a break."

"Sir—?"

"*Do* it, damn you," Quinn snarled. "Don't you see? They set this capture up *themselves*."

O'Dae gulped and spoke urgently into his mike, a look of incomprehension on his face.

He was too late. By the time the guard team reached the infirmary all they found was a handful of wounded Security

men and unconscious medics . . . and from the exit the
guards were ominously silent, as well.

The general alarm came through on the Security van's
radio five minutes into their mad drive toward the fence and
freedom. "Great," Caine muttered.

"They had to catch on eventually," Lathe said from behind the wheel. "Frankly, I didn't think we'd get even this
much of a head start. I guess the limpet mines Mordecai
planted rattled them more than we expected."

Caine looked at him, wincing in spite of himself at the
comsquare's horrible "head wound" and the "blood" coat-
ing his face. "I suppose I should be grateful that you told at
least *some* of us about this one," he gritted, putting as much
sarcasm into the words as he could. "It's an improvement
over Argent, anyway."

Lathe sighed, rubbing ineffectively at the makeup on his
face. "I'm sorry, but it had to be done this way."

"Why? Because I couldn't be trusted to react properly
when Pittman betrayed us? What about the rest of you? *You*
ought to have been as angry as I was."

"Perhaps. But since Pittman was your teammate, you and
the others would naturally have been expected to react the
most strongly. You, particularly, were the one Galway was
watching closest—I don't know whether you noticed that."
The comsquare shrugged fractionally. "Besides which, Pittman
had to be able to say in complete honesty that you didn't
suspect him when he made his phone calls. They were almost
certainly analyzing his voiceprint patterns, and any lies would
have been picked up on immediately."

Caine turned away and glowered out the windshield. Once
more Lathe had played fast and loose with both the game and
his own allies . . . and once more the fact that logic was on
his side didn't help a damn.

Lathe turned a corner, and a few blocks ahead Caine saw
the fence at Athena's perimeter. "I hope you have some way
to get through the Security troops they're bound to have at the
gate up there," he said tartly. "It'd be a shame to waste a
perfectly good double agent getting into a place you can't get
out of."

"I've got a plan," Lathe said evenly.

"One that takes the lasers up on Green Mountain into
account?"

"If you'll notice," Skyler's voice came from the crowded

compartment behind him, "we've been taking a route that gives us minimum exposure to those lasers."

"Which probably wasn't necessary," Lathe added. "I doubt the lasers can be set to shoot at ground targets inside the fence—too much danger of misfires or enemy mischief. But there was no point in taking chances."

"What about when we hit the fence proper?" Anne Silcox asked, a noticeable tremor in her voice. "We're not going to try and bluff our way past the guards, are we?"

"Not with the word already out," Lathe assured her. "Actually, I'm rather hoping the lasers *will* react to an attempt to ram the fence from the inside."

Caine took a deep breath against the butterflies beginning to congregate in his stomach. "I trust you're bearing in mind that Anne is still wearing all our flexarmor."

"Against *those* lasers?" Jensen grunted from the van's rear. "That bandage over her hair will protect her about as much as the flexarmor will. Lathe—we've got company coming. One of the spotters is swinging around in this direction."

"Has he got us fingered?"

"I don't think so, no. He's turning pretty casually, as if he's just coming in for a closer look. But if we don't want him to spot the grand exit, we'd better get out fast."

"Right. Next corner—everyone get ready to climb out."

The next corner turned out to be a short two blocks from the fence and what could now be seen to be a heavily guarded gate. Skyler herded the others into the relative concealment of an arched doorway in the cross street while Lathe and Hawking worked together at the driver's side of the van. A moment later they were finished, and as the two blackcollars jumped clear the vehicle lurched forward and sped off toward the gate.

"Make yourselves invisible," Lathe murmured as the two blackcollars joined the others under the arch. "And cross your fingers."

"It's veering off line," Colvin pointed out tensely as the vehicle vanished from sight beyond the buildings across the street from their shelter. "It was starting to shift toward the other lane."

"A little of that'll be all right," Hawking assured him. "As long as it hits the fence somewh—yowp! There goes the spotter."

It was, Caine thought, the understatement of the evening.

The aircraft screamed past them at streetlight level, chasing after the empty van like a mad Valkyrie.

"Everyone across the street—up against the building over there," Lathe snapped.

They'd barely reached the other side when there was a crash of metal on metal from around the corner as the van plowed into the fence—

And without warning the entire landscape lit up like the inside of a sun and there was a thunderous explosion.

Followed immediately by darkness and unearthly silence. Cautiously, Lathe took a look around the corner. "Come on, everyone," he said, and disappeared around the building at a dead run.

Ahead, the scene by the fence was stomach-churning impressive. Torn metal lay scattered everywhere, some of the pieces barely recognizable as being from the van or the spotter, others too distorted for even that much identification. At least five meters of the fence were gone or crumpled; the concrete around the crash site—what of it was visible—was blackened and blistered. Of the guards that had been standing at the gate there was no sign at all.

"What *happened*?" gasped Anne Silcox, running beside Caine.

"Looks like Lathe was right," he told her. "The van must have triggered the defense lasers when it rammed the fence. I guess the spotter was too close and got caught in the blast—either that or the laser got it directly."

"My God." She shook her head, as if not believing it.

"I'm sure Torch has done things equally messy," Lathe commented from her other side. Caine looked across at him, struck by the intensity in his voice. "It's part of any war, guerrilla or otherwise . . . and if you're really determined to be a part of it, you'd better get used to this sort of thing."

She glanced at him, then turned silently away. Caine caught Lathe's eye, nodded at the fence. "You have some special magic to keep the lasers from frying *us*?"

"Shouldn't need any magic," the comsquare said. "I doubt the things are set for antipersonnel applications. Too wasteful, not to mention dangerous—all the more so now with all the sensors in the area having been fried. The only real question is whether or not we'll make it to the cars waiting in the next block before Quinn recovers enough to send out more troops."

Apparently Quinn was indeed adequately shocked; or per-

haps he believed the escapees had perished in the blast.
Whatever the reason, the cars were well away from Athena
and driving sedately north before fresh spotters belatedly
appeared in the night sky.

Chapter 29

The spotters were still buzzing around the city—mostly far
to the south of their quarry—when Lathe pulled the car into
an alley and shut off the lights. "What're we doing here?"
Caine asked, his stomach tensing again. He'd had enough
surprises for one night.

"I need to make a quick phone call," the comsquare
replied as the second and third cars pulled up behind them.
"Ms. Silcox, I'd like you to accompany me. Pittman, come
up here and get behind the wheel, just in case a fast exit is
required. Caine, you stay with him; I'll have the rest of them
spread out in loose shield formation."

"It might help if we knew exactly what kind of trouble you
were expecting to run into here," Caine told the comsquare in
a low voice as the others began clearing out of the van.

"No trouble anticipated," Lathe assured him. "Just a pre-
cautionary measure. Really."

"Right," Caine muttered under his breath. He and Silcox
got out as Pittman went around and climbed into the vacated
driver's seat. Caine listened as the footsteps faded into the
night . . . and for the first time since their capture he was
alone with Pittman.

For a long moment neither man moved or spoke. Then
Pittman took a deep breath. "Whatever you're going to say to
me, I wish you'd go ahead and get it over with."

"All right," Caine said. His eyes flicked over the younger
man's face, noting the tension lines there—lines he'd never
really paid attention to before. "You've been playing this
game for quite a while, I understand. Why?"

"You mean how did the Ryqril force me to—?"

"No, I mean why did you go to Lathe instead of simply
playing along with them?"

Pittman turned to face him, a vaguely bewildered look on his face. "What the hell else was I supposed to do? Betray all of you for real?"

"Why not? Whatever they had on you must have been a real sun-cruncher for them to trust you so fully." Caine frowned, a sudden thought striking him. "Unless they thought they'd gotten you loyalty-conditioned?"

Pittman snorted. "Galway's not stupid enough to try something *that* obvious. It takes fifteen days to condition someone that thoroughly, and if they'd tried keeping me out of circulation that long they might just as well have phoned Lathe and announced their intentions."

Caine nodded. He knew all that, of course, but for a moment he'd dared to hope Pittman might have stumbled on a way to break the Ryqril's loyalty-conditioning technique. "Then back to question one: why didn't you simply play on Galway's side?"

Pittman dropped his eyes, turned back to face the windshield. "Because I couldn't," he said simply. "You're my friends; my comrades-in-arms, if you want to get sentimental about it. I couldn't betray you, no matter what it cost."

He swallowed, and Caine saw his jaw muscles tighten momentarily. "What *is* it going to cost?" he asked quietly.

"With luck . . . nothing. At least, that's what Lathe's promised me."

"And you trust him to come through?"

Pittman turned back to face Caine, a wry smile on his lips. "Why not? *You* do."

Caine snorted. "That's hardly an apt comparison. I never get to choose whether to trust him or not."

"Sure you do. You don't have to put up with all of his high-handed finagling—not really. You could go to him right now, tell him he's pulled one too many fast ones at your expense and that you're taking off. But you're not going to, and we both know it. Why not?"

"Because he's the best tactician I've ever known, I suppose," Caine said, almost grudgingly. "Because—hell, *I* don't know why."

"In other words, because you trust him to get the job done right, with the least hazard to your own skin . . . and you're smart enough to prefer getting bruises on your pride to watching your teammates die around you."

Pittman broke off abruptly. Caine studied his face for a

long moment, then snorted. "Yeah, I guess you're right. We both trust him . . . and we both hate it."

Pittman shrugged fractionally. "It beats getting killed with dignity. I guess. The hell with it." He nodded toward the alley mouth. "Who do you suppose he's calling? Quinn?"

"I sure hope not. This town's going to heat up enough as it is without him waving red gloves under someone's nose."

"Yeah. Well . . . maybe he's just calling Reger. Someone safe, anyway. That would be a change."

"It would be nice," Caine agreed heavily. "But somehow, I doubt it."

Kanai had just finished his dinner, and was wondering without any real enthusiasm what he should do for the rest of the evening, when the phone twittered.

He paused, turning to look at it, his hand falling to his *shuriken* pouch. There were perhaps a dozen people who might be calling him, most of them mad at him, none of them anyone he really wanted to talk to. Glaring at the phone, he willed it to shut up.

But the person on the other end was persistent . . . and Kanai had been the blackcollars' contact man too long to easily ignore a phone call. With a sigh, he picked up the handset. "Yes?"

"Kanai?"

The blackcollar squeezed the handset with sudden pressure. "*Lathe*?"

"Right. Your line being tapped?"

"Certainly not," Kanai answered, automatically giving the old blackcollar code response for *yes*.

"Okay. I want to talk to Bernhard—let him know how things went tonight. Can you arrange that?"

"Probably," Kanai said cautiously. *How things went tonight*? A smokescreen for Security's benefit, or was Bernhard working some sort of game behind his back? "When do you want to talk to him?" he asked Lathe, forcing his voice to remain casual.

"There's a street six blocks north of last night's popbox— we'll be at a house two blocks west of that intersection. Got that?"

"I think so." *Popbox*—that had to be the place they'd popped up out of Anne Silcox's tunnel. Visualizing a map of Denver . . . "Yes, I know where it is. You want me to bring Bernhard there tonight?"

"Affirmative. Alone, of course."

"Of course." Translation: no Security tails. Possible, but only if he worked fast. "We'll be there shortly."

"Good. Oh, and you might tell Bernhard that Anne Silcox will also be here."

"Right," Kanai said, stomach tightening with sudden uncertainty.

The line went dead, and for a couple of heartbeats Kanai stared unseeing at the instrument. *Anne Silcox?* But that was impossible—less than twenty-four hours ago Bernhard had indicated he would be turning her over to Quinn.

"Damn," Kanai hissed between his teeth. Something strange was happening here, and whatever it was, he already didn't like it. Gathering up his gear, he grabbed a coat and slipped out the door.

The Security man at the monitor bank shrugged helplessly. "I'm sorry, Prefect Galway, but there's nothing more I can tell you. There were four high-power comm-frequency laser pulses in each of these three directions, each pulse consisting of the single word 'Christmas.' We've got the source pinpointed to an area a short way out into the mountains, but until and unless General Quinn releases the spotters from search duty over Denver, there's nothing I can do about looking for it."

Galway clenched his jaw with frustration. "And if the damn thing is mobile, it could be packed up and back in someone's garage before we find it."

"I'm afraid that's about right," the officer agreed.

"Damn." Galway stared at the star images displayed on the monitors, his eyes shifting among the three superimposed circles. At the end of one of those vectors was the mysterious spacecraft that had been skulking out there ever since Lathe's team had landed on Earth. Clearly, it was the intended recipient for the unauthorized message; just as clearly, at least to Galway's thinking, the message itself had come from Lathe. A prearranged signal to action . . . but action of what sort? *One way or another, it'll all be over soon*, Lathe had said, referring to the consequences of Pittman's actions. What could he have meant by that?

"Oh, hell," Galway muttered as a sudden thought struck him. Crazy—utterly crazy—but it was exactly the sort of thing Lathe would do—

"Galway!"

The prefect jerked around, startled, to see Quinn and two other Security men stride into the situation room. "General," he said, stepping toward the other, "there's been a signal to the ship out there—"

"Galway, pending a full investigation through the Ryqril officials on Plinry, you're confined to quarters," Quinn cut him off. "Your alleged double-agent scheme has been a total fiasco, resulting in loss of life, damage to government property, and the escape of valuable prisoners. Escort him to his quarters, men."

"*What*?" Galway stared, unable to believe his ears, as the two Security men stepped to his side. "You're not *serious*. All right, so Lathe and Pittman pulled the sheets over our heads. We haven't lost the whole—"

"What do you mean, *our* heads?" Quinn snarled. "*You're* the one they fooled."

"Me *and* the Ryqril on Plinry," Galway shot back. "Let's not forget they were the ones who initiated the whole project."

"We've got only your word and some possibly forged papers for that," Quinn said icily. "Maybe when we do some inquiries we'll find out you had more to do with it than you claim. Eh?"

Galway felt his stomach tighten up. This couldn't be happening—it just *couldn't*. Had Quinn gone totally insane? He looked to the man at the monitor for support, saw only carefully measured blankness in the other's eyes. "General," he said, forcing his voice to remain calm as he turned again to face Quinn. "A signal's been sent to the enemy ship out there, and if I'm right we're on the verge of losing any last bit of leverage we might still have on Pittman—"

"To hell with Pittman!" Quinn thundered. "He had his chance to cooperate—now he can damn well roast with the rest of them. And when we've dealt with them, it'll be *your* turn in the pit. Go on, get him out of here."

Hands curled into impotent fists at his side, Galway let them lead him from the situation room. *It'll be all right*, he told himself, trying with only limited success to believe it. *It'll be all right. He's sending word to Plinry—that's the important thing. Maybe it'll get there in time. Until then—*

Until then he would just have to sit quietly by and hope Quinn came to his senses soon. And hope to hell that Lathe didn't shred the city into ribbons before then.

The city, and any chance of survival for Plinry.

Chapter 30

The two blackcollars arrived three minutes after Hawking's tingler alerted the group inside—Bernhard was wary and grim as death itself as he slipped through the safe house door, Kanai behind him looking only marginally more comfortable. Standing off to one side beside Anne Silcox, fingers resting casually on the grips of his *nunchaku*, Caine watched as they stepped to the middle of the room where Lathe waited, and he saw, for the first time, the depth of hostility in Bernhard's eyes as he gazed at Lathe.

Once, Caine remembered with a trace of bitterness, he'd hoped to find allies among these same Denver blackcollars. Seldom had he ever had a dream shattered quite so thoroughly.

Bernhard broke the brittle silence first. "I hear through the grapevine that you've been busy tonight," he said, his voice deceptively casual.

"A bit," Lathe replied, matching his tone. "The grapevine provide any details?"

"It says your entire team was captured trying to break into Athena." Bernhard's eyes flicked across to Caine, lingered on Silcox before returning to Lathe. "I see the operation didn't take."

"No, it didn't. Any hints as to how we got out?"

"Not really, except that you took a lot of guards and part of the perimeter fence with you when you left."

"There were some explosions elsewhere in Athena that provided a diversion for us," Lathe told him. "Nothing but timed limpet mines designed to spread out the opposition . . . but Quinn doesn't know that. He thinks we had help. Help that was able to sneak into Athena on its own to stir up trouble. You want to take a guess as to who the likely suspects will be?"

Bernhard's expression didn't change, but suddenly the room seemed colder. "Quinn's not that stupid," he said softly. "He'll recognize a cheap frame-up like that for what it is."

"Maybe." Lathe shrugged. "But to be perfectly blunt, I

don't think you can afford to take that chance. Not after agreeing to help Quinn capture us.''

Bernhard glanced again at Silcox. "So you know about that. Well, I warned you, Lathe—don't say I didn't. I warned you at least twice to get out of Denver while you could.''

"And I told *you* we weren't ready to go. But that's old business. More important at the moment is how you're going to convince Quinn that you haven't double-dealt him. And it won't be easy—we've already shown him one alleged traitor that was still on our side.''

"Well, then, I suppose we'll just have to take you out as promised,'' Bernhard gritted. "That ought to convince him, don't you think?''

"Very likely,'' Lathe agreed. "But how are you going to do it? You don't know how to find us, you don't know where or when we're going to strike, you don't even know why we're here. So how are you going to capture us?''

Bernhard's eyes flicked to Caine and Silcox. "At the moment it's two against one,'' he said pointedly. "Whatever guard shield you've got outside would be too late to help.''

Beside him, Kanai stirred. "I won't fight him, Bernhard,'' he said softly. "I told you that last night.''

"Offhand, I'd guess a lot of your other blackcollars will feel the same way,'' Lathe told Bernhard. "How many can you rely on, do you suppose? Two? Three?''

"Enough,'' the other said shortly. "Blackcollars who take as many stupid chances as you do shouldn't be too hard to take out.''

Lathe shook his head. "You've completely missed the point of what we've been doing. The whole campaign was designed to force Quinn to admit he couldn't keep up with us and to hire or force you to go after us. Now you've got the job, whether you like it or not—and that puts you square in the nutcracker with us. If you don't deliver damn fast, Quinn's bound to come to the conclusion that you've come over to our side . . . and he knows where to find *you*.''

"Not if I don't want him to,'' Bernhard ground out.

"Only if you're willing to leave Denver entirely.'' Lathe shook his head. "And I'm guessing you'd just as soon stay in your comfy little sinecure.''

"All the more reason to take you out,'' Bernhard said, but Caine could see the confidence beginning to fade. "But all right, then; let's hear *your* solution to the mess.''

For a long moment Lathe gazed at him. "You can do what I asked when we first met. Help us carry out our mission."

Bernhard snorted. "Oh, that *would* be a grand idea, wouldn't it? *Exactly* the thing to get Quinn off our backs."

"You give us the help we need," Lathe continued, as if the other hadn't spoken, "and we'll provide you with some bodies to show Quinn. Bodies that even the experts won't be able to prove aren't us."

"What?" Silcox whispered at Caine's side. "He didn't mention any of that part to *me*."

He hadn't mentioned it to Caine, either. "Just stay cool," he whispered back. "He knows what he's doing."

If Bernhard found the suggestion outrageous, it wasn't immediately evident. "That's a damned big risk for us to take," Bernhard said, shaking his head. "Safer to just take you on."

Lathe shrugged. "That's your choice. But I'll tell you straight out: if you don't help us, you'll soon wish you had. We can take this city apart—you know it and I know it. And every raid we pull will nudge Quinn a step closer to ordering your own destruction."

"Suppose *I* offer to help you?" Kanai spoke up suddenly. "There's no need to take all of us down just because Bernhard won't cooperate, is there?"

Bernhard threw his companion a glance, but even as he started to speak Lathe shook his head. "Sorry, Kanai. We may be able to use your help later, but first of all we need something only Bernhard can provide. Well, Bernhard?"

The other glowered at him. "I don't take well to blackmail, Lathe. Or to threats."

"I don't like them much myself," Lathe came back. "But our options at this point are limited, and I haven't got time for anything with more finesse."

"Damn you—"

"I suggest you think it over—you'll probably have at least a couple of days before Quinn gets impatient and drops the sky on you. Discuss it with your team; certainly with your boss, Sartan. In fact, maybe I ought to talk to him myself."

Bernhard's eyes narrowed. "Leave Sartan out of this—it's none of his business."

"Why not? I'd think he'd have a vested interest in protecting his roughneck squad. Well, no matter. If you don't tell him, there are other ways to get a message there."

"Oh, really?" Bernhard's lip twitched in an almost-smile. "Well, you go right ahead, then, and give him a call."

Lathe cocked an eyebrow thoughtfully. "You really *don't* care if I feed him my version of all this, do you? Interesting." He shrugged. "Well, anyway, between Quinn and Sartan I think you'll eventually change your mind about helping us. I'll be in touch for when you do."

Bernhard pursed his lips. "Lathe—"

"No, don't try it," the comsquare said. "I have a man through the doorway over there with a sniper's slingshot trained on you, and I don't think you'd like fighting me on your back."

A disbelieving look flashed across Bernhard's face, followed by a rueful smile. "I begin to see why Quinn is always underestimating you. You're good, Lathe . . . but in the long run it won't be enough." Turning on his heel, he strode out the door. Kanai sent a last, unreadable look at Caine and Silcox, then followed.

Lathe inhaled audibly, let the breath out in a whoosh as he turned to Caine. "And that is that," he said. "For now, anyway. Well, Anne?"

She nodded. "He's the one," she said with a sigh. "Strange; they always referred to blackcollars so positively. Maybe he's changed since they vanished."

"'The one'?" Caine asked, frowning. "The one what?"

"The blackcollar she occasionally saw with her Torch friends," Lathe told him. "More to the immediate point, the one who was there the day before they set her up in the Shandygaff and all disappeared."

Caine focused on Silcox. "Why didn't you say anything about that earlier?"

"Because it wasn't any of your business," she retorted. "And because if Torch is doing something special, I didn't want a group of self-appointed heroes charging in and shaking up the cart."

Caine snorted. "Nice of you to come around a little, anyway."

"I don't have a lot of choice," she shot back, throwing a glare at Lathe. "I don't like the way you're bulling around Denver any more than Bernhard does. The sooner you get out of here, the better it'll be for all of us."

Caine looked at Lathe. "We just make friends everywhere we go, don't we?"

The comsquare shrugged. "Get used to it. There aren't a lot

of people like Torch around who are willing to risk their comfortable existence for the chance to be free someday.''

Silcox bristled. "If that's a slap at *me*—"

She broke off as Skyler slipped in through the door. "Well?" Lathe asked.

The big blackcollar nodded. "No problems. They're both on track."

"Who are on what?" Caine frowned, a familiar suspicion tightening his stomach. "Lathe, what're you up to this time?"

Lathe's lips compressed momentarily. "I promised our . . . local benefactor that in return for sending a laser message to a scout ship Lepkowski left us we'd find out who the mysterious Sartan is that Bernhard's blackcollars are working so closely with."

"So you've got two of your men tailing Bernhard?" Silcox asked. "That's crazy—he'll spot them within five minutes."

"Of course he would," Lathe said. "That's why they're tracking Bernhard from inside his trunk."

Caine felt his mouth drop open. "You *are* kidding. Aren't you?"

"It's the only way, Caine," Skyler said with a shrug. But he, too, looked uncomfortable. "The state Bernhard's in, it'll probably never even occur to him to check a trunk that obviously hasn't been touched."

"Unless there are alarms or warners on it—"

"There were. Hawking took care of them."

"Great," Caine muttered. "Just great. That laser message better have been damn important, Lathe."

"It was part of my promise to Pittman," the comsquare said quietly. "Come on—we'd better call the guard ring in and get out of here. Anne . . . ?"

She hesitated, then shrugged. "Sure, why not? I haven't got anywhere else to go . . . and I guess I'm pretty well committed now, anyway."

Lathe smiled faintly at her. "Welcome back to the war," he said.

Chapter 31

Mordecai hadn't really liked the idea from the start, and his opinion of it had been going steadily downhill ever since then. There were a limited number of ways in which two men in full kit could wedge themselves into a car trunk, none of them comfortable for both straight-line travel and sharp turns. Gritting his teeth, he did the best he could, hoping like hell Bernhard wasn't headed somewhere on the far side of town.

In that, at least, they were lucky. They'd been riding for no more than fifteen minutes when the car glided to a halt and both doors opened. Two sets of footsteps, on concrete or something equally hard . . . a door opening and closing . . . the whine of a sliding door's motor . . . and then nothing. Mordecai gave the silence three minutes, then carefully popped the trunk.

They were, as expected, in a garage, though its generous dimensions were something of a surprise. A sliding door exited—presumably—to the street; more ordinary doors led out one side and to the rear, probably to an attached building and outside, respectively. There were no windows, and a quick flashlight scan of the walls and ceiling turned up no likely cameras or other monitors.

"A good low-tech blackcollar hideout," Jensen murmured as they eased out of the trunk and worked the kinks out of their muscles. "Nothing to attract Security's notice."

Mordecai stepped over to the building door, pulling a sound-catcher from his kit and pressing it against the panel. A low hum was all he could hear. "They've got a bug stomper going in there," he told Jensen, putting the instrument away. "I guess we do this the hard way."

Jensen nodded and stepped to the other door. He listened for a moment, then cracked it open carefully. Some light, not much, filtered in, and as the blackcollar opened it enough to slip out Mordecai saw that it indeed led outside. He gave Jensen a five-second lead, then followed.

They were at the back of what appeared to be a fairly large

middle-class house. Several lights were showing in various windows; Jenson was already moving cautiously toward the largest of them, a ground-floor solarium set in the center of the wall. Mordecai took the other direction, circling the garage to try to find out just where they were.

The street out front matched the house: well lit, smoothly paved, with even some trees and other attempted landscaping in the narrow median strip. The surrounding houses, too, had the same reasonably well-off look as the one he was standing beside. He gave them a cursory scan, then peered down the street, looking for a street sign. He'd located one, and had just stepped away from the garage toward it, when a pair of cars glided down the street and came to a halt two houses down.

Mordecai dropped into a crouch and froze, trying to squeeze into what little shadow was available. *Security,* was his first thought; but as a single figure emerged from each of the vehicles he began to breathe easier. A Security car would have been packed to the gills with armed men.

Abruptly, his lip twitched. The way the men walked—their feline grace, the sense of invisible awareness about them . . .

They were two of Bernhard's blackcollars.

Mordecai grimaced, aware that he was completely exposed to anyone coming up the walk, but to his surprise and relief, the newcomers didn't come any closer to Bernhard's house. Instead, they walked up to the house they'd parked in front of, two down from where Mordecai was standing. At the door they paused briefly, as if working a key, then disappeared inside.

Mordecai took a careful breath and permitted himself a smile. So Sartan at least was smart enough to play it cool: two houses, with a tunnel between them, to avoid having large crowds show up at his doorstep for everyone to see. It wasn't an especially clever trick, but it usually worked well enough. Rising out of his crouch, he headed back to Jensen.

The other was lying propped up on his elbows outside the solarium, peering inside through the bottom pane of glass. "Company's starting to arrive," Mordecai whispered. "Two blackcollars, using the old shell-game approach."

Jensen grunted. "Wondered where they came from. Can't see much, but I heard two new voices join the party."

"How many in there so far?"

"Sounds like just your two plus Bernhard and Kanai. If Sartan's with them, he's being mighty quiet."

Mordecai chewed his lip. "Maybe this isn't his house after all. Well, we're here; might as well get something out of it. You stay put and keep counting; I'll go back and watch for visitors and bandits."

"Sounds good."

They stayed at their posts for nearly half an hour more. In that time a grand total of three more blackcollars arrived.

"That *can't* be all the troops Bernhard's got." Jensen shook his head when they met again and compared notes. "I got the impression he had at least a squad, more likely two or three of them. We're talking, what, seven men total here?"

"Maybe he's just called in his top circle," Mordecai suggested. But something about that felt wrong. "Or just the ones he thinks will cooperate in taking us out."

"No." Jensen was positive. "I can't hear any words out here, but the tones are clear enough—and that's *not* a nice simple war council. They're having a good healthy argument in there. Besides, if these are the troops he's going to hit us with, why is Kanai with them?"

"Point," Mordecai admitted. "And no sign of Sartan either way. Are you tracking the logic the same way I am?"

"Bernhard's got barely six blackcollars he can trust, even counting Kanai, or only six blackcollars period," Jensen said promptly. "He knows we've got at least five blackcollars plus Caine's team, and that we've got the advantage of being the defending party. He therefore needs all the forces he can get if he wants a chance in hell of stopping us—and those forces ought to include all the street troops Sartan can offer him. If he isn't talking to Sartan . . ." He spread his hands.

"Then either Sartan has already backed out of the operation," Mordecai concluded, "or else Sartan doesn't exist at all."

Jensen cocked an eyebrow thoughtfully. "Hard to avoid that conclusion, isn't it? So what the hell is Bernhard trying to pull with his Sartan game, anyway?"

"Control of some of the criminal underground, maybe," Mordecai offered doubtfully. "Or he could just be muddying the waters for Security's benefit. I don't know—this sort of stuff is Lathe's forte, not mine. We've seen enough—let's get out of here and report."

"Just a second," Jensen said, an odd look on his face. "If this really *is* all Bernhard can bring to bear, and if they're not flocking to his banner as it is, maybe a gentle push would do some good."

"A gentle *what?* Jensen—"

"Why not? A nice, civilized talk with them—surely they aren't going to attack two emissaries here to deliver a message. He's clearly under some pressure from them already; a little more may get us Bernhard's help without our having to run amok all over Denver. You can stay out here as backup if you want, but I'm going to give it a try."

Without waiting for a reply he started back toward the garage. Mouthing an old Hebraic curse he'd been saving for just such an occasion, Mordecai followed. If Jensen's erratic behavior of the past few months had finally played him false . . . well, at least he wasn't going to die alone.

The others heard them coming, of course. A flurry of barely audible movement began as they stepped through the garage door into the house proper and continued as they crossed a large kitchen, and by the time they reached the living room off the solarium only Bernhard was still sitting there.

Still, the look of astonishment that appeared on his face made the entrance worthwhile. "What the hell?" he gasped, mouth opening with shock. "You! But—"

"Hello, Bernhard." Jensen nodded gravely. "We thought we'd drop by and see how you're coming with the job of persuading your team how easily we can be taken." He glanced around the room. "Nice place. Sartan get it for you?—sorry, I forgot; Sartan doesn't exist. I guess mercenary work is profitable enough even without a sponsor."

For a long moment Bernhard was silent, a whole spectrum of emotions chasing each other across his face. Then, with a sigh, he reached for his tingler and tapped a brief message: *All clear; return.* Almost immediately the others started filtering in, and in under a minute Jensen and Mordecai were standing inside a circle of seven blackcollars.

"Nice group," Jensen said, glancing around. "You want to make the introductions, Bernhard?"

"Not especially," the other growled. "I could order you killed for this, you know."

Jensen shook his head in disgust. "Bernhard, how long are you going to play this game? Haven't we proved that *you're* the ones who're going to get hurt if you keep up this nonsense?"

One of the others growled something under his breath, and Mordecai braced himself for combat. He understood what Jensen was trying to do, but baiting someone like Bernhard took a lot of skill—and even when it was done right it could backfire at the turn of a gyro.

But Jensen either didn't notice the danger or didn't give a damn. "How can someone who claims to be a blackcollar roll over and play dead just because Security asks him to?" he continued. "Have you forgotten that we're supposed to be *fighting* people like Quinn?"

"We haven't forgotten," Kanai said. "All right, you know about the Sartan screen—but you don't know *why* we're doing it."

"So tell us," Jensen invited.

"Because we need money if we're going to pick up the war effort again. *Lots* of money, coming in on a regular basis. For that we need part of the Denver territory and to get it we need Sartan."

"Ingenious," Jensen said, not sounding overly impressed. "And after you have your nest egg?"

"We take the fight back to the Ryqril," Bernhard said.

Jensen looked at him for a long moment. Then he shook his head. "No. It'll never happen. No matter how much money or territory you get, it'll never be enough. Maybe it would have been once—maybe while Torch was still around and you had to face the fact that they were doing your job for you. But not any more. You're too comfortable, Bernhard. Too content with your role here—particularly too comfortable with your special dispensation from Quinn. Left to yourselves you'll just sink deeper and deeper into the garbage of the underground, until you're no better than any of the other bosses or underlings in town. And that's how you'll die."

Slowly, his eyes locked like targeted weapons on Jensen, Bernhard got to his feet. "You're wrong," he said, each word as hard and precise as if cut from hullmetal.

"Then prove it," Jensen told him. "Come back with us. Now."

Bernhard's expression didn't change, but suddenly Mordecai felt something new in the atmosphere. A sense of thoughtful anticipation had been added to the antipathy there, as if Jensen's analysis had found a resonance with thoughts and fears some of the others had also had. Thoughts they'd perhaps tried to bury but never completely killed.

And it was clear that Bernhard felt it too. "Cute," he said, lip quirking as some of the tension seemed to leave his body. "Very cute. I don't have to let you herd me into that kind of box, you know—not even if my own men are helping you do it," he added, glancing around. "But you're right on one count: bucking you won't do anything but grind down both our forces needlessly." He took a deep breath. "All right. Let's go."

"Just like that?" Mordecai asked, not quite believing it.

"I said so, didn't I?" Bernhard snapped.

He started toward the garage, and as he did so Kanai stirred. "I'd like to come along," he said.

"No," Bernhard said over his shoulder.

"Yes," Jensen said.

Bernhard spun back to face him, his face furious. "Damn it, Jensen, I'm still doyen of this group," he snarled. "*I'm* in command of these men, and if I don't want him along, he doesn't come. Understand?"

"No, I don't," Jensen told him. "What difference does it make whether or not he's along? Unless you're planning to betray us and don't want any witnesses."

"Take that back," one of the others growled, taking a step toward Jensen. "Take it back *now*."

"Easy, Pendleton," Bernhard said. For a long moment he locked eyes with Jensen. "We take insults very seriously on Earth," he said at last. "You're damn lucky we've built up a good resistance to them—Pendleton used to be a lot more impulsive. All right, Kanai, you want to come, you can come. Pendleton, you're in command until we're back."

"Right," Pendleton growled, still glaring at Jensen.

"I suppose we're ready, then," Bernhard said, his voice almost conversational. "Shall we go?"

"Sure," Jensen said . . . and for the first time Mordecai recognized the other hadn't been nearly as confident about all of this as he'd appeared. "We'll take your car, Bernhard— I'll drive."

"Fair enough. Can I assume I'll finally get to meet whoever the local is who's been helping you since you arrived?"

Jensen smiled slightly. "Why not?" he said, very softly. "I'm sure he'd like to meet you, too."

Minutes later, they were on their way, and seated next to Kanai in the back seat, Mordecai had time to play back Jensen's last comment. His comment, and the way he'd said it. *I wonder*, he thought, *what that was all about*.

He couldn't tell. But somehow, he didn't think he liked it.

the corridor beyond.

the sector or two the distance of their position [...] be[...]
could, for safety. Which definitely meant—turned out—[...] don't
think the major directing the operation really knew where he

Chapter 32

"You took a hell of a chance out there. I hope you realize that."

Lathe paused, looking away from the mirror to the edge of the sunken tub where Reger had seated himself. "Not that much of one, really," he told the other. "A little strategically applied makeup, a lot of genuine blood in case they were being thorough enough to use type analyzers, and the rest was pretty much of a given. You'd be surprised at how few people will really *look* at a face that's covered with blood."

Reger snorted, and Lathe turned back to the sink and the last remnants of the makeup from their prison escape, glad the tedious job was almost done. The dried blood had been easy enough, but the false head wound had been composed of non-water-soluble materials and the solvent's odor reminded him of some of the worst days of the old war.

"I assume," Reger said, "that there was method to the rest of it, too, that you didn't just improvise as you went along? The Silcox woman—why did you have her wear all of your flexarmor? Just to bulk her out?"

"Partly that, and partly because all the rest of us were supposed to be unconscious from head wounds." He caught Reger's puzzled look in the mirror and continued, "She established early on for the assault team that her injury was one where she could fade in and out of consciousness, right? Okay; that meant she could conveniently fade out if someone started asking awkward questions, but could also fade in if the medics started to check her out for any problems besides her head wound—specifically, problems below neck level."

"Ah." Reger nodded. "I see. With your flexarmor elsewhere, they were welcome to examine the rest of you as much as they wanted."

"Right," Lathe said. "And the symptoms fit with her supposedly having bandaged her own head, anyway—"

"Which she needed to have done to hide her hair."

"Right again. Also, with the in-out fading, she would have

been able to provide diversion or misdirection if it had become necessary. Which it didn't, as it turned out—I don't think the major directing the operation really knew what he was doing.''

Reger snorted. ''You put a hell of a lot of trust in her.''

Lathe took one last swipe at his forehead and thankfully tossed the cotton ball aside, turning to face Reger again. ''We're having to do a lot of trusting on this mission, it seems. Well, now—enough of these preliminaries. You've probably heard the whole story from Caine or one of the others by now, anyway. So what did you *really* come here to talk about?''

The other pursed his lips. ''Caine tells me he wanted to get those two truck drivers out, too, while you were there—spun me some sort of story about you not trusting them to cooperate with you on the escape.''

''He's right; we couldn't have. But it's actually simpler than that. The Dupres and Karen Lindsay had no connection to us at all, aside from having been forced to help us in a couple of minor parts of the operation. A fast interrogation will show they're innocent pawns, and they'll be released. If we'd broken them out, on the other hand, they'd automatically have come under more suspicion, and when they'd been recaptured they'd have been put through the whole gauntlet. By ignoring them when we made our break, we actually did them a favor. Though Caine still has a hard time seeing that.''

Reger grunted. ''Maybe with good reason. Because as it turns out, they're not quite as unconnected as you thought. I own the trucking company the two women drive for.''

''What?'' Lathe felt his eyes narrow. ''Why didn't you tell me this before?''

''I didn't *know* it before,'' the other retorted. ''You never mentioned those people before tonight. Anyway, it may not be an immediate problem—I own the company, but through several levels of bureaucratic paper. It could take Quinn days to dig his way through it, even after it occurs to him to look.''

''Yeah. Unfortunately, Galway's here, too, and if Quinn doesn't think to look, *he* sure as hell will.''

''Caine told me a little about Galway,'' Reger said. ''Sounds like a dangerous opponent.''

''If the Ryqril and other assorted idiots didn't keep interfering with him, he might have nailed us long ago,'' Lathe said frankly. "If Quinn gives him free rein . . . well, there's nothing we can do but try to move up the timetable as best we can."

"By running amok in Denver." Reger exhaled between his teeth. "I can't say I like that idea at all, Lathe. The inherent advantages of the attacker notwithstanding, there are a hell of a lot of Security men at Quinn's disposal. And that doesn't count Denver's *real* bosses, who're going to be damned annoyed at a progressive gunfight shaking up their territories."

"We need Bernhard's knowledge." Lathe shrugged. "As long as he's unwilling to rock his own personal boat, the only way to get his help is to make it even more dangerous for him to sit on his hands. Tonight's little play in Athena will have pushed things a long way toward that goal—that's the main reason I took the risk in the first place—but if he's going to be stubborn, we'll just have to keep stirring the fire."

"Maybe if you told me what you wanted to know, I could find it out for you."

"Sorry." Lathe shook his head. "You I could probably trust to keep quiet about it, but the rest of your people I couldn't. And if Security gets wind of it, they're likely to overreact. Badly."

The intercom in Reger's pocket beeped. "Yes?" he said, pulling it out.

A second later, his eyes widened, and, bounding from his seat, he stepped close to Lathe, holding the instrument so that both men could hear. ". . . says that Lathe'll want them put up here, at least for the night. What do I tell him?"

"It's Jensen and Mordecai," Reger hissed into Lathe's ear. "With Bernhard and Kanai."

Lathe plucked the instrument from Reger's hand. "This is Lathe—put Jensen on."

"Uh—yes, sir."

"What the hell does he think he's doing?" Reger snarled into the pause.

"I don't know, unless they've persuaded Bernhard to help. Somehow."

A moment later Jensen's voice came on. "Lathe? What's up?"

"That's my line, isn't it?" the comsquare said. "Reger and I were just wondering why you brought Bernhard out here."

"You wanted him here, didn't you?" Jensen said, sounding surprised. "Wasn't that the basic idea of this operation?"

"Yes, but—well, we were rather hoping to keep Reger's assistance to us out of the general news."

"Ah. Well, we weren't followed, if that's what's worrying you. And we stopped off at our number-three safe house before leaving town and went over the car and both of them with a bug stomper. They're perfectly clean."

"Glad to hear it." Lathe thought hard for a second, trying to hear beyond Jensen's words and figure out what the other had in mind. "Uh . . . the sensor net and death-house setup you were building for Reger—how far along are they?"

"Essentially finished, at least the visible parts. There's some wiring to be done yet, but I should be able to finish all of that tonight. You—uh—weren't planning to mention the death house to Bernhard, were you?"

Lathe pursed his lips. "Not that or the sensor net either. Should I make it an order?"

"I think it would be a good idea."

Lathe looked at Reger. "Is there some part of the house you can put Bernhard and Kanai where they can be watched around the clock?"

The other had a sour look on his face, but he nodded. "Yes, if you really think it's necessary. And safe."

"It's probably both. As long as they know where we are now, I want to have them right here where we can keep an eye on them." He caught the look on Reger's face and added, "And as long as there are five blackcollars in the house on your side, he's not likely to try anything against you personally."

"I hope you're right. Barky"—this into the intercom—"go ahead and let them in. Don't bother with the usual escort; there'll be a group of blackcollars here to meet them."

"Yes, Mr. Reger." The instrument went dead.

"You'll get some of your men out there right away?" Reger suggested mildly to Lathe.

In answer, the comsquare reached for his tingler.

For Caine, the confrontation at the steps to Reger's house turned out to be rather anticlimactic.

Not that he was really expecting trouble. With Lathe and Skyler waiting with Reger and him and with Jensen and Mordecai walking behind them, the two Denver blackcollars would have had to be crazy to start anything. Still, given Bernhard's attitude at their earlier meeting that evening, such a complete reversal struck Caine as damned odd, to say the least.

But a reversal it apparently was. Neither Bernhard nor Kanai showed the slightest sign of hostility as they walked up to where the reception committee waited.

"Lathe," Bernhard said, eyes cool as he looked over at Reger. "So. Reger. I should have guessed you were the one playing patron for them."

"Accident of history, actually," Reger told him. "Not that it matters. You really here to help, or was this just a childish ploy to smoke me out?"

Deliberately, Bernhard turned back to Lathe. "Is there some place where we can talk?" he asked. "Somewhere we won't be disturbed or eavesdropped on?"

"My room's got a bug stomper in it," Lathe said, stepping back and gesturing the other forward. "Mordecai, escort Commando Kanai to his quarters, will you? Reger will tell you where. Caine, Skyler, come with us."

The comsquare led the way inside and down the various hallways to his room. "Make yourselves comfortable," he told the others as he folded a table out from the wall and then stepped to a bookshelf where a stack of maps was sitting.

"The security here seems to be tighter than the last time I came by," Bernhard commented as he pulled a chair up to the table and sat down. "Your doing?"

"We helped a bit," Lathe said briefly. "Here we go." He stepped back to the table, unfolded a map of the Aegis Mountain area, and laid it out. "Recognize it?" he asked Bernhard.

"Aegis Mountain," the other said. "So?"

"I want you to get us in."

Bernhard twisted his neck to look up at Lathe. "*That's* what you wanted? Damn it all, Lathe, I told you once the mountain was locked up tighter than a Ryqril base. How the hell—"

"Yes, I know the official story," Lathe interrupted him coldly. "I also know it's a load of cockroach slime. You were a blackcollar assigned to the base—whatever back doors there were in and out of it, you know about them. So scrap the sheep bleatings and tell us where they are."

For a long moment the two men remained frozen where they were, gazes locked. Caine licked his lips, without noticeable effect, as the tension in the room grew steadily more oppressive. He desperately wanted to look over at Skyler, to see how the other was reacting to the standoff, but was afraid to move even that much . . . and at long last Bernhard dropped his eyes.

"Give me a map of the area northwest of the mountain," he said with a tired sigh. "It won't do you any good . . . but I'll show you the only way in."

"It's one of the fifteen ventilation tunnels into the base," Bernhard said, tapping the map at a spot alongside an intermittent creek. "Two meters across at this end, but it gets bigger later on as a bunch of the intakes connect together. It cuts horizontally into the mountain for a dozen meters, then shifts to vertical, dropping a hundred meters or so before leveling out again and heading in toward the base, several klicks away. It's an intake tunnel, fortunately; if it was an exhaust tunnel you'd find your way blocked by the groundwater heat-exchange system."

"Seems straightforward enough," Skyler commented, peering over Bernhard's shoulder. "What's the catch?"

"The catch is that these are too obvious a back door for even military bureaucrats to miss," Bernhard told him sourly. "So they made sure no one could use them."

"Booby-trapped?" Caine hazarded.

Bernhard snorted. "That's a mild way of putting it. It's an extremely nasty three-stage defense system." Snaring a pencil and pad from the bookshelf, he began to sketch. "Stage one is in that first dozen meters at the mouth of the tunnel and a few meters of the vertical shaft. It's remote-operated, for the most part, though there are some pressure and proximity defenses there, too."

"At least the manual weaponry won't be any trouble," Caine remarked. "No one in there to fire them."

"Stage two," Bernhard continued, ignoring the comment, "is at the midpoint, where the smaller tunnels join into one large thirty-meter one. That part's more or less passive, with bulkheads that were supposed to seal down the tunnel when the base was abandoned."

"Were they activated?" Lathe asked.

"I don't know, but I'd guess so. And even if you've really got the time and equipment to cut or blow through all those, there's still stage three . . . and I guarantee you won't survive that one."

"Let me guess," Skyler said. "Automated defenses, right?"

"Automated, self-contained, and utterly pure poison," Bernhard said heavily. "Lasers, particle and flechette weapons, gas, explosives and scud grenades, and a microwave flamer that would lock the joints on battle armor while it cooked you. If you *had* any battle armor."

"In other words, an area of the tunnel to be crept through with caution," Lathe said. "How long is it?"

"About a hundred meters—and you're missing the point. You aren't going to creep through it; nor are you going to run, fly, or drive through it. You enter that section and you're dead. Period."

For a moment the room was silent. Then Lathe leaned over the table and made a small mark on the map, one valley away from and due north of the spot Bernhard had indicated. "I presume the entrance to the tunnel is camouflaged," he said. "You'll need to help us find it."

Bernhard stared up at him. "Haven't you been listening? I just told you the tunnel was lethal."

"Yes, you did," Lathe said. "But security systems decay with age, and it's possible even something this sophisticated has fallen apart sufficiently to let us get by it. Regardless, we need to check it out in person." He straightened up. "If you'll come with me, I'll take you to the room Reger's got set up for you. We'll lie low here a couple of days to let Security run themselves ragged out in Denver, then head out and see just what we've got to work with out there."

Caine cleared his throat as Bernhard got to his feet. "Lathe, I'd like to talk to you when you've got a moment."

"Of course." Lathe caught Skyler's eye, jerked his head toward the door.

"Sure," the big blackcollar said. "Come on, Bernhard, I'll show you to your quarters."

Bernhard looked as if he wanted to say something, but apparently changed his mind. Together, he and Skyler left the room.

Lathe turned to Caine as the door closed behind the others. "Well? Bernhard's scare story getting to you?"

"A little, maybe," Caine admitted. "But that's not what I wanted to talk to you about. Is it my imagination, or is everyone suddenly becoming very cooperative around here?"

Lathe pursed his lips. "You noticed that too, did you?"

"It's a little hard to miss. First Anne Silcox admits she knows at least a little more about Torch than she originally let on, then Bernhard does a complete one-eighty on helping us—to the extent that he doesn't even argue about your dragging him along into the mountains. And last but not least, Reger is willing to let him and Kanai stay here, despite the fact that they'd probably like to see him dead and vice versa. It seems to me just a little too good to be true, and I'm not sure I trust any of it.''

"Hm. Well, as for Silcox, I don't think there's anything necessarily suspicious there—she wasn't going to trust us on our word alone until we basically proved we were on her side by getting her out of Athena.''

Caine snorted gently. "On her side, sure. After basically dragging her into this mess just so there'd be someone for Bernhard to go after that we could rattle Security by saving—''

"Who told you that?'' Lathe asked sharply.

"Oh, come on, Lathe—I may not be as good a tactician as you are, but I've got hindsight with the best of them. Your hope of getting to Torch through her fizzled, so you left her dangling in front of Bernhard so that you'd have an excuse to pull the Grand Athena Escape Stunt. You want to argue any of that?''

For a moment Lathe stared at him in silence. Then, ruefully, he shook his head. "You're better at this stuff than I thought," he admitted. "I always knew you had tactician talent. Would it help if I told you I was hoping Bernhard wouldn't take the bait and that I'd have to get my lever on him somehow else?''

Caine shrugged. "Actually, I don't feel as bad about her as I still do about the Dupres and Karen Lindsay. After all, Anne volunteered for duty here—why should she expect any different treatment than the rest of us get?''

Lathe shorted. "Thanks a lot.''

"Don't mention it. You were talking about suspicious cooperation . . . ?''

"Right. As for Bernhard . . .'' Lathe hesitated. "I suspect he's using his change of heart as camouflage while he sets up a game of his own on the side. Add to that—'' He broke off abruptly. "Never mind. The point is—''

"Add to that Jensen's move in bringing Bernhard back here in the first place?'' Caine suggested.

Lathe gave him a lopsided smile. "You're *definitely* better at this than I thought,'' he said. "Yes. On the surface that doesn't seem like a very smart move on my part . . . but there's something in his attitude that makes me think he also may have a plan of his own in the works, something that he needed Bernhard's presence here to accomplish.''

"You going to ask him what it is?"

"No—at least not right now. When and if we get into Aegis, maybe it'll be time then. But not yet. Some of Jensen's attitudes and perspectives may have changed since the Argent mission, but his basic skills and intellect haven't. You may not have noticed, but as we were escorting Bernhard here earlier, he and Reger were heading off into a huddle by themselves, so it's possible Jensen's cooked up something with him that'll help protect our flanks while we concentrate on the main mission."

"In other words," Caine said slowly, "you *do* have an idea of what he's up to. But don't want to tell me what it is."

Lathe gazed off into space. "Caine . . . if I'm right, it's something I don't really want to be involved in. And I'm pretty sure you won't want to know about it in advance, either."

"Or in other words, I should trust you. Just this once." Caine grimaced for a moment, then sighed. "I *knew* I shouldn't have agreed to let you take command."

Lathe chuckled. But the laugh lines stayed only briefly, and didn't reach his eyes. "Come on, let's go talk to the others," he said, folding up the map. "We need to discuss this, decide who'll be coming along to the mountain in a couple of days."

"Blackcollars only?"

Lathe eyed him, shook his head. "No, I don't think so. Your team's earned the right to be in on the kill."

"I agree." Caine grimaced. "I just hope you're not being literal about it being a kill."

The comsquare nodded grimly. "So do I."

Chapter 33

They stayed at Reger's mansion for the next two days, recovering from the Athena escape and waiting for a reasonable lull in Security activity. Caine found the delay almost intolerable; but he had to admit they would have been foolish to try moving any sooner. Spotters and fighter aircraft literally swarmed over Denver and the nearby mountains, obviously watching for any even remotely suspicious activity. The reports coming in from Reger's informant net showed the situation inside the city was even worse, with heavily armed Security troops patrolling the streets and poking into any place they could think of where the blackcollars might be hiding. For a while Caine worried that they might go so far as to begin a house-to-house search of the entire region, but Skyler pointed out that even if they did, Reger's high-priced neighborhood was likely to be low on the list of probable hideouts.

Still, he was relieved when Lathe decided on their second evening of idleness that the overhead patrols had thinned sufficiently to risk a short sortie the next morning. "We don't have to actually *do* anything out there tomorrow," the comsquare reminded them. "Just locate the place and maybe loosen whatever grating is closing it down. We've got another six days or so before I want us out of the area entirely."

"Why six?" Colvin asked.

"Because that'll make it eight days since we sent the message out to the scout ship," the comsquare told him. "That's round-trip time between here and Plinry for the Corsair Quinn should have sent right after our break."

Caine glanced at Pittman's carefully controlled expression, noticing as he did so other surreptitious looks that were headed that way. So far Pittman hadn't shown any willingness to talk about his involvement with Galway, and up till now no one had felt the need to press him on the subject. But now Braune cleared his throat. "Round trip to Plinry . . . with bad news aboard?"

"You could say that," Lathe acknowledged. "Project Christmas will be bad news for *someone*—and if it's the Ryqril who get the hot end, they may go a little berserk here trying to find us."

"Does Bernhard know about this?" Colvin asked.

"No. Why? You think he might stall in hopes Quinn will drop the roof in before he has to do anything concrete to help us?"

"The thought had crossed my mind."

Lathe shook his head. "Actually, I think Bernhard's lost his last chance to betray us directly to Security. Remember, he presumably doesn't want Ryqril in Aegis Mountain any more than we do—else he could have told them about the back door years ago when he was making his tacit peace with them. After tomorrow, though, if he turns us over to Security the secret will be out—and if Quinn can't get the back door's location from us, he'll chase Bernhard down for it. No, Bernhard's much more likely to try killing us himself if he still wants us dead.''

Hawking grunted. ''Cheerful thought. On the way to or from the soft probe tomorrow, you think?''

''He'll wait until the main expedition,'' Jensen said quietly. ''Tomorrow he'll be surrounded almost entirely by blackcollars. He'd know enough to wait until the rest of Caine's team is along, in hopes they'd get in our way in a fight.''

Almazad snorted. ''Thanks a lot.''

''He's right, though.'' Lathe nodded thoughtfully. ''And it leaves us with only one practical approach—which I was going to recommend anyway. Suppose we do the following. . . .''

The sounds of soft conversation filtered through the heavy door: Jensen and Alamzad, presumably. ''I hope,'' Pittman murmured as Caine reached for the doorknob, ''you know what you're doing.''

''Me, too,'' Caine answered frankly. ''But this is *our* mission, remember. We have a right to know what's going on.''

The room was considerably smaller than Caine had realized, more like a vertical crawlspace than a room per se. Alamzad and Jensen were indeed there, crouched over some sort of mechanism at the far end but looking back at the newcomers. ''You should have announced yourselves,'' Jensen growled, sliding a *shuriken* back into his pouch.

Caine swallowed the automatic apology that came to mind. ''We had other things on our minds,'' he said instead. ''Your private scheme, to be specific.''

Jensen cocked an eyebrow. ''So Lathe's caught on, eh? Knew he would, eventually. Is he really so worried about me that he sent you to snake out the details?''

''He doesn't know we're here,'' Caine said. ''This is on my authority as head of the mission.''

For a long moment Jensen gazed at the two of them in silence. Then, slowly, he nodded his head. ''All right,'' he said. ''But not for you personally, and not because you're my titular commander on this. I'll tell you because Pittman's earned it.''

"Pittman?" Caine frowned, shooting a look at the other.

"That's right. Pittman stayed loyal to you and all the rest of us, no matter what it might cost him." Jensen's mouth was tight. "That's the mark of a true blackcollar, Caine: loyalty. Loyalty to your teammates, to other blackcollars . . . and sometimes even to allies you don't approve of."

A shiver went up Caine's spine. "You're talking about Reger, aren't you?"

"Lathe's the one who makes our deals and alliances," Jensen said, his eyes focused elsewhere. "That's the doyen's job, and commandos don't expect to have much voice in those decisions. Fine. But there are other ways I can influence events."

"Such as by building a death-house gauntlet in Reger's mansion?" Pittman asked quietly.

"You've got it," the blackcollar said grimly. "Think of it as a loyalty test . . . with death as the punishment for failure."

Caine focused on Alamzad. "Did you know what he was planning?"

Alamzad shook his head. "I still don't," he added. "But I think I should."

"It'll cost you," Jensen warned. "All of you. If I tell you, I'll want your assistance in carrying out what'll essentially be an execution."

Caine took a deep breath. Far back in his mind, the thought occurred to him that this, too, was part of what it meant to be a leader. "You'll have it."

They set off before dawn the next morning: Lathe, Caine, Skyler, Bernhard, Kanai, and one of Reger's drivers, riding in tight discomfort in a car that had been designed for at least two fewer passengers.

"Why the hell didn't Reger give us a decent vehicle?" Bernhard growled as they headed out into the moutains. "Even a van would've been better than this."

"True," Lathe agreed. "But we've been using vans a lot lately, and I thought it might be a good idea to throw Security a minor curve in that area. They know how many of us there are and so will probably be watching most carefully for vans or large cars."

Bernhard snorted and fell silent.

Whether Lathe was right or whether the Security spotters were simply not watching the right place at the right time, they made it to the jump-off spot the comsquare had chosen without incident. "Everyone out," Lathe ordered, heading back to the trunk. "Get your kits and let's get started—we've got a long hike ahead of us."

Caine glanced around in the predawn glow, a strange sense of déjà vu tickling the back of his mind. The creek trickling quietly alongside the road, a particularly striking bluff rising above the hills to the south . . . and he caught his breath as the landscape clicked. "Lathe, do you know where we are?"

"A couple of klicks northwest of the Aegis Mountain entrance," the comsquare said. "As good a spot as any to strike out overland from. Why?"

"Oh . . . no particular reason, I guess. Only that we're just a ridge or two northwest of the spot we headed out from when we checked out the base."

"Ah. Well, at least this time you won't have to worry about your car being stolen."

The words were barely out of his mouth when the car beside them pulled away, making a U-turn and heading down the road in the direction it had come. Caine swallowed as he watched it disappear around a curve, knowing it was the best way but still not really liking the arrangement. A vehicle parked here would be horribly conspicuous, true; but on the other hand they had only Reger's promise that the car would indeed come by twice a day until they rendezvoused with it.

If the others were worried, though, they didn't show it. "Which way?" Skyler asked as he tightened the straps of his pack and hunched his shoulders a couple of times to settle it.

"Through there," Lathe told him, pointing along a rock-strewn cut between two steep hills. "Single-file, and keep an eye out for aircraft overhead."

They'd been hiking for just over an hour when a Security man stepped out of the undergrowth fifty meters ahead directly onto their path.

All six men froze into statues as Lathe, in the lead, flashed the appropriate hand signal back to them. The Security man, Caine noted uneasily, was heavily armed, with both a holstered paral-dart pistol and a shoulder-slung laser assault rifle. Radio headphones peeked out from under his mountain cap, and infrared-enhancement goggles were slung around his neck.

Caine gnawed at his lip. The soldier wasn't looking their way at the moment—was, in fact, facing ninety degrees away from their line of approach. But balancing that was the fact that the terrain and sparse foliage near him precluded any kind of quiet approach. They'd have to take him out from where they stood.

But Lathe was making no move to draw either his slingshot or a *shuriken*—was making no move at all, in fact. "When are we going to take him?" he whispered to Skyler as the seconds crept by.

"Just relax," the other whispered back.

And to Caine's surprise, the soldier turned and walked casually away.

"What . . .?" he hissed, totally confused now.

"You weren't paying attention to his stance and equipment," Skyler explained as they started forward again. "Both were more appropriate to a sentry than to someone on bush-beating duty. Bernhard, what's out here that anyone might want Security protection for?"

"No idea," the other said with a puzzled frown. "Kanai?"

The other shook his head slowly. "Nothing I know of. Possibly a major intake to the city water supply?"

"That's right—you got a map of that network a few days ago, didn't you?" Skyler commented to Caine. "Maybe they still think we're out to sabotage the system."

"Doesn't matter," Lathe put in. "From his positioning I'd guess the center of the ring is a ways south, off to our left. We'll veer north and see if we can avoid any more contacts."

"Right," Caine said. He glanced at Skyler, caught the other's signal. "Bernhard, Kanai—do either of you know what those things were around the guard's neck? I've never seen goggles quite like those before."

Bernhard snorted and launched into a rather condescending explanation of infrared-enhancement equipment. Caine kept the whispered discussion going for several minutes longer as they continued on, plying both him and Kanai with more such naive questions. It was an annoying role to play, but as a diversionary tactic it succeeded remarkably well. By the time the conversation ended, Skyler had returned to the group as quietly as he'd left it, without either of the Denver blackcollars having noticed his absence.

The sun rose higher in the sky, eventually passing zenith, as they continued to hike. "It sure didn't look this far on the map," Caine complained once as they broke for a ten-minute lunch.

"Uphill climbs never do," Kanai puffed, as out of breath as any of them despite his high-altitude acclimation. "For your full expedition out here, Lathe, I suggest you make the jump-off point a little closer. Reger isn't really going to learn anything useful about your destination, no matter where along the road his driver lets you off."

"You may be right," Lathe conceded. "Anyway, the worst part is over. I read the entrance as being just on the northern side of the peak over there." He pointed.

Caine looked and sighed. "What's that, another two or three hours?"

"One hour tops," Lathe promised. "Let's go. I want to find the entrance, figure out what we'll need to get it open, and be back at the pickup point before dark."

Lathe's estimate turned out to have been on the optimistic side, but not by too much. Exactly an hour and fourteen minutes later they came to a halt beside a rocky overhang and the ventilation tunnel intake.

Caine had wondered how the hell a two-meter grille could have remained unnoticed all these years, but now that he was here he realized that it wasn't nearly as unlikely as he'd imagined. Shielded from above by the rock overhang, its surface covered by strategically placed grasses and other plants, the actual intake openings scattered in an irregular pattern instead of a normal crosshatching—the more he studied it, the more he realized that even someone searching for the damn thing could walk right by without noticing it.

Lathe might have been reading his mind. "Lucky for us you knew precisely where this was located," he commented to Bernhard. "Wasn't it?"

"Yes," the other said shortly. "Hadn't you better get busy on your studies?"

"Yes, well, we're actually not in as much of a hurry—"

"Shh!" Kanai cut him off. Caine froze with the others, straining his ears. . . .

"Behind us," Bernhard murmured, drawing a *shuriken*. "Someone's coming."

"A lot of someones, actually," Skyler told him stepping over to examine the grille. "It's Mordecai and the rest of the group."

"What?" Kanai frowned, peering into the distance. "But you said—"

"I guess he lied, didn't he?" Bernhard snarled, jamming his *shuriken* back into its pouch. "That's all. Lathe's just making sure we all know who the boss is around here. All right, Comsquare; we're properly impressed. You going to level with us now?''

"Sure." Lathe nodded at the grille. "We're going in. Now."

"In other words, you never planned to make any preliminary studies." Kanai's face was beginning to redden with anger. "I thought we were allies now—you had no cause to lie to us."

"Maybe, maybe not," Skyler put in before Lathe could answer. "But we've been at least as truthful as your leader was. Haven't we, Bernhard?"

Kanai spun on him. "And I've also had about enough of that—"

"This supposedly hard-welded grille's already been cut free," Skyler interrupted him coldly.

"What?" Kanai frowned, his anger cooling into confusion. "That's impossible . . . isn't it?"

"Done fairly recently, too, I'd say—certainly since the war," Skyler continued. "It's being held on by twisted wires at a dozen or so places."

"Twisted from . . . ?" Caine asked.

"The outside."

"Well, well." Lathe turned back to Bernhard. "This remarkably well-hidden door, and someone managed to find it. Any ideas on how they might have done that, Bernhard?"

Bernhard's face had become a mask. "As you said, someone else must have stumbled on the place."

"Someone else who?"

"How should *I* know?" the other countered.

Lathe snorted. "Right." Turning his back on Bernhard, he joined Skyler and Kanai by the grille.

Fifty meters back, Hawking came around a clump of scraggly evergreen trees, the other blackcollars and Caine's teammates following in his wake. "Any trouble?" Caine asked as they approached.

Hawking shook his head. "Saw another of those Security guards after Skyler came back to warn us about them."

"Did you have to take him out?" Lathe asked.

"No, he was way to the south of us, sitting on a flat rock jutting out from the hillside. They're definitely guarding *something*, though."

Lathe grunted. "Well, whatever it is, it shouldn't be our problem. Braune, Colvin, Pittman—get busy assembling those rope ladders. We're going to need them right away. Hawk-

ing, Alamzad—come up here and check this thing out for
booby traps and alarms.''

But whoever had jury-rigged the entrance apparently hadn't
thought to leave any hidden deterrents behind. By the time
Caine's teammates had the rope ladders ready, Hawking and
Alamzad had removed the grille and made a visual examination of the first part of the tunnel beyond.

"You see that mesh lining the inside?" Hawking pointed it
out. "Looks like a multistage electric barrier, with potentials
starting at the slight-jolt stage out here and going up to lethal
on the last ring.''

"Sensors?'' Lathe asked.

"Between the rings—there and there. Probably mostly passive types: sound and motion detectors and maybe photobeam
or laser bounce reflectors. You don't want sensors this close
to the surface that use lots of current or throw off detectable
electromagnetic fields. That stuff will be deeper down.''

"What about the stage-one weapons Bernhard mentioned?''

Hawking pointed. "Right at the end there, where the tunnel starts going vertical. At least one reasonably heavy laser
and what look like a pair of flechette repeaters. Probably got
gas and acid jets hidden behind the electrical mesh, too—I
think I see where the metal has been acid-protected.''

Caine licked his lips. "How likely is it the stuff's running
on automatic?''

"It's not," Bernhard said. "Everything but the electric
mesh was manual control, and the fuel cells for the mesh
probably drained themselves years ago.''

Lathe cocked an eyebrow at Hawking. "True?''

"Probably." The other shrugged. "Hard to tell until we try
going in, though. The mesh, at least, doesn't seem to be
responding to pressure anymore.''

"In other words, we've learned all we can from out here,"
Lathe said. "Let's suit up, then—full flexarmor, including
gas filters.'' His eyes shifted to Bernhard. "And we'll let our
guide go first.''

Kanai gave the comsquare a long, hard look. "I thought
we were going to be allowed to leave once we got here," he
said. "Just another lie?''

"The grille's been opened,'' Lathe told him. "Bernhard's
the only one we know of who knew how to find it. You can
draw your own conclusions.''

Bernhard snorted. "Oh, I see—you think I came up here
five years ago and added new traps to the tunnel in case

someone from Plinry forced me to let him in someday. Come on, Lathe—you're being ridiculous."

"You're right, of course," Lathe said. "Let's just say I've grown accustomed to your company." He hesitated. "Though on second thought, there's no real reason you have to come along, Kanai. If you want, you can leave now."

Kanai seemed to consider that. Then, with a glance at Bernhard, he shook his head. "Thank you, Comsquare. But as long as I'm here anyway, I might as well see it through to the end."

"All right." Lathe took a deep breath, glanced around the group. "Mordecai, you'll stay up here on guard duty. The rest of you . . . let's go."

Chapter 34

Bernhard went first, unrolling the rope ladder before him as carefully as if setting out a fur-skinned runner for a visiting eminent. But nothing fired at him, blew up under him, or sprayed lethal fluids toward him, and by the time he tilted the rest of the bundle over the edge of the vertical shaft Caine was starting to breathe again.

Or he was until the uncoiling ladder hit the scud mine.

"You *did* say all these were set on manual, didn't you?" Skyler commented after the slender needles had buried themselves in the shaft walls and ceiling and the echoes of the blast had faded into silence.

"I also told you some of the mines were on automatic," Bernhard growled back.

"Looks like we hit one," Lathe said, glacially calm. "We'll have to watch ourselves on the way down. Avoid contact with the shaft walls, and don't touch anything that's protruding. Got that, everyone? Let's get moving, Bernhard."

The other took a deep breath and started down the ladder. Lathe went next, followed at twenty-second intervals by Hawking, Caine, Pittman, Braune, Colvin, and Alamzad, with Skyler bringing up the rear.

A hundred meters down, Bernhard had said, but to Caine

the trip seemed much longer. Suspended in almost total darkness, the faint glow from his armband light barely showing him the section of ladder before him, he found a strange sense of disorientation gripping him, as if his directional sense had disappeared. *Like the blind man combat test*, he thought; only this was much worse. The ladder's swaying seemed to be increasing in amplitude. . . .

"Everybody hold it a minute," Lathe's soft voice floated up from beneath him. "Stop where you are, lock your arms around the ladder, and take some deep breaths. Something funny is happening here—a low-level sonic, feels like, playing games with our inner-ear balance. Whatever, take a second to reorient yourselves."

"Use the other lights as reference," Hawking suggested. "Sorry, Lathe—I should have caught on to this earlier."

"Forget it," the comsquare told him. "Everyone okay? Let's keep going, but take it easy."

The effect seemed to get worse as they approached the bottom of the shaft, but Caine found that simply knowing it was an attack and not something internal made it easier to handle. Focusing on the lights above, listening to his other kinesthetic senses, he was actually startled when Lathe's goggled face suddenly appeared beside him and his feet hit solid ground.

"Oops," he said, prying his fingers from the ladder. "Sorry—concentrating on something else."

"No problem. Get into the tunnel before you get stepped on."

Caine nodded and moved away from the ladder. Ahead, the tunnel opening was visible in the sleeve-light glow, a dim figure—Bernhard?—already there. On the far side of the shaft another figure was crouched over a collection of wires and components. "What's that?" he asked, stepping over.

"Our confuser," Hawking's voice answered. "Lathe was right—it's a sonic broadcast unit of some sort, aimed upward along the shaft."

Caine glanced upward. "Seems a little silly, with all the armament already up there."

"It wasn't put here by the designers," Hawking replied. "It looks very much like it was hand-made. By an amateur."

Behind his gas filter, Caine licked his lips. "Ah-*ha*."

"Don't let it worry you," Lathe advised. "If this is the worst we'll have to face, we should be fine."

Somehow, that wasn't much comfort. Caine stepped into the tunnel proper, fingers taking automatic inventory of his weaponry.

The rest made it down without incident, and a few minutes later they were walking along the tunnel, again spread out in a loose line in case of trouble. There was little conversation; everyone seemed more interested in careful listening than in idle chatter. But aside from their own footsteps there was apparently nothing to hear.

Nothing to hear, and no impediments to their progress . . . and they had been walking for nearly half an hour before anyone noticed that there was something odd about that. "Bernhard," Alamzad called softly from near the back of the line. "Didn't you say this was an intake tunnel for the ventilation system?"

"Yes. Why?"

"Well . . . shouldn't we be running into filters of some sort along here somewhere? There ought to be at least a sensor mesh or bio-kill screen this far down the tunnel."

There was a long silence from the front of the line. "How about it, Bernhard?" Lathe prompted. "They didn't leave *all* the filtration work to the innermost tunnel section, did they?"

"I doubt it," Bernhard said at last. "There should have been at least the sensors he mentioned, and probably one or more micron filtration screens, too. I've been watching along the walls, and I think I've seen a couple of places where something like that would have been mounted."

"And you didn't say anything?" Colvin growled.

"Maybe he didn't find it significant that someone went to all the trouble of taking the stuff out," Pittman said icily.

"What significance do you want it to have?" Bernhard shot back. "I told you once I've never been down here. Everything could have been taken out of this end before the war, for all I know."

Colvin snorted his opinion of that.

"All right, ease up," Lathe put in mildly. "Bernhard never promised to take us by the hand and point out the sights along the way. It's up to us to keep our own eyes open."

The group went on, again in silence. Now that he was watching for them, Caine noticed more of the filter mountings Bernhard had mentioned: rings of heat-bruised metal running the circumference of the tunnel. " Looks like they were taken out with a torch," he muttered to no one in particular.

Hawking, ahead of him, half turned around. "And notice that they took the *entire* filter—they didn't just cut a hole so they could get through it. Might indicate it was done by scavengers, bringing stuff out of here back to Denver."

But then why didn't they also take the laser and flechette guns from the entrance? Caine grimaced, but kept quiet. The others were sure to have thought of that themselves anyway.

And finally, after walking for nearly an hour, they reached a thirty-meter cavern were a dozen tunnels like theirs met and combined. Ten meters inside it was the first of the stage-two passive defenses.

Or, rather, what was left of it.

"Class-four hullmetal," Hawking muttered, examining the edges of the man-sized hole that had been cut through the half-meter-thick bulkhead blocking the passage. Beyond the hole, off to one side, the missing piece lay warped and blackened on the tunnel floor. "Harder than hell. They were sure deadly serious about getting in."

"Serious and a little crazy, too," Alamzad said, leaning into the hole to peer at its edge. "There's gas-pocket honeycombing every five centimeters or so."

"What would that have been for?" Pittman asked. "Poison gas under pressure?"

"Or else something flammable to incinerate the cutter operator with," Hawking said grimly. "The fact that they got through anyway implies they knew what they were doing."

"Or had a lot of cutter operators," Lathe said. "Bernhard, what other defenses are there in this section?"

"Two more bulkheads," Bernhard said mechanically, peering beyond the barrier into the darkness swallowing up the rest of the vast chamber. "From the evidence, I'd guess they're gone, too."

"Um." Lathe seemed to consider, turned to Hawking. "At a guess, how long would it have taken to do three bulkheads like this one?"

"With the proper equipment . . ." Hawking pursed his lips. "Maybe a month or two. Without it, most of a year. At least."

"Hence the little sonic gadget back at the shaft?" Skyler suggested. "Something to guard their backs while they worked?"

Hawking shrugged. "Reasonable enough. Still . . . you *did* say stage three was totally unpassable, didn't you, Bernhard?"

"It was supposed to be," Bernhard said. "But I wouldn't have thought . . . whoever it was would have had the patience for this stage, either."

Jensen snorted. "Oh, come on, Bernhard, let's quit the wide-eyed innocent act, okay? *You* know who did this, *we* know who did this, so let's drop the bush-waltz."

For a moment Caine thought Bernhard was going to keep up the facade to the very end. But after a moment of silence, the other sighed behind his gas filter. "How long have you known?"

"We've *known* since we got to the intake tunnel," Lathe told him. "Suspected for a lot longer. After all, everyone we've talked to agrees that Torch disappeared without a trace—where else could they have gone but into Aegis Mountain? And who else might have known a way in that the Ryqril weren't blocking?"

"Pretty faulty logic," Bernhard said.

"Not really," Lathe said. "Anne Silcox remembers you as being held in much more esteem than your actions lately would warrant, which implies you were more help to Torch than you've let on."

"The real question," Skyler added quietly, "is whether or not you really *were* helping them on this one. In other words, whether you told them about all the defenses or made them find out the hard way."

Bernhard gazed steadily at the big blackcollar. "I told them everything I knew about this deathtrap," he said, his voice flat. "I told them their chances weren't good, that they'd be here for months just getting in." He took a deep breath and turned back to the cavern. "What can I say? They were fanatics."

"So you brought them here and just turned them loose?" Braune asked.

"That's what they wanted."

"You could have come down with them," Braune shot back. "Shown them the way, pointed out some of the traps."

"It doesn't look like they needed me, does it?" Bernhard retorted, waving a hand around him. "They got as far without me along as they would have with me here to hold their hands."

"And stage three?" Alamzad asked.

There was a long silence. Caine looked off into the darkness, wondering what they'd find down there. Bodies, most likely. An involuntary shiver ran up his back, and he turned to find Lathe's eyes on him. "We can quit now if you'd like," the comsquare said quietly.

Caine bit his lip. All this way . . . through the frustrations with Karen Lindsay and the Dupres . . . the humiliation of being plucked bodily from a Security trap . . . the loss of his command, willingly or not, to Lathe, and the price that had exacted from his ego . . . all of it for nothing? "Let's go on," he told the other. "See if they found a way through. If they didn't . . ."

Lathe nodded understanding. "We'll find out soon enough."

Within half a kilometer they'd come to the two other bulkheads Bernhard had mentioned, both of them cut through as the first had been. The tunnel narrowed down after the last one, though not to the point where they had to walk in single file again. The floor became inexplicably crunchy underfoot, suggesting to Caine that there were probably sonic detectors nearby using the sound of crackling gravel to track the intruders. But there was nothing he could think of to do about it except to stay alert and hope like hell that the first trap the tunnel threw at them would be something their flexarmor could handle.

But the tunnel didn't seem to be in any hurry, and they got another uneventful kilometer or so before Bernhard called a halt. "Stage three starts a little way ahead," he warned, gesturing to the curve just ahead. "From here on the tunnel will do a lot of twisting."

"Probably so you won't see the lasers until you're right on top of them," Lathe said grimly. "Back to single-file order. Bernhard and I'll go first."

"Until we reach the pile of corpses, anyway," Bernhard amended. "After that you're on your own."

"Move," Lathe nudged him.

They disappeared cautiously around the curve . . . and as the next in line, Hawking, started to follow there was a sudden exclamation from ahead.

"Lathe?" Hawking snapped.

"It's okay," Lathe's voice came, his tone a combination of relief, awe, and amusement. "Come ahead, everyone, and see how Torch beat the stage-three defenses."

A walking tank suit? was Caine's first thought—surely nothing larger could have been brought down the narrow entrance tunnel. He hurried to catch up with Hawking, and came to a confused halt beside Bernhard and Lathe, standing beside a man-sized hole in the wall.

"A secondary intake?" He frowned, leaning in to peer down it. It headed out at right angles from the ventilation tunnel for perhaps fifty meters and then seemed to turn toward the base ahead.

"It is indeed," Lathe said. "But not one the original designers had in mind."

"Torch?" Alamzad asked.

"Who else would have had the patience to dig a tunnel through a hundred and fifty meters of rock?" Bernhard said. But even he seemed a little awed. "Damn crazy fanatics, all of them."

A sudden revelation hit Caine. "So *that's* what we've been walking on—they just spread the rock chips from their digging on the tunnel floor back there."

Jensen cleared his throat. "Yeah. Fanatics. You realize, Lathe, that this means they're almost certainly still in there. And they may not like being interrupted."

"That's the main reason I wanted Bernhard along," Lathe said. "Let's hope they still remember you fondly, Bernhard." The comsquare glanced around the group. "Caine, you and I'll go with him; the rest of you stay here for now. No sense risking everyone until we've got some idea of what's ahead—that tunnel's too cramped to maneuver in if there's trouble."

The tunnel was narrower than it had looked from the entrance, frequently forcing them to sidle along crab-style. "What kind of wall would they have had to break through to get in?" Lathe asked as they sidled along.

"Four or five meters of reinforced concrete," Bernhard said, "with probably a few centimeters each of lead and soft iron for pulse protection. After cutting through the stage-two bulkheads and all this rock, I doubt it would have slowed them down significantly."

The three men continued on in silence. A few minutes later Bernhard's prediction was borne out, as they passed through an archway of torch-blackened concrete and half-melted metal at the tunnel's end and exited into a large, dark chamber.

They were in Aegis Mountain.

Chapter 35

For a long minute the three men just stood there, the faint glow of armband lights showing only the vaguest hint of their surroundings. *We made it*, Caine thought. *We made it. We're really here. Inside Aegis Mountain.* The biggest single obstacle to his quest . . . and yet, to his surprise, he found himself unable to generate any of the satisfaction he should rightfully be feeling at such a triumph.

But then, this was hardly his own personal victory. Beneath the foggy sense of unreality was the knowledge that without Lathe this would never have happened. Lathe, his blackcollar team, and the comsquare's other allies. With a lurch, Jensen's private scheme came to mind, and Caine grimaced behind his gas filter at the part he had yet to play in that plan.

But that was still in the future. For now, there was the Backlash formula to be found. Unfastening his light from its armband, he flipped it to higher power and played it around. A short distance away to both sides were stacks of plastic crates, extending away from their wall for at least fifty meters. "Supply storage?" he hazarded.

"Right," Bernhard said. "Level nine. Above us are three levels of officers' and enlisteds' quarters, the rec/med level, training level, command, munitions, and the fighter hangar. Some of those levels are considerably higher than this one, with actual freestanding buildings and landscaped rec areas—well, you'll see."

"Where's power generation handled?" Lathe asked.

"Beneath us," Bernhard said. "Twin fusion reactors, with gas turbine and multiple battery and fuel-cell backup. All of them probably long dead or tripped."

Lathe looked at Caine. "Presumably Torch has something running wherever they've set up shop—they won't have spent the last five years hunched over flashlights."

"Just as long as they've got power to the computer records," Caine muttered.

"Records?" Bernhard frowned. "*That's* all you wanted here? I thought you were looking for unused weapons or electronics."

"Don't worry—if it works out it'll be well worth the trouble," Caine assured him. On his wrist his tingler came on: Lathe signaling the others to join them. "Where would the best place be to get onto the computer?"

"Command level. Assuming Torch got enough power to the access control system to get the doors there open."

"If not, they probably just blasted them down."

"If they did, you can say goodbye to the computer," Bernhard growled. "That whole level is doomsdayed up to its roof."

"There's no point in speculation," Lathe said. Behind them, the faint scrape of boots on stone signaled the arrival of the others through Torch's bypass tunnel. "Let's get upstairs and find out where they're hiding."

There were no lights in operation on the supply level—no lights, no doorways, and no elevators. Fortunately, all the relevant doors had already been forced and jammed open and the backup stairways weren't hard to find. Using them was something else again; with their open spiral design and slightly uneven footing, they'd clearly been designed for easy defense, and with every level they ascended the prickling sensation between Caine's shoulder blades grew more and more uncomfortable. The fact that Torch hadn't attempted communication implied to him that the fanatics had decided on a no-warning ambush . . . and they'd have no better spot than along the staircase.

But the group reached level three without incident, found their way along the darkened halls to the main command center and found it untouched.

"All right, then," Lathe said, turning to Bernhard. "Where's the *next* best place to tie into the computer?"

"Down the hall," the other said, pointing. "The computer rooms are also on this level. But without power they're as useless as this place is."

"So maybe we'd better concentrate on finding Torch instead," Skyler said quietly. "If they're still here."

Lathe nodded, looking around them. "I'll admit the place seems deserted. But they *were* here . . . so where did they go?"

"Back outside?" Colvin suggested. "Maybe they just stuck around long enough to ice their trail and then took off for parts unknown."

"This is an awful lot of work to go to just to hide out," Alamzad said. "Unless they've just taken off temporarily to avoid seeing us."

"How would they have known we were coming?" Jensen asked.

"Oh, the base's phone lines are probably still operational," Bernhard said. "Maybe your friend Anne Silcox knows more about where her comrades went than she lets on."

"There may be a simpler explanation," Lathe said slowly. "Bernhard, where did you say the medical facilities are?"

They found them there, thirty-eight of them, in various parts of the brightly lit level-five medical complex. Men and women both, ages ranging from young adult to late middle age.

All of them dead.

"Damn," Braune whispered as they walked carefully among the bodies. "Damn."

"What happened?" Lathe asked Hawking as the latter rose from a brief examination of one of the bodies.

Hawking shook his head. "Vale's the one with the real medical knowledge, but it looks to me as if they were poisoned. You'll note there's been no visible decay—that's characteristic of some types of poisons. If I had to guess, I'd say it was something low-level they ingested over a long period of time."

"Not ingested," Bernhard said from across the room. "Inhaled."

Alamzad swore under his breath. "The gas attack that knocked the base out in the first place. *And* the missing filters from out in the tunnel."

"They knew," Skyler murmured. "We'll probably find the filters set up in their living quarters somewhere around here. They knew they were dying and tried to fight back."

"And yet they didn't leave," Lathe mused. "I wonder what they were doing down here that they considered that important."

"Never mind them," Pittman put in. "What about *us*, now that we're here? Will our gas filters be enough to protect us?"

"We won't be here long enough to build up a real dosage of the stuff," Lathe assured him. "Caine, there must be a separate computer for the medical section. It's a long shot, but let's see if they might have put your information in it." His eyes found Skyler. "The rest of you, spread out, see what else is around here."

The medical computer turned out to be across an untended environmental area in a building that also housed the main labs and several more bodies. "At least it's got power," Caine said, wincing as he rolled a corpse-laden chair out from in front of the console and tried a couple of commands. "Let's see if I can get on."

"If you can't, we'll ask Bernhard if he knows any special passwords," Lathe told him. "I'm going to take a look around the rest of the building. Signal if you find anything useful."

He left. "All right," Caine muttered, snaring another chair and sitting down before the keyboard. Computer usage had been fairly standardized throughout the TDE before the war, and his Resistance tutors had given him the most common military passwords. Keying one in, he began his search.

It took only about an hour to try all the passwords he knew and to run through the directories they accessed, and when he'd finished he leaned back in his chair and sighed. Nothing. No mention of Backlash; no files tied in with the word *blackcollar* except for a few medical records.

Which meant that Lathe's hoped-for long shot hadn't panned out. If the Backlash formula was indeed in Aegis, it had to be up on level three.

Caine glared at the screen. Getting in there would be a major project all its own—and a dangerous one, if Bernhard could be believed. Still, military computer systems often had overlapped files. Perhaps he could at least find out how to reenergize the command level from here. He was just beginning a second search of the directories when his tingler came on. *Caine: Come to the number-two lab—fourth door down the hall.*

Lathe met him at the lab's door, an odd expression on his face. "Any luck?" the comsquare asked.

"None," Caine told him. "Looks like we're going to have to get into the main machine upstairs after all."

"Maybe, maybe not. Come take a look at this."

Frowning, Caine stepped past him into the room . . . and stopped short with surprise.

Another twenty or more bodies were inside, most of them

lying in cots but a few slumped over lab tables. The lab tables
themselves . . .

"What the hell were they *doing* in here, anyway?" Caine
asked. "Place looks like a robotless genetics assembly line."

"It does at that," Lathe agreed. "I'd expected to find what
was left of Torch on this level, because they'd have come to
the med section to fight against their poisoning. But it looks
now as if they were set up here from the very beginning."

"That long?" Caine frowned.

"The indications are here. But hang on to your teeth—the
real kicker is over here."

Lathe led the way around one of the long tables to a
cluttered desk squeezed between a pair of chem-assemble
machines. A man lay across the papers and disks there,
looking for all the world as if he'd settled down for a short
nap and never awakened. A ledger-type book sat open before
him, and it was to the heading on the left-hand page that
Lathe silently pointed. Caine leaned over and read it . . .

"PRODUCTION SCHEDULE," was written there in a bold,
firm handwriting. "DOSAGES OF WHIPLASH PER DAY FOR WEEK
ENDING . . ."

"Whiplash?" Caine frowned. "What the hell is—"

He stopped abruptly. "Are you thinking," he asked the
comsquare slowly, "the same thing I am?"

"We won't know for sure without a real test," Lathe
cautioned. "But it's just barely possible we've found a short-
cut to the end of the mission."

Caine snorted gently. "Only if you believe in miracles,"
he said. "I gave those up about the same time I stopped
believing in Santa Claus."

"Nothing wrong with accepting miracles that come your
way," Lathe murmured.

Something in his tone made Caine look up at him. The
comsquare's face was tight, his eyes focused on infinity.
"What's wrong?" Caine asked.

"Oh . . . nothing. Nothing I can do anything about, anyway." Lathe took a deep breath, released it slowly. "You
just reminded me that Project Christmas is being activated
about now back on Plinry."

"Project Christmas? What's that?"

"Ask me another time," the other advised. "Come on,
let's get back and find the others. And see if we can come up
with a safe way to figure out just what the hell this little
Christmas present of Torch's really is."

Chapter 36

It was three in the morning, and Haven was collecting his gear for another sortie outside the equipment shed, when the scout ship from Earth reached Plinry orbit and sent its prearranged radio signal . . . and from the outer parts of Capstone, Dayle Greene activated Project Christmas.

Haven paused, listening as three distant explosions came faintly to his ears: one each from the Hub's eastern, southern, and western gates, Greene's signal to him and the nine other hidden blackcollars that the climax of the operation had begun. The blasts weren't particularly powerful, Haven knew, certainly nothing that could actually bring the gates down. But Security under Hammerschmidt's command was eminently predictable, and within minutes the Hub's forces would be racing to the wall to prepare for invasion.

Which would leave the Chimney virtually undefended against the blackcollars arrayed against it. Undefended, that is, except for a cadre of Ryqril guards and four multimegawatt lasers.

Haven gritted his teeth and eased out onto the roof. The whole thing was coming down a few days ahead of the anticipated schedule, but his force was really about as ready as it ever would be. The only question still hanging over them was whether or not the lasers had been adequately dealt with . . . and unfortunately there was only way to find out.

Security's reaction began as the blackcollar sidled to the corner of the equipment shed and carefully laid out his equipment. In the near distance cars started up and roared off toward the wall, and as Haven unfolded his sniper's slingshot he saw a spotter craft southward shoot off to the west. The spotters were a potential problem, he knew, but one they would just have to live with. At least the rows of Corsairs sitting on the ground at the 'port would be out of the way soon, assuming that the scout pilot up there played his role properly.

And if he did, Haven knew, odds were good those Corsairs

would blast him out of the sky. The blackcollar winced once, then put the thought firmly out of his mind. Some of the blackcollars waiting silently nearby would likely be dead within the hour, too, and dwelling on either possibility was counterproductive.

He had just set a large, silvery ball into his slingshot's pouch when the city lit up around him.

Dropping flat to the roof, he eased a goggled eye around the shed in time to see one of the wall-top lasers swivel upward and fire.

He grinned tightly. The drone pods the scout pilot was dumping out by the hundreds over the city were perfectly harmless, but the Ryqril had no way of knowing that. The laser swiveled fractionally, fired again; a second later the other three joined in the battle as the cloud of falling pods came within their respective ranges. Aiming, firing, reaiming— all of them operating at blinding electrical speed.

Or rather, two of them were, the ones at the back corners of the Chimney. But the two nearer ones, the ones that he, O'Hara, and Spadafora had spent over a week pelting with radioactive putty . . .

They were slow. Incredibly slow. The kind of slow that could only mean they were being aimed and fired manually.

In other words, Hawking's damn crazy trick had actually *worked*.

Haven took a deep breath and set his slingshot brace against his arm. Slow against distant specks in the sky would still be fast enough to vaporize blackcollar commandos trying to scale the Chimney wall. One last shot . . . and if it wasn't perfect all the rest would have been for nothing.

He waited with forced patience, watching the laser's movements for just the right moment, and as the weapon twisted upward and paused momentarily he let the pellet fly. Through his binoculars he saw it hit squarely in the middle of the exposed gimbal mechanism—

And squeezed his eyes shut as it flared with blue-white light.

There wouldn't be any direct damage, of course—the hullmetal gimbal ring was designed to withstand attacks by other high-power lasers, and Haven's simple thermite bomb would hardly even strain its heat sink. But high-power lasers didn't splatter molten metal all over the place—molten metal that the laser's own heat sink would help solidify. And with the weapon on manual control, it was likely to sit in virtually that same position long enough for the metal to congeal.

It was doubtful that the laser's operator even realized anything was wrong with the gimbals until the first of the grappling-equipped ropes caught on the wall next to the weapon and he tried to lower its aim. Haven held his breath as the laser strained against the strands of metal bracing it into its upward position . . . but the delicately balanced mechanism had been designed for speed, not power, and it struggled in vain. A quick glance at the Chimney's next corner showed the other laser had similarly been rendered helpless.

And a quarter of the enclave's perimeter wall was suddenly defenseless.

Reaching for his tingler, Haven tapped out a quick message. But the ground troops had already figured out that their keyhole was clear and four more ropes snaked their way to the top of the wall. *Spadafora, O'Hara: Stay on backup,* Haven signaled; and with one last quick assessment of the ground situation he headed back for the stairs at a dead run.

By the time he reached the dangling ropes and climbed up the Chimney wall, the other blackcollars had gone down the inside, and from the sounds and laser flashes coming from the enclave the battle was in full swing. "Situation?" Haven asked Charles Kwon, the latter stretched out under the disabled laser with a sniper's slingshot in hand.

"Most of the resistance is coming from that building over there," Kwon reported, nodding toward a squat blockhouse near the heavy gate. "Three Ryqril got through the gate, but since they haven't shown up down below I presume O'Hara and Spadafora have them pinned down. Three of ours are blocking any further sortie attempts; the other three went that way, toward the housing unit."

Haven nodded. "Any sign of Corsairs yet?"

"No, but from where I was it looked like the whole Plinry contingent was heading up to deal with the scout ship and pods before we made our move. If we hurry—"

He broke off, shifting aim and firing his slingshot toward a shadowy figure that had appeared around a building below. The Ryq jerked with the impact, his laser shot going wild. Before he could recover, a *shuriken* flickered across the courtyard from one of the half-hidden blackcollars. The alien flopped backward and lay still. "If we hurry," Kwon continued, reloading his slingshot, "we may get out of here before we have to worry about the Corsairs."

"We can hope." Haven tapped at his tingler. *De Vries, Anderson: Situation?*

De Vries; minimal Ryqril warrior presence—all forces effectively pinned down.

Anderson; have gained access to civilian quarters; objective not in sight.

"Maybe we should just go for a straight trade," Kwon suggested. "Their civilians for—"

De Vries; objective sighted in warrior blockhouse.

Haven grunted. "Cute. The roaches probably hustled 'em over there when the scout started shoveling out the pods. You called it, Kwon—got the hailer handy?"

In answer the other blackcollar pulled out a small box, set it to his lips. *"Khray hresakh tlahiin, Ryqril-ahz,"* he called, his voice booming from the tiny amplifier. *"Razenix ylay-kiy qhadi . . ."*

Haven listened with half an ear, the rest of his attention on the situation below. There was no guarantee the Ryqril commander would go for this; the other could just as easily decide to try to hold out until the Corsairs could bring firepower to bear from the air. Twisting his head, Haven took a quick look at the gimbal mechanism of the laser towering over him. It was supposed to be incapable of firing into the enclave itself, but with sufficient leverage at the proper places it might be possible to swivel it past its restraints. "Remind them we have two of their defense lasers at our disposal up here," he instructed Kwon. "We can probably turn it against the enclave directly; we can certainly shoot holes in their returning Corsairs if they choose to be stubborn."

Kwon nodded and cut loose with another long stream of jaw-cracking Ryqrili. Haven gnawed at his lip, painfully aware that time was on the aliens' side. If they didn't crack quickly, the blackcollars would have not only the Corsairs but also the full brunt of Capstone Security to deal with.

Abruptly, a faint alien voice drifted out of the blockhouse. *"Tlesahae—khreena,"* it said . . . and Haven let out a long sigh.

"Now," Kwon cautioned, "let's see if they really mean it."

They apparently did. A moment later two figures emerged from the blockhouse and headed toward the gate. *O'Hara,* Haven signaled, *objective moving our way. Confirm Ryqril still pinned.*

Acknowledged. Warriors still pinned.

"I'm going out to take fall-back position," Haven told Kwon, sheathing his slingshot and reaching for one of the ropes. "Pull our people out carefully—I don't want any last-minute cuteness on the cockroaches' part."

"Got it. Watch for tricks out there, too."

But the Ryqril made no attempts to renege on their deal. It was almost, Haven thought, as if the invasion of their supposedly impenetrable enclave had so rattled them that thoughts of resistance never entered their minds. Whatever the reason, it reduced by one the number of obstacles they had yet to face. Keeping half his attention on the ground and the other half on the sky, he watched and waited.

Minutes later the exchange was complete. The two figures were outside the enclave, the failed Ryqril sortie back inside behind the closed gate. Haven hurried forward, knowing that as the blackcollars pulled out the danger of enemy retaliation increased dramatically. The blackcollar assault force was appearing over the wall now, and as the first of them slid to the ground Spadafora and O'Hara drove into sight with the cars they'd appropriated from a nearby parking area. They headed for the two figures too, arriving at the same time as Haven.

"Who's that, Taurus Haven?" the older woman said, voice tense and quavering slightly as she peered at Haven's goggled face. "It's about time—we were starting to think you'd forgotten all about us."

"Don't be silly, Mrs. Pittman," Haven chided her gently, ushering the two women toward the waiting cars. "It's just that some things take time."

The tally was impressive, and beyond Haven's most optimistic expectations: no one dead, only one incapacitated, and only a few other injuries that could be considered major. A definite and almost complete victory, he thought as they wheeled around and drove like banshees away from the Chimney.

The trick now was to get them all out of the Hub alive.

There hadn't been much real discussion on this phase of the operation, mainly because contingency planning didn't mean a hell of a lot when the assault team was going to have to get through both Hammerschmidt's forces and whatever the Ryqril had on hand to throw at them. It was going to be strictly a play-by-ear escape, and all of them knew it. Security's edge was in numbers; the blackcollars' was in superior training and a firm grip on the initiative.

It wasn't until they were halfway to the gate that it suddenly occurred to Haven that the expected Security forces had yet to show up.

"Where the hell are they?" he muttered to O'Hara, hunched over behind the wheel. "The Ryqril must have alerted them by now that we're here."

"Yeah, I've been wondering the same thing," O'Hara said. "Mrs. Pittman, Davette—did the Ryqril communicate with Security at all during the time you were in the blockhouse?"

"I'm afraid we don't understand Ryqrili," the older woman murmured, her eyes locked on the deserted street ahead.

"But they would've talked to Security in Anglic, Mother," the girl pointed out. Her attitude, Haven noticed, was almost serenely calm in the face of their danger—a toughness he'd often seen in her brother, as well. "None of them said anything in Anglic while we were in there, Commando Haven."

O'Hara cocked an eyebrow at Haven. "Maybe they really *didn't* alert Hammerschmidt. Could be they were so embarrassed at their fortress being breached that they wanted to handle things themselves."

"Or else they weren't sure they trusted Security not to take advantage of the opening themselves," Haven mused.

"Everyone in Security is loyalty-conditioned—"

"Yes, well, if blackcollars came charging into *my* fortress, I think I might suspect Security anyway," Haven said. "Or maybe they've just decided on a simple old-style ambush. Just keep your eyes open."

Haven didn't believe it himself, any more than O'Hara seemed to, and he was as surprised as any of them when the two cars arrived within sight of the south gate with still no signs of reaction. "At least," O'Hara commented as they glided to a halt by the curb a block from the metal mesh, "we've found where all the guards went. I was starting to wonder if they'd dropped off the planet."

"Um," Haven grunted. They'd found Security, all right: four carloads of them, anyway, grouped in defensive position around the gate as if still expecting an attack from outside the Hub. "At a guess I'd say Greene and his merry men have been keeping up the diversion pressure out here."

"Another good reason to have left us alone," O'Hara suggested. "Conventional wisdom would say the Ryqril could handle us themselves."

"Which begs the question of where the hell the Ryqril

reaction is,'' Haven growled. Outside, the blackcollars from
the second car were flitting shadowlike along the street
toward the Security positions. If they really didn't know the
blackcollars were behind them, they wouldn't have anyone
watching their backs. . . .

The results were inconclusive, but if there were sentries
posted, they clearly weren't up to the job. Minutes later, the
entire Security force adequately neutralized, the cars sped
through the gate and out into the relative safety of the city
beyond. O'Hara turned at the first corner and pulled into a
garage that opened before them, and as the car rolled inside,
Haven caught a glimpse out the window of a dark craft riding
high in the sky above them.

He smiled tightly. So the Ryqril *had* sent a Corsair or two
after them. But if they'd held off attacking to avoid damaging
their puppets in the Hub, they'd gambled away their last
chance. Out here, among the common people and the laby-
rinth escape route he and Greene had set up, the aliens hadn't
a hope in hell of catching them without burning down all of
Capstone.

Which, it occurred to him, they might be willing to do. But
that was out of his hands. His part of Project Christmas had
been a success; the future repercussions were up to the universe at large.

Chapter 37

''Backlash.'' Colvin said the word slowly, as if tasting it.
''Backlash. So *that's* what this whole thing was about. Damn.
No wonder you kept it secret, Caine—the Ryqril would probably have preferred blowing up Denver to our getting hold of
it.''

''We haven't got it yet,'' Skyler warned. ''Speaking for
myself, Lathe, I don't believe it. If Torch reconstructed the
formula for Backlash, why did they give it a different name?''

''Why not?'' Lathe countered. ''After all, there's no guarantee they ever knew the correct code name to begin with.''

''In which case,'' Hawking put in dryly, ''they hit mighty

close to it accidentally. I agree with Skyler, Lathe—I think we should avoid getting our hopes up at this stage."

"Agreed," Lathe said. "But whether Torch's drug is Backlash or not, we still need some way to test it out. Suggestions?"

There was a minute of silence. Caine sent his gaze around the room, to Colvin and Braune as they stared off into space . . . to Alamzad as he whispered quietly to Hawking . . . to Pittman, who finally knew why the tightrope he'd been walking all these months had been so important.

And as his eyes drifted to Skyler and Jensen he could see that they, too, were watching his teammates—were judging, perhaps, their reactions and potentials. *We're still in school as far as they're concerned*, he thought with a touch of bitterness. *Cadets—trainees—junior members of the team. Well, that's going to change soon. Just as soon as we're true black-collars ourselves.*

"What sort of documentation was there for this Whiplash stuff?" Hawking spoke up. "Anything either on the computer or hard-copied?"

"The book had a lot of stuff in it besides production listings," Lathe told him, "but I couldn't make much sense out of it. You and Alamzad can take a run through it, but I suspect we'll need a biochem expert to really figure it out."

"In other words," Pittman said quietly, "the only way to really test it will be to try it out on someone. All right; whenever you're ready, I volunteer."

"Thanks," Lathe said, "but we're a long way from that point yet. We first have to look through the book and the medical computer, and then see if we can get into the main computer upstairs. And even then we aren't just going to inject anyone with an unknown drug."

"Eventually, you'll have to," Pittman said. "And you know it. I'm just getting my bid in early."

"Pittman . . ." Skyler hesitated. "Look, they're going to be all right. Project Christmas—"

"Was impossible from the start," the younger man said with a touch of bitterness. "Don't kid yourselves—I didn't. But that doesn't mean I don't appreciate the effort."

"Pittman—"

"No, it's all right, Lathe." Pittman got to his feet, headed for the door. "I'll be ready whenever you want me."

He left. "Damn," Braune murmured under his breath.

"He'll be all right," Lathe said. "If he wasn't as tough as he is, I wouldn't have let him play this double-agent game in the first place. The best thing we can do for him now is to finish up here as quickly as possible and get back to Plinry.''

"Where I trust the news about this Project Christmas will be good," Caine said.

"We all hope that," the comsquare agreed grimly.

"Well, then, let's get to it." Hawking sighed, standing up. "We're talking at least a couple of days of steady work here. Incidentally, anyone know where Kanai and Bernhard are?''

"They're over in the isolation ward, looking through the records there," Jensen said. "I can see the only door into the place through my window here, and they haven't left."

Lathe cocked an eyebrow. "You making a second career out of keeping track of them?" he asked mildly.

"Someone has to," Jensen replied.

"Point," Lathe admitted. "Okay—the job's yours. The rest of you, let's get to work."

"Try it now," Hawking grunted, wriggling his way back along the ceiling cable tray and dropping to the medical-lab floor.

Caine tapped in the password; a moment later a new directory appeared on his display. "I'm in," he announced. "I don't believe it, but I'm in."

Hawking shook his head as he stepped to Caine's side. "I don't believe it either, but I'm not too proud to accept gifts from the universe. Maybe Torch was smarter than we thought.''

"Oh, I agree. Why take the risk of breaking into the command level when you can tap into the computer files through the medical system down here? What I'd like to know is how they physically got the storage disks upstairs into the readers."

"Maybe they found a back-door crawlway someone could use," the blackcollar said. "Maybe they got one of the remotes in there started. Or maybe the last Aegis survivors even left it set up this way. Whichever, I'll be happy to take it."

"Yeah." Caine found a likely-looking file and accessed it. "Did we ever establish whether or not we'd recognize the Backlash formula if we do run across it?"

"I'll take any formula at all at this stage," Hawking replied candidly. "Four days in this hole has me just about at my limit. How the hell did they expect people to hold out here for years on end?"

"Having lights and companionship around would probably help," Caine said. "Look at this, will you?"

Hawking pulled over a chair and peered at the display. Caine expelled a tired breath and let his gaze drift to the lab's window. He hated to admit it, but four days in Aegis had about done him in, too. The emptiness and silence were just too unnatural; the lack of light everywhere but the stairway and medical level was downright spooky. Only out in the open area between buildings—

His thoughts froze in mid-grumble. Braune was coming across the open area toward the lab complex at a dead run, and he looked worried. "Back in a minute," Caine told Hawking, getting out of his seat and heading out the door.

He met Braune at the building's entrance. "What's up?" he asked.

"Trouble," the other puffed. "Bernhard's attacked Jensen and gone into the stairwell."

"He *what*? Jensen all right?"

"I think so—Colvin's over with him now, by the stairway door. Jensen had me tapped as backup man, but I was too far away to help."

"Show me," Caine ordered. "Have you alerted Lathe?"

"I didn't know where he was," Braune said as they headed off, "and I thought that Bernhard might have left Kanai down here as backup, so I didn't want to use the tingler."

"But if Bernhard's lost us—"

"He hasn't. I grabbed Pittman and sent him out on Bernhard's tail before I came for you."

Pittman. Great. The man with the martyr leanings. "We've got to find them right away," he growled.

"I know. Over here."

They skidded to a halt at the stairway door. A few meters beyond it, Colvin was kneeling over a prone Jensen. "How is he?" Caine asked, dropping to one knee and checking the other's pulse.

"Out cold, but I don't think he's badly injured," the other replied. "I waved Alamzad over a minute ago and I sent him after Pittman, okay?"

"Yeah." Caine glanced around, but none of Lathe's team was in sight anywhere. "Braune, get back to the lab where you found me and tell Hawking. Colvin and I will go after Bernhard."

"Watch yourselves," Braune warned as he headed off again.

Inside the stairwell, all was quiet. "Which way?" Colvin whispered.

In answer, Caine pointed to the *shuriken* lying on the second step up. "My guess is the command level. Let's go."

They started to climb, as quietly as possible. Once again, Caine found himself thinking of how well designed for ambushes the staircase was, but again his fears proved unfounded. At each landing they found another throwing star pointing the way farther upward, but that was the only visible indication that anyone had even come this way since their arrival. No sounds other than their own footsteps; no glimpses of either their quarry or their fellow teammates. As they passed the command-center level and still the *shuriken* led upward, Caine began to wonder if perhaps Bernhard had caught and eliminated his new shadows and left the stars himself as decoys.

But they kept on, and just inside the level-one stairwell door Alamzad was waiting, his *nunchaku* gripped in his hand. "Where are Lathe and the others?" he hissed as Caine and Colvin stepped to his side.

"Braune's getting them," Caine said. "Where are Pittman and Bernhard?"

"Inside the hangar—straight down the hall and out the double doors," the other said. "Bernhard went right over to the main control station, we think. Pittman's watching from a distance, but he'll probably take some action on his own if you don't get in there quick."

"Hell," Colvin whispered. "Caine, the hangar is where the main tunnel exit starts. Do you think . . .?"

"That Bernhard's going to let the Ryqril in?" Caine's stomach knotted. "I sure as hell hope not. But whatever he's up to, we've got to get in there and stop him." He pulled the door open.

"Hold it," Alamzad said suddenly. "I thought I heard something on the stairs."

Colvin stepped to the railing, took a quick look down. "I don't see anything," he said. "Could be Lathe and reinforcements. Should we wait?"

"No." Caine shook his head. "Besides, this is *our* job— *we're* the ones Jensen picked for his backup, remember? Come on."

They slipped through into the darkened hallway, and from there past the large double doors into the hangar proper . . .

and as they took their first tentative steps in the pitch-darkness, Caine realized they were in trouble.

The hangar was *huge*. The supply storage room they'd entered Aegis through had been comparable in size, but with boxes and crated machinery all around it had seemed more likely a cozy maze than anything else. In contrast, the hangar had an overwhelming sense of emptiness about it, an emptiness that, combined with the darkness, gave Bernhard a hell of a combat advantage.

"Where's this control station, Zad?" Colvin hissed at Caine's side.

"Straight across the hangar," Alamzad whispered back.

Caine took a deep breath. It was the blindfold test all over again, this time for real. "All right," he said, forcing calmness into his voice. "We'll use the Plinry recognition code system—try not to take each other out in the fight. Do you know where Pittman is, Alamzad?"

"Afraid not."

"Okay. Colvin, you hang back near the door until we've got Bernhard localized. Give us a hundred-count, then signal Pittman with the recognition info."

"Via tingler? That'll alert Bernhard."

"Can't avoid it. Besides, by then we ought to be in position to jump him."

"Right. Good luck."

Alamzad to his right, Caine set off. *Open your senses,* Lathe's old instructions came back to him. *Relax, and allow your subconscious to process the information your ears, nose, and skin are sending it.* He concentrated . . . and as he slipped into the necessary mental state the small bubble of perception around him began to expand. *There,* off to his right—something large, with a stubby appendage stretched out toward them. One of the fighter craft, somehow still safely inside when the rest were locked out by the base's fall? Probably. Ahead, the sounds of a low voice were becoming audible—Bernhard talking to himself? Odd; but it was the best directional marker the hunters could have asked for. He stepped up his pace; with luck they'd be on top of the blackcollar before Colvin's tingler signal alerted him that he had company.

Caine: Bernhard on phone at far end of hangar.

"Dammit!" Caine snarled to himself, slapping at his tingler. But it was too late; Pittman's ill-timed message had sent the balloon up for good. "Attack," he snapped, charging forward.

Beside him, he sensed Alamzad vectoring off from his direction, swinging wide to flank Bernhard and present a more diffuse target. Caine snatched out his *nunchaku*, sent the flail swinging in a wide defensive arc ahead of him. Somewhere very near here—

With a *crack* of hardwood on hardwood the *nunchaku* leaped in his hand, almost tearing itself from his grip. He had barely time to realize he'd just hit Bernhard's own *nunchaku* before a foot snapped out toward his chest.

Snapped out much too fast to counter; but if Caine's reflexes weren't those of a blackcollar they were still adequately fast. Twisting at the waist, he managed to turn far enough for the kick to hit him obliquely, the toe of the boot scraping across his chest as it went by. Off-balance, his own counterkick was weak and of dubious aim, but it still connected solidly enough to elicit a grunt of pain from his opponent. Caine let the momentum of Bernhard's kick throw him backward, flipping himself over into a crouch. "Bernhard?" he called into the darkness. "Give it up, Bernhard—you can't get out of here."

The other didn't answer . . . but abruptly there was a crash of bodies off to his side. "Got him!" Alamzad gasped, the last word cut off into a *whuff* of expelled air. Caine took a long step toward the sound, dimly sensing someone else moving in from behind. "Bernhard!" he snapped, and as the faint swish of cloth on cloth telegraphed the blackcollar's coming attack, Caine ducked his head, rolled into a flat somersault, and kicked both feet straight out toward his unseen opponent.

He caught Bernhard square in the chest, from the feel of the impact, throwing the other backward to the floor. Caine's *nunchaku* was still in his hand; rolling into his knees, he swung it whistling over his head.

The hardwood slammed into bare hangar floor, the crack echoing in the vast room. Caine flipped the flail horizontally, trying to find where Bernhard had rolled to. "Over here!" Colvin called from ahead of him, and Caine was scrambling to his feet when his tingler suddenly went on: *Stand by for nova.*

Nova; Plinry code for a flare. Caine halted in midstride, squeezing his eyes down to slits . . . and suddenly the room blazed with light.

Bernhard was caught flat-footed. Even as he twisted his head away from the glare and tried to leap back, Colvin's *nunchaku* lashed out to catch him hard across his abdomen.

Bernhard folded over with a choked gasp, falling heavily to the floor. Colvin raised the *nunchaku* for a final blow to the head—

"Hold it!" Caine snapped. "Don't kill him. We need to know who he was talking to on the phone."

Colvin caught the flailing half of the *nunchaku*, brought both sticks down to a guard position. Caine glanced around, spotted Alamzad dragging himself slowly from a prone to a sitting position. "You all right?" Caine asked, stepping toward him.

The other nodded weakly, clutching his stomach . . . and only then did it penetrate Caine's conscious mind that the light bathing the tableau was far too clean and steady to be coming from a flare.

He turned, squinting against the glare. A pair of spotlights of some sort. He stepped out of their direct line, in time to see a shadowy form climb out and away from a larger shadowy bulk.

The bulk he'd tentatively identified earlier as a leftover fighter craft. "Pittman?" he called.

"Here," Pittman replied, coming around into the light. "What do you know? The damn trick actually worked. I was afraid nothing would happen when I flipped the switch."

"*I'm* glad you didn't get the laser cannon controls by mistake," Caine countered. "Good move, though. All right, Bernhard—you've had enough time to get your wind back. Who'd you call and what did you tell him?"

Bernhard's face was still pained, but he managed a tight smile anyway. "I called for revenge," he said in a hoarse voice. "You're finished, Caine—you and your whole crowd of troublemakers. I've just burned your last bridge out of here."

Chapter 38

"What the hell is *that* supposed to mean?" Caine growled, his throat suddenly tight.

"It means I've taken out your base of operations," Bernhard said. Still holding his stomach, he eased himself into a sitting position. "You probably didn't know it, but while we were at his house Reger was stupid enough to tell me that he'd had Jensen redo his sensor net. Thought it would be a deterrent, I suppose. The fool. So. In an hour it'll be dark outside; half an hour after that he'll be dead meat."

Alamzad snorted weakly. "*You're* the fool," he said. "I worked with Jensen on that net, Bernhard—Security won't get within half a klick of Reger's house."

"Security?" Bernhard's lip twisted in contempt. "Quinn's trained idiots couldn't find their way through a garden patch. No, Security won't be called into the act until Reger is dead and his house a smoking ruin—though after that I imagine they'll find enough evidence linking him to you to take his organization apart down to the bedrock."

"So it was your blackcollar team you called," Caine said quietly, an odd feeling of sadness flowing in to replace some of the tension. He'd hoped Bernhard wouldn't do this. "All right, Bernhard—on your face on the floor. Lathe'll want to talk to you."

"Oh?" Abruptly, the pain left Bernhard's face, and in a single fluid move he was on his feet again. "And I suppose you beginners are going to take me down to him? Forget it, Caine. I go where I choose—and you haven't got a snow-flake's chance of stopping me."

"No, he doesn't," a new voice came from the shadows behind the fighter craft. "But I do."

Caine turned, combat reflexes tensing.

And Kanai walked forward into the light.

"You spoke of bridges," Kanai said, taking a few more steps forward to stand facing Bernhard. Peripherally, he knew that Caine and Pittman had shifted position to bring *nunchaku* to bear against him; that Alamzad, still on the floor, had quietly drawn a *shuriken*. But at the moment none of that mattered. All that mattered was Bernhard and the shame he was bringing upon them all. "Another bridge is at risk here," he told his leader. "The bridge of friendship between us. If you value my loyalty—my presence in your team—you'll call Pendleton back and withdraw the order."

"So you're joining this band of suicidal fools?" Bernhard sneered. "I thought you had more sense, Kanai."

Kanai felt his lip twitch. "I have no intention of joining them, Bernhard—I don't especially like them, and some of Lathe's methods make me ill. But that's not the point. Like them or not, they *are* blackcollars . . . and I cannot simply stand by and allow you to betray them.''

Bernhard returned his gaze steadily, and in the other's expression Kanai could see that there would be no turning back. Not for him, not for anything else. Bernhard had chosen his path, and nothing but death could turn him from it.

And Kanai felt infinitely old.

"You're getting worked up for nothing." Bernhard said softly. "I haven't betrayed any blackcollars—not really. But without Reger as a base, Lathe'll have no choice but to pull out as soon as they're done here." His eyes flicked back to Caine. "I warned him to get out of Denver, Caine. This is the price of ignoring me.''

"So you pay Reger back for your anger at Lathe?" Alamzad growled. "How noble. True blackcollar spirit.''

Bernhard's expression hardened. "And what would *you* know about blackcollar spirit?" he countered. "Or about warfare, for that matter? Reger's going to be an object lesson; when he breaks, the rest of the criminal underworld will fall into line that much faster.''

"So that you can get your slice of the gravy pie?" Pittman said contemptuously.

"So that we can have the resources to continue the war," Bernhard told him.

Kanai shook his head. "No, Bernhard. Jensen was right— you haven't any real intention of taking us back into the battle. You're just playing games, pretending you're more than just the dead husk of what you once were.''

Bernhard's eyes flashed anger. "And you, of course, are too noble to admit defeat when a cause is lost? Face reality, Kanai—we have each other and that's it. Either we stick together or Security takes us apart one at a time. If we can't win the war, we can at least survive.''

"To what end? Survival for its own sake? That's no better than death.'' With an effort Kanai stifled the tirade building up inside him. Now was not the time for a philosophical discussion. "Call Pendleton back. This is your last chance.''

"No," Bernhard shook his head.

Kanai let his hand rest on the ends of his sheathed *nunchaku.* "Then I will.''

"You can try. You'll have to get by me first.''

Kanai took a deep breath. "I know," he said softly, and started forward. One step . . . two. . . . Bernhard brought his own *nunchaku* into fighting position. . . .

"Stop," Caine said suddenly. "Kanai, back off. It's not worth risking your life for. Reger's not in any danger—all Bernhard's done is to send his own men to their deaths."

Bernhard snorted. "Because of Jensen's big bad sensor system? I see you're not familiar with the term 'keyhole.' "

"You mean the setting up of a section of sensor net that can be deactivated from the outside?" Caine said calmly. "Oh, there's a keyhole there, all right. I presume that's why Reger and Jensen let you know that he'd done the work, so you'd know to look for a keyhole if you decided to betray us."

Bernhard's eyes narrowed. "You're slidetalking," he said flatly. "Reger shot off his lungs, and you're just trying to talk your way out of the hole."

Kanai turned to see Caine shake his head . . . and something in the other's face sent a shiver up his own back. "You're wrong," Caine said. "Jensen did more than just revamp Reger's sensor net, Bernhard. He also built a death-house gauntlet into the mansion."

"What?" Bernhard's hands visibly squeezed down on his *nunchaku*.

"You heard me. A death house, one capable of taking out even blackcollars. So leave him be, Kanai. If they obey him, what happens is on their own heads."

For a long moment Bernhard stared hard at Caine, indecision rippling across his face. "And you think it's too late to warn them, do you?" he at last. "Well—"

Without warning, he turned and sprinted back to the hangar wall and snatched up the phone headset. Caine snarled something, but it was clear he'd been caught off-guard and his reaction would be too slow. Across the way Pittman hurled his *nunchaku* at Bernhard, which missed, and Colvin charged forward, scrabbling for a *shuriken*—

And something inside Kanai broke.

A *shuriken* seemed to leap of its own accord into his hand; all the frustration and shame of the past years welled up in his arm to send the black throwing star burning across the gap like an avenging angel—

And Bernhard jerked backward with a yelp as the *shuriken* sliced cleanly through the phone cord and ricocheted from the metal wall into the darkness.

"No," Kanai said into the sudden silence. The word was heavy on his tongue—heavy, but strangely clean. "With your actions you've forfeited the right of command. Caine is right; the others must now make their own choice as to whether or not to accept your betrayal.''

Slowly, Bernhard laid down the handset and started to walk toward Kanai, his eyes alive with madness-tinged hatred. Kanai licked his lips, but stood his ground without fear. He had no doubt he would die in the coming fight, but death wasn't really that hard to face. Not for a man who'd been allowed one last chance to regain the manhood he'd thought gone forever.

''Don't try it, Bernhard.''

The voice came from the shadows behind Kanai; and as Bernhard jerked and a low guttural growl escaped his lips, Kanai thought he would attack right then and there. Slowly the madness left the other's eyes, and with a deep, pain-filled breath he straightened from his fighting stance and lowered his arms to his sides.

And stood there, his face a mask, as Skyler and Hawking stepped forward into the light to take him under control. Behind them, Lathe paused beside Kanai. ''Welcome back,'' the comsquare said, searching the other's face.

Kanai locked eyes with him. ''You were waiting to see what I'd do, weren't you?'' he said, anger at Lathe stirring in him again. ''To see whether I'd side with him.''

''As you said, each of you has the right to make his own choice,'' the comsquare said quietly.

Kanai took a deep breath, eyes flicking to where Bernhard's hands were being secured behind him. *Why doesn't he try to escape?* he wondered . . . but the question wasn't hard to answer.

Even half insane with anger, Bernhard was still first and foremost a survivor.

Kanai closed his eyes briefly and turned away . . . and wondered why that thought should so fill him with pity.

Chapter 39

"Where will you go?" Caine asked as Skyler removed the makeshift shackles from Bernhard's wrists and stepped back to stand by the entrance to Torch's bypass tunnel.

Bernhard rubbed his wrists for a moment in silence before fixing Caine with a cold glare. "Do any of you really care?" he asked. His eyes flicked from Caine to Lathe, lingered on Kanai. The latter seemed to Caine to stiffen slightly, but he didn't shrink from Bernhard's gaze.

"We all care," Lathe said. "It's not too late even now to get back into the fight."

"Alone?" Bernhard snorted. "Dead or deserted, I've lost what's left of my team."

"You were trained to be able to fight alone," Lathe reminded him. "And there are organizations like Torch all over the world you could link up with. You're a valuable quantity, Bernhard—I'd hate to see you throw yourself away."

The other held Lathe's eyes for a long moment. "It's you, Comsquare, who's throwing himself away. You'll never get off this planet, you know, and if Quinn doesn't get you the Security chief in the next city will. You're dead, Lathe—all of you are. Remember that, Kanai. Remember it when the Security troops are moving in on you . . . and remember that *I* kept you alive and healthy in enemy territory for thirty years."

Kanai didn't reply, and after a moment Bernhard turned to the tunnel entrance. "Before you go," Skyler said, holding a folded piece of paper out toward him, "you'll need this."

Bernhard frowned down at the paper. "What is it?"

"Your departure pass," the big blackcollar told him. "Mordecai's guarding the entrance, remember? He won't let you leave alone without this."

Bernhard spat a curse in reply. "I suggest you take it," Lathe said mildly. "Mordecai's a better fighter than any of us, including you . . . and he takes his orders very seriously."

275

Bernhard snatched the paper out of Skyler's grip and, without another word, disappeared down the tunnel.

Caine took a deep breath. "I hope there's no way he can set up any booby traps on his way out."

"There won't be," Lathe assured him. He nodded, and with an answering nod Skyler slipped into the tunnel behind the departing blackcollar.

"Bernhard will spot him," Kanai murmured.

"Perhaps," Lathe said. "But he won't do anything about it. Come on, gentlemen—let's finish this project and get the hell out of here."

"No other conclusion?" Lathe asked, his eyes flicking between Hawking and Caine.

Caine shook his head wearily. "It's not listed on any file we can access. The code-check program Hawking wrote can't find any overlaid codes of the sort we found in the Plinry archives. There's no hard-copy data anywhere we can get to. The Backlash formula simply isn't here."

Lathe sighed, and for a long moment the room was silent. "Well," he said at last, "that's the way things go sometimes. The universe doesn't give any guarantees that there are even answers to the questions we ask, let alone that we can find them."

Hawking stirred. "I take it, then, that the Torch drug is not, in fact, Backlash?"

"I wish we knew," the comsquare said. "We've gone through every scrap of documentation we could find—we've got the calculated dosage amount, the formula, the manufacturing sequence, and even the estimated lifespan of the drug. But as to its purpose, not a whisper. Apparently they didn't think it necessary to mention that, as if anyone likely to find it would already know what Whiplash refered to."

"Then maybe Anne Silcox will be able to tell us something," Hawking suggested.

"Maybe," Lathe said. "Assuming she and Reger did indeed survive the attack Bernhard called down on them, which is by no means certain. I've been thinking we might do a quick test before heading back there, just to see if the stuff does anything obvious."

"No," Caine said firmly. "Absolutely not. Pittman's already suffered more than his fair share for this mission, I'm not having you risk his life with some witch's brew a group of fanatics came up with."

"Agreed," Lathe said. "But who said anything about testing the stuff on Pittman?"

Caine stared. "You mean . . . *you?*"

"Do I look crazy?" the other countered. "I'd prefer to use someone a little more expendable. Come on, let's get the gear packed up. If we hurry, we should be able to make it back to Reger's tonight."

The first thing Miro Marcovich noticed as he drifted toward consciousness was that somewhere his body was hurting like hell.

It took a while longer for the pain to localize into his neck, and as it did so the rest of the sensations began falling into place. He was lying on his back on a prickly surface . . . his left arm inexplicably bare . . . and there were footsteps and murmurs of conversation around him. *Did I faint?* he wondered, searching his mind for a clue as to what had happened. But the last thing he could remember was standing outer sentry duty in the woods surrounding Ivas Trendor's mountain home. Carefully, wary of hurting something else, he opened his eyes—

And nearly had a heart attack. Standing and milling around within his view were a half-dozen men, but not in the Security uniforms he'd expected to see. Dressed in civilian clothing, with black shirts peeking through at the open necks. And their faces—

Instinctively, his right hand twitched toward his paral-dart pistol, even though he knew the holster would be empty. Perhaps the emergency alarm on his belt—

"How do you feel?" one of his captors asked, kneeling down beside him.

Marcovich sighed with defeat and let his hand drop back to his side. "My neck hurts where you hit me," he said. "I'm . . . surprised I'm still alive. If you're hoping to get some inside information about Trendor's place, you can forget it—I'm not talking."

"What's a Trendor's place? Never mind—we're not here for information. And we're not going to kill you, either. At least I don't think we are."

Marcovich grimaced. "Oh, that's comforting. Really." His eyes flicked away from the face he'd seen so often these past days on Trendor's guardroom wall, over to where his laser rifle was resting against a tree. His communicator and emergency alarm were piled around it, along with the rest of his weapons and other gear. So near. "When does the final decision get made?"

"Right now," a new voice broke in.

Marcovich looked back just as a hypospray tingled against his arm. He frowned—and then gasped as a red-hot flame seemed to course up the limb. "Damn," he breathed. "What're you doing to me? What *is* that?"

"To be perfectly honest, we don't know," the second man—Hawking, the name drifted up from his memory—said, frowning at a medical reader already strapped around Marcovich's upper arm. "We needed someone to test it out on, and as long as you Security people were hanging around the mountains doing nothing anyway, we thought we'd borrow one of you for a while."

The fire was pouring like slow lava into Marcovich's chest now, and a mottled haze was beginning to creep across his vision. His muscles trembled uncontrollably; with an effort he licked dry lips and wound up nearly biting his tongue. "How do you feel?" Hawking's voice came dimly to his ears.

"Like I'm dying," Marcovich managed to snap. Maybe there wasn't any way to stop them, but he was damned if he was going to *cooperate* with them. "Go away and let me die in peace."

"Well?" the other blackcollar asked.

Hawking shook his head slowly. "Sorry, Lathe. I remember well enough what kind of reaction the . . . proper stuff caused. This isn't it."

"Damn." Lathe gazed down at Marcovich, and even through his own haze of agony Marcovich was struck by the depth of raw disappointment on the other's face. "You're sure?"

Hawking didn't even bother to answer, and after a minute Lathe seemed to pull himself together. "Well, then, what *is* it doing to him?"

"Damned if I know." The other shook his head. "I don't think he's dying—his vital signs are holding steady—but beyond that I haven't even got a clue."

A third man stepped up to Lathe. "What's the word?" he asked, his voice practically dripping with suppressed eagerness.

"Apparently, it's no," Lathe said. "I'm sorry."

The disappointment that Marcovich had seen moments earlier on Lathe's face appeared on the newcomer's. "You sure? I understood several injections were necessary—"

"But there should be a particular physiological reaction on

even the first one," Hawking said gently. "It's simply not there."

"And you'll remember the instructions specified a single dose, anyway," Lathe said. "Still, there's one more thing we can try."

Abruptly, a fist snapped out at Marcovich's face. He twitched away, trying to bring his rebellious arm up to defend himself; but even before he'd moved the punch had stopped centimeters away from his nose. "No." Lathe shook his head, withdrawing his hand. "No enhancement at all."

The third man took a deep breath. "Yeah. Well . . . we'd better be moving along, then, hadn't we? Eventually someone's going to miss him."

Lathe frowned. "Hawking?"

"I think he's going to be okay," the other assured him. "It'll be several more minutes before he can go anywhere, but the initial reaction's already passing. He's not going to die out here, if that's what you're worried about."

"I was," Lathe acknowledged. Briefly, his right hand clutched at his left wrist. "All right, get moving. I'm going to gag you and tie your feet together," he added to Marcovich, producing a cord from somewhere. "By the time you can get loose, we ought to be long gone."

Marcovich nodded understanding as the two others disappeared off into the underbrush. Already the fire in his blood was fading away, and with it the immediate fear of death. "I didn't think you blackcollars cared about people like me," he told Lathe, struggling to get the words out.

"We don't," the other said flatly, busying himself with the cord. "At least, not very much. But we don't kill even Security men indiscriminately, and certainly not when it isn't necessary. Though I doubt you'd show similar restraint."

Marcovich thought it over, decided it wasn't worth lying about. "No, I wouldn't," he admitted.

Lathe grunted and finished his work in silence. Carefully, Marcovich tried moving his arms, but it was clear that his muscles were still a long way from full control. The blackcollars were going to get away . . . unless . . .

"By the way, my men took the batteries out of your communicator and emergency beacon when they picked you up," Lathe said, getting to his feet and inspecting his handiwork. "Same for your laser. We thought your friends might try to track you that way once they noticed you were missing. Of course, you can try to get back and alert them, but since you don't know where you are, I wouldn't recommend it. My suggestion is to just sit here and enjoy what's left of the sunshine until they come to find you."

Marcovich gritted his teeth, his last brief surge of hope evaporating. "You blackcollars read minds, too?"

Lathe smiled faintly. "It's how we survive. Thanks for your help, Security man."

"Marcovich is the name," he said, moved by an only dimly understood desire to be more than just another gray-green uniform to this man. "Miro Marcovich."

Lathe nodded to him. "Thanks for your help, Marcovich," he said. Producing the gag—a length of permatape—he carefully applied it across Marcovich's mouth and around behind his neck. Then, turning away, he disappeared behind the trees.

And Marcovich was alone.

It took him the better part of an hour to get enough fine-motor control back to untie his feet. A quick inspection of his equipment showed the blackcollars had indeed left him no way to signal the rest of the Security cordon, and a few minutes of careful reconnoitering confirmed that he hadn't the vaguest idea as to which way Trendor's grounds were. And a permatape gag he knew better than to try to remove without the proper solvent.

With a tired sigh, he found a flat rock and propped himself up against it. There'd be a search party out eventually, and he wouldn't be that hard to find. Though they probably wouldn't be fast enough to catch the blackcollars and find out what the hell they'd injected him with.

Behind the permatape, he grimaced. Deep within him, he could feel the drug churning and grinding, tearing at his system like a canal digger. Changing his whole being . . . and gradually he came to realize that Lathe had been wrong.

The stuff was indeed going to kill him.

Leaning back against the rock, he closed his eyes and waited for the search party to come.

Chapter 40

Anne Silcox was waiting in a faint pool of starlight outside Reger's mansion as the two cars drove up. "The gate guards called and told us you were back," she said as Lathe got out and trudged with the others up the steps. "I was hoping to talk to you—when you have time, of course."

Lathe nodded and took her arm. "Let's go inside," he said. Signaling Skyler to take the others back to their quarters, he led Silcox in the other direction to the quiet and privacy of the main living room.

"Reger told me you were going to try and get inside Aegis Mountain," she said as they sat down on a couch together. "I . . . did you . . . meet anyone?"

Lathe rubbed his forehead tiredly. "I'm sorry, Anne, they were all dead when we got there. A couple of months ago, from the looks of things."

She took a deep breath, swallowed visibly. "I didn't lie to you," she said quietly. "I really *didn't* know where they'd all gone. It wasn't until Reger told me where you'd headed and I had time to think . . . Did you find out why they were there?"

"Yes and no," he said. "They were manufacturing a drug called Whiplash, but we never figured out what it was supposed to do. Does the name mean anything to you?"

Her eyes seemed to come back from somewhere else. "No, not really," she said dully. "They sometimes talked about Whiplash as a sort of sky-pie breakthrough that was supposed to free Earth from the Ryqril. But of course most of the projects had that as their goal. How . . . how did they die?"

"They were poisoned by leftover gas from the war." Easing the pack off his shoulders, Lathe leaned back onto the couch and closed his eyes. He was tired—more tired than he could ever remember being since the end of the war itself. *So much for retirement*, he thought, half bitterly. *The last of the blackcollars. Maybe Bernhard was right, after all. Maybe we're the ones throwing our lives away for nothing. . . .*

"You realize, I hope, that you're making a mess of my couch."

Lathe opened his eyes. "Hello, Reger. Nice to see you alive."

The other grunted as he sat down in a chair across from them. "Yes, I'm rather pleased to be that way myself."

"Tell me about it."

"About the way Jensen said it would happen," Reger said with an uncomfortable shrug. "Five of them came in, two nights ago, right along the keyhole path and loaded for mountain lion." He shook his head in memory. "I tell you, Lathe, it was the goddamnedest thing I've ever seen. Like shooting cats in a box. They never even had a chance."

Lathe sighed. "If you expect me to be proud about it, you're going to be disappointed. Blackcollars shouldn't die like that."

"But it wasn't your fault, was it?" Silcox frowned. "I mean, it was Jensen who set the death house up and Reger who suckered Bernhard's men into it. You shouldn't feel guilty about it."

"Leaders are responsible for what their men do," Lathe told her. "You'll understand that someday. Especially now that you're in charge of Torch."

"Me?" She looked startled.

"Who else? *Someone's* got to rebuild the organization, and you're the most reasonable candidate. Though if it helps any, you probably won't have to start exactly from level zero. Isn't that right, Reger?"

Reger scratched at his ear. "I don't know, Lathe. You're talking a hell of a lot of risk for not much gain. I'm in this business for the money and power, not to play Quixote for the nobility of it all."

"What about the power that'll be available when the Ryqril are thrown off Earth?" Lathe said. "You'll be in a clear position to grab some of that when it happens."

"*If* it happens," the other countered. "You don't have to go through all the arguments again—I remember them well enough. It's just that I don't see a hell of a lot of indication the roaches are busy packing their bags."

"Wait a second," Silcox said. "If you're talking about me linking up with Reger's streetlice operation, you can forget it. I've got higher standards than *that*."

"You can't afford to be choosy," Lathe told her bluntly.

"What, you think you and Kanai can start things up all by yourselves?"

"*Kanai?* Who said I was going to take *him* on, either?"

"Listen to her." Reger snorted. "This is the patriot who's going to lead all of us to freedom? You have to submit a full pedigree to even get in on the revolution."

Silcox glared at him. "I can find more trustworthy teammates than you under the rocks in your yard," she growled. "I may be young and inexperienced, but I'm capable of managing without you, thanks."

Lathe sighed. "Anne, don't be ridiculous. Maybe Reger's current organization won't work, but he's got the contacts and information net to both find the people you need and to pull in all the other data a successful resistance group has to have. You, on the other hand, know more about the basic techniques of undercover operations than he does—and you've got access to the Torch safe houses, where I'd bet heavily there are some duplicate records and material hidden. Kanai, along with his obvious blackcollar training, knows where the back door to Aegis Mountain is if and when you ever find a real use for the place."

"In other words," Reger said heavily, "you're saying that together we're a reasonable team, but singly we're just spinning our wheels. I suppose I agree—but only if all of us have the same goal. You still have to convince me there's something in all of this for *me*. Spectacular political assassinations are fine in their place, but as a means of throwing the Ryqril off the planet I doubt they're all that effective."

"Who's talking assassinations?" Lathe frowned. "I'm talking operations against Security forces and government installations."

"Yes, and you've proved your point," Reger said. "But remember that you had a whole flock of blackcollars on hand to help you infiltrate Trendor's house—"

"To infiltrate *what?* Trendor who?"

"He's the former Security prefect you assassinated this evening," Silcox said. "Didn't you even know his name?"

Lathe stared at her, shifted his gaze to Reger. "What are you two talking about? We didn't kill anyone this—"

And suddenly it all clicked. "My God," he whispered. "My *God.*—Reger give me the details. What exactly happened to this Trendor?"

"He was shot down in his home in the mountains." Reger's face had an odd expression on it, as if he were wondering about Lathe's sanity. "There was a massive laser fire fight in his defense—three of his Security guards were killed in that—but the intruders apparently escaped without anyone else seeing them. Are you saying it wasn't you out there?"

Lathe took a deep breath. "Have your people find out which Security men died in the battle," he told the other. "I'll guarantee you Miro Marcovich will be one of the names."

"You know him?" Silcox asked.

Lathe turned to her. Her face, like Reger's, was wary . . . but behind the confusion the first hint of understanding was beginning to appear. "Yes," he told her. "We kidnapped him this afternoon to test your friends' Whiplash drug on . . . and he's Trendor's assassin."

"That's impossible," Reger said. "Security men are loyalty-conditioned to be incapable . . ."

He trailed off. "My God," he said, very softly.

Lathe let the silence hang in the room for a half-dozen heartbeats. Then, picking up his backpack, he got to his feet. "If you'll excuse me," he said, "I need to go and discuss this development with my men. You two might want to do the same, perhaps concentrating on the best ways to get Torch revitalized."

Silcox took a deep breath and looked across at Reger. "Not Torch," she said quietly. "Phoenix. A living torch, revived from its own ashes."

Reger nodded thoughtfully. "Silly, really. But I suppose that kind of symbolism is important to such a group's morale." He hesitated, looked up at Lathe. "On your way out, Comsquare, would you mind asking Commando Kanai to join us?"

Lathe smiled faintly. "I'd be glad to."

Epilogue

It was Colonel Poirot, not General Quinn, who eventually came to release him from detention—or rather, *General* Poirot, Galway noted, eying the other's new insignia with some surprise. "Promoted just in time for the trial?" he said sourly as Poirot led the way down the hall.

Poirot grunted. "Not funny. The whole damn unit is in turmoil since Trendor got burned. You heard about that, I suppose?"

Galway nodded. "One of my guards filled me in."

"Yeah, well, I don't suppose he mentioned the Ryqril reaction to it all. There's a Ryq in charge in the main Security office right now—a *khassq*-class warrior, no less. Quinn's been taken away, God only knows where, and everyone in the entire upper command's either been promoted or removed."

Galway felt his jaw clench momentarily. So he'd been right, all the way down the line . . . and yet, even now he still had trouble believing it. Somehow, assassination just didn't fit Lathe's character. "So where are you taking me?" he asked Poirot. "They sending me home or down the hatch with Quinn?"

"I don't know," the other said heavily. "All I know is that there's a Ryq fresh in from Plinry who wants to see you."

"Oh, hell." That scout ship that had left orbit right after the blackcollars' big escape, destination almost certainly Plinry. Galway had almost forgotten about that, but whatever its mission had been, he had a strong suspicion he wasn't going to like hearing about it.

There were two Ryqril standing stiffly by the rear corners of Quinn's desk when they arrived, indistinguishable to human eyes except for the differing patterns in the ornate baldrics crossing their massive chests. " 'Re'ect Galray?" the one on the left said as Galway and Poirot paused just inside the office door.

"I am Galway," the prefect identified himself, speaking with some difficulty around the sudden lump in his throat. On both alien baldrics were the distinctive patterns of the *khassq*-class warriors, the highest stratum of Ryqril society.

"I an Taakh—rarriaer *khassq*," the same Ryq identified himself with a brief touch of his paw to his baldric. The laser and short sword on his belt jiggled with the motion, and Galway swallowed again.

"Other nan—lea' us," the second Ryq said. Poirot bowed briefly and backed hastily out.

For a moment the aliens eyed Galway in silence. Then Taakh stirred, gesturing to a cassette lying on the desk. "The re'el shuttle has lekht Earth," he said, giving the words their usual Ryqril mangling. "Did the 'lackcollars go rith it?"

Galway licked his lips, resisting the impulse to say that he had no idea. Obviously, they knew that. What they wanted was for him to look over the available data and give them his opinion on the matter. A test of some sort. . . . Stepping forward, he picked up the cassette and slid it into the reader.

It was a complete record of the shuttle pickup from Denver that morning, including both tapes from the 'port and Athena's radar records of its departure path. Galway studied it closely for several minutes, acutely conscious of the silent aliens towering over him a bare meter away. But this wasn't something he could afford to rush.

Finally, he looked up. "I can't prove it," he said carefully, "but the blackcollars *could* have left with the shuttle."

"Ex'lain," Taakh ordered.

Galway took a deep breath. "Here—at the 'port—they took on several large crates, one of which contained a fully assembled high-powered winch. While they were flying over the mountains here"—he located the spot on the record— "they claimed to have temporarily lost power and dipped below the intervening mountain peaks almost to ground level. They were out of your view long enough to have grabbed a snag-equipped pod and to winch it aboard. Again, I don't know if they actually did so or not."

"They did," Taakh said. "Satellite 'hoto shor it 'eyond do'rt. Too late to sto' they. Yae are the nan re can use."

"The man—use for what?" Galway asked cautiously.

The second Ryq stirred. "On 'Linry the 'lackcollars 'enetrated the encla'e and took the hostages."

A shiver went up Galway's spine. The enclave. Once again Lathe had pulled off the impossible, right under the Ryqril's collective snout . . . and in the process had hung Plinry from a thread. "I didn't know what they'd done," he said quietly. "I thought they might try to free Pittman's family, but . . ." *I thought they were well enough guarded*, he finished the thought to himself.

"Yae think like they." The Ryq nodded, the very human gesture looking totally out of place on his alien physique. "Yae rill hel' us ca'ture they."

It took several heartbeats for the significance of that to sink in—and as it did Galway felt a surge of relief flood through him. *Capture*, not destroy . . . and capture implied no mass destruction on Plinry. "I—yes, sir, of course I'll help in any way I can," he managed. "But capturing them will be extremely hard, if not impossible. Wouldn't it be easier to just try and eliminate them?"

The two Ryqril exchanged glances. "They dae the in'ossi'le," Taakh said, as if that was explanation enough.

Galway opened his mouth . . . then closed it again as it suddenly made sense. Lathe's men invading the allegedly impregnable Ryqril Enclave; Lathe himself getting to Trendor despite all the guards. There was no way to pretend anymore that Argent had been a fluke. The blackcollars were, pure and simple, breakers of impossible odds . . . and in the war against the Chryselli perhaps such odds were beginning to stack up. The Ryqril had tried twice now to trail the blackcollars in hopes of snatching whatever they might be after, with disastrous results both times. But the Ryqril were clearly not ready to give up . . . and somewhere in the upper echelons of their military, the blackcollars' status had apparently been changed again.

From seekers of usable goods to combat resource. And as the main source of that resource, Plinry had been given a new foothold on its tenuous existence.

Provided, of course, that Galway did his job properly. "I will be honored to assist you," he told the Ryqril. "And I know just the right man to go after first."

"Lath'?" Taakh asked.

"Yes," Galway said.

"Not exactly the result we'd all hoped for," Lathe said, his eyes drifting to the starscape painting adorning the *Novak's* lounge wall. "But certainly nothing to be ashamed of, either."

Caine nodded silently. *Thus endeth my first command,* he thought . . . and while it too was nothing to be ashamed about, it was hardly bragworthy, either, with all the small failures and half-failures along the way. He winced as the memories went drifting by.

Beside Lathe, General Lepkowski cleared his throat. "Don't be too hard on yourself, Caine," he said. "You kept your team alive. All in all, that's a pretty good scoresheet for a newcomer to the game."

Caine managed a rueful smile . "Perhaps."

"If that's not good enough," Lathe suggested, "try remembering that if you hadn't come up with this mission in the first place Torch's supply of Whiplash would probably never have left Aegis Mountain."

"Yeah. Well, I suppose being the inspiration to others' greatness is better than nothing." Caine straightened up in his seat, shaking the memories firmly from his mind. "So. Have you two figured out yet how we're going to use this stuff to throw out the Ryqril?''

"Oh, we've got a few ideas," Lathe said offhandedly. "Create havoc in key areas, pick up some new allies—that sort of thing.''

"Allies?" Caine snorted gently. "If you're looking for names, I can give you one right now.''

"Oh, he's already at the top of our list," the comsquare told him. "After all, we'll want to start out right away with the brightest and best the opposition has to offer.''

"Galway?" Caine asked.

"Yes," Lathe said.